Praise for

After reading *Salvaged* in one sitting, I fell in love with it and dubbed it as one of the best books I've ever read. I used to hope that one day I would have a guy like Edward Cullen from *Twilight*, but now I can't wait to meet my own Riley Bennett. Stefne Miller has opened my eyes to new ways of looking at my relationships with my friends and with Christ.

—Rachel, seventeen years old

I thought the story line of *Salvaged* was amazing. I couldn't stop reading it! I thought it was better than *Twilight*! Stefne Miller has great writing skills, and she proved it with this fantastic book.

—Amanda, fourteen years old

I loved *Salvaged*; it was a great book. I didn't want it to end, and I can't wait to read the second book!

—MaKenzie, thirteen years old

Salvaged was something I could plug into because I could see this happening in my life. Love, Christianity, and humor made it hard to put down. I loved it!

—Kerrigan, twelve years old

With her captivating voice and genuine characters, Stefne Miller has hit a home run with this book! This inspirational story is one that grabs the attention of the reader from the very first line and doesn't let go until the end then leaves the reader wanting more. It is a must-read for young adults and grown-ups! As an English and literature teacher, this is a book I would definitely teach in my classroom. It has a clear message we all should hear whether as a teenager or an adult.

—Shelley, mother of three young adult girls
and teacher of grades five through nine

salvaged

Best wishes
and
many blessings !
Stefne
Miller

Stefne Miller

a love story

Tate Publishing & Enterprises

Published by Tate Publishing & Enterprises, LLC
127 E. Trade Center Terrace | Mustang, Oklahoma 73064 USA
1.888.361.9473 | www.tatepublishing.com

Tate Publishing is committed to excellence in the publishing industry. The company reflects the philosophy established by the founders, based on Psalm 68:11,
"The Lord gave the word and great was the company of those who published it."

Book design copyright © 2010 by Tate Publishing, LLC. All rights reserved.
Cover design by Kellie Southerland
Interior design by Blake Brasor

Published in the United States of America

ISBN: 978-1-61663-028-7
1. Fiction, Christian, Romance
2. Fiction, Coming of Age
10.2.11

dedication

For Shaun and our children: My very own dreams come true and proof that God gives amazing gifts.

For Tammy, Anne, and Jennifer: Evidence that allowing God to choose your friends makes the world of difference.

For Mom: You are a shining example of the unconditional and unending love that a parent has for their children. I hope my children feel as loved as you've always made me feel.

For Kerrigan: You were the first "Young Adult" to read this book. Hearing you say "I loved it" will forever be one of the most memorable moments of my life. Thank you for taking the time to read it.

"What I tell you in the dark, speak in the daylight;
what is whispered in your ear, proclaim from the roofs."
                                    Matthew 10:26 (Life Application Bible)

chapter 1

Looking back, some might think it was the summer I turned seventeen that changed my life for the better, but I beg to differ. As impossible as it sounds, in one very important way, it was actually the summer before.

As it turns out, the accident that could have taken my life ended up being the tragedy that saved it. If it weren't for the events of that day, I never would have experienced the dream that set my life on a new path—a new adventure.

It was the dream, his presence, and the events that followed that prepared me for the biggest blessings of my life; and even though I didn't know it, those blessings prepared to unveil themselves as the old Ford made its way toward home.

As each mile marker passed, it felt as though the knot in my stomach would double in size. For returning to a place so familiar, the unknown that lay ahead left me terrified.

"You know they can't wait for you to arrive." Gramps noticed my apprehension and talked nonstop during our drive from the airport. "Molly's been talkin' about you constantly, and she's made sure to tell everyone at church that you'll be livin' with 'em this summer."

Although my exhaustion level reached its max and I wasn't in the mood to talk, I sensed his growing concern, so I chose to appease him by attempting to speak my first words since climbing into the truck almost an hour before. "Has she?"

"She sure has. I hope you're prepared for the welcome wagon. You know you'll be gettin' a lot of visitors."

"Ah, people want to come see the freak show, do they?"

He chose to ignore my comment. "Heck, I hear even Riley's lookin' forward to seein' you."

"That's highly doubtful," I refuted with a groan. "Who in their right mind decided we should spend another summer under the same roof?"

"Now, Atticus—"

"Attie."

"—it's the best we could come up with under the circumstances. It was this or you would end up sleepin' on a cot alongside the animals in my clinic."

"That would be better than having Riley torture me for three months. I could swear that boy lives to make me miserable." My face felt warmer, and I knew it wasn't the heat of the Oklahoma summer that caused the discomfort. Just thinking of Riley Bennett made my blood boil.

"Oh now, you're just bein' silly."

"Oh no I'm not. Remember the time he shot me in the eye with that arrow? Or the time he locked me in the dirty clothes hamper?" I ignored the laughter flowing out of my grandfather's throat. "To this day the smell of dirty socks makes me feel claustrophobic. If it weren't for Melody, her brother would have kept me in that hamper for days."

"You were in there for less than five minutes."

"It felt like an eternity."

"You were no angel either. I seem to recall you doin' some harassin' yourself."

"It was self-defense. Survival instinct at its best."

"You two were young and he was ornery."

"Ornery? Try devil-child."

"Atticus," he scolded. "You shouldn't talk like that."

"I only speak truth."

"You speak exaggerated truth. You always did have an active imagination and a bend toward the dramatic."

"Active imagination my rear. Thank God for Mr. Bennett coming to my rescue a hundred times a day; there's no telling what would have happened to me. That boy hated me before, and I don't even want to think about how he must despise me now."

"He doesn't blame you, Atticus—"

"Attie."

"Nobody blames you. Really, don't worry. He's changed a lot, grown up. Heck, who wouldn't given the situation."

"Great, another thing to hold against me. Let's see, ruin boy's summer before junior year—check. Cause boy to have to grow up faster than necessary—check, check. Now ruin boy's summer before senior year—check, check, check."

"Well, I apologize," Gramps offered.

"Apologize for what?"

"Here I thought we were havin' a welcome home party, but it seems to me that you're much more interested in havin' a full-blown pity party. Do they make balloons for that kinda shindig?"

"You're right; I'm acting like a turd."

"Yeah, you are. Luckily, I love you anyway."

"Thank you." I started to gnaw on my thumbnail. "I'm just nervous and scared."

"I know you are, but I promise, you're gonna be pleasantly surprised."

Making our way up the drive, I realized that not much had changed appearance-wise. The home had the same pale yellow exterior with white trim and charcoal gray shutters. Weathered white wicker furniture sat on the patio, and green ferns hung above the railings between round white wooden columns. The only new addition that I could see was a porch swing, which now hung on the left side of the patio. The old oak front door with its large oval window beckoned guests to enter the once happy home, but I was hesitant to oblige.

Pulling down the visor and flipping open the mirror, I checked my appearance.

"Ugh, what's the point? There's no hope for me."

"Shush now, Atticus." My eyes turned to Gramps as he scolded me. I noticed his crumpled forehead slightly showing under his old brown cowboy hat and knew instantly that my comment bothered him. "God made you perfect."

"Yes," I grumbled. "God made me perfectly plain."

My mother's beautiful almond-shaped eyes and dainty nose or my father's olive skin coloring definitely hadn't passed down to me. I looked more like my Gramps than either one of my parents. He and I had small builds and paler complexions. Like his, my face had no distinct features. If someone were to draw a portrait of me, all they'd need to do is draw a large circle, two dots to represent my beady eyes, an inverted heart for my pug nose, and two thin, straight lines to replicate my lips. Heck, if they really wanted to outdo themselves, gluing some yellow yarn to the top of my head would make it a darned near perfect reproduction. I'd resigned myself to the fact that I was a very plain-looking girl and always would be. For some reason, God wanted me that way, and although I didn't know why, it wasn't as if I had a choice.

Looking back into the mirror, I realized that my dirty blonde hair hung flat on my head, looking stringy, and my dreary green eyes reflected a tiredness that made me look much older than my sixteen years. A lack of sleep was catching up with me.

I slammed the mirror shut and flipped the visor back against the roof just as Mr. and Mrs. Bennett entered my line of vision. My apprehension dissolved as I noticed Mrs. Bennett jumping up and down clapping her hands as Gramps pulled the truck to a stop. Mr. Bennett stood motionless but wore a large grin on his face. The appearance of the odd couple caused me to laugh.

"Attie." Mrs. Bennett was practically running in place. "Get out here and let me give you a hug."

"Yes, ma'am," I said through the window. Mr. Bennett opened

the truck door and grinned as an air of excitement rushed into the truck cab.

"Look at you," she shouted. "Look at her, Tom; doesn't she look amazing?"

"Yep, she sure does."

If there were any two people more opposite in the world, I couldn't imagine it. Thomas Bennett, being at least six feet six inches, with a stocky build, simply towered over his much shorter and slimmer wife, Molly. And his quiet nature balanced her constant state of excitement.

Being the same age as my dad meant that they weren't quite forty years old, and with Riley going off to college next year, they had a whole new life ahead of them. They were both wonderful people, and they loved me.

Riley caught my eye as he walked out onto the porch. Never one to hide his emotions, his body language spoke volumes. With shoulders slouched, he kept his head down, which caused his moppy brown hair to partly cover his face. He refused to so much as make eye contact with me, and as if I were on a roller coaster, my anxiety level rose again.

"Thanks for letting me come stay with you, Mr. and Mrs. Bennett. I know this can't be easy on you."

"Now don't you talk like that, Attie," Mrs. Bennett said. "We're thrilled to have you here."

"That's right, Attiline," Mr. Bennett added. "This'll be the highlight of our year."

Hearing Mr. Bennett call me Attiline instantly calmed my nerves back to a more manageable level. He'd called me Attiline for as long as I could remember, and the fact that he still referred to me with his special term of endearment meant that his feelings for me hadn't changed.

I continued to study Riley as he shoved his hands into his blue jeans and tensely curled his toes over the edge of the porch step. He was annoyed, and I felt guilty for intruding on his life.

Unfortunately, the time had finally come, and I couldn't go on ignoring him any longer.

"Good grief, it's Riley Bennett," I teased.

"Hey, Charlie," he muttered.

I never understood why in the world he called me "Charlie." He'd been doing it for years, and more than any other reason, I could only assume he did it to drive me crazy. Normally it worked, but today I refused to let it get to me.

"Are you happy to see me?" I asked.

"Sure, why not."

Looking down, I noticed his feet shuffling on the patio. He was agitated by my arrival and turned to go back inside, but his mother's voice stopped him in his tracks.

"Riley, get Attie's bags and take them up to her room. Make yourself useful for cryin' out loud."

If nothing else, no one could call Mrs. Bennett dull. She talked like a crazy woman, with arms flying around in the air and her eyes all buggy. Melody and Riley had always found her to be a constant cause for embarrassment. I, on the other hand, had always found her to be a breath of fresh air—just like me.

Slowly turning on his heels, Riley rolled his eyes and glanced at me. In an attempt to convey a certain amount of solidarity, I rolled my eyes as well. I couldn't help myself; I felt bad for him. He obviously didn't want me here in the first place, and now he was stuck having to haul my bags inside.

"Sorry," I whispered.

"It's all right," he muttered.

Growing up, torment and torture had been Riley's game plan every time I visited. He'd pulled my hair, locked me in closets, thrown ants in my sleeping bag, and blown up several of my Barbie dolls with an arsenal of firecrackers. Now, here we were about to spend the summer together. If nothing else, the next three months would be interesting.

chapter 2

Gramps thanked the Bennetts for letting me stay with them and then turned, grabbed my hands in his, and prayed. "Lord, thank you for bringin' Atticus back to Guthrie. I'm so blessed to have her as a part of my life. Thank you for the Bennetts and their willingness to allow Atticus to stay with 'em. Please bless 'em in return for lovin' this precious child. In Jesus's name. Amen."

"Amen."

"I love you, Atticus Elizabeth Reed. Welcome home, princess."

"I love you too, Gramps, and I'm glad to be here, even if I don't act like it."

His heavily calloused, rough hands still cradled mine. "All's forgiven."

"Thank you. But can I ask one little, teensy, weensy favor?"

"You can ask me anything, although I may not give you the answer you wanna hear."

"Could you call me Attie from now on?"

"But your name's Atticus."

"My horrendous, forced-upon-me name is Atticus. My preferred name for years now has been Attie."

"Atticus Finch was a great man. You should be pleased to be named after someone so brave and honorable."

"Good grief, he's not even real. Try telling your friends that it's worth having a name like Atticus just so you can honor a completely fictional character. It's utterly ridiculous."

"Enough of this silliness. You'll always be Atticus to me, and I'm way too old to be tryin' to start a new habit."

"Pff." A blast of air escaped from between my lips and caused a tuft of my hair to soar.

"Get on now. Be a good girl and be sure to get some sleep. You look a little tired."

"Yes, sir."

A little tired? He was being polite because I actually looked like a school bus backed over me several times. I was falling apart at the seams, and nothing but my glue-white skin was holding me together.

Maybe a new location would do me some good after all.

Even standing just inside the front door, a sense of security engulfed my body. I was home and I felt safe and loved—except by Riley of course.

Directly in front of me, the staircase sat in all its old craftsman-style grandeur. The dark brown oak wood stood out against mossy green covered walls. I noticed the same fake plant sitting on a tall planter in the corner of the landing, and Mrs. Bennett's framed postcard collection dotted the stairwell walls.

I sent several of the postcards during our many family trips around the country. Every time Dad was invited to speak at a university, he would turn the visit into a family vacation. I'd seen practically every state in the continental U.S. but had yet to leave the country. Every time we found ourselves somewhere new I made sure to purchase two postcards: one for myself and another for Mrs. Bennett.

Turning left, I headed toward the kitchen and made it halfway through the family room before noticing a new television sitting next to the old gray stone fireplace.

"Get yourself a new television, Mr. Bennett?"

"Isn't it great, Attiline? It's a fifty-inch flat screen HDTV." His chest puffed out, and a large grin spread across his face. "It was the family Christmas gift this last year."

"It's awesome." I nodded enthusiastically. "I guess I know where I'll be watching football this year."

"Oh, you'll love it." He spoke with as much enthusiasm as I'd ever heard him use. "The picture is so clear you can see each individual blade of grass."

"I can't wait."

Football season was my favorite time of year, and Saturday through Sunday nights ran together as I sat and watched game after game. My ritual usually started Saturday mornings with "College Game Day" and then progressed through the weekend. College football was by far my favorite, but I watched professional football as well, seeing as how there weren't any college games on Sundays.

"A lot of great players are returning to the Sooners this year, Mr. Bennett. It should be a great season."

"Dang straight. Everyone on the *Sports Animal* is already talking about a National Championship. I think it'll be exciting, and you can come over and watch it all on that huge screen."

"I'll bring the chips and dip. You supply the beer."

"Very funny," he said dryly just as Mrs. Bennett yelled for me to join her in the kitchen.

"Let's have some girl talk. It's been awhile since there's been another girl in the house."

"You poor soul." Mr. Bennett grabbed me and gave me a bear hug. "She's been preparing for this moment since she knew you were coming. It could be a very long night, so I hope you got some rest on the plane."

I couldn't bear to tell him that I was tired and only wanted to crawl in bed. I hadn't slept since the night before, and even then I'd spent much of the night awake. A bad dream woke me up, and I never fell back to sleep.

Mr. Bennett gently squeezed my shoulders and pushed me into the kitchen as I braced myself for what was going to be hours of listening to Mrs. Bennett have "girl talk."

I took my usual seat at the kitchen table as music played from the laptop sitting on the kitchen counter.

"Bon Jovi?" They were her favorite.

"Of course. Riley taught me how to download music and videos from iTunes, and I'm telling you, Attie, I've spent a fortune on all kinds of old music. I have over four hundred songs on that thing."

"That's impressive." I gave an approving nod. "I may need to check it out and download some songs onto my Shuffle."

"You should. And I hate to brag, but I'm totally hip."

"Hip?"

"Oh yeah, I've got a lot of newer stuff on there too. Justin Timberlake, Fergie, all kinds of stuff. Some of it's a little racy, but I pretend I don't notice."

"Sounds good. You're definitely hip," I confirmed sarcastically.

"Riley and some of his friends caught me in here dancing the other day while I was doing the dishes. I thought he was gonna die of embarrassment, but I think I move pretty well for my age. I mean, I was a cheerleader in my heyday, but Riley said he thought I might blow out a hip or something."

"He clearly underestimates your talent."

"You always did speak the truth, Attie. I'm gonna love having you home."

"So I guess teaching at a high school means you get to hear all kinds of new music."

"Oh yeah. The girls make sure I'm up-to-date. It helps me stay young. I'm not the old fuddy duddy type."

"No, you definitely aren't that."

I glanced around the red kitchen as she talked about her favorite students. She'd always been a collector, so knickknacks filled every available space. Her decorating style perfectly matched her personality—busy. Handmade gifts from Riley, Melody, and years of students littered shelves that she'd hung randomly on the walls, and trophies of all sizes, shapes, and types filled the china cabinet. Funny, I didn't actually see china.

While looking around the room, I noticed for the first time that behind every item she displayed there was a story. These weren't just knickknacks, they were memories. The items kept her attached to her past and now, in many ways, attached to Melody.

Her continued flurry of words caught my attention, and although I wished we would simply get it over with and acknowledge the extremely large elephant in the room, we continued to make small talk as she unloaded and reloaded the dishwasher. I wondered how long it would be before someone in the house mentioned the name "Melody."

Mrs. Bennett began fanning herself in an effort to cool down. "So, Attie Reed, let's get caught up on your life."

Riley suddenly appeared and entered the kitchen, but she held out a hand and shushed him away. "We're having girl talk in here. You get on out."

He ignored her and continued on his path. "I need a drink."

"Drink your spit," she said, giving him a gentle shove back toward the living room. "You can get a drink later."

"Mom, seriously, I just need a drink, and then I'll leave you two alone."

"Fine," she said, throwing her hands onto her hips. "You've got fifteen seconds."

He rolled his eyes for the second time since I'd arrived and grabbed a water out of the fridge before walking back out of the room in a huff.

Mrs. Bennett turned up the music and then turned to face me. "So do you have a boyfriend?"

She wasn't wasting any time trying to get to the good stuff, and I was immediately embarrassed.

To avoid her gaze, I reached for an oatmeal cookie from the plate in front of me. "No, I don't have a boyfriend."

"You're kidding? No boyfriend?"

"I don't mind really. Guys just don't seem to pay me any attention."

I noticed Riley's head snap in our direction, and by the look on his face, he didn't seem surprised by my admission. Luckily, he quickly lost interest and turned his attention back to the TV.

"I've always known I wasn't one of the pretty girls. I think boys see me more as buddy material. You know, like someone they want to hang out with but don't necessarily want to make out with. I'm beginning to believe that's my lot in life, every guy's best buddy."

Mrs. Bennett's head shook so violently from side to side that I was surprised it didn't fall right off. "I don't believe a word of that, Attie. You're gorgeous; you always have been. I bet the boys are just intimidated by you. You're self-confident, and you know what you want. That scares boys off."

"I wouldn't say I'm self-confident. Clueless maybe, but definitely not self-confident. And anyway, you know what boys want, and I don't have them."

Her eyes grew wide in anticipation. "What do boys want?"

"You know…they want girls who have big boobs, and I don't have those."

A clammer rose from the living room, and I realized that Riley's chair had fallen over and he was sprawled onto the floor.

"Stupid chair," he said, getting up off the floor, giving it a kick, and moving to the couch.

Mrs. Bennett laughed. "Oh, Attie, if there's one thing boys want more than big boobs, it's a challenge. Stand your ground, hold on to your values, and make 'em wait. You do that and you'll have boys falling all over you."

"That's what Mom always said. 'Boys like a challenge.' But I don't think I'm trying to be a challenge as much as that I just am one. By nature I'm a challenge. Mom always said I was a handful and it would take a very special boy to put up with me."

"She said that?"

"Well, that and that if anyone ever kidnapped me they'd let me go after only a few hours. I guess she figured I'd drive them crazy with all my talking."

"She always did have a sense of humor. You'll find a special boy one day, and he won't care that you don't have huge boobs, although yours are perfect. Not too much and not too little. Just right."

I grabbed another cookie while sneaking a look at my chest. Mrs. Bennett was wrong; they were too small and far from perfect.

"Riley, get on in here and open this jar for me," she screamed.

"Mom, I'm watching TV."

"Don't start with me," she threatened.

I noticed him shiver at the sound of her voice and remembered he'd once said her voice was so shrill it was like the sound of fingernails dragging down a chalkboard. "Get your butt in here right now before I call your dad in here to make you do it."

He threw himself off of the sofa, stomped into the kitchen, and opened the jar before slamming it onto the counter and starting to walk back out.

"Wait just a minute, mister. I'm not finished with you yet."

He threw an angry glare my direction, which caused me to pull my legs up to my chest in defense.

"Where do you think you're going?" his mom asked.

If there's one thing she excelled at, it was intruding in other people's lives. Nothing was sacred or secret as long as she was around. Knowing other people's business was what she lived for.

"Answer me, Riley. Where are you going?"

He removed his stare from me and transferred it to his mother. "I'm goin' for a walk for cryin' out loud," he snapped.

"To where?"

"What is this, an interrogation?"

"Don't get smart with me, Riley Bennett."

"Probly Joshua's."

"Well, why don't you invite Attie to go along? She's been cooped up in airplanes all day, and I'm sure Joshua would love to meet her."

She wasn't merely making a suggestion; she was pretty much giving him an order, and we both knew there would be hell to pay if he didn't comply.

"Fine," he said rudely. "Wanna come, Attie?"

"You go ahead," I replied. "I wouldn't want to intrude. I think I'm doing that enough already."

"Riley!" she yelled.

He glanced back at me, and his eyes practically begged me to let him off the hook.

"It's okay, Mrs. Bennett; I've got to unpack anyway."

"Sorry," he mumbled.

As I got up and walked toward him, I realized just how tall he was. The top of my head barely reached his shoulders, and I was instantly aware that if he wanted to he could break me into a million pieces in a matter of seconds.

I reached up and gave him a pat on the head. "It's all right, Riley; I'm a big girl. If I want to go for a walk, I can go by myself."

And with that, I skipped up the stairs toward my room.

Riley Bennett had tried to get the best of me and failed miserably. I'd won round one.

chapter 3

I needed some serious alone time, so I threw my hair into a ponytail and washed my face. The Bennetts kept their house colder than I was accustomed to, so I threw on some sweats in an effort to ward off the chills and made my way toward my new space.

Nothing had changed in Melody's room. One summer while I visited we painted the walls hot pink and all the trim and furniture black. Her mother hated the idea but allowed us do it anyway. Melody was proud of the room once we finished it, and now here I was taking it over as my own for the summer. If I'd known that I would be staying here, I would have encouraged her to use different colors.

Not even the bedspread had changed.

My chest tightened, I was beginning to get short of breath, and my heart raced.

I couldn't do it; I couldn't sleep in her bed—not tonight.

"You're all right. I'm right here," a gentle voice soothed.

"So you followed me all the way to Oklahoma?"

"Of course."

My eyes searched until they found Jesus sitting on Melody's bed. Just as he'd been the first time I saw him standing in my hospital room, he wore blue jeans, a simple t-shirt, and his feet were bare.

"Rough day?" he asked rhetorically. Of course, he always knew how I felt.

"Not the best, but not the worst."

He smiled at me. "What's on your mind?"

"As if you don't already know."

I sat in silence for several moments as he waited patiently for me to continue.

"I don't know if I can do this tonight. Sleep in Melody's bed, I mean. Just being in this room makes me miserable. It's all very painful. Literally and physically painful."

My heart ached, and my eyes filled with tears.

"I can understand that. Melody was a special friend. I know how well you fit together, how much you enjoyed each other."

I was angry and confused. "Why did you give her to us only to take her away?"

"Would you rather you never knew her?"

I shook my head. "Of course not."

"It's complicated," he whispered.

My mood was turning somber. I knew that my mind would never grasp how or why anything happened, let alone the deaths of innocent people, but I still wanted answers.

"Attie, you'll never understand why my Father and I allow the things we do. You just have to remember that all things work together for good."

"Good? The death of innocent people?" My mind couldn't even reconcile the thought.

"Not that, no. But out of your walk through that pain, good will come. You're stronger now, more compassionate, and you value human life more than most people your age. Those are all good things."

"Couldn't you teach those things another way?"

"Yes." He was now sitting next to me on the floor. "You've done well, Attie. You've done most everything I've asked of you. You *will* see the good one day, I promise."

"I guess I'll just have to trust you on that?"

"Yes. I never said this journey would be easy; I just asked you to join me on it."

"Before agreeing I guess I should have clarified further," I teased.

"Perhaps." A sweet smiled formed on his face as we sat next to each other under the window. "You're going to make it, Attie. You and me together, just as we've always been. You can do this."

"How am I going to do this is the question."

A slight smile filled his face, and his head shook as a small laugh escaped his lips.

"What's so funny?" I asked.

"You remind me of Philip."

"Philip who?"

"One of my original disciples. He was so full of faith, but he always asked for explanations. He practically wore me out with the questions. It's one of the things I loved the most about him. He had a curious mind and so do you. You want answers—to everything."

"Do you think you would have chosen me as a disciple?"

"Attie, a disciple is someone who simply chooses to follow me. You've made that choice. I asked you to follow me, and here you are, one of my chosen. My disciple."

His voice was so gentle and relaxing that I wished I could have climbed into his lap and have his arms wrap around me. Sitting on my mother's lap always brought me more comfort than her words alone could, and for almost a year I missed the security that a loving touch provided.

Changing the music on my iPod to Chris Tomlin, I closed my eyes and pictured myself in my mother's lap as we were both wrapped in our heavenly Father's arms.

Just as I drifted off to sleep, something latched onto my toe, and out of instinct, I kicked my foot in an effort to remove it and ended up coming into contact with something solid.

Throwing open my eyes, I realized that it had been Riley, and he was laid out on the floor in front of me.

"Riley!" I threw my iPod onto the bed and ran to his side. "I'm so sorry."

"You kicked me in the face," he said in a daze.

"Well, you startled me. Good grief, you snuck up on me."

"Did not, I called your name three freakin' times. Seriously, do you have to be so violent?"

"Well, I said I was sorry."

"Holy moly, are you in karate or something? That kick was hard." He rubbed his chin and grimaced. "What, are you like a third degree black belt or something?"

Mr. Bennett must have heard my screams because he came barreling up the stairs and stopped in the hallway. He probably thought we were killing each other.

"What's going on in here?" he asked.

"She kicked me in the face."

"It was an accident. He snuck up on me."

"I did not. I was sent up here to check on you."

Mr. Bennett stood just outside the doorway, never entering the room. "Is he bleeding?"

"All of my injuries are internal," Riley accused sarcastically. "Call the paramedics."

"Let me look at it," I said.

Riley sat up, so I placed my hands on his face and smiled just before I threw his head back with an intentional jolt.

"Ow. Seriously, Charlie, settle down already."

"No, sir, he isn't bleeding."

"Dad, tell her to leave me alone."

I slapped him on the forehead before shoving him back onto the ground. "Give me a break, you big baby."

His dad stood back and laughed. "You could've given him a scar to complement the other one you gave him."

"Excuse me?" I asked.

"That scar on Riley's chin. You hit him with a baseball bat when you were six."

I watched Riley as the tips of his fingers clumsily felt around for the scar until he found the slight indention just below his chin. "You did this?"

"Good grief, I was six. Cut me some slack." A quiet giggle escaped me, but I regained my composure just before slapping him on the forehead again and making my way to my spot under the window.

"For such a little thing, you've always packed quite a punch, Attiline. And you've gotta toughen up, Riley; you're getting your butt kicked by a girl. Maybe Attiline can teach you a thing or two."

Little by little, Mr. Bennett was ripping out Riley's self-esteem, throwing it on the ground, and stomping on it. I have to admit it was fabulous to watch, but I ended up having to tuck my head behind my knees to hide my laughter.

"Thanks a lot, Dad. I appreciate your concern."

"No problem, son. All right, Attiline, you gonna be okay tonight?"

"Yes, sir."

"If you need anything just make Riley get it for you."

"I'll be fine, thank you." I didn't bother to look up. "I think he's had quite enough of me for one day."

"No doubt," Riley huffed.

"Well, all right then. Good night, kids."

We sat in silence for several seconds as Mr. Bennett made his way back downstairs. I peeked out from behind my knees and caught Riley moving his jaw in circles.

I lightly nudged his leg with my bare foot. "Anything broken?" I asked.

"You mean besides my pride? No."

"You big baby," I teased as I lightly kicked him again.

"Shut up."

"Relax; I won't beat you up anymore. As a matter of fact, you'll hardly even know I'm here. I'll make sure to stay out of your way."

"That sounds perfect." He threw his arms over his face in disgust, and I sat and watched as he lay lifeless on the floor.

"I think it was my physical therapy."

"Your what?" he asked, sitting back up.

"My physical therapy," I muttered.

He crawled over to the window and sat down next to me. "Your physical therapy what?"

"I think that's where the powerful kick came from."

"Oh. You must've had a great therapist."

"I'm sorry, Riley, really I am. I hope you accept."

"For which time?" He was now laughing. "Evidently you have a history of aggression toward me. You must have a subconscious desire to kick my butt."

"Only because you've tortured me for so many years. Remember the arrow you shot into my eye?"

"There was a plastic suction cup on the end for cryin' out loud. It didn't even do any permanent damage."

"It still hurt."

"So this is payback?" he asked.

For the first time since my arrival that day, he smiled at me, and I couldn't resist smiling back. "I guess."

"Just don't let it happen again. Please, I hardly have any pride left as it is."

"Although I do have a very active imagination, I'll try my darndest to contain my sadistic subconscious mind."

"I'd appreciate that."

He got up and began to leave the room.

"I'm really, really sorry, Riley."

"Quit saying you're sorry," he said over his shoulder. "It's getting annoying."

"Sorry."

As I watched him leave the room, my line of vision met the bed, and fear instantly filled my body. There was no part of me that wanted to sleep in Melody's bed tonight. I wasn't ready.

"Okay, come on."

"What?" I asked, looking back up at him.

"Come with me." His voice had softened, and he held out a hand in my direction.

"Where to?"

"My room," he said, grabbing my hand and pulling me to my feet. "You can sleep in my bed."

I stopped cold in my tracks.

"I'll sleep on the floor, Charlie. What kinda guy do you think I am?"

I thought back to the time he held my face in the oven and pretended he was going to turn it on.

"Wait,"—he laughed—"you probly shouldn't answer that."

"Probably not."

• •

(*Riley*)

I led Attie toward my room. "Thanks so much, Riley. I'll be out of your room first thing in the morning. I just don't want to upset your parents, not sleeping in Melody's bed and all. Cool room," Attie said as she plopped herself onto my bed.

I dug through my closet as she raved about being back in Oklahoma. Although she spoke quickly, her voice was soft, and her words were formal and polished. She probably thought I sounded like a country hick compared to all the hoity toity New Yorkers she usually hung out with.

I would be sleeping in the same room as Attie, and put bluntly, I was a nervous wreck. Closing my eyes, I took a deep breath and turned to face her. She'd already made herself comfortable by lying on her stomach, and she watched as I unrolled the sleeping bag and lay on my back with my arms folded behind my head. Peering over at me, I could tell she wanted to say something.

"Yeah, what is it?" I asked, slightly curious.

"Nothing."

"Good gosh, just say it."

Placing her chin on the mattress, she looked down at me with a scowl but didn't speak. I'm not sure how it happened, but before I knew it I was sitting in front of her, and even though we were only inches apart, I lowered my head so that I could see her eyes. She didn't startle or pick up her head; she slowly rolled up her eyes so that she could see me.

"What already?" I demanded.

"Why have you always called me Charlie?" she asked. "Nobody else does. Good grief, you and your dad sure have a thing for nicknames. In this house alone I'm called three totally different things."

My body relaxed as she talked. "Does it bother you?"

"Yes ... no, I don't know. I just don't see how you can get Charlie from Atticus."

"I didn't."

"Why then?"

Her eyes looked drowsy, and it was clear that she needed rest, but my eyes remained locked on hers. "You remind me of the Charlie Brown cartoon."

Her eyes narrowed and a crease formed between them as her lips twisted into a crooked frown. "Why Charlie Brown? Other than a big skull, I don't look a thing like him—do I?"

"No, and you don't have a big skull. You don't look a thing like him. It's no big deal."

She waited for me to answer and somehow managed to look intensely through tired green eyes.

"You say 'good grief' all the time, just like on the Charlie Brown cartoon."

"I do?"

"All the time, you always have."

The scowl turned slightly softer. "One more question?"

I sighed in an effort to act annoyed.

"You're unhappy that I'm here, aren't you?"

"Huh?"

"I could tell from the moment I got here. I realize that you don't want me here. Why do you dislike me so much? Did I do something, or maybe it's that I'm here and she's not."

I shook my head vigorously. "No. No, you're talking all crazy. I don't dislike you, I just—I don't know, it's just weird."

"What's weird?"

"Oh…uh…having a girl in the house again. I kinda got used to the quiet."

"Well, I can be quiet."

"I don't want you to be quiet."

"You don't?"

"No, of course not. You'll just take some getting used to, that's all. It'll be all right."

"Just let me know if I'm being too loud or if I talk too much. I haven't had anyone to talk to in a while, so I may go a little crazy."

"Well, I'll let you know if you start to get on my nerves."

"Good. I don't want to wear out my welcome."

"Well, you're gonna if you don't stop talking and go to sleep."

"All right, sorry."

"And stop saying you're sorry all the time."

"But I am." Her voice was hushed and the words trembled. "I'm more sorry than you could ever know."

It was clear that we were no longer on the topic of her incessant talking.

"You don't have to say another word, Charlie. You have nothing to be sorry for."

She nodded her head as tears filled the lower part of her eyes. I watched until they fell freely and then looked away. "You're gonna do just fine." My own voice shook, but I refused to cry in front of her, on the first night anyway. "You can relax now; you're home."

"Thanks, Riley."

I glanced back at her. "You're welcome."

Attie rolled over, and after only a few minutes of lying in silence, I heard her begin to breathe softly as she drifted off to sleep.

I was in shock. Attie Reed was gonna be living in my house for the summer. What were my parents thinking, putting an all-American hormonal boy and girl in such close proximity for an extended period of time? This couldn't be good. To make matters worse, she looked just as pretty in person as she did in the Christmas card we received just five months before she arrived on our doorstep.

It wasn't your normal family photo, the one with the annoying sweaters and fake, tense smiles. This picture was different, as if the photographer had caught a private family moment and those of us who received the card were getting a peek into their private world.

Attie and her dad were wearing jeans and the same white long-sleeve turtleneck with an OU logo on the front. Dr. Reed sat on the floor cross-legged as Attie sat on his right knee turning sideways with her bare feet resting on his left knee. His arms wrapped around her waist, and hers were around his neck. The photographer must have snapped the photo while they were laughing about something, and I wondered if maybe Attie had told him a joke. Her hair rested on her shoulders, and her nose scrunched as she smiled at her father. It would have been the perfect picture had her mother been in it as well. At the time, I thought the picture was meant to proclaim to everyone that they were okay, they'd survived the darkest time in their lives, and they were happy again. I hoped the picture portrayed the truth.

chapter 4

(Attie)

Apparently my body thought I was still on East Coast time because I woke up extra early. Riley was asleep on the floor below me, and I realized that he gave the impression of being much nicer when he was sleeping. I didn't remember having any nightmares during the night, and if I did, I didn't wake him. Maybe the night-mares stayed behind in New York and they wouldn't be bothering me any longer. One could only hope.

Sliding out of bed as quietly as possible, I quickly made the bed. Wanting to leave a note thanking him for letting me borrow his bed, I searched the room and found a notepad and pen on his desk. He had scribbled drawings on most of the pages, but I found a blank piece toward the back, scrawled him a note, and left it lying on the bed.

Gramps would be there at eight fifteen to take me to take my driver's license test. This time I felt confident that I was going to pass, so not wanting to look too unsightly in my license picture, I dug through Melody's drawers until I found some of her old makeup. I wasn't exactly sure what I was doing, but I'd seen plenty of women put makeup on, so I figured I could do it. Plus, the few days Melody and I spent together the summer before, I would sit on her bed each morning and watch as she carefully transformed her face. I took mental notes so that I would be prepared a few months later when my sixteenth birthday finally arrived and I was allowed to start wearing makeup myself.

I'd secretly been jealous. Her mother was letting her wear makeup, and my mother was still treating me like I was twelve. Even worse, Melody was so naturally beautiful she didn't even need makeup. I was the one that needed serious help. I did, however, find one loophole—ChapStick. I wore it religiously and whether I had chapped lips or not. It was the closest thing to lip gloss I'd ever come into contact with, and wearing it made me feel like I wasn't a complete square.

I swiped some powder onto my eyelids, but it was too dark, so I rubbed most of it right back off. Taking the mascara wand out of the tube, I carefully applied it to my eyelashes. Applying it was much harder than it looked, but the end result was acceptable.

I also threw on some lip gloss and curled my hair. Looking in the mirror, I decided that I didn't look half bad. I threw on some clothes and ran down the stairs just in time for Gramps to pull into the driveway.

"Atticus." Gramps greeted me with a big kiss on the cheek. "Wow, are you wearin' makeup?"

"I want to look good for my driver's license picture."

"I see." He wore a small smirk on his face. "So how'd you sleep?"

"Good. No nightmares or anything."

"Praise God. Maybe bein' home is helping to ease your mind."

"Yes, maybe it is."

That or the fact that Riley was sleeping next to me on the floor. I felt guilty although I wasn't sure why. It wasn't as if we'd done anything wrong or even wanted to.

After arriving at the examination office, Gramps said a small prayer before escorting me into the office so that I could face my fate, but within thirty minutes I was back in the truck with Gramps. I'd blown it. The truck was much taller and wider than Dad's coupe, so I was unable to see a couple of curbs that I should have avoided. I also failed miserably at parking.

"Well, Atticus, it looks like you'll be driving a golf cart around town for the next few years."

Although he was trying to be funny, I didn't think the situation called for humor at all. As a matter of fact, I was desperately fighting back tears. I could feel my chest start shaking as tears were just on the edge of release.

I was almost seventeen and still didn't have a driver's license. I was now, in fact, a confirmed loser.

He interrupted my pity party. "Oh, I forgot. I have something for you."

"A gift?" A gift would cheer me up.

"Not a gift so much, but it's something you've always wanted."

"What?" I squealed like a three-year-old. "What did you get me?"

"I'm signing my OU football tickets over to you."

"Get out?"

"Is 'get out' kinda like saying 'No way'?"

"Yes, it's just like that."

"You're gonna have to get me up-to-date on all this stuff, Atticus. I haven't been around teenagers since 'righteous' was popular."

"Righteous?" I shrugged. "Anyway, where are the seats?"

"Oh, they're good seats, Atticus; you'll love 'em. They're under the upper deck so you don't get sunburned or rained on. Perfect for a princess."

"Awesome. How many are there?"

"You can have three, and your dad and I will get the others. The first game is around Labor Day."

During our drive home, he shared stories about many of the Sooner games that he attended. A few of them didn't sound that fun—they sounded miserable. He called one of them "The Ice Bowl" and said that he almost got frostbite, but the excitement of the game made it well worth it.

Other than the Lord, my grandmother, and animals, OU football was his greatest passion, and he'd passed it down to me. Believe it or not, he taught me the words to "Boomer Sooner" before "Jesus Loves Me." He'd be ashamed of himself if I reminded him of it.

"How do I handle going to Oklahoma State for vet school?" I asked as we pulled into the Bennetts' driveway.

"Sometimes you just have to grin and bear it. There's no reason you can't root for OSU when they aren't playing us."

I wasn't so sure about that. If there was one team I hated more than Texas, it was Oklahoma State.

"Gramps, when Jesus talked about loving your neighbor, I don't think he was referring to OSU."

I'd made him laugh, and he seemed proud. Prejudice against OSU Cowboys and Texas Longhorns was the only form of prejudice promoted in our home. "I love you, Atticus Reed."

"You too, Gramps. Thanks for everything."

I hopped out of the car, slammed the door, and as I ran inside the house, Mrs. Bennett yelled my name.

"Yes, ma'am?"

"Breakfast is about ready. Come on so it doesn't get cold."

"Yes, ma'am."

I walked into the kitchen and noticed the family dog, Boomer, sitting in my usual spot. He looked as if he didn't have any intention of moving, so I sat in Melody's seat. Mr. Bennett was absorbed in the newspaper, and Mrs. Bennett stood at the stove making gravy and singing along to Rick Springfield blaring from her laptop.

I'd never gotten the whole "gravy with breakfast" thing, but it did taste good. I liked it over hash browns. I'd learned that Okies would put gravy on just about anything. They also liked to fry their food—vegetables especially. I'd eaten fried okra, fried zucchini, fried squash, fried pickles, fried green beans, fried broccoli, and fried cauliflower. In my opinion, the okra and squash were the best. One summer I'd even tried fried bacon with gravy, and I hated to admit it, but it was incredible.

Picking up a portion of the paper, I occupied my time until breakfast was ready.

• • • • • • • • • • • • • • • • • • • •

(Riley)

A small throbbing under my chin woke me up. Reaching up to touch it, I winced in pain. Attie kicked me harder than I'd originally thought.

I looked to my bed hoping that she would still be there, but my heart sank when I saw that she was gone. A piece of paper sat on the pillow. It was a note.

> Thanks so much, Riley. I slept really great. I'm sure I'll be fine to sleep in Melody's room tonight. I might as well get used to it, right? Yea, you get your bed back!
> Sorry again about your chin.
>
> —Charlie

I didn't fail to notice she signed the note "Charlie." Feeling a grin fill my face, I reread the note a few more times before the smell of greasy bacon broke my haze, and I raced to wash up and get dressed.

I wanted to walk into the kitchen as unassuming as possible, and evidently it worked because no one bothered to acknowledge my existence. They were each reading a section of the paper and were absorbed in the news of the day. My dad read the front section, my mom "Life and Style," and Attie was reading the sports section.

I started to make myself a plate of food. "Good morning, everyone. Wow, Mom, biscuits and gravy, eggs and bacon—all my favorites. Thanks so much."

As I leaned over and kissed her on the cheek, she about fell out of her chair.

"We...we...well, thanks, Riley." Amazingly, she was nearly speechless for once in her life. Unfortunately, it didn't last long. "What's gotten you in such a good mood?"

"Nothing really."

She believed me and moved on to questioning Attie. "What got you out of the house so early this morning?"

Our eyes looked toward Attie as we waited for a reply. She lowered the paper and laid it in her lap, and I'm pretty sure we all inhaled when we saw her. Her hair curled a little as it lay on either side of her face, there was a little bit of color on her eyelids, and she'd used some of that black stuff girls put on their eyelashes. I think I even noticed that she was wearing something shiny on her lips. Although she looked pretty, I preferred her without all the goop on her face.

"Well…" Attie bit her thumbnail and kept her eyes looking down at her lap. "It's rather embarrassing."

She peeked up as we all leaned in to hear her explain what was causing her so much discomfort. We were captivated.

Her eyes squeezed and her nose scrunched up. "I went to take my driver's test."

Dad set his paper down onto the table. "Well, why is that so embarrassing?"

"I've failed three times now." She tried to remain composed but failed miserably and began to sob. Tears poured down her face, and unfortunately the stuff on her eyes didn't stay on her lashes. I handed her a napkin so she could wipe the black streaks off her cheeks.

As Attie continued to cry, my parents and I sat stunned and horrified. None of us knew what to do with a sixteen-year-old girl that was inconsolable, and I panicked.

"I want my mom," she wailed.

That was it, my heart shattered. The sound of her voice was the most pitiful sound I'd ever heard, and worse was the fact that the sound came from her tear-stained face.

Before I knew it my mom was at her side, and tears were flowing from her eyes as well. "I know, Attie, I know you miss your mom. I wish I could take your pain away. I wish I could take all of our pain away."

Attie instantly stopped crying, and her body turned rigid. "Oh, I'm so sorry."

Dad rubbed her knee. "Sorry for what, Attiline?"

"I'm sitting at your table, eating from Melody's chair. She should be the one sitting here, not me. I'm being selfish and not even considering your pain." Her shoulders shook as she tried to catch her breath. "All I can think about is how much I miss my mom." She threw her head onto the table, and luckily, I caught her hair just before it landed in the gravy.

My parents and I glanced at each other as Attie struggled to contain herself.

Before I knew it, tears filled my eyes. "Oh great." I threw my hands up in disgust. "It took less than twenty-four hours, and now we're all crying."

"I didn't even get to go to their funeral," Attie continued. "I've never even seen their headstones."

Getting up, she walked away, leaving us to watch as she left our presence. After she made her way upstairs, my mother went to sit on my dad's lap. They were crying not only because they felt badly for Attie but because they also missed my sister.

I'd caught them crying about Melody on a regular basis, so seeing their grief was nothing new, but I never knew how to help them. I couldn't even help myself.

• • • • • • • • • • • • • • • • • •

(Attie)

Somehow I ended up locked in the upstairs bathroom sitting on the side of the bathtub trying to calm myself down. It wasn't helping, so I decided to splash cold water on my face to see if that would bring me around. But when I walked up to the sink and saw my face in the mirror, my sobs became heavier. Black mascara was smeared down my face, causing me to look like a deranged clown, and what was worse, the Bennetts witnessed it.

Confirmation: I was, in fact, a loser.

I was scrubbing my face when Riley's muffled voice penetrated through the bathroom door. He was talking with a sweet voice and sounded concerned. After washing the paint off my face, I turned off the water and mustered up all the composure that I could before opening the door.

He clumsily fell onto the bathroom floor and stared up at me in disgust.

"Good grief, Riley, you look more ridiculous lying on the bathroom floor than I did with my clown face."

"I guess I'll have to learn to appreciate your brutal honesty," he snapped.

Stepping over him, I walked into his bedroom and sat on the bed. I hoped he would follow, but he never did; he simply lay there looking like a pile of dirty clothes someone left on the floor.

"You should never talk like that, Charlie, like it should have been you instead of her. It just isn't good. Surviving is something never to feel guilty about. God spared your life for a reason. You're supposed to be here."

Honestly, I didn't remember a thing that I said downstairs because I burst into tears and started having verbal diarrhea. They probably thought I'd lost my mind. Little did the Bennetts know they had welcomed a girl into their home that was prone to hysterics, and I was certain they didn't quite know what to do with me.

Riley didn't look like he was going to move, so I strolled back into the bathroom and lay down on the floor with the top of my head against his. I closed my eyes and rested my cheek on the cool tile floor, and my body relaxed as Riley reached over his head and began stroking my hair.

I reached over to return the favor but, as graceful as ever, ended up poking him in the eye.

We were forced to get up off the bathroom floor when Mr. Bennett called upstairs and told Riley to march his butt outside and get his chores done.

He sat up in a huff. "I can't wait to move away for college so I don't have to listen to anyone tell me or my butt what to do."

Once downstairs, none of us mentioned the incident that took place over breakfast, but I caught Mr. Bennett shoot Riley a look or two of concern. He wanted to know if I was all right, but all Riley could do was give him a quick nod before getting his slave labor butt outside to mow the lawn.

Eventually I followed him outside and sat on the porch step as he made the first few passes of the lawn mower. Once he started bagging the grass clippings, I walked up and started to help.

"You don't have to help with this," he said, trying to stop me.

I grabbed a hold of the trash bag and held it open. "I need to earn my keep around here somehow … and I wanted to apologize for my behavior this morning. I completely overreacted. Unfortunately, I tend to do that often, so prepare yourself. It was unfair of me to get you and your parents so upset."

"You don't need to apologize to me. We're your family; that's what family's for."

"Is it?" The concept of family felt foreign to me for some reason. "Did you and your parents have a pow-wow or something? They said the exact same thing."

"Nope. No pow-wow."

"Thanks." I closed my eyes and inhaled deeply. "This is one of my favorite smells, you know."

"What?"

"Fresh cut grass. I don't know what's so alluring about it, but I love it, don't you?"

"Maybe when you're the one cutting the grass, the smell loses its appeal. It does nothing for me."

"Makes sense I guess. To get so wrapped up in the job you can't enjoy the small rewards."

He stopped bagging and looked up at me with a small scowl. "You think the smell of cut grass is a reward for cutting it?"

"Idiotic, huh?"

"Strangely, no. Do you think the accident causes you to appreciate little things more?"

"Maybe. I didn't experience this smell last year, so it could just be the restoration of that memory. Who knows?"

"Do they hurt?" he asked as he dumped the grass into the open bag.

"Pardon?"

"Your scars."

"Oh, those?" I looked down at one of my arms. "No, not really. They itch every once in a while, but they don't hurt anymore. They're ugly, aren't they?"

"No. I don't think they're ugly at all."

"Jesus calls them battle scars."

"Jesus what? You talk to Jesus now?" he asked with a laugh.

"No. Remember, I happen to have a very active imagination." Looking around the yard, the mowing job seemed monstrous. "Good grief, this job's going to take us all day."

We continued to work together in a comfortable silence until Mrs. Bennett brought out lemonade.

Sitting on the porch swing, I laid my head back and closed my eyes as we swayed back and forth. "I could sit like this forever. There's something about summer. It's like you're in a different world, even if just for a small amount of time. Everything slows down, and life just seems easier."

I opened one eye and peeked over at him. "I've lost my mind, haven't I?"

"No. Not at all."

"Then why are you staring at me?"

"Sorry, I didn't realize I was." He looked back out at the yard before laying his head back against the swing. "I guess I wish I could see things the way you do."

"Have a near-death experience and then spend five months in a hospital; maybe that'll do it for you."

"I think I'll pass. Maybe I'll just try to start seeing life through your eyes and see if that works for me."

"Sounds good." I closed my eye again. "Do you have any big plans this summer?"

"Two-a-days start soon. They keep me pretty busy."

"What position do you play?"

"Tight end."

"I can see that; you've got the build for it. I guess you've got some speed then too?"

"I guess."

"Keith Jackson and Trent Smith were great tight ends for OU. Maybe you can play for the Sooners."

"I doubt it. I'm not that good."

"Sure you are."

"No, if I'm lucky I can play at a small college somewhere. Maybe get a little bit of school paid for."

"That would be helpful, wouldn't it?"

"Sure would."

"Do you like going to the OU football games?"

"Yeah. What about you?"

"I've never been, but my Gramps just gave me his season tickets. You'll have to go with me sometime. I can't wait. I've always wanted to go to a game."

"That'd be great."

"It would be fun, wouldn't it?"

"Yeah, thanks for inviting me."

"No offense, but who else am I going to ask?"

"None taken. But don't worry, you'll make some friends soon. But until then, what are your plans for the summer?"

"I'm going to work at Gramps's vet clinic. He said if I would help out over the summer he would buy me a car before school started."

"Sounds like a deal to me. What kind are you gonna get?"

"An old junk heap. The way I drive it would be nonsensical to spend a lot of money. It probably won't take me long to get in my first wre…" I stopped myself. "Well, you know what I'm saying."

"Yeah."

We sat quietly for several minutes. I wanted to sit there for the rest of the afternoon but knew that we needed to continue our mission.

"Should we get back to work?" he asked. "Otherwise we'll be doing this all day."

I opened my eyes and jumped to my feet. "Let's go."

"You should wear shoes, Charlie. It's dangerous to mow in bare feet."

"Oh, Riley, I didn't get to walk in grass last summer. Can't you just let me enjoy it?"

"Sure, who am I to spoil your fun? Just don't get too close to the mower. You end up losing a toe, and with our history the way it is, my dad'll think I did it on purpose."

chapter 5

(Riley)

I made my way toward my room and saw Attie sitting on the floor in her usual spot under the window.

"We need to get you a chair, Charlie."

"I'm fine. I like sitting under the window."

The phone rang, and within moments Mom was screaming up the stairs telling Attie that the phone was for her.

I got a whiff of perfume as she ran past me, threw herself into my chair, and rolled across the floor until it slammed into the wall. She smelled amazing, and I hardly cared that she'd thrown her feet onto my desk.

Her toenails were red.

"Hello?" She spoke into the receiver and grinned as she listened to the voice on the other end of the line.

I instantly knew who it was. Other than my mother, Anne was one of the loudest talkers I'd ever heard, and even through a phone and across the room, I could hear her warmly greet Attie.

Anne was a regular at my house while Melody was alive, and when Attie visited, the three were inseparable.

I got out my iPod, stuck the buds into my ears, and was just about to push play when I heard the word *boyfriend*.

Okay, I reached a moral dilemma. Should I leave the room and give her some privacy or stay in the room and try to ignore her by occupying myself with something?

It was a difficult decision, but I chose to stay in the room, pretend I was ignoring her, but actually listen to every word she said. It probably wasn't the most moral choice, but I was certain that what I heard would be interesting.

No, she didn't have a boyfriend.

This was not news to me, seeing as how I'd heard her tell Mom the same piece of information when I was eavesdropping on *their* conversation. I realized that I was becoming very nosy but continued to eavesdrop anyway.

Yeah, some of the boys from her school were pretty cute. No, she didn't date very much. No, she didn't miss New York; she didn't have many friends left after the accident, she said.

I noticed that she was about to start flipping through my sketchbook, so I quickly got up, grabbed it from her, and threw it under my bed.

She pointed to the phone next to her ear. "A little privacy, please?" She obviously wanted me to leave the room.

"No," I shot back. "You're in my room!"

I pretended to turn up my iPod and picked up a book as she gave me an evil stare before rejoining her conversation.

"Riley adorable?"

I almost dropped my book but then realized she was asking a question more than making a statement.

Attie glanced back at me, but I pretended not to notice.

"Jealous? Why would girls be jealous of me? Well, that's just foolish. It's not like that at all."

I secretly watched as her eyes grew large while she listened to Anne speak from the other end of the line.

"What do you mean he's 'with' her?"

Her jaw dropped.

"Sex?" She threw her small hand over her mouth and then turned to see if I was listening. Trying very hard not to express any amusement at the conversation, I focused my eyes on the book in front of me.

She turned back around.

"Riley…a lot of girls?" Her voice sounded disappointed.

Evidently the news wasn't good because she looked a little woozy, and before I knew it she threw herself over and put her head between her knees. I sat up slightly so that I could hear more clearly.

"What?" she squealed.

She threw her body straight up against the back of the chair, causing it to roll back into the wall. It was like I was watching *The Exorcist* or something.

"Virgin?"

My entire body froze in fear of getting caught just as the conversation was getting good.

She was trying to whisper, but I could still hear her quivering voice. "I'm only sixteen, Anne. Of course I'm a…virgin."

Just as I was beginning to feel relieved, she dropped her head back between her knees and miserably failed at whispering again.

"Seduced?" Attie looked like she was about to pass out again, and it was becoming nearly impossible for me to act like I couldn't hear her screams.

"I've got to get out more," she said, dazed as she sat back again and put her head in her hand. Poor thing looked like she'd just come off of a roller coaster that beat her to a pulp.

After talking for a few more minutes, she hung up the phone and sat in a trance-like state as she stared at my closet door. "Sex, seduction…good grief, where am I, *Dawson's Creek*?" Finally gaining her composure, she stood and walked out of the room.

That was by far the strangest half of a conversation I'd ever heard, and Attie Reed was getting more and more interesting by the minute.

chapter 6

(Attie)

As I sat cross-legged on the floor under the window, my mind replayed the phone conversation with Anne. Riley was with some girl named Tiffany, and she was probably gorgeous and had big boobs, although I'm not really sure why I cared. It wasn't as if I was interested in having him for myself, but the thought of him being with that kind of girl didn't settle well with me.

Given the phone conversation, it was obvious that he and I had less in common that I'd originally thought and once school started I'd be on my own.

"What's bothering you?" Jesus asked as he appeared sitting next to me.

"Nothing. Nothing we should talk about anyway."

"Since when do we not talk about things?"

"Since they're inappropriate."

"Nothing's off limits between us, Attie. You can talk to me about anything. Come on, out with it."

Going way outside of my comfort zone, I dug down deep, finally mustered up the courage, and dove right in. "I talked to my friend Anne on the phone today, and she gave me some scoop about the school I'll be going to and the kids that'll be there—and Riley."

"And?"

"And they're all into stuff that I'm not into. I realize I was out of it most of last year, but I don't remember everyone around me being so promiscuous. From the way Anne makes it sound, she and I are in the minority—big-time minority. It sounds like everyone is having sex or wants to or have basically done everything but. Some guy even tried to seduce her at a party once. I don't know if I'm ready to deal with all that. I'm already a freak and an outsider; what are they going to do when they find out I'm also a major prude? I feel like I'm walking into a lions' den and everyone's going to be ready to pounce. I'm not going to fit in, I know it."

"It's never been easy to do the right thing. Ask anyone who's done it."

I nodded, although I wanted to cry. Hearing him say that doing the right thing wasn't easy wasn't helping my situation or relieving my anxiety in any way.

"Do you remember the story of Daniel from the Bible?" he asked.

"Daniel? Was he the one who was thrown into the lions' den?"

"Yes. The story seems appropriate seeing as how that's where you feel you're heading. Do you remember what happened to him?"

I thought back to a coloring page that I'd been given in Sunday school when I was little. It was a picture of a man dressed in a robe, and he was sitting on the floor with a big smile on his face as he petted two lions. I remember wishing that I could pet a lion and right then and there decided that when I became a vet I would take care of lions and other zoo animals.

"Nothing," I finally answered. "Nothing happened to him."

"Why not?"

"God sent an angel that closed the lions' mouths. When they pulled him out, he hadn't been injured at all. The lions hadn't touched him."

"That's right. He'd called out to God, and God protected him. Now, I can't guarantee you that when you walk through the halls at school people won't say bad things about you or accuse you of things that aren't right or fair. But what I can promise you is that I'll walk through those doors with you and that I won't leave you alone—ever.

I'll protect you, Attie; I'll protect your spirit. Nothing they say or do can have an effect on you unless you let it."

"I appreciate that."

"Do you feel any better about it?"

"Yes, a little." It still bothered me to know that Riley was just like the other kids, but there was no sense in mentioning it. That was between Riley and Jesus, not Riley, Jesus, and me. I was pretty sure that Jesus was aware of the situation, and he didn't need me bringing it up.

"As time goes on you're going to have a lot of questions about those kinds of things, and I don't ever want you to think it isn't safe to talk to me about them. Trust me, there isn't anything you can say that I haven't heard before—or worse."

"That's good to know." He was right. I was sure there'd be plenty of things I had questions about or complaints that I wanted to file with him. As a matter of fact, one was burning in my mind as we sat there, and although it was a much lighter subject, it still weighed heavily on my mind.

"Why didn't you give me bigger boobs?" I asked.

"If the man we have picked out for you wanted that, my Father would have given them to you."

"Most boys like big boobs," I pouted.

"Most boys don't know what they want, let alone need," he replied. "At least until they're twenty-five or so."

"Does that mean I'll be waiting until I'm twenty-five to get a date?"

"Maybe."

"Elizabeth and Mr. Darcy got together when she was about my age. So did Anne and Gilbert from *Anne of Green Gables*."

"Back then they also died when they were forty." His sarcasm wasn't helping to improve my mood. "Look, you shouldn't worry so much about what boys think of you anyway. No one can love you like I can. My love is pure, complete, and unconditional. You're precious and you're perfect—just the way you are. Just the way you were created."

"Thanks a lot." I wasn't being sincere, but at that moment all I wanted to do was end the conversation. I knew what he was saying was truth, but there was still that part of me that wished that some-one—some human—would think I was beautiful.

"And by the way, you are beautiful." He'd read my mind.

"Thanks," I murmured.

"Attie, even when you find that boy who believes you're beautiful and falls head over heels in love with you, the love won't be perfect. It will be flawed, just like the boy who gives it."

"I understand." Disgusted with myself, I shook my head. "I don't know, maybe I'll just become a nun or something. That way I don't have to deal with any of this. Do you see a convent in my future?"

"I'm not a fortune teller."

"I know, it would just be nice to have a clue about my life in the future."

"Okay, Attie, I never do this—"

I leaned close to him. "Do what?"

"Tell people about their future."

"You're going to tell me about my future?"

He nodded. "Part of it."

"Sweet!"

"Oh, I don't know if you can handle it." He enjoyed teasing me. "Maybe I shouldn't say anything."

"Oh yes, you should," I squealed.

Jesus was about to reveal part of his master plan, and I was like a dog with a steak in front of it. I was practically salivating at the prospect of getting a glimpse into my future.

Jesus glanced around as if to make sure that no one was eaves-dropping, and for some reason I did the same.

"I can't believe I'm doing this."

"Tell me already," I begged. "I can't stand the suspense."

"Okay, here goes. You ... "

I hung on the word.

" ... are not going to be a nun."

"What? That's it? I'm not going to be a nun, that's the big news?" My disappointment was evident.

Jesus shrugged. "Hey, you asked and it's better than nothing."

"An old maid?"

"No. Go to bed, Attie. You're tired and you're talking foolishly."

"Don't I always? Talk foolishly I mean."

"Not all the time—just much of it. It's one of the many things I love about you. Now go to sleep."

• •

Mom glanced over at me from the driver's seat. "You girls are so funny. I'm glad you're together for another summer."

"It's just Attie, Mrs. Reed. She makes me seem funnier," Melody said, laughing from the backseat. She leaned toward the front of the car so she could join the conversation. "Oh look! It's Meg Patton and her new baby. She just had it and she's only seventeen." Melody pointed out my window, and I turned to look at the girl. The new mother pushed a baby carriage and talked to a woman who was walking beside her.

"She's a cute girl." Mom's voice sounded sweet.

I turned to talk to them, but a scream escaped my throat instead.

Everything became dark. Muffled sounds filled my ears, but I wasn't able to make sense of them. I wanted to move but couldn't; something held me down, and a sharp pain throbbed in my stomach.

My hearing returned to normal, but nothing made sense.

"Get them out of the car!"

"Help me grab her. Hurry! Her arm is stuck; I can't get her out."

There was more screaming from many different voices, but they were being drowned out by crackling and popping sounds.

"Attie!" Mom screamed. "Melody! Get them out first! Please get the girls out!"

My body was being torn apart, and my stomach felt as if it exploded. The pain was excruciating, and I was aware that I was dying.

Mom continued to appeal to anyone who would listen. "Somebody, please!"

"Mom?" My vision was murky, but I could see her face. It was bloody, and her eyes were large and full of fear.

Her voice calmed. "Get out of the car, Attie." Her words sounded crisp and clear.

I looked into the backseat in search of Melody and found her lying covered in blood in a twisted heap on the floor. I turned my attention back to my mother and out of the corner of my eye saw fire.

"Get out, Attie!"

"Mom?"

Everything went dark.

chapter 7

(*Riley*)

I jolted out of bed at the sound of someone screaming, and it only took a second to realize the scream came from Attie.

I threw sweatpants on over my boxers and sprinted to her room. Throwing on the bedroom light, I found her sitting on the floor screaming for her mother and Melody. Her eyes were closed, her fists were tight, and her body was shaking.

Running to her, I knelt down, grabbed her shoulders, and gave her a gentle shake. She needed to wake up and end the nightmare. "Attie, wake up, Attie."

Her eyes finally opened, but she looked up at me as if she didn't know me at all.

"You're all right." I tried to sound reassuring. "You're not alone. I'm here; you're safe."

My parents came charging up the stairs behind me and stopped in the doorway. They both looked terrified.

"Is she all right?" Dad asked in a breathless voice.

I held out my hand signaling for them to stay back. "Yes, it was a nightmare. She's all right; she just needs to sleep. Go back downstairs. We'll be fine."

They stood back and watched as Attie shivered in my arms. Seeing her gripped in fear was agony for them.

Attie's eyes focused on me. "Riley?"

"Yes." Sitting down, I pulled her onto my lap. "I'm here."

"I almost didn't recognize you." Her voice was tired and soft. "Why are you calling me Attie?"

"'Cause you scared me to death and I couldn't think straight, that's why."

Mom rushed over, wrapped us in a blanket, and then kissed Attie on the top of the head.

"It's okay, Mom. Go on, you don't need to watch this," I urged quietly. "Go downstairs."

Dad started to take a step into the room but stopped himself. After staring at Attie for a moment, he finally walked into the room for the first time since Melody's death. He gently pulled Mom away from us, and then the two of them slowly went back downstairs. My mother wailed all the way down the stairs.

I rocked back and forth in an effort to soothe Attie back into a deep sleep, but just as she started to fall asleep, her eyes opened again and looked up at me. "You aren't trying to seduce me, are you?" Her voice was hushed and her words sounded mumbled. "Anne said you seduce girls and have a lot of sex."

Well, that explained the phone conversation I overheard.

"No, I'm not." I laughed. "I don't."

"I'm not like that," she muttered.

"I know you're not." I instinctively stroked her cheek with my fingers, and the more I caressed her soft skin, the more she relaxed in my arms. "I'm not like that either, Charlie. I'm not."

"You called me Charlie." A small smile inched across her face. "You really are Riley; I thought that was you."

"Of course."

"I haven't been kissed." Her mumbling made her difficult to understand. "That makes me a freak."

I looked into her tired eyes. "You're not a freak. You're wonderful; now go to sleep."

Her eyes closed, but after a few moments she opened them again. "Help me stay awake." Her voice trembled. "I'm afraid."

Tears ran down my cheeks, and the speed of my rocking increased as I protectively pulled her closer to me. "You're already asleep. I'm right here." My voice cracked. "It's gonna be all right."

She was afraid to sleep because she was afraid to dream. It was similar to an eighties horror movie I'd watched with my parents, except Attie's nightmares were once real. She'd seen her mother and best friend die, and she was left to live with the guilt of surviving. The memory of their pain was torturing her.

Within a few minutes Attie's breathing was rhythmic and gentle. I sat holding her in my arms and crying for what felt like hours. The last time I cried was the day of Melody's funeral, and it felt good to let it all out.

Eventually, my legs went numb, so I moved our bodies until we were lying on the floor.

She slightly came to and looked around. I spoke softly into her ear. "It's all right. I'm still here."

"Thank you, I don't want to be alone anymore."

"I won't leave you, Charlie. Not until you're ready."

"Poor Riley," she whispered, "that could be a long time."

"I'm not going anywhere."

Attie needed me, and nothing could drag me away.

• •

(*Attie*)

My eyes opened and immediately closed again. The sun was bright and my room was full of light. Opening my eyes again, I looked around until I noticed Riley sitting under the window. He was reading.

"Riley?" My voice was groggy, so I shook my head to force myself to wake up. He looked up and grinned at me.

"Hey, Charlie, did you sleep well?"

"Ha, ha, very funny." I moaned.

"You didn't wake up again after the nightmare. You slept peacefully."

I sat up quickly. "Were you here all night?"

"Yeah." He shrugged his shoulders. "I slept in here on the floor."

I lay back down and covered my eyes with my hands. "Good grief, I'm so sorry. You didn't need to do that." I peeked back at him to see if he looked bothered.

He shook his head and gave me a smile. "It was no problem." His eyes were warm. "Really, it's fine."

"I didn't talk in my sleep and say anything stupid, did I?"

"Nope. Your lips were sealed. Why?" He smirked. "Is there anything I should know?"

Relief filled my body. "No. Nothing that you would find interesting anyway." I rolled over onto my stomach and looked up at him. "How long have you been awake?"

"A few hours."

"Riley! You did not have to stay." I rolled back over and covered my face with my pillow. "I'm so sorry I'm such an emotional basket case."

"It's fine. I know I didn't have to stay; I wanted to. It's no big deal. Don't lose any sleep over it or anything." His voice sounded like he was smiling.

I spoke from under my pillow, "Boy, aren't you the jokester this morning."

"Really, I wouldn't have done it if I didn't want to. Eventually you'll have to survive without me, but it didn't necessarily have to start last night."

I rolled back over onto my stomach. "What are you reading?" I asked. He held up a *Seventeen* magazine so I could see the cover. "Oooh, any good?"

"Yeah." He nodded enthusiastically. "As a matter a fact, right now I'm reading an article called 'What Boys are Really Thinking.'"

"Oh yes." I nodded. "I read that. It didn't help me figure you out in any way."

He let out a carefree laugh that made me feel very at ease. "That's because I'm a man, not a boy."

"Ah, I should have made the differentiation."

"Well, according to the article, boys are pretty much pigs."

"I hate to tell you this, Riley, but I didn't need an article to figure that out."

He ran his fingers through his already messy hair. "You agree? You think boys are pigs?"

"Not all, but most are until they're at least twenty-five or so."

"Oh yeah, where'd you hear that?"

"A pretty reliable source."

I certainly wasn't going to tell him where I'd heard it. After last night, if I told him I was having nightly conversations with Jesus, he would have advised his parents to lock me away in an insane asylum.

"We aren't all pigs, you know."

"Oh no?"

"You can't believe everything you hear, Charlie."

"I'll take that into consideration."

My mind traveled back to my conversation with Anne, and I wondered if what she said was true. She sounded as if she knew for sure, but Riley would be the only person that would know. The question was whether or not he would be honest about it.

Sitting in a partial ball, his left leg was tucked underneath him, and his right was bent up in front of his chest. He shyly hid part of his face behind his knee.

"How often do you have them?" he asked.

I'd gotten lost in thought. "What, boys?"

He threw his head back and laughed. "No, not boys. Why, do you have boys often?"

I laughed along with him. "No, not quite," I admitted.

"The nightmares? How often do you have nightmares?" His shyness escaped as he rested his chin on his knee.

"A lot more than I have boys, I can tell you that."

One of his eyebrows raised and his look became stern. "The nightmares?"

I shut my eyes. "Pretty much every night."

"What have you done about it before now?"

"What do you mean?"

"If I wouldn't have come in last night, it could've gotten even worse. Did your dad come in and help you before?"

"Our house in Ithaca had three stories. I slept in the bottom story, and my dad slept in the top. I don't know if he ever heard me. I told him about the nightmares, but I don't know that he ever understood. Sometime I would set my alarm for every hour and a half. That way I never fell deep enough asleep to dream."

"How can you survive with that little sleep? Isn't that bad for you?"

"Look at me, Riley. There are bags under my eyes, and I look about twenty years older than I actually am. Sometimes I feel like I'm falling apart. Other times I'm just so drained that I can barely function. It's been going on for a while now, and my body is becoming accustomed to it … somewhat."

"You don't look as bad as you think. You hide your exhaustion well."

I smiled at him. "Well, thank you."

He looked back at me with sadness in his eyes. "Are the dreams the same or different?"

"Almost always the same. Always of the accident, always of my mom's face."

"It must be terrible. From what I saw last night, they seem bad."

"I guess I'm used to it."

"Is it normal? I mean for them to last this long after the accident?"

I shrugged my shoulders.

His questions kept coming. "Have you seen someone about this? Like a therapist or counselor or something?"

"No, I just assumed I would grow out of it at some point." That was a lie. I was actually afraid that they would never go away.

His shoulders slumped and his eyebrows turned down. "You're sleep deprived, and worse than that, you're tortured on a nightly basis." His concern was growing. "There's nothing wrong with getting help. I should know; I've gotten plenty. You need to talk to someone."

"You've seen someone?"

"Oh yeah, no big deal. I've done both individual and family counseling. We started just after Melody died. It helped a lot."

I remained silent. I couldn't believe he admitted that he'd been to therapy.

"It's not something to be ashamed of or anything. I'd hate to think about where I'd be without it."

"Yes." I giggled, "You could be a total nut job like me."

His eyes rolled as he shook his head at me. "You aren't a nut job, Charlie. You're just grieving. I would think that type of thing would be normal." His voice sounded full of distress, and I appreciated his concern. Unfortunately, I wasn't sure I agreed with him. I wasn't at all normal. I was tired and scared, and all I wanted was to wake up from my never-ending nightmare. I was sad, and I didn't want to be sad anymore.

We sat quietly for a few minutes before he decided that we needed to go down and get something to eat.

"Heck, we've already missed breakfast. I don't wanna miss lunch too." He was up and halfway down the stairs before I even got untangled from my blanket.

We made our way to the kitchen, and I saw Mr. and Mrs. Bennett sitting at the table deep in conversation. For the first time since arriving, there was no music coming from the laptop.

When I walked in, they both looked up. Their faces wore the "concerned parent" expression. I glanced at Riley wondering if they knew what happened the night before, and as if he could read my mind, he somberly nodded his head.

"Oh boy," I muttered under my breath.

Mrs. Bennett broke the silence. She was nearly crying. "Attie, are you all right?"

"Yes." I tried to sound reassuring. "I'm fine. It's just a nightmare, no big deal. Honestly, they sound worse than they are."

I glanced back at Riley hoping that I would be able to tell whether or not I was being convincing. The sadness on his face was a sign that nobody was buying my act.

Mr. Bennett stood and hugged me. "Can we help you, Attiline? Is there anything we can do to help?"

"Oh no, I'll be fine." At this point I didn't even sound convincing to myself.

"Are you sure?"

I waited a few moments before I replied. "Well, there's one thing." I bit the corner of my thumbnail and looked up at Mr. Bennett out of the corners of my eyes. This technique always got me what I wanted from my dad.

"I'll try." He wasn't promising anything without hearing my request.

"Can you get me off the cheerleading squad?"

"What? Attiline, last month you flew all the way here just to try out, and practices haven't even started yet. Why would you wanna up and quit now?"

Everyone's eyes were on me, and I felt completely uncomfortable. He placed his hands on my shoulders and looked me in the eyes.

"If that's what you want, I'll consider it. But first tell me why. Why do you wanna quit doing something that you love so much?"

I'd realized he wasn't going to stop the interrogation until I gave an acceptable answer. After all they were doing for me, I knew that I needed to be honest. I motioned for everyone to sit down and then joined them.

"Sadly, you all got a glimpse of what my nights are like—at least for the time being anyway. I've gotten pretty used to them, but they tend to terrify anyone within hearing distance." I looked at Riley apologetically, and he gave me a small smile. "I hoped that being back here would somehow make them go away, but that clearly didn't happen."

Noticing the Bennetts' growing concern, I continued with my reasoning.

"I don't think that spending six nights away would be a good idea right now, and cheer camp is less than a week away. I wouldn't get much sleep, and there's a chance that none of my roommates would either."

Mr. and Mrs. Bennett were nodding as I spoke, so I must have been making sense.

"Not to mention, it's embarrassing," I admitted.

Mr. Bennett spoke first. "I understand that. But wouldn't it be more logical to just get out of cheer camp but stay on the team?"

"It wouldn't be right, Mr. Bennett. If it is a requirement that the team attend camp, then I should either attend or no longer be on the team. It's only fair. Plus, for totally selfish reasons, the last thing I need is another reason for people to dislike me. Preferential treatment doesn't bode well in high school."

Riley didn't agree with me. "Screw what other people think."

"Riley Bennett," Mrs. Bennett scolded. "You cut that talk out right now."

He apologized to his mother and then turned back to me. "Who cares what anyone else thinks? Missing camp is no big deal." He grabbed my elbow to give it a slight squeeze. "Stay on the team."

"I care what people think. I'm already an outsider. I'm already the freak."

"Attie." Now Mrs. Bennett sounded angry with me. "You stop talking like that. Nobody thinks you're a freak. Why would they?"

Yanking my elbow away from Riley, I sat back in my chair and crossed my arms across my stomach. They would never understand.

"Never mind." My jaw grew tight.

Riley leaned toward me and gently placed his hand on my arm. "Who cares?"

My voice rose as I spoke. "That's easy for you to say, Riley."

He removed his hand from my arm and sat upright. "Whaddya mean?"

"Good grief, you're the most popular boy in school. You're smart, athletic, good looking…"

He raised an eyebrow and grinned.

"I mean, not to me necessarily…"

He quickly frowned.

"But evidently to everyone else. Every girl in school and some probably not in school want to go out with you."

At first he blushed, but then he crossed his arms and shook his head. "Not true, not at all."

"Yes true. It is true. Imagine being in my situation." I stood up and threw my hands on my hips. The dreaded drama queen was coming out. "Let's see, the bizarre girl from the accident who claims an angel saved her life goes off to cheer camp where she wakes up screaming at the top of her lungs every night. Throw on top of that the fact that our cheer uniforms don't hide any of my scars, and then I become Frankenstein. Kids are cruel, Riley. Do you think they won't make it hell for me?"

He was silent. There was nothing he could say. Kids were cruel, and they could show no mercy. He placed his elbows on the table and put his face in his hands.

I lowered my voice. "I don't want sympathy. I just don't want to subject myself to more anguish." Tears surfaced, but I shook my head in an effort to keep them at bay. I didn't want to cry in front of the Bennetts again. Sitting down, I tried to regain my composure. "Honestly, I don't care about cheering anymore. I only tried out because my dad wanted me to. I prayed that I wouldn't even make the team. God didn't seem to hear that particular plea."

"But you did make the team," Mr. Bennett spoke again. "You made the team because you're good and because you love it."

"But Mr. Bennett—"

He interrupted me. "Okay, Attiline, it's my turn to speak." His voice was stern.

"Yes, sir." I bit the fingernails on my left hand and looked down at the table as I fumbled with the napkin ring in my right.

"Your dad wanted you to try out because he knew you would enjoy it, among other things."

"What other things?" I mumbled.

"Look at me, Attiline."

Out of the corner of my eye, I could see him lean toward me, and my tears fought their way to the surface again. I shook my head.

His voice was stern but gentle. "Atticus Elizabeth Reed, look at me."

I sat still as he waited, never releasing me from his gaze. I could hear Mrs. Bennett crying but wasn't sure what Riley was doing. After what felt like hours, I realized I wasn't going to win the battle and lifted my eyes to meet Mr. Bennett's.

"Thank you," he whispered. "It's time for you to move on, Attiline. It's time for you to enjoy your life again. Your dad...all of us want you to participate in life again."

Mrs. Bennett sat sobbing across from me. I still couldn't see Riley.

"Nobody said this would be easy, and nobody said this would be painless. It just is what it is. It stinks." His eyes filled with tears, and his voice cracked. "Your mom and Melody are gone."

Feeling like I'd been slapped in the face, I inhaled quickly.

"They're gone; they died." He spoke the words as if he thought I didn't already know they'd been killed.

I heard a small moan leave my body. It was as if a knife stabbed into my heart. I physically ached.

"They're gone, Attiline. You lived, but you're living as if you're gone. Can't you see that God spared your life for a purpose? There's no reason, evidence-wise, that you should be here. That you should have or could have lived. But you did; you're a miracle."

"I don't want to be a miracle if this is what it's like." The floodgates opened and my tears ran free.

Mr. Bennett continued, "You can't go through life as if you died or should have. You miss your mom and Melody. We do too. We lost our only daughter, and Riley lost his twin sister. There isn't a day that goes by that we don't grieve for our loss.

"We could all shut down, write off life, but where would that get us? Who would that benefit? It won't bring them back." Mr. Bennett was full of emotion and his voice shook, as did my body. "God saved you, Attiline. You're here for a reason. You aren't gonna fulfill that purpose hiding away from people. Hiding from life."

For one of the first times in my life, I was speechless. I could think of nothing to say; there were no words in the English language that could be used to disagree with him. He was right.

Mr. Bennett relaxed and sat back in his chair. "Riley's right, Attiline; screw 'em."

I'm fairly certain that my eyes popped out of my head, and Mrs. Bennett's jaw came unhinged. He could see that we were shocked, but he didn't seem concerned about it.

"So a few jerks don't like you; screw 'em. What if some boys are turned off by your scars? Screw 'em. If stupid high school girls don't like you—"

"Screw 'em." Mrs. Bennett finished his sentence and giggled. Mr. Bennett looked proudly at his wife and nodded his head.

He laughed as he looked back at me. "That's right, screw 'em. There's nobody on this planet that's perfect, Attiline. You'll never please everybody—no matter how long you live. The sooner you figure that out, the better off you're gonna be. Your only responsibility is to be the best person you can be. Obey the Lord and give your life as a sacrifice to whatever God has in store for you. And if people don't like that, well then—"

"Screw 'em," Mr. and Mrs. Bennett said in unison.

I snickered.

"I'll get you out of cheer camp because you have a real medical condition. But you'll stay on the team. If anyone has a problem with you or looks at you wrong or says anything inappropriate, just smile at 'em, and then we'll go have Riley beat 'em up." He grinned and then grabbed my hands and bent down and kissed them. It was the sweetest gesture anyone ever gave me, and it caused me to cry again.

"Oh sweetie," his voice was tender, "you're gonna be okay. We're here for you, and we're gonna walk through this with you. You're not alone, do you hear me? We will all walk through this together. None of us are completely healed yet. We all need each other."

I nodded my head. No one spoke for several minutes. All I could hear were the sniffles that accompanied our crying.

"Attiline, your dad's not here right now, so I'm gonna take over his role until he gets back."

"Okay."

"Here's the plan: first, I want you to consider getting some counseling with Joshua Crawford twice a week. I've already talked with him, and he'd be more than happy to meet with you. Joshua did an amazing job with Riley, and I know he'd do the same for you.

"Second," he said, looking up at everyone. "All of us will go to church every Sunday morning. We've become too relaxed about it, and it's time to be more faithful. We can't expect the Lord to fully bless our lives when we can't even give him two hours a week.

"Third." He looked back at me. "You're gonna start holding your head up high. You are who you are and it isn't gonna change, so you might as well get comfortable in your skin—perfect, flawless skin or not.

"Fourth, you've got to think of something else to call us other than Mr. and Mrs. Bennett. You're like a daughter to us, and Mr. and Mrs. seems a little cold and unfamiliar. Deal?" He held his hand out to me.

I grabbed it and shook it a few times. "Deal."

"Good. Anything else we need to discuss while we're all here?"

"I would just like to say a few things," I admitted.

"Shoot."

I took a deep breath. "First, thank you for everything. For letting me live with you and for putting up with my emotional outbursts and for loving me unconditionally. I appreciate it more than you can know. I haven't had that in a long time."

Mr. and Mrs. Bennett smiled at me, and I finally snuck a peek at Riley. He sat with his elbows on the table, and both of his hands held tissue, which he pressed to his eyes.

"And secondly…" I looked back at Mr. Bennett. "I'd like to add that I've never heard you say that many words in all my time of knowing you, which evidently is forever."

From beside me I heard Riley chuckle. Mr. Bennett threw his head back and laughed. "I've been saving up all my words for such a time as this. I'll go on record right now as saying that I'm now officially talked out, so don't plan on hearing anything out of me for a while."

With that he stood, leaned over to give me a kiss on the forehead, and told me he loved me.

"I love you too."

I did.

chapter 8

I spent much of the week helping the Bennetts spruce up their flow-erbeds, and for hard work it was a lot of fun.

Mr. Bennett had already talked to the cheerleading coach, and she reassured him that all would be fine and it would be handled diplomatically so as not to cause problems with the other girls. I was glad to have one less thing to worry about.

While we worked, we took turns telling stories about Mom and Melody. It was refreshing to focus on happier memories rather than the accident. I hadn't done it in a year. I even felt like the worst was behind me and I was doing better and moving on.

I suffered from nightmares every night since the second night at the Bennetts'. Riley started sleeping in my room so that he could wake me up if necessary. Against his wishes, I decided that tonight I would attempt to sleep in the room all by myself. I needed to start dealing with the nightmares on my own. But when Mr. Bennett announced that we should start cleaning up because it was getting dark outside, my heart sank, and I feared the approaching night.

Mrs. Bennett happily sang the Barney song as she cleaned up the mess we'd made. She sang it over and over until Riley finally told her she was ruining the whole day and begged her to stop.

After finishing up, we showered, ate dinner, and sat down to watch a movie. Riley begged for us to watch *I Am Legend*. The movie had just come out on video, and he hadn't gotten to see it while it was in the theaters. I agreed to his movie choice, wrapped myself in a blanket, and settled in on the couch next to him.

"This movie better not give me nightmares," I said.

His lips spread across his face in a toothless grin. "Hey, at least it would be a change of topic."

I never imagined dreaming about something different. For so long having dreams that told a different story didn't even seem possible.

Mrs. Bennett put a bowl of popcorn between us on the couch, and we started the movie.

Watching a horror movie with Mrs. Bennett in the room was like watching two movies in one, with the other being a comedy. She talked back to the screen as if Will Smith were going to hear her suggestions and follow them, and she constantly added her own dialogue when it was a horrible time to do so. Luckily, the movie became too much for her to watch, and she excused herself from the room, leaving us to watch the drama unfold in peace.

I became completely engrossed in the amazing character of Legend. He was a noble man who tried to do the right thing, so much so that he lost everyone that he loved and began to lose himself in the process. No matter the circumstances and the uselessness he must have felt, he continued on his mission. Legend was willing to sacrifice his life to fulfill his purpose.

I could relate to the depths of despair he was feeling when he begged a store mannequin to speak to him. He'd just lost his best friend, and all he wanted was for someone to talk to him. Maybe he longed for someone to tell him that he wasn't alone and everything would be okay. For me, that one-minute clip was the most powerful scene in the entire movie because it wonderfully showed that everyone, even a hero, needs someone to talk to.

At that moment I made the decision to agree to counseling with Joshua. I knew that I needed someone to talk to, and I needed to talk to someone whose pain wouldn't increase as I tried to decrease my own. Dad, Mr. and Mrs. Bennett, and Riley couldn't be the ones I shared my grief with because they each carried enough grief of their own.

My attention went back to the movie. Legend became tired of being alone and was ready to allow the monsters to devour him—the monsters that only came out at night. He was going to let his enemy be the one to put him out of his misery, and he went looking for them so they would quickly accomplish their goal.

Amazingly, just before the monsters won, God sent someone, another survivor that Legend could connect with and fight the monsters alongside. Although the movie didn't credit God for bringing him his new companion, I knew that's exactly what had happened. Just when Legend couldn't take one more step alone, God sent someone who reached in, pulled him out of his pit, and joined him in his battle. Now that he was given a companion, the trajectory of the movie, of this character's life, changed. And because of that change, Legend was able to fulfill his purpose after all.

I looked over at Riley, who was totally engrossed in the drama, and couldn't help but realize the parallels of our stories. I was haunted at night by monsters of my own, and just when I couldn't take another night, another moment alone, God sent me a friend. He sent me someone who would help me fight my monsters. God sent me Riley, and I was certain that the trajectory of my life was changing as well.

"Great movie, kids." Mr. Bennett stood, stretched, and let out a large yawn. Riley and I looked at each other and rolled our eyes.

"Old folks," Riley chided while pointing his thumb toward his father.

"Hey now, no making fun of the senior citizen in the room," Mr. Bennett teased. "It's way past my bedtime, and I've got to get some sleep. See you guys in the morning, and don't forget about church tomorrow."

"All right. Good night, Dad."

"Good night, Pops," I added.

Mr. Bennett stopped and turned around to face us. "Pops?"

"Pops, that's my new name for you."

"Pops," he repeated as he tried to decide if he liked my new name for him. He smiled and nodded his head. "I like that. I sound young and cool, not old and out of touch. Yeah, that's a cool name. Okay, good night, kids."

Riley and I slowly made our way up the stairs. I knew that we were both afraid of what the night might bring, and once we made it to the top landing, we stopped outside Melody's room to contemplate the unknown.

As I took a deep breath and began to walk into the room, Riley put his hand on my shoulder and turned me toward him. "Look, you don't have to do this alone." He looked frightened for me. It was sweet.

"Riley, this isn't your burden. I've got to do this."

"I don't know."

"What?" I winked at him. "Are you going to sleep on my floor every night for the rest of your life?"

He gave me a sly grin. "Don't even go there. You might be afraid of my answer."

I chuckled at his sarcasm.

His face turned somber. "We can give it more time, Charlie. I can stay with you until you don't need me anymore."

"Let me try. I'll be okay." I tried to sound confident and reassuring. "If I need you, I'll come get you."

He glanced into Melody's room and grimaced. "You promise you'll come get me? I don't want you to hurt anymore."

"I know you don't."

I patted his shoulder before walking backwards into the bedroom. I was trying to be funny, but he didn't find it the least bit amusing. Giving him one last small smile, I closed the door and continued to walk backwards until I could see the crack under the door. I stood waiting for several minutes until Riley's shadow finally walked away.

I slowly turned to face the night alone, and like Legend did in the movie, I tried to prepare myself to face the monsters when they came out of hiding.

· ·

(Riley)

Wanting to make sure that I woke up to check on Attie a few times during the night, I set my alarm for three hours later, but when the alarm went off at one o'clock, my eyes were still wide open. I'd never fallen asleep.

After getting out of bed I crept toward her room and saw light escaping from under the door. Slowly, so as not to make any noise, I opened the door and looked in.

My heart stopped beating.

I didn't see her anywhere. She wasn't on the floor or in the bed. I turned to go check downstairs but caught a glimpse of her red toenails peeking out from beside Melody's dresser. Walking into the room and setting my eyes on Attie, my heart broke. She'd crouched herself in a corner between the dresser and the wall. Her legs were pulled up to her chest, and her head rested on her arms, which were draped across her knees. Her body trembled, and as I moved slightly closer, she startled.

"It's okay, Charlie." My hands were shaking as I reached out to her.

"Riley?" She sounded exhausted.

I moved closer to her. "Yes, I'm here." Stroking her hair with my hand, my trembling stopped as she laid her head back against the wall, looked at me with heavy eyes, and tried to give me a small smirk. "I guess I'm not as brave as I thought."

"Why didn't you come get me?" I whispered. "Silly girl, I told you to come get me if you needed me."

She now gave a small, tired laugh. "Good grief, Riley, you need your sleep."

I moved my hand to her cheek. "You thought I was sleeping?"

"Weren't you?"

"Not a chance."

She tilted her head so that it rested in the palm of my hand, and her eyes slowly shut.

I didn't want to rouse her, but I needed to remove her from the corner. "Charlie?"

"Hmm?"

"Wait right here. I'll be right back."

She opened her eyes. They were full of fear.

"I'll be right back. I'll only be a minute. I'm not leaving you alone, Charlie. I'll be right back."

After she nodded at me, I ran into my room, dug through my closet, yanked out two sleeping bags, and laid them out on the floor before returning to her as fast as I could.

I knelt down and touched her face. "Come on, come with me."

She was wedged so tightly into the corner that I was forced to pull her up by the arms to release her from the grip of her hiding place. Grabbing her hand in one hand and her pillow in the other, I led her to my bedroom.

"Riley, I—"

Assuming that she was about to try to talk me out of watching over her for the night, I didn't let her get another word out. "This isn't a debatable issue. I don't wanna hear it. I'm not letting you torture yourself anymore."

Attie nodded and then without any warning walked up to me and put her forehead on my chest. She was beyond the point of exhaustion.

"Thank you, Riley. I don't think I can fight the monsters alone."

I wrapped my arms around her and kissed the top of her head. "You aren't alone. I'm right here. I'll keep fighting the monsters with you."

She sighed as her small frame melted perfectly into my welcoming body. After only a few moments, she relaxed, and her breathing became soft.

"Charlie?"

There was no response.

"Charlie?"

She didn't answer; she'd fallen asleep standing up. I drew her in closer to my body and whispered into her ear, "Wake up, and let's get you in the sleeping bag."

"Sleeping bag?" she mumbled. Her face nuzzled into my chest. "No, I'll sleep right here."

I let out a small laugh. "No, you can't sleep standing up; you need to lie down."

Slowly and wobbly she pulled away from me, but rather than get into the sleeping bag, she climbed into my bed.

"Charlie? That's my bed. We need to sleep on the floor."

It was useless; she was already asleep.

Making myself comfortable on the floor, I listened to her breathing until I drifted off to sleep.

I was near, and no more monsters would come for her tonight.

chapter 9

(Attie)

"It's not like that."

"This is inappropriate. You're seventeen, Riley. Sleeping with Attie next to you every night is asking for trouble."

"Dad, you have no idea what you're talking about."

"Don't tell me that I don't know what I'm talkin' about."

"You're right; I'm sorry. But I don't think you understand."

"Son—"

"You don't see it; you don't see the terror she lives through at night. I feel compelled to help her. She needs me. Nothing's gonna happen. Trust me, please."

"I don't know, Riley."

"She needs someone to pull her out of the nightmares. It's torture for her. I'm just trying to help. There are no ulterior motives here. I swear, and she certainly doesn't have any romantic feelings toward me. Really, you don't need to worry."

"Okay, son, but you watch yourself."

It was silent for a few moments.

"You do know that she's eventually gonna have to face this alone?"

"I realize that, Dad, but don't you think she should have the chance to get some counseling done first, start working through it all?"

"Maybe you're right."

"Please trust me. I need to help her walk through this. I know it sounds extreme, but I believe that's why she's here. I believe God brought her here this summer—because she needs me." His voice was tender.

"You're taking on a lot here, Riley. She's got a lot to process, and you still haven't finished walking through your own grief."

"I know."

"Well, do you also know that your mom's gonna kill me if she finds out that I allowed this? She could have a heart attack right on the spot." Pops was almost joking.

"I know."

"And Eddie, what in God's name am I gonna say to him? 'Uh, hello, Eddie, uh, I just thought you might wanna know that while your sixteen-year-old daughter is living with us I'm letting her sleep with my seventeen-year-old son.'"

"Well, when you say it like that—"

"Not a word of this to your mother, do you understand me?"

"Yes, sir."

"If you get caught, I didn't know a thing."

"I understand."

"You better be a gentleman."

"I will."

"I swear, Riley, you lay one finger on that girl and—"

"Dad, seriously, trust me."

I could hear Pops begin walking back down the stairs. "The door stays open at all times. You hear me?"

"Yes, sir."

A few moments later Riley was back in his room.

I looked at him apologetically. "I got you in trouble, didn't I? I'm so sorry."

"Nah, he's fine now." He shrugged. "He came upstairs to wake us up for church and there you were in my bed. I think his imagination went a little wild."

"Oh yes, I guess that would be quite a shock."

He smiled encouragingly at me. "I explained everything to him, and he's fine now. Really, don't worry about a thing."

"Okay." I lay in bed and watched him start to roll up the sleeping bags, but I didn't move. "You know, you can be sweet when you want."

He rolled his eyes. "Do me a favor, and don't tell a soul. I'd never hear the end of it from the guys."

I nodded at him. "Deal. I'm sorry I fell asleep in your bed. I don't know how that happened."

"You're one stubborn girl, Charlie, even when you're asleep."

"So I've heard."

He cocked his head as his eyes squinted slightly.

"Nobody has told me I'm stubborn in my sleep, just that I'm stubborn," I clarified. "Trust me. I've never slept in a bed with some-one before."

"Me either."

"No?"

"No. Now get out of my room." He winked at me. "You don't live in here for cryin' out loud."

After everyone finished getting ready, we all piled out of the house and headed off for church.

"I'm gonna take Attie in my car with me."

"Riley," Pops said sternly. "Remember our talk?" Although he thought that he was talking cryptically, I heard an accusation in the tone of his voice.

"Dad, settle down. It's no big deal. Some of the kids usually get together for lunch after church. I was hoping that I could take Attie and she could get to know some people."

Pops nodded. "All right, I guess."

Riley merely snickered at him as he opened the car door for me and I climbed in.

As he walked around the front of the car on his way to the driver's side, he looked at me through the windshield and gave a big grin. My eyes followed him until he climbed into the car and buckled up.

"Are you a good driver?"

"I'm an excellent driver," he said in a strange voice.

"Pardon?"

"Oh, come on!" He was shocked that I didn't understand the joke. "*Rainman*? The movie *Rainman*?" His eyebrows rose.

I shook my head.

"Don't tell me you've never seen *Rainman*. Dustin Hoffman and Tom Cruise? Gosh, we've got to rent that movie. You'll love it."

"I'm not a Tom Cruise fan. I think he's a little strange."

Come to think of it, I wasn't one to talk.

"Yeah, I know, but this was pre-Oprah freak-out. You know, *Top Gun* days."

I remained silent.

"Seriously, you haven't seen *Top Gun* either?"

"No, sorry." I felt bad about it for some reason.

"What am I gonna do with you? I mean, all those nights of staying awake and you didn't bother to watch any classic movies?"

"Are movies from the eighties considered classics?"

"To me they are."

"I'll give it a better effort." I laughed. "I promise."

He looked over and winked at me. "Good."

"Eyes on the road, Riley Bennett," I warned as I pointed out the front window.

"Oh." He looked back at the road in front of him and laughed. "Good grief, Charlie, my hands are sweating. Having you in the car is making me a nervous wreck. It's like I'm carrying precious cargo or something."

I laughed at his misery. "You are; I'm pretty darn precious if I may say so myself."

He rolled his eyes but smirked. "You have no idea."

"You do realize that you so much as hit a curb and I could very well have a breakdown."

"Lord, help me!" He laughed. "In that case you better wipe my brow. I'm freakin' sweatin' bullets over here. We've got to get your driver's license."

"Good luck. I'm the world's worst driver. Looks like you'll have to carry the burden a bit longer."

"Last night you told me not to carry your burdens."

"We'll have to make an exception in this particular instance."

"Works for me; I'll carry any burden you ask."

Leaning over, I kissed him on the cheek. "Such a sweet boy."

The car jerked slightly.

"Riley!"

He was laughing. "Don't do that while I'm driving or we really will wreck. Shame on you, getting me all hot and bothered like that."

"Yeah right. Just drive."

chapter 10

Church service was fantastic. I hadn't been to church since before Mom died, so all of my time with the Lord had been alone in my room.

After the accident, as I drew closer to God, my dad pulled away from him. Growing up my Gramps's son, Dad was always at church, so he had a strong spiritual foundation and was saved at the age of eight. I knew Dad would eventually come back around. He'd be another sheep found by his shepherd and returned to the fold.

"Attie!" I heard a voice call my name and turned to see Anne in the back of the sanctuary motioning for me to join her. As I went toward her I noticed two girls standing beside her, and all of their eyes were on me as I made my way to join them. The three girls could not have looked more different.

Anne's short blonde hair was slightly spiky, yet neat, and her classically beautiful facial features matched the way she dressed. I don't know if you could call her style preppy as much as it was classic. My guess was that she bought most of her clothes at Ann Taylor, and I assumed her purse always matched her shoes. Her appearance certainly matched her personality. Friendly, energetic, and well mannered.

The girl standing to Anne's right was the total opposite of her in terms of dress and the way she carried herself, but she possessed a certain beauty all her own. Her complexion was fair with light red freckles, and with one look the phrase that came to mind was "free spirit." I knew instantly that we would be friends. Her hair was short and spiky, and even from afar I could see red, brown, and blonde tufts all over her head. She dressed like she shopped at Goodwill not out of necessity but because she wanted to. She reminded me of a very young version of Shirley MacLaine's character in *Steel Magnolias*. Unconventional but beautiful.

The girl on Anne's left looked like a simple t-shirt and jeans type, and I honestly would have killed for her complexion. Her black hair was cut into a bob that hit her shoulders, and whereas the other two girls seemed more outgoing, she acted more reserved.

I made it through the crowd to join them, and Anne started the introductions. The free spirit's name was Tammy, and the other girl was Tess.

After visiting for a few minutes, all the girls' eyes left my face and looked at something behind me. They were in awe.

"Hi, Riley," Anne greeted.

As he walked up behind me, I felt his hand rest on the small of my back. "Hey, Anne," he replied.

"Do you know Tammy and Tess?" I asked.

"Yes, I do. Hey, girls, how are you?"

"Pretty good, can't complain." Tammy didn't act interested in the fact that Riley joined us.

"Good." Tess's voice was soft.

Riley's attention turned to me, and as he talked, he reached up with his free hand and brushed some hair away from my eye. I wasn't certain, but I thought I heard Tess sigh.

"A group of us are gonna take a road trip to El Reno for lunch. You girls wanna go?"

I looked back at the girls and noticed that Anne's and Tess's mouths were hanging open. Part of me desperately wanted to reach over, place my hand on their chins, and shut their mouths. Tammy, on the other hand, was still unfazed. "Sounds like fun. Why don't you girls go ask your parents if you can go?" I suggested.

Within seconds they all took off in separate directions to find their parents. Riley Bennett just asked them to lunch, and they weren't going to waste any time.

Riley and I stood with our shoulders almost touching and slightly turned toward each other. As I smiled up at him, I realized his hand was still protectively resting on my back.

"You do realize you just made their year?"

He lowered his gaze and pulled on his ear. "No, I didn't."

"Riley," I whispered, "I'd be willing to bet that every girl standing here has a crush on you."

He tilted his head. "Except one?" Looking up at me out of the corners of his eyes, he gave a sly grin. "Do you have a crush on me, Charlie?" His voice sounded strangely hopeful.

"No. I know you too well."

He laughed. "Is that so?"

His eyes still smiled on me as the girls made their way back to us. I couldn't put my finger on it, but I was fairly certain that I hadn't seen him look at me like that before.

He finally turned to the girls. "Ready?"

"Yes!" Anne and Tess squealed.

Tammy rubbed her hands together. "Let's do this thing."

Leaving his hand on my back, he led me out of the sanctuary, through the foyer, out the door, and toward his car. The girls followed behind us like little chicks.

He opened the passenger side door, and after the girls slid into the backseat, he stuck his head into the car and told them to buckle up. Once the front seat was back in position, I went to get in, but he gently grabbed my arm. "I'm gonna go talk to the guys for just a minute. I'll be right back, okay?"

I rolled my eyes at him. "Good grief, Riley, I'll be all right. I'm a big girl. Besides, the sun's still out, so I shouldn't turn psycho for several more hours."

He gave me a small smirk, placed his hands on either side of me onto the car, and leaned forward until our faces were mere inches apart. Our eyes locked. "I'm actually looking forward to sundown," he whispered.

My heart raced as he held my gaze. It was as if dragonflies were fluttering around inside my chest—it was a sensation I'd never felt before. I tried to think of something to say, but before something came to mind he pulled away, gave me a wink, and motioned for me to get into the car. When I was safely inside, he closed the door and ran toward his friends. I watched him in the side mirror as he gracefully sprinted toward the boys who were making fun of him as he approached. Riley slapped one of them on the head.

"What in the world was that?" I asked myself out loud. "And why did I like it?"

Anne began jumping in her seat. "OMG."

The backseat erupted in squeals of delight.

"He's hot; there's no doubt about it," Tammy said dryly.

Tess fanned herself with her hands. "And so romantic. Did you see how his hand rested on her back? Oh my gracious."

"Oh my gosh," Anne gushed. "You never told me that you and Riley were together."

"We aren't together."

"And milk doesn't come from cows." Tammy sneered.

"Honestly! He's just being protective. He's not interested in me or anything."

Tammy glared at me cynically. "You don't try to protect things you don't care about. But, allow me to add, Riley Bennett can protect me anytime."

Tess sighed. "Tell me about it."

We were all silent until Anne spoke again. "Oh my gosh!"

The car filled with squeals and laughter until Riley opened his car door. At once we sat stone-faced and quiet.

"Let's go," he said over his shoulder while he started the car. "Everyone buckled up?"

"Yes, Dad," Tammy chided.

He looked over at me and winked. "We wouldn't wanna upset Officer Attie over here."

I heard Tess sigh again. I wished she'd be a little less obvious.

Riley glanced into the rearview mirror. "Tess?"

She looked shocked. "Me?"

"Chase is in the car with the guys."

"Oh yeah, Chase. I forgot about him."

"Who's Chase?" I asked.

"I don't remember." She sat in a daze for a moment before a fit of giggling erupted.

I definitely liked these girls.

Tammy leaned forward and, in a dry tone that I assumed was normal for her, started talking to Riley. For a split second I fought the image of Melody leaning forward in the car just before the accident. I shook my head and tried to focus on the girls and Riley.

"You're one hunk of a boy, Riley," Tammy said flatly.

"Gimme a break!" He tried to act cross but actually laughed.

Tammy shrugged her shoulders and sat back. "I'm just sayin'."

I turned to face the girls in the backseat. "Okay, Tess. So who is this Chase person?"

"He's my boyfriend."

I laughed at the way she spoke. As words left her mouth, they seemed to float on air. Every word sounded like a dream.

"They've been together since sophomore year." Anne took over the rest of the explanation. "They're the cutest couple you've ever seen."

Tammy raised her eyebrows at me. "Until now."

I gave her a quick glare and then looked over at Riley to make sure he wasn't paying attention. He wasn't. His face was expressionless, and his hands were tightly gripping the steering wheel. The sight reminded me of the conversation we'd had earlier in the day.

"Do I need to wipe your brow, Riley?"

He grinned. "Maybe in a minute. I'll keep you updated."

I looked back toward Anne, who was still talking. As my gaze fell on all the girls, I pictured *The Three Stooges*. Like the famous trio, the girls were very different, but when you put them together, you got a slapstick comedy routine. I was sure that Anne's always-excited personality; Tammy's mellow, dry wit; and Tess's life in a dreamlike state were going to make my life a lot more fun.

We talked easily with each other until finally pulling into the parking lot.

"We're here," Riley announced. "Johnnie's."

I couldn't be certain, but I thought Riley might be salivating already.

"We have Johnnie's in town, Riley," Anne spat.

"Not this Johnnie's we don't. They have nothing to do with each other. This place has been here forever."

My door opened, and a very mild-mannered, brown-headed boy smiled down at me. He grabbed my hand to help me out of the car and then continued to remove the remaining girls from the backseat. As Tess got out, he gave her a small kiss.

I smiled. "You must be Chase."

"Yes."

"Anne has told me all about you."

Anne broke in. "Shut up, Attie. Chase, your girlfriend couldn't tell your story fast enough, so I did it for her."

"Big shocker," Tammy chided as she cut between all of us and made her way inside. "I'm getting me a burger."

Riley grabbed my hand in his and led me inside as Anne gave me a curious glare.

While the boys slid tables together and we got comfortable, Riley made the introductions. "Matt and Curt, this is Attie. Attie, this is the guys."

The African-American boy with shoulder length dreadlocks and shockingly blue eyes shook my hand. "Nice to meet you, Attie, I'm Curt. You ready for Coney time?"

"Coney time?"

Matt, a redheaded boy with freckles, shook my hand next. "Oh yeah. It's heaven on earth. You'll be sorry you've been missing out your whole life."

My curiosity was rising. "Okay, Riley, what exactly is a Coney?"

He took the seat directly across from me. "It's an amazing hot-dog with coleslaw on it."

"Coleslaw on a hotdog? Oh, I don't know, just thinking about it makes my stomach churn."

Tammy threw her feet up on the empty seat next to me. "I'm in," she announced. As I gave her a quick pat on the foot, I noticed that her socks were striped. She was one of a kind.

Riley stood and reached out, offering Tammy his open hand. "That's my girl, Tammy. High five."

"You know me, I'm up for anything," she answered as she slapped Riley's hand.

"Now we just gotta get Attie to give it a try." Sticking out his bottom lip, he batted his eyes at me. "Come on, Charlie, give it a try. Please."

"That look is totally unbecoming," Tammy scolded before turning her attention to me. "Just eat the dang dog, Attie. It's not gonna kill ya."

"Fine! Bring it on," I conceded. "What about you, Anne? Are you going to do it?"

She waved her hands in front of her. "Don't look at me. I'm not touching that stuff."

"This used to be a little hole in the wall. All they had was a counter with some stools. The line would stretch out forever to get a seat, but people would wait as long as it took. The original building burned down, and they rebuilt it then moved to a new spot and then back here. Just recently they added to the joint by taking over the spot left vacant by the Dollar Store." Curt filled us in on the history of the restaurant as Riley ordered everyone a "Fried," "Coney," and a Dr Pepper.

"Don't forget the fries," I reminded.

"No!" Riley and Curt yelled simultaneously.

"You don't waste precious stomach space on fries," Matt added in disgust.

"He's right, Charlie." Riley said. "You've gotta save room cause you'll want more Coneys."

"Charlie? Is he calling you Charlie?" Tammy asked, hiding an accusation inside of a question.

"It's a long story."

She raised an eyebrow and tilted her head. "I'm sure it is."

"Tammy—"

She cut me off by shaking her head at me and throwing her hands in the air. "I'm just sayin'."

Riley was oblivious to Tammy's curiosity as he shared stories of taking family road trips to El Reno for a Coney every chance they got.

I took a big sip of my soda. "They don't really have Dr Pepper in New York."

"What?" Anne was shocked. "Whaddya mean they don't have Dr Pepper?"

"It's very hard to find. I guess it's a southern thing, kind of like biscuits and gravy."

"They don't have biscuits and gravy either?" Chase asked. "Man, that's rough."

"Well, mark my words, by this time next year you'll be twenty pounds heavier," Tammy added. "Oklahoma is like the fat food capitol of the world."

"Do you mean fast food?" I asked.

"No, I mean fat food. We like food that makes you fat. You'll definitely pack on the pounds."

I laughed, and Dr Pepper spit out of my mouth. "Thanks a lot, Tammy."

Riley tossed me a napkin.

"Thanks, Riley."

"Just watching out for you," he said proudly.

Out of the corner of my eye I could see the amused look on Tammy's face. Her imagination was probably running wild. I'd definitely need to clear things up the first chance I got.

As the waitress set the food onto the table in front of me, I looked down onto my plate and saw a cheeseburger with fried onions spilling out from under the bun and a bright red hot dog with brown chili and bright yellow-colored slaw on top. Glancing over at Riley, I noticed he was already halfway done with his Coney.

"Do I pick it up or use a fork?"

He wiped chili from his chin. "Either one."

"This is amazing," Tess said in a dreamlike state. I looked down the table as her voice became stern. "Chase, go get me another one."

I scrunched my face and gulped as I grabbed my fork, cut off a piece of the hot dog, and prepared to bring it to my mouth.

"Make sure you get plenty of chili and slaw on each bite," Riley suggested.

"You've got chili on your face," I said as I threw him a handful of napkins.

"Oops, thanks. Come on, Charlie, you'll love it. I promise."

"Oh, all right already." I scooped the colorful mess up and shoved it in my mouth. Within moments I realized it was by far one of the best foods I'd ever tasted.

Everyone sat waiting for my reaction, so I nodded my head wildly while chewing.

Riley grinned. "Good, isn't it?"

I took a sip of my Dr Pepper. "That's freakin' awesome!"

Standing up, Riley pointed a finger in my direction. "I told you! I knew you'd love it!"

I glanced down the table just as Chase prepared to take another bite. "I need another one."

"I'm on it." He jumped up and ran back up to the counter.

"Make that two," Tammy added. "That thing rocks."

"Three," Riley yelled with his mouth full and chili still dangling from his chin.

"Four," Matt added.

"Make that five," Curt announced.

"Six." I glanced toward the voice and found Anne looking ever so guilty. "What? I don't want to be left out."

As we ate, the boys began talking football. "Well, I heard Berman say that they wouldn't have any kind of defense this year," Curt announced.

"He drives me crazy," I muttered to myself.

"Who?" Riley asked.

"Chris Berman."

Matt looked at me with a shocked expression on his face. "You know who we're talking about when we say Chris Berman?"

"Of course."

Curt leaned toward me. "Why does he drive you crazy?"

"He's a long talker."

"A what?" the quartet of boys asked.

"A long talker." I took a deep breath and began my dramatization. "You know, instead of stopping to take a breath every once in a while he just keeps on talking and talking and talking just like this until he's about out of air, but he just keeps on talking and talking and talking, and his voice starts to shake and he doesn't have an ounce of air left and it sounds annoying just like this and drives me crazy." I quickly took in a deep breath just as my lungs felt like they were about to explode. "He just needs take a breath every once in a while and cut it out with the run-on sentences."

"Oh my gosh!" Chase shouted. "Come to think of it, he is a long talker."

"You guys watch for it next time," I suggested. "You'll never be able to watch him the same way again. From now on, every time he talks you'll be thinking, *Take a breath. Take a breath. Berman, take a breath.* That's what I do. I can't even stand to listen to him anymore. Watch him and then report back to me; I swear you'll hear it.

"I don't like Jim Rome either. I find him totally arrogant. He acts like he knows everything, but he looks like he's never played a sport a day in his life because he wouldn't want to mess up his hair. And the 'Sports Reporters,' don't even get me started on those losers. That one weasel-ey looking guy hates OU. He never has anything nice to say about us, and I think he has some vendetta against Bob Stoops. You know for a fact he's never played a sport. He was probably in the band—played the piccolo or something."

"Dude," Matt elbowed Riley. "The girl watches ESPN."

Riley grinned at me. "Yes, she does."

"That's a dream girl right there," Matt added.

"Yes, she is," Riley concurred.

"My momma raised me right, Matt." I winked.

Riley leaned across the table and motioned for me to join him. "Is there such a thing as a piccolo?"

"I have no idea," I admitted as I leaned toward him. "It just came out. It sort of sounds like it would be a wimpy instrument."

Grinning, he sat back and took another bite of his Coney.

"Hey, you know Anne likes sports too," I said.

"I do!" Anne came to life. "I really do."

"What about you?" Riley asked Tammy.

She shot him a look of disgust. "If there's a party with food involved, I'll watch it. Other than that, forget it."

Chase started talking from down at the end of the table. "Tess loves football, but she'd choose a chick flick over it if she had the chance."

"I love chick flicks," Tess said with a sigh.

"Me too," Anne and I agreed and then looked at Tammy, waiting for her to respond.

"I'll go watch them if I can have Milk Duds."

"I'm with you, Tammy," Riley murmured.

"What's your favorite chick flick, Attie?" Tess asked.

"The latest *Pride and Prejudice*."

"Me too!" Tess gushed.

"Oh gosh," Chase sounded exasperated. "Do not get this girl started on *Pride and Prejudice*."

Tess ignored him. "I wish I were Elizabeth Bennet."

Riley quickly stood up and started for the door. "Okay, party's over. When we start talking chick flicks, I'm out."

The other boys agreed and stood up to leave.

Anne ignored the boys and stayed in her seat. "Isn't Mr. Darcy the most wonderful thing ever? So sexy! That brooding, smoldering scene in the rain…Oh Lord!"

Riley plugged his ears. "I'm not listening to this. I don't wanna hear this."

"Well, you started talking about sports!" Anne snapped.

"You just said you liked sports!" Matt snapped back. "We never said we liked this Pride and Jealousness thing."

"Prejudice," Tammy corrected.

"You've seen it, Tammy?" Tess asked.

Tammy shrugged. "I heard Mr. Darcy was hot, so I decided to check it out."

"He's definitely hot." Tess sighed.

"Let's go, boys!" Riley yelled over his shoulder as he walked out the door. "You girls cool off and then meet me in the car."

chapter 11

"I'm not quite ready to head home yet, are you?" Riley asked after we dropped the girls off at their respective houses.

"Not really."

"Wanna go get a soda?"

"Sure. Whatever you want to do."

We drove in silence until pulling into a vacant spot at Sonic. He ordered two Route 44 Diet Cherry Cokes and turned to face me. "So did you have fun today?"

I unbuckled my seat belt and twisted slightly so I could face him. "I had a wonderful time. Thanks so much for inviting us to come along. It was really nice of you. I really liked everyone."

"No problem. Wait until you meet Kent. It'll get even better."

"Who's that?"

"Tammy's boyfriend. He's a great guy. They're perfect for each other."

"By that I suppose you mean he's able to put up with her crap?"

"Oh yeah. He matches it word for word; it's a blast."

"She's great."

"Nothing like having someone around who tells you exactly what they're thinking. You two are alike in that way."

"I prefer girls like that over fake ones any day of the week."

"I can't blame you."

"So when will I get to meet Kent?"

"Not until school starts. He's out of town until then."

"Why? Where is he?"

"Weatherford. He spends his summers working on his grand-parents' farm."

"I look forward to meeting him."

"You seemed really happy to make some new friends."

"I hope we can hang out more often. Maybe you'll get lucky and the girls will start asking me to hang out with them every once in a while."

He looked confused. "Why would that be lucky for me?"

"You'd be off the hook. You wouldn't have to keep me enter-tained all the time. Given the fact that you get stuck with me every night too, you must be getting pretty sick of me by now."

"Actually," he said with a shrug, "not at all."

The carhop knocked on the window. He quickly paid her, grabbed our drinks, and turned back to me. I unwrapped both straws and put them in our drinks before grabbing my drink out of his hand.

"Good grief, this thing is huge. If I drink all of this I'll be up all night."

"What else is new?"

I punched him in the shoulder as I took my first swig.

"I had to say it. You set it up perfectly."

"True, I did."

Riley watched as I took another sip. He was acting strangely—he had been all day—and I was getting suspicious.

Closing my eyes, I took a deep breath and laid my head back against the headrest.

"What's the matter? Are you feeling okay?" he asked.

"Can I ask you something without you getting upset or taking it the wrong way?"

"Uh…"

I turned my head and looked at him.

He set his drink into the cup holder and immediately ran his fingers through his hair. "I would hope so. I guess it depends on what it is."

"It's not that it's any of my business or anything. I just don't want to think something that's not true," I said.

"Go ahead; just lay it all out there."

My mind raced as I played with my straw.

"Please just get it over with; I'm dyin' here."

"Someone told me that you've had sex with a lot of girls and you have the reputation of being a player. Again, not that it's any of my business or that it should even matter to me, but—"

"But what?"

I shrugged my shoulders, looked down at my drink and wished I'd never said anything. He was obviously uncomfortable.

"Just say it."

I looked back up at him. "Are you playing me, Riley?"

"What?"

"Being so nice, spending all this time with me. Is this a game for you? A summer challenge?"

His eyes were large and full of shock. "Is that what you think?"

"I don't think so, but I don't know. I mean it isn't as if we've ever been extremely close before, and now all of a sudden we're attached at the hip."

"That's not true, Charlie. We've always been close."

"We hated each other."

"No, we enjoyed torturing each other; there's a difference."

He laid his seat back and covered his eyes with his fists.

"You're upset with me. I knew I shouldn't have said anything."

"Yes, I'm upset, but not with you. And yes, you needed to say something. Good grief, if that's what you've been thinking all this time … Geez, the thought of it makes me sick."

I touched his arm and then quickly pulled my hand away. "It hasn't been 'all this time.'"

"Have I been acting like a complete jerk and didn't know it?"

"No, I just started wondering today."

"So I was a jerk today?"

"Of course not."

"Then what in the world happened today that made you start doubting my intentions?"

"You acted different."

"Different how?"

"It was the way you looked at me. It was just, I don't know, different." I nervously plunged the straw up and down in my soda. I'd never been a fan of confrontation, and I certainly wasn't enjoying this conversation. "I'm sure I could have totally misread it. It's not like I'm an expert on this or anything. Good grief, Riley, just forget I ever brought it up."

"No, it's okay."

"Is it all true, Riley?"

"I don't even know where to start."

As I watched him shake his head, I realized his face had paled. "So I'm right?"

"Yes."

I doubted my facial expression hid my disappointment.

"I mean no."

"No?"

"Okay, here goes. First, I do not have sex with a lot of girls. As a matter a fact, I've never had sex with anyone."

"You haven't?"

"No."

"I thought Anne and I were the only ones."

"Apparently not."

"Well, that's a relief."

"Now, the whole 'player' thing, I can sorta understand that. I do tend to go out with a lotta girls and then not ask them out again. But it's just because I don't like 'em enough to go out a second time. Honestly, I don't even kiss most of 'em. I don't know who says I've had sex because I've never told anyone that I have."

"Have you told anyone that you haven't?"

"Just you," he confided. "Maybe some people just assume, who knows? The guys on the team talk about sex all the time, and some-

times I joke around with them about it, but I've never claimed to
have had sex with anyone."

I sipped on my soda but kept my eyes on Riley.

"The last date I went on was a couple of days before you got
here. It was the girl I took to prom."

"Tiffany?" I asked.

"How'd you know that?"

"Sources."

"Anne?"

"How did you guess?"

"Do you remember when you had that phone conversation with
Anne, the one where she asked if you were a virgin—"

"You heard that?" I screamed.

"The entire thing. I couldn't help myself."

"But you were listening to your iPod."

His forehead scrunched in a look of complete guilt.

"You weren't listening to your iPod?"

"No, I was listening to you."

"Oh good grief."

"And when you and my mom were talking in the kitchen that
first night and my chair tipped over?"

"Yeah."

"I was eavesdropping on your conversation then too. I leaned
back so far trying to hear you that the chair tipped over."

"Are you serious right now?"

"There's more."

"There's more?"

"Yes."

"What?"

"When you had your first nightmare and you were half asleep—"

"Oh no. I don't think I want to hear this … what did I say?"

"You told me you'd never been kissed."

"Oh my Lord!" Without thinking I threw the car door open and
jumped out.

"Charlie, wait."

It was too late; I was already walking across the parking lot.

"Charlie—" I heard his footsteps running up behind me.

"I asked you the next day if I said anything and you said no." I paced back and forth between two picnic tables.

"I know. I didn't wanna embarrass you."

"Yes, finding out this way is so much less embarrassing," I said, full of sarcasm. "I can't even think right now…what else did I say? Wait, don't answer that."

"You told me that—"

I threw my drink at him, and it exploded on the ground in front of his feet. "I said don't answer that."

"You asked me if I was a player and if I had sex with a lot of girls."

"You knew the whole time? You knew I thought that about you?"

"Yes, I tried to say something that night after your nightmare. I told you it wasn't true—you just didn't remember the next day. Ever since then I've been waiting for a way to tell you. It was killing me to know that you thought all that stuff about me."

"Why do you even care, Riley? As long as you aren't playing me, what difference does it make if I think you're playing someone else? It isn't my business."

"I want it to be your business. I want you to know that's not who I am."

"Why?"

He rolled his eyes and sighed as he plopped down on picnic table bench. "How honest do you want me to be here, Charlie? This may not be something you wanna hear right now. Maybe we should save the rest of this conversation for a later time."

"No." I sat down across from him. "Go ahead."

He covered his face with his hands, took a deep breath, let it out, and the words "I like you" popped out as the air left his mouth.

"Pardon?"

"I like you," he whispered from behind his hands.

"Well, I like you too. I mean we've known each other forev—"

"No…I mean I like you like you." His hands lowered, and he looked me directly in my eyes. "I'm crazy about you actually."

"Am I being punked right now?" I looked around to see if someone was watching and ready to jump out laughing at my expense.

"No, of course not. I like you, what else can I say?"

"Well, when in the world did that happen?"

"Uh … pretty much the second you pulled into our driveway."

"You have got to be kidding me."

"No."

"Riley, that doesn't make sense. I saw you—you looked miserable when I showed up. You didn't even want to be around me. You fled the house for God's sake."

"I wasn't miserable, I was a nervous wreck. I left to go see Joshua so I could talk to him about you."

"What the … ?" My mind was spinning. I tried to think back to that first night, but my mind was foggy.

"Please don't freak out."

"I'm not. I'm just confused."

"Honestly, this isn't a game to me. I like you, and I genuinely wanna help you get through all this stuff that you're dealing with. You've got a lot on your plate, and I wanna help; that's all. I don't have ulterior motives of any kind, and I don't have any intention of acting on my feelings. We were so relaxed today that I think I let my guard down and my feelings were more noticeable."

I was speechless. I wouldn't have guessed he felt the way he did in a gazillion years.

"Are you upset?"

"No. Just shocked. I didn't see this coming."

"I can understand that."

I looked down at my busted Route 44 cup and wished that I hadn't thrown it at him. My mouth was going completely dry.

"You can have mine when we get back in the car." How he knew what on earth I was thinking was beyond me. The boy was definitely tuned in.

"Thank you."

"Since I've been so honest, I might as well tell the rest."

"There's more? Good grief, Riley."

He ignored me and continued. "I promised myself that I wouldn't try to start anything with you as long as you were living in our house. I plan on keeping my word, but once you've moved into your new place, I'd like to ask you out on a date."

"You would?"

"Yes."

"That's over two months away; your feelings will more than likely change by then. You'll probably be sick of me."

"If my feelings change at all, I can assure you that it won't be in that direction."

"What if I'm not interested?"

He laughed. "I hadn't even considered that a possibility."

"Oh yeah? Being a bit arrogant, aren't you?"

"We have a connection, Charlie. I feel it—don't you?"

"I suppose. I feel something; I just never thought about it."

"Well, don't get so excited about it." He was obviously disappointed in my lack of enthusiasm.

"Maybe your feelings aren't romantic ones. I mean, it's not like you have to fight off being physical with me or anything. We've spent a lot of time together including many nights of sleeping right next to each other, and I didn't feel any kind of tension or anything."

He laughed again. "I wouldn't say that."

"You wouldn't? You haven't tried to kiss me or touch me in any way."

"It's strange. What happens in that time together—at night and how I feel about you then is very different than I feel at other times, like right now for instance. I take my job very seriously."

"Your job?"

"Helping you feel safe. I realize that your need to feel safe is much more important than my personal or physical interests."

"So you do have a physical interest in me?"

"Oh yeah, I'm a seventeen-year-old boy. I'm human, you know."

"How human?"

"Let's just say that if I were Catholic, I'd spend much of my time in a confession booth."

"Oh." I was shocked by his bluntness. He was laying it all out there for me to know, and I was completely caught off guard by his honesty—and by his feelings.

"Look, right now I just wanna be your friend. I want us to hang out and get to know each other. I want you to know me so that when I do ask you out you'll say yes. I don't ever want you to think that this is a game for me because it isn't."

"When are you planning on asking me out?"

"Depends on what time of the day you move out."

"Gotcha."

"But for right now, we're just friends; nothing changes, all right? Don't worry about anything. Don't act weird or uncomfortable."

"All right. And once I move out?"

"Katy bar the door."

"You best prepare yourself, Riley, I may say no."

"No, you won't."

"I could."

"You could, but you won't."

"Hmm."

"Do you really think you might say no?"

"No. I'm a sixteen-year-old girl; I'm only human."

"Oh trust me, I know that all too well."

· ·

Jesus appeared as soon as my ear buds were in and the music was on. "Did you have a good day?"

"I did. It was a great day."

He smiled at me. "I could tell."

"Church was great. I've never spent time with you when so many other people were around. It was powerful."

"Both forms of communication are important, Attie."

"What do you mean?"

"Well, when you spend one-on-one time with me, we're building an intimate connection; we're making you stronger and building your faith. You come to know who I am on a more personal basis.

"When you take part in corporate worship, it's less about you and more about worshipping me, lifting up my name so that I might pour out my blessings on the church as a whole.

"Following me isn't just about having one-on-one time with me. It's about walking out this door and being my hands and feet out there in the world. It's when my flock joins together that my work can truly begin.

"You miss out on all that I can do in your life when you limit our relationship to just you and me. I created people to be relational creatures, to need others who they can share experiences with."

"That makes sense. I'm more than willing to get involved in church."

"It's more than just church, Attie. Do you remember the dream you had in the hospital?"

"Of course."

"I asked you to go on a new journey with me."

"Yes."

"That journey is going to take place outside of these four walls. This isn't just about us, our relationship. It's about you being willing to do whatever I ask of you."

"I can do that."

"Following me isn't easy, but it *is* rewarding. Up to this point, I've allowed you to take time to heal, to get to know me, and trust me more. I can only teach you so much of that here, under the confines of our conversations. For you to completely heal and to learn to trust me, you're going to have to walk it out, and that means taking the risk of involving yourself in other people's lives. Not only that, but allowing other people to be involved in yours."

"I'll do whatever you ask."

"Good. I'm sure I'll be reminding you that you said that," he teased.

"Probably," I conceded.

"So what about this whole Riley thing? How do you feel about knowing that he likes you—as more than a friend?"

"I don't know."

"Do you feel the same?"

"I don't know. I hadn't thought about it. I didn't think it could be like that between us, so the possibility never entered my mind."

"I've noticed your heart rate goes up a little when he's around."

"What are you, a doctor now?"

"Well, I've been known to heal the sick and raise people from the dead. You know, that kind of thing." He was being sarcastic but truthful at the same time.

"What do you think about it? Do you see a problem with it? With Riley and me?"

"No. I think you need to be careful. You're both young and hormonal, and you're in situations that can make avoiding physical contact very difficult. I believe that he's being very respectful to keep his distance until you're out of the house. It shows that he knows his limitations and that he's willing to give himself boundaries. There aren't many seventeen-year-old boys that are willing to do that."

"I hadn't thought about it like that."

"I think you're in very good hands, relatively speaking of course. I believe that he's good for you. You're good for each other."

"So I have your blessing if I end up becoming interested?"

"You have my blessing once you have his parents blessing. And by the way, I don't think that there's any doubt whether or not you're interested."

We talked more about the day and my new friends, and then at ten o'clock there was a knock at my bedroom door.

"Come in."

"Are you sure you're ready for me?"

As I made my way to the door, I heard growling. "What in the world?" I swung open the door. "Riley?"

He was wearing a football helmet, shoulder pads without a shirt, cutoff sweatpants, cleats with no socks, and a baseball bat rested on his right shoulder.

"Um, excuse me, ma'am," he said in a deep voice. "Did someone call about needing me to come kick some monster butt tonight?" He was trying to be serious and keep himself from laughing, but I couldn't hide my amusement. He looked completely ridiculous.

I decided to play along and started fanning myself with my hands before throwing my arm across my forehead. "Why yes, sir, I did." It was a very bad Scarlett O'Hara impression. "I need a big strappin' young man to save me."

"Well…" Riley doubled over laughing but tried to regain his composure. "I'm here to save you!"

I dramatically sighed. "Oh thank God!"

Before I knew what was happening, he scooped me up and threw me over his left shoulder. One of the shoulder pads poked into my rib, but I was laughing too hard to care.

"I've got you, Miss; you'll be safe tonight," he said, stomping toward his bedroom.

As he swung me around I saw his dad standing at the bottom of the stairs looking up at us like we were crazy.

"Hi, Pops!"

He shook his head and rolled his eyes.

Carrying me into his room, Riley threw me onto his bed and started beating his chest with his fists. "Bring it on!"

"Riley!" At this point I was laughing so hard that tears were streaming down my face.

He hopped onto the bed and jumped while still beating his chest.

"Riley! Stop, Riley! I can't laugh anymore! My stomach hurts!" I felt like I was falling and then realized we were lying on the floor. The bed had collapsed, and we were sprawled out on the ground.

"What in God's name is going on up there?"

"We're just havin' some fun, Dad."

"What kind of fun, Riley? Never mind, don't answer that!"

"It's okay, Dad; we're just playin' around!"

"Your dad probably thinks we're up here doing some weird teenage mating ritual."

Riley wiped tears from his eyes. "There's no telling what's going through that man's mind."

I jumped up and raced to my room. "Don't move, Riley. Don't

move!" Throwing open my dresser drawer, I grabbed my camera and ran back to his room. "I've got to get a picture of this!"

Riley stood up and posed in various positions while I snapped away.

"Enough up there already! People are trying to sleep down here for crying out loud!"

"Yes, sir."

Riley removed his cleats. "He's probly been sitting on the bottom step this entire time. He's so freakin' paranoid."

"Well then, I guess it's a good thing he doesn't know how you really feel about me."

He looked at me over his shoulder and raised an eyebrow. "Oh, you're gonna bring that up, are you?"

"No. Subject dropped."

"Thank you. It was embarrassing enough the first time."

"So do I get a performance like this every night?"

"I don't think so. I already broke the bed, and I think I pulled a groin muscle."

"Don't tell your dad; he really will lose his mind."

He laid the sleeping bags onto the floor and climbed in.

"You can sleep on the bed, Riley. It isn't fair for you to have to sleep on the floor too."

"Need I remind you that we broke my bed?"

"*We* didn't break your bed; you did!"

He shrugged and then propped himself up on his elbow. "Sleeping on the floor is no big deal. I go camping all the time, and that's much harder. You wake up and you've got a rock in your back and a twig up your butt or something."

"Ooh, sounds so appealing. I'm sorry I've been missing out." I threw my hair into a knot and then climbed into the sleeping bag next to him. "I really do love sleeping in a sleeping bag. It's the most comfy thing ever. It's got to be the closest thing to actually being in the womb."

"I can't believe you've never been camping. You'd love it."

"You think so?"

"I know so." He grinned and pumped his eyebrows up and down. "I was right about the Coney, wasn't I?"

"Yes, Riley, you were right about the Coney."

"So, will you go camping with me if I plan a trip?"

I raised my eyebrows back at him. "Will you wear the helmet and pads again?"

"Not while I'm camping, but I'll wear it again … when you least expect it."

"I can't wait. That was the highlight of my day."

He frowned. "*That* was the highlight of your day? I think you just shattered my heart into a trillion little pieces."

"It was one of them—*one* of the highlights of my day."

He smiled again. "Go to sleep, Charlie."

chapter 12

"Atticus, don't you look beautiful this morning! And so well rested."

"Thanks, Gramps!" I gave him a kiss on the cheek. "I slept all night last night."

He waved his right hand in the air. "Praise the Lord! I've been prayin' that God would send a guardian angel to protect you at night."

I pictured Riley in his hero costume. "He did, Gramps. God sent me a guardian angel."

"God is good, Atticus. Isn't he faithful?"

I couldn't have agreed more. "Yes, Gramps, he is. He's very faithful."

"So Thomas tells me that you'll be startin' counseling with Joshua Crawford tomorrow mornin'."

"Yes, I will, so I won't be in for work until about nine thirty or so."

"That's not a problem, Princess. I can't tell you how glad I am that you'll have somebody to talk to, especially with the anniversary of the accident right around the corner."

I groaned. I'd been trying to forget that the anniversary was next Monday. I was hoping it would come and go without anyone noticing.

"Are you plannin' on doing anything special on that day?"

"I hadn't thought about it, Gramps." That was a lie of course; I'd probably spent hours debating whether or not I should mark the day in some special way.

"You know, you don't have to do anything if you don't wanna."

"I know. We'll see." It was time to change the subject. "So what's on the agenda at the clinic today?"

"Well, we've got a lot of boarded animals right now with it bein' summer vacation time and all. I was thinkin' you could start with feedin' 'em and playin' with 'em a little."

"Sounds great."

"Later this afternoon I've gotta head on over to the Truman place to check out some horses. You can join me if you'd like."

"Awesome."

As we pulled in behind the clinic, I could hear the dogs barking. This was always one of my favorite moments of the day. The animals got excited because they knew that people were arriving and they were about to get some company.

Walking into the clinic felt like entering heaven. Among the crazy, hectic, and cruel world sat this clinic—a refuge. Within its walls was a man who loved me more than life itself, and I could spend my time caring for the wonderful creatures who visited.

The clinic hadn't changed at all. Just inside the door sat a bucket of dog treats. He must have been using the same brand because when I picked one up and smelled it, the scent was familiar.

Eight orange plastic chairs lined the walls, and there was a small coffee table with animal magazines and a Bible stacked on top. The wall above the chairs was decorated with a scripture:

> And God said, Let the earth bring forth the living creature after his kind, cattle, and creeping thing, and beast of the earth after his kind: and it was so.
> And God made the beast of the earth after his kind, and cattle after their kind, and every thing that creepeth upon the earth after his kind: and God saw that it was good.
> Genesis 1:24–25 (KJV)

I smiled at the memory of my grandmother standing on a ladder and painting the words. I'd been sitting on the floor watching her as I played with a new litter of puppies and she sang hymns.

Me-Maw worked at the clinic every day answering the phone, cleaning cages, and anything else that needed to be done. She did it all because she loved working alongside her soul mate. Seeing as how she spent all her time here, so did my dad. He was literally raised in this clinic. My grandparents had a small bedroom, bathroom, and kitchen added to the back of the clinic so that Me-Maw could care for her child and assist her husband simultaneously. After Me-Maw passed away several years ago, Gramps moved into the clinic permanently. Aside from my family visiting over the summers, he didn't have any other family, so he figured he'd move in with the animals and they could keep him company.

As I walked past Gramps's office, I saw Me-Maw's white vet coat still hanging on the back of Gramps's desk chair.

As we walked toward the back of the clinic, the noise became almost deafening. I walked amongst the cages greeting all the animals. Smaller breed dogs were always my favorite, but there were several larger ones that I felt compelled to pet as well. I noticed one small dog in a cage, and unlike the other dogs, it wasn't clamoring for attention. The small dog (which looked like a poodle mix) huddled in the back of its cage, and its rear leg was in a small cast.

"Gramps, what's wrong with this one?"

"Oh, I call that one Baby. Someone stuffed it in a paper bag and threw it in the trash. Connie West was walkin' by and heard the poor thing cryin', so she got it out and brought it to me."

I opened the cage door. "Poor Baby."

"Be careful, Atticus, she's very skittish. She dudn't like people much."

"Well, who can blame her?" I slowly reached into the cage and placed my hand just an inch or so from her nose so she could get used to my scent. "Hey there, pretty Baby. Are you going to let me pick you up?" Reaching in with the other hand, I slowly removed her from the cage. As I held her close to my chest, she fell asleep.

"Well, look at that, she likes you," Gramps whispered. "You've always had a way with animals."

He brought me a sheet and fabricated a sling so that I could keep her close by for the rest of the day, and then I got to work.

The morning passed quickly as Baby and I fed the other animals and sterilized equipment. I was lost in thought when Gramps interrupted to tell me that I had visitors.

Walking into the reception area, I was greeted by Anne, Tammy, Tess, and a cheery blonde-headed girl that I'd never met.

"Oh, look at the puppy!" Tess squealed, running over to me.

Anne made the introduction. "This is Jennifer. She's on the cheer squad with us. I thought you might enjoy making a new friend."

"Hi!" Jennifer said excitedly. "I'm so happy to meet you. The girls have told me so much about you."

I shook her hand. "Nice to meet you too, Jennifer."

"And don't worry," she added. "I'm on Team Attie."

"Team Attie?"

"Yes, the squad is sorta dividing into two camps. Team Attie or Team Tiffany," she explained. "So far, Team Attie is bigger."

"Why the two teams? Shouldn't a cheer squad be one team?"

"Well, evidently Tiffany doesn't think so. She's already trying to cause problems for you."

"She's never even met me. What's she upset about?"

"Who knows? She likes to be the talk of the town, and now that you've arrived, she's losing ground."

"Oh." Unfortunately, my fear of being the enemy of the girls on the cheer squad was coming to fruition. At least part of the team anyway.

Anne interrupted my thoughts. "We came to see if you wanted to get some lunch with us."

"I don't know. I need to ask my Gramps."

"Gramps says go ahead." His voice bellowed from the back room. He'd been eavesdropping.

"Give me just a minute. I need to put Baby back into her cage."

As I entered the holding room, Gramps was busying himself by putting away supplies.

"Gramps, are you sure it's okay? You don't mind?"

"Go, Atticus. Don't you worry about me."

"All right then." I carefully placed Baby back in her cage and told her that I would be back soon.

Walking back out into the reception area, Tammy hopped up out of her chair. "Let's get moving."

"Thanks for inviting me, girls. I appreciate it."

Tess gave me a small hug. "We couldn't stand the thought of you having to work all day. It is summer, you know."

"It's not that bad. I get a car out of the deal."

Tammy nodded. "Cool. Does he need any more help around here? I could use a car too."

We hadn't been sitting at our table for thirty seconds before the interrogation began.

Tammy started them off. "Okay, chick, spill the beans."

Anne leaned toward me with wide, excited eyes. "We want to know all the details."

I tried to act like I didn't know what they were asking me. "What are we talking about here, girls?"

"Do I have 'DUMB' written on my forehead?" Tammy asked. "Spill it, sister."

"What's the point? You don't believe me anyway. I'm being honest when I say that there's nothing going on between Riley and me. Nothing interesting anyway."

Tammy threw her arms up in disgust. "Oh, come on!"

"I don't believe it," Tess said. "He looks at you like he wants to lay one on you."

Tammy made a clawing motion with her hand. "Reeoow."

"Good grief, guys. Aren't you exaggerating a bit?"

"No!" they replied simultaneously.

Anne pointed at herself. "I've known Riley for years, and I've never seen him act this way over anyone before."

"He's in love." Tess's voice was wishful.

"Dang straight," Tammy agreed. "Bom-chicka-wah-wah."

I rolled my eyes as I felt my face begin to warm. "You guys are embarrassing."

Tammy laughed. "Embarrassing my friends is what I live for."

I looked over at Jennifer in hopes that she would be a voice of reason amongst the craziness. "Are they always like this?"

"Yes. But who can blame them? We are talking about Riley Bennett, the most popular boy in school."

"Oh good grief, not you too?"

Jennifer gave me a sympathetic grin. "Sorry. I used to have a huge crush on him, but he never gave me the time of day."

"Sorry." It felt weird to know my new friend once had a crush on the boy who now had a crush on me. I felt guilty about it actually.

Jennifer continued. "Matt says Riley talks about you all the time. 'Attie this and Attie that.' There's no doubt about it, Riley's hooked."

"Honestly, Attie, you don't like him at all?" Tess's disappointment was obvious.

"I didn't say that exactly."

"I knew it." Anne squealed.

"You *do* like him!" Tess now sounded delighted.

Anne moved her plate out of the way, placed her elbows on the table, and leaned toward me. "Does he like you?"

I sat back and started chewing on my thumbnail. "You'd have to ask him."

"Oh, I plan on it."

I sat straight up. "Don't you dare, Tammy. I would die."

"Okay, already, I wouldn't want you to die over it."

"Look, girls, as soon as there's more to know, *if* there's more to know, you'll be the first I tell. Can we change the topic now?"

They obliged and spent the next hour filling me in on mustknow scoop about the school and the people who inhabited it.

I wasn't quite finished with my meal when Anne announced that she, Tess, and Jennifer needed to take off.

"You go," Tammy said. "I'll stay with Attie."

Within moments they were off, Tammy and I were alone, and I was afraid, very afraid. Her radar was like nobody I'd ever known, and she could smell a rat in my Riley confession.

"Okay, Attie, it's just us. Tell me what in the heck's going on with you two."

Now normally I wouldn't tell a person I hardly knew my deepest, most intimate secrets, but there was something about her that made me feel I could trust her.

"Oh, Tammy, it would take forever for me to fill you in."

"I've got all day. Spill it."

So I did. I told her everything. About the accident, recovery in the hospital, moving to Oklahoma, the nightmares, Riley sleeping next to me, and his confession. All of it right out there for her to know.

She sat silently listening to the whole story and waited until I was completely finished before saying a word. "If I were you, I'd jump his bones."

"Tammy!"

"I'm just sayin'."

● ●

The Truman Ranch had always been one of my favorite places to visit. They were extremely wealthy and their home was amazing. It was by far the largest house I'd ever seen. My favorite part of the property was the stables. The family owned dozens of beautiful stallions, and the facilities were incredible.

A strange voice echoed through the metal building. "Hey, Doc Reed."

"Well hello, Cooper." Gramps walked over to the blonde boy who called his name. "You 'bout to head back to school?"

The boy looked over at me. "Yes, sir, as soon as break is over."

"Good. Are you enjoying your summer?"

"Yes, sir, very much." His eyes stayed on me. Although I couldn't put my finger on why, I felt weird. Maybe it was the way he was looking at me. I imagined that it was the same way I looked at homemade rice crispy treats every time my mother had made them for me—full of longing. The gaze is completely acceptable when one is looking at dessert but not so much so when a guy is looking at a girl he just met. He was giving me the creeps.

"Who is this you have with you, Doc?"

"Oh yeah, sorry. This is my granddaughter, Atticus."

I reached out to shake his hand. "It's Attie."

"Well hello, Attie. I'm Cooper. It's very nice to meet you."

"You too." We shook hands, and as I pulled my hand back, I wiped it on my jeans. Where was antibacterial gel when a girl needed it? "Uh, your horses are beautiful."

I started walking toward a horse in an attempt to break his stare.

"Yes, they are." He followed me. "They're my dad's passion. I think he loves the horses more than his children."

I looked for Gramps in hopes that he would rescue me, but he was busy examining one of the horse's hooves. "Oh, I doubt that. They are amazing though."

"So are you here visiting your grandpa for the summer?"

"My Gramps," I corrected. "Well, actually my family is moving back here."

He gave me a big smile. "Oh, great."

I was fidgeting. "Yes . . . great."

"Are you in high school or college?"

"I'll be a senior in high school. And you?"

"I'll be in my second year at Cornell."

"Oh. How nice for you," I mumbled under my breath. He was full of himself, and I'd had quite enough of his pompous, overly friendly attitude. I silently prayed for him to go away.

"Atticus, could you come over here and help me please?" Gramps finally came through and rescued me.

"Nice to meet you, Cooper. Maybe I'll see you around."

"Are you not coming to my pool party on Friday? I think most everyone else is."

"Oh, is it your party? I've heard about it."

He grinned. "You should come. I'll make sure to look for you."

"Great." I tried to sound enthusiastic.

"Hope to see you around, Attie."

"Uh-huh." I quickly walked away from Cooper and joined Gramps. "What can I help you with?"

"Nuthin', you just looked like you needed a little rescue."

"I did. Thanks for saving me."

"That's what I'm here for, Atticus."

After examining the horses, we headed back to the clinic to shut down for the day and found Riley's car parked in the clinic parking lot.

"Wonder what Riley's doing here?"

"Did he not tell you that he'd be picking you up?"

"No."

"Well, we've got a plan, the Bennetts and I. We're coordinating your transportation so we can get you where you need to be. Until you get your license anyway."

I watched as Riley got out of his car and was making his way toward us.

"I'm sorry that I'm such a moron and I've become a burden to everyone around me."

Riley arrived at the truck with a large grin on his face, and I felt my spirits lift.

"Oh, you're not a burden to any of us, Atticus. Anyone would be happy to have you keep 'em company during a car ride. Isn't that right, Riley?"

"Yes, sir," he said with a wink.

"That kid you met today sure looked like he'd enjoy keeping you company. He'd probly drive you anywhere you wanted to go."

"What kid?" Riley asked as he leaned onto the car window and grinned at my Gramps.

"That Truman boy. He took a likin' to Atticus."

"Oh really?" Riley asked, looking over at me with a frown.

"No, not really," I corrected.

"Oh yeah, he did," Gramps responded. "Who could blame him though, right, Riley?"

"Not me, Dr. Reed." Riley opened the truck door so that I could get out. "I couldn't blame him at all."

He opened his mouth to say something more, but I pointed my finger in his face. "Shut it, Riley. Not another word out of you about this subject."

"Yes, ma'am. I'll be nice."

I walked toward his car. "Thank you so much."

He ran past me to the passenger side door and opened it. "You're welcome very much."

Riley shut the door behind me, trotted around the front of the car, and got in the driver's side. A grin filled his face. "Good day?"

"Yes."

"Tell me about it."

"Well, this morning when I got to the clinic, there was this adorable little puppy named Baby. Somebody'd thrown her in the trash..."

I told him the full day with details but left out the conversation that I shared with the girls and then Tammy individually.

"So what about Cooper Truman?" he asked.

"You know him?"

"Oh yeah. Should I be worried?"

"No," I said with a roll of my eyes. "He was a pompous jerk."

A cheesy tooth-filled grin filled his face. "Good."

"How about you, Riley, how was your day?"

"Good."

"Did you do anything?"

"No, not really." He shrugged. "Just hung around the house."

"You need to get out more."

His dimples appeared as he laughed. "Yes, I do. I definitely need to get out more."

We arrived at home, and as I went to open my car door, Riley snapped at me. "Don't you dare."

"What? Oh, good grief, Riley, I can open my own car door."

"I know you can open your door. I just don't want you to. I wanna do it." He jumped out, ran around, and opened the door for me. "How can I compete with Mr. Darcy if you won't even let me open your door?"

I patted his smiling face and walked toward the house. "Well, Mr. Darcy doesn't actually exist, so odds are in your favor."

"Sweet."

Riley's parents stood in the foyer as we made our way inside. "Why don't you go wash up for dinner?" Mrs. Bennett suggested.

"Okay. I'll do that and then be right back down."

I started up the stairs but only took a few steps before realizing that the Bennetts were following me.

"Everything okay?" I asked, turning to face them.

They all nodded with large grins plastered on their faces.

"All righty then."

I turned back around and continued my assent with their footsteps continuing to follow mine up the stairs. Making it to Melody's room door, I turned to them again. "Okay...well here I am. I'm going in now."

Mrs. Bennett was grinning and bobbing her head. "All right!"

They didn't budge.

"What's going on? You guys are freaking me out!"

"Just open the dang door, Charlie."

"Fine." I obeyed, and as soon as the door opened, cheerful yellow walls greeted me.

I gasped. "What in the world? What did you do?"

It was no longer Melody's room; it had completely changed. The walls were now a cheery pale yellow, and the wood trim had been painted white. All of Melody's old furniture was painted white as well, and a brand new daybed with new bedding sat in front of the window.

Mrs. Bennett jumped up and down. "It's 'shabby chic', Attie. Do you like it? Do you like it?"

"Do I like it? I love it!"

I walked into the room and directly to the wall where the bed previously sat. Several charcoal sketches hung on the wall framed in whitewashed frames with moss green linen borders. They covered almost the entire wall. It was breathtaking. The largest, in the middle, was a drawing of the Christmas card picture that we had taken last year. I looked at the others: Gramps and Me-Maw leaning up against the side of his truck; my parents' wedding portrait; Melody, Riley, and I at about six years old sitting on the porch eating popsicles; Mr. and Mrs. Bennett and my parents gathered together at a table; Riley in his costume from last night; and a rolled up sleeping bag. The last frame that I laid my eyes on held a sketch of my mother and me. She looked happy and beautiful.

"This is the most amazing and kind thing anyone has ever done for me."

Mrs. Bennett came up and stood behind me. "We wanted you to have a place of your own while you were here."

Turning around, I threw myself into Mrs. Bennett's arms. "Thank you so much." I was sobbing. What else was new?

"You're very welcome, Attiline." Pops walked over and gave me a kiss on the top of my head. "Do you like where we put the bed? Riley said you liked to sit under the window."

I glanced over at Riley. He was leaning against the doorframe with a large grin on his face.

"I love where you put the bed. I love all of it."

Mrs. Bennett released me and clapped. "Oh goody!"

I turned back to the pictures. "Who drew these? They're so beautiful."

"Oh, that was Riley. It doesn't take him any time at all."

"Riley? You drew these?"

I spun around and saw him walking toward me. "Yeah."

"I didn't know you were an artist."

He reached out and pulled me to his chest. "Hmm, I wonder what else you don't know about me."

I squeezed his neck as he hugged me. "Thank you so much. I love them."

"I'm glad that you like them. You're welcome."

Pops loudly cleared his throat, and Riley released me from his grip and shoved his hands in his pockets.

"Well, we'll leave you to look around," Pops announced.

"Dinner in thirty minutes," Mrs. Bennett added.

I felt my body droop when I discovered that Riley was following his parents out of my room. "You aren't staying, Riley?"

"Hold your horses, I'll be right back."

"Good." Sitting on the bed and taking in the view of my room, I realized that not all of the frames housed pictures. "What's with the empty frames?" I yelled.

"I've got a plan for two of them, but it's a secret." He walked back into the room with a wrapped gift in his hands. "The others are for pictures from the future. Like maybe one of us."

"Sounds great to me. Future romance or not, you're my best friend." I eyed the gift. "Even more so if that's a present for me."

He smirked as he handed it to me. "It sure is."

"Oooh, I love gifts!"

"Figured as much."

I tore open the wrapping paper, causing shreds of paper to fly into the air. Riley tried to catch them as they fell back to the earth, but most of it landed scattered on the bed. "You got me a cordless phone? I love it!"

"Correction, I got *us* a cordless phone."

"Same difference." I quickly hugged him. "Oh, Riley, thanks."

"I figured I had to do something to get you out of my room every once in awhile."

I opened the box and removed the phone.

"So did you mean what you said about me being your best friend?" he asked.

"Yes, you are my best friend." I set the box down and looked at him. His eyes were full of admiration. "I don't know what I would do without you, Riley. I believe God sent you to me."

"I do too. No doubt." He hesitated. "But have you ever thought about the fact that God could have brought you to me too?"

"Pardon? What do you mean?"

"Well, you act like you're the only one who needed someone. Maybe I needed someone too."

"You? But you've got it all together."

"Well, that's not true." He ran his fingers through his hair. "I was struggling. Not to the same extent that you are, but I was having a hard time. My faith was shaken pretty badly, and I didn't have anyone who believed what I did, or to the same degree anyway. I didn't have anyone to support me living out what I believe God's called me to. A higher standard for myself, I guess."

"I see." I nodded. "Doing the right thing can be difficult. Especially when it's because you feel like God told you to. People just don't get that."

"No, they don't." He was quiet for a few moments as he picked up my hand and traced the lines in my palm with his finger. "You're good for me, Charlie. I'm a better person when I'm around you."

My hand warmed at his touch. "You were already a good person. You just needed someone to be a good person with. It's more fun that way."

"Well . . ." He looked back up at me and smirked. "We certainly have fun together."

"We're agreed then. We're good for each other, romance or no romance."

"Actually—we're perfect for each other." He winked. "And I'm still betting on a romance."

• •

Later that evening, I lightly outlined each and every line of the sketches hanging on the wall. I think I was somehow hoping that tracing the lines of my parents' faces would connect me with them.

"Am I gonna have to clean that glass every day?" Riley asked from the doorway behind me.

"Probably."

"You okay?"

I nodded.

"Do you want me to leave you alone?"

"No," I whispered.

He walked in and stood a few inches behind me. Although my eyes were on the wall in front of me, I could feel his eyes on me, and his concern was palpable.

Within moments I reached back and touched the top of his wrists with my fingertips. His hands flinched at the surprise of my touch, but they instantly rested again. Looking down, I watched as my fingers slid down the front of his hand until our fingers entwined.

The top of my hand didn't come close to comparing in size to his, and I noticed that my skin looked pale white against his sun-kissed tan. I wrapped our arms across my body and allowed myself to lean back against his chest.

For the first time in a year, I felt I was where I belonged. In his arms, I was safe and home.

"I can't believe you drew these for me. I love them more than you could ever know."

"I loved drawing them for you."

Our voices were hushed.

"Making me happy seems to come naturally to you, Riley. You're very good at it. Why do you believe that is?"

"There are so many reasons I could probly write a book about it. All I know for sure is that seeing you happy makes me happy. And being like this, just standing here like this, makes very me happy."

"Then I'm going to try to stop being such an emotional wreck all the time and just be happy." I turned my head and looked up at him. "I want you to be happy, Riley."

"When I'm with you, I am happy." He pulled me more tightly to him. "So keep spending time with me."

"You don't know how much I needed some happiness in my life."

"Oh, I don't know. You look pretty happy in that picture with your dad."

I looked back at the sketch but couldn't respond.

He placed the side of his face against mine, and I could feel my eyelashes brush his cheek when I blinked.

"Ever since the picture came in the mail, I've been wondering what you were laughing about. Do you remember what was so funny?"

"No." Honestly, I didn't want to think about it. I didn't want to go back there, not now. I didn't want to lose the happiness I was feeling, and going back there would cause my joy to evaporate. "But I do know we haven't laughed like that since."

In one final brush of his cheek, I let my eyes close.

"Are you asleep?"

I didn't know how much time had passed. "I was until you talked," I admitted.

"Well, let's get you tucked in. Your place or mine?"

"Mine. I want to sleep by my beautiful pictures."

Within minutes Riley had the sleeping bags laid out, and feeling sleep quickly approach, I climbed inside.

I sensed the monsters as they crept out of hiding.

During the night I experienced another nightmare. It was worse than any other I'd experienced while in Oklahoma, and Riley wasn't able wake me out of it quickly enough to keep me from experiencing the anguish at the end of the dream. For what might have been the three-hundredth time or more, I watched my mother and Melody die, and Riley was powerless to help.

chapter 13

"Hello, Attie. I'm Joshua, and this is my wife, Nicole."

"Hello."

"We've heard a lot about you, Attie," Nicole added.

"Uh-oh." I grumbled and rolled my eyes.

"All good," she corrected. "All good."

"Thank God."

"Have a seat, Attie." Joshua motioned to the chair next to the fireplace. "Please, make yourself comfortable."

"Can I get you anything to drink, Attie?" Nicole asked.

"Nope, I'm good. I might need Kleenex, though; I'm a crier."

Joshua took a seat on the sofa. "Right there on the table next to you."

I saw a box of tissue sitting on the table and put it in my lap just in case they were needed.

Joshua began. "I'll start by telling you a little about us. Okay?"

"Sure."

"Attie, I'm a licensed and practicing psychiatrist, and I also hold a seminary degree. So, while psychiatry and counseling is my primary occupation, I feel called to youth ministry, and I do that in my spare time."

"Wow, you're a busy man."

"You don't have to tell me that," Nicole joked.

"My wife joins me occasionally if I need a female perspective, and she's also always close by when I counsel females. I feel like it helps them relax and feel safer. So is it okay with you if she hears our conversations?"

I nodded.

"Trust me, Attie, my lips are sealed. I would never share anything I hear," Nicole promised.

"I trust you."

"Good."

Joshua continued, "Nicole and I have been married for eight years, and so far, we don't have any children."

"One day soon hopefully," Nicole interrupted.

"I've been in the ministry for six years, but we've only lived here for nine months. From what I understand, your family is very well respected in this town, but that's all I know. Mr. Bennett only told me that you would be staying with them for the summer and that you were dealing with some difficult issues, and he's hoping that I can help. He didn't give me any more details than that."

"Sounds fine."

"Okay, any questions?"

I shook my head.

"Well then, it's your turn. Please, why don't you tell us about yourself?"

"Oh gosh, are you ready for this?"

He grinned. "Yes. I've heard just about everything, so nothing you can say will scare me."

Before I spoke, he picked up a notepad and pen.

"I'll be seventeen in August and a senior when we start school later this summer."

Joshua was already taking notes.

"A year ago this coming Monday, I was in a car accident with my mom and best friend, Melody. They both died, but I didn't. I should have—or so the evidence suggests, but here I am.

"I was pinned in the car, and bystanders were unable to get me out. My left arm and leg were jammed into some metal, so they couldn't pry me loose.

"The car was on fire and the flames became too intense, so the people were forced to give up and leave us to die. Nobody knows for sure how I got out; all they know is that when the fire was put out and the smoke cleared, they found me lying about ten feet from the car. The doctor said that the water they were spraying on the car kept me from suffering burns. Based on the physical evidence, my seat was crushed around a pole, and there was no logical explanation to me freeing myself from the vehicle. Evidently, as they loaded me into the ambulance, I mentioned something about a man in white carrying me from the car.

"I was unconscious in the hospital for a little over three months. While I was asleep, I had a very vivid dream.

"Jesus and I were taking a walk together, enjoying each other's company when all of a sudden everything went dark. All I could see was Jesus, in his bare feet, standing on a stepping stone. He asked me if I was ready to follow him on a new journey. At first, I wasn't sure if I wanted to or not. I was afraid to say yes. But eventually, after some prodding, I agreed. I took a step onto the first stepping stone, and next thing you know, I woke up.

"My dad was working through his own grief issues and never came to the hospital. So I spent almost all of my time alone unless someone from the clergy or a nun stopped by.

"After I woke up, I began to see Jesus in my hospital room. Sometimes he was alone, and sometimes he had angels with him. He and I would have conversations with one another, but the angels never spoke to me. They spent all of their time praying. There was one particular angel that looked familiar to me, and Jesus told me that he was who pulled me from the car."

Nicole gasped. I looked up, and Joshua was no longer taking notes. He just sat with his mouth hanging open.

"Oh wait, it gets better," I assured them. "Even to this day I have conversations with Jesus. I actually see him dressed in blue jeans standing in my room. We talk about everything from school to boys to boobs. Although, I must say that he didn't like the boob conversation very much.

"Anyway, I also suffer from terrible nightmares almost every night and have since I woke up in the hospital.

"I'm currently living in my dead best friend's bedroom and have a crush on her brother. Oh, and he sleeps on the floor next to me every night so that if I start to have a nightmare he can wake me up before it gets too bad. Don't worry, there's nothing kinky going on or anything like that. It's totally innocent."

Joshua let out a small chuckle.

I thought I was finished and then thought of something else. "One more thing, I've failed my driver's test three times now. I think that un-unknowingly I'm afraid of driving a car, so I do poorly on purpose but don't know it. Kind of a subconscious thing."

I took a deep breath. "Okay, I think that about covers it." I nodded and waited for their reaction.

They sat stunned and silent.

"Oh, you don't have to worry. I already know that I'm a nut-job, so don't be afraid to say exactly what you're thinking. It couldn't be any worse than what I've already told myself."

"Do you really want to know what I'm thinking?" Joshua asked.

"Isn't that why I'm here? For you to make all this craziness go away?"

"Oh, I don't know," he responded. "Why are you here?"

"Is this like a trick therapist question?"

"Nope. I will not ask you any trick questions," he said reassuringly. "So tell me, do you want all of this so called craziness to go away?"

"I want the nightmares to go away." I knew that for sure.

"The rest? What about your visions of Jesus? Do you want them to go away?"

I might as well be honest. "Not really. I kind of like those."

"I can understand." He nodded as he and his wife looked at each other.

I was certain that they didn't know what to do with me.

Joshua looked back at me. "Attie, I'm going to be brutally honest with you because I believe that you can handle it."

"Bring it on," I encouraged.

"I don't think there's one thing wrong with you."

"Pardon?"

"Other than the nightmares anyway."

"You don't?"

"Nope." He turned to his wife. "Do you?"

"Not at all."

My mind was spinning. "Huh? I'm confused."

"Attie, I've been a Christian for fourteen years and a pastor for six, and I must be honest with you and tell you that I'm jealous." He was dead serious, and his wife was enthusiastically nodding in agreement.

"Huh?"

"You have a faith and relationship with the Lord that I would literally die for."

"Me too," Nicole agreed.

I was in shock. "Huh?"

"Don't you see? God revealed himself to you in such an amazing, wonderful, and loving way that you can't help but believe he's as real as the three of us sitting here in this room."

"He's in the room too," I stated.

"He is?" Joshua asked excitedly. "Where?" He frantically looked around.

"I was just joking. I thought I'd freak you out."

"Good one. Cruel, but good."

Nicole snickered at him.

"Seriously, Attie," he continued, "the truth of the matter is that he is that real, the rest of us just aren't willing to see it. Whether it's the Holy Spirit or Jesus or God, or even your imagination could be debated forever, but the fact of the matter is, he's here and you see him. You see him because you want to and because you're willing to do whatever it takes to keep yourself that close to him."

"I don't understand."

"God reveals himself in various ways. But to see him, and I mean see him spiritually, not necessarily in the physical, it usually involves a lot of sacrifice on the part of the follower. There must be a willingness to go through the very difficult times and walk out the other side still believing that God is good. Most of us are willing to go to church on Sunday and maybe Wednesday. A few will go above and beyond that and will serve in some way or another, but the reality is that most of us are unwilling to give up everything if that's what he asks.

"You may not have chosen to lose everything, but you did, and rather than turning your back on Christ, you ran *to* him. Look at your reward, Attie. It's amazing. You have a very real, very loving relationship with the Creator. With your Savior. I wouldn't give that up for anything if I had it."

"Me either," Nicole said as tears rolled down her face and dripped from her chin.

I took her the box of Kleenex. "You need these more than me."

"Thank you," she whispered.

Joshua continued, "Other people, many of them fellow Christians, won't understand. They may in fact call you crazy, but if that's crazy then sign me up."

"So to clarify here, you don't think I'm crazy?" I asked.

"I'll be glad to clarify. No, Attie, I don't think you're crazy at all," Joshua answered.

"What about the nightmares?"

"I don't know yet. We need to pray about it and see what the Lord will reveal about them. What concerns me is that you seem detached from your emotions."

"Pardon?"

"You sat right there in that chair and told me one of the most horrific stories I've ever heard. You lived through it, but yet you told the story as if none of it affected you. That concerns me. It may be that you haven't truly dealt with your grief, and your nightmares are a way for your subconscious mind to work its way through your emotions. Since you don't deal with your grief when you're awake, you end up having to tackle it while you sleep."

"I guess that makes sense. But if I thought about it all the time, I'd be a walking basket case. I don't want to deal with it anymore. Nobody would be able to be around me I'd be so darned depressing."

"I completely understand that. Look, the Bennetts lost their daughter on that same day, and the only reason they're doing as well as they are is because through counseling they forced themselves to deal with their pain. You haven't been given the opportunity to heal. You haven't talked it through with anyone. Nobody can expect to completely heal without working through their grief. I may be totally off base, but I don't think so. I do know that if we ask God to reveal what's behind the nightmares, he will. God's faithful, Attie."

I laughed. "Oh, I know that!"

"Yes, I'm sure you do," Joshua agreed. "Better than most."

"What about the driving thing?"

"I can understand your fear there. It's very common for people that survive vehicle accidents to no longer want to get in cars, let alone drive them. That's a normal fear that we can work through. Baby steps.

"Attie, you're not crazy, and I don't want you walking around thinking that you are."

We spent the rest of the session in prayer. I found this form of "communicating" with Jesus very intriguing. Other than short prayers with Gramps and the church service on Sunday, I'd never prayed with anyone else around. Joshua seemed to know what he was doing. I figured he must have taken a prayer class in seminary or something. He used beautiful words and terms that I'd never heard before. I found myself wishing that I had a tape recorder so that I could play it back, but then I felt guilty because I was thinking about recording the prayer and not listening to it live. I tried hard to concentrate and not let my mind wander again.

Joshua asked that the Lord "grant me peace of mind both during the day and while at rest" and that God might "reveal to us how to bring the nightmares to an end." My favorite part was when he asked that my "struggles and pain would be used to bring glory to God and to be a witness to others that when you're faithful to God all things are possible."

He also used the word "intercede." I would have to look that one up when I got home because I had no idea what it meant, but it sounded good when he said it. He asked for the Holy Spirit to "intercede on Attie's behalf."

Nicole also prayed. Her words were sweet, and she was very emotional. She expressed thankfulness that God had revealed himself to me in such a sweet yet powerful way. She even thanked him for bringing me into their lives. That was neat. All in all, the prayers could have won an award if there was an award for such a talent. The only thing I knew for sure was that when prayers were that beautiful, God would surely have to answer them. I believed the odds were in my favor and the nightmares would be over soon.

"I wish I could talk to Jesus the way you do," I exclaimed when they finished.

"And I wish I could talk to him like you do," Joshua replied back.

"Me too," Nicole added.

"Maybe we can all rub off on each other," I suggested.

"I truly hope so." Joshua gave me a hug. "I truly hope so."

There was a honk from outside, which meant my ride was there.

"One of my many chauffeurs." I rolled my eyes and made my way to the door.

"We'll work on the driving thing on Thursday, okay? It's my new goal in life to have you driving by the end of summer."

Saying my good-byes, I ran to join Mrs. Bennett in her Suburban. As I opened the door, Bon Jovi poured out of the speakers. She yelled a thank you to Joshua and Nicole, who were standing on their patio, and then pulled away.

"Okay, I've had a very hard time, but I think I finally came up with your new name," I said.

"Oh goody. Let's hear it."

"It's from *Little Women*. I might as well stick with the whole names-from-literature theme."

"All right."

"How about Marme?"

"Oooh, I like that! That's a good name. I love that book."

"Good. So, Marme, do you happen to have any big plans tonight?"

She laughed. "Attie, I'm old and have no life. No, I have no plans tonight and hardly ever do."

"Well, would you be at all interested in going shopping with me? I need an outfit for the pool party Friday night."

She glowed. "Oh, I would love to, Attie! I would just love to!"

During the rest of the drive she talked nonstop about the stores that she wanted to take me to and the type of clothes she would wear if she had my "cute and dainty" figure.

She pulled in front of the vet clinic. "I'll pick you up after work and we can get busy shopping."

"Great, Marme. Thanks."

She let out another squeal and drove away. I'd made her day, but I was slightly disappointed that it wouldn't be Riley who was picking me up after work. He'd gone to the gym before I woke up, so I wouldn't get to see him until late in the evening. I looked forward to telling him all about my counseling session.

The reception area already had three dogs and their humans waiting for the doctor to see them, so I immediately got to work behind the desk checking in each "patient."

"Everybody's checked in, Gramps," I announced as I made my way to the back.

"Well, Atticus, I didn't know you arrived already," he said, giving me a kiss on the cheek. "So how was it?"

"Good. Maybe we can talk about it over lunch?"

"Not today. Riley has already requested that you go to lunch with him."

My heart almost exploded. "Really?"

"He's anxious to know how it went."

"Oh, okay." I tried to act normal, but the look I got from Gramps made me believe that he wasn't falling for it. I changed the subject. "So how's Baby?"

"She's waiting for you."

I grabbed the homemade sling, put it on, and went to retrieve Baby from her temporary home.

"Hello, Baby. It's me, Attie. I'm back."

After placing her in the sling, she quickly fell asleep.

"She didn't sleep well last night," Gramps informed me. "She whined quite a bit. I hope her leg isn't hurtin' her."

"Oh, poor Baby." I rubbed her head. "Don't tell me that you have nightmares too. Are you thinking of the mean man who threw you away? That would certainly give me nightmares."

"Can you call 'Theo' back please, Atticus?"

"Yes, sir, I'm on it."

I spent the majority of the morning at the desk answering the phone and setting appointments. Baby slept quietly and never whimpered.

The phone rang again. "Reed Clinic, may I help you?"

"Is this Attie?" a male voice asked.

"Yes, it is."

"Attie, this is Cooper Truman."

I slightly gagged.

"We met yesterday at my ranch."

"Yes, I remember you. How can I help you?"

"Well, actually this is a personal call. I was wondering if you might want to join me for lunch today?"

I silently gagged again. "Oh, that's so nice of you, but I already have plans."

"Disappointing."

"Yes," I lied.

"I'm going out of town for the rest of the week and won't be back until the party." He was thinking out loud. "You will be at the party, won't you?"

"Yes." Although now I wished I wouldn't be.

"Then I guess I'll just have to wait to see you then." He sounded disappointed.

"Unfortunately," I lied again.

"Well,"—I could tell he didn't want to hang up—"I'd better let you get back to work."

"Okay, Cooper. Thanks for calling and I'll see you Friday." I hung up the phone. I think I heard him trying to say something just as I was about to set the handset down. I felt a slight satisfaction from sort of hanging up on him.

I noticed Baby start to whimper. "I know, Baby, that gross boy is freaky, isn't he?" She looked up at me and then laid her head back down.

At 11:50 Riley came strolling into the clinic with a movie star grin spread across his face and wearing khaki shorts with a purple polo shirt. The purple enhanced his tan skin, and his green eyes sparkled under his hair, which was lying in disarray on his head.

"Hey, Charlie."

"Hi, Riley."

He pointed to the bundle draped across my midsection. "Is that Baby?"

"Yes, do you want to meet her?"

He walked toward me. "Of course."

Slowly and gently I removed her from the sling and handed her to him.

"Holy moly, she's adorable." He held her up in front of his face so that he could get a good look at her. "I can't believe some jerk threw something this precious away."

"I know."

"Look at how fragile she is."

"She won't be fragile for long now that I'm looking after her."

"Do you take her everywhere in that thing?"

"Yes. She sleeps better when she's close to me."

His jaw dropped slightly before a small laugh escaped his throat. "Sounds familiar."

"Yes, I guess it does."

He carefully handed Baby back to me. "Well, don't get any ideas. I'm not gonna start carrying you around in one of those harness things."

"Har, har," I said, punching him in the shoulder. "It's a sling."

"Whatever."

"While I put her back in her cage, why don't you go say hello to Gramps?"

I placed Baby back in her prison, and she whimpered for a few moments before making her way to the back of the cage. "I don't know why she's always in that corner. She looks so sad and lonely back there."

Riley walked up behind me and peeked into the cage. "Nobody puts Baby in the corner."

"Pardon?"

"Oh come on, you haven't seen *Dirty Dancing*?"

"Gross, I don't watch those kinds of movies."

"It's not 'that kind of movie.'" He laughed. "It's rated R at the most. You know, it's a Patrick Swayze movie."

I shook my head. I didn't know who he was talking about.

"Patrick Swayze? *Roadhouse*?"

I still had no idea whom he meant, so I shook my head again.

"He was the dead guy in *Ghost*."

"Oh, *Ghost*, I love that movie." Finally, a movie I recognized.

"Of course you do, it's a chick flick. You're completely hopeless."

"As are you."

"True. Are you hungry?"

"Famished."

"Let's get out of here then."

I started toward the exit. "Be back in a bit, Gramps."

"Can we get you anything, Dr. Reed?"

"No thanks, I've got my lunch in the fridge just waiting on me."

We made our way to the car, and as Riley opened my car door, he grabbed my arm and grinned at me. "For the record, I don't watch 'those kind of movies' either."

"Good to know."

"I can't even believe you would think I did. I'm a little hurt quite honestly."

"I'm sorry. You just never know what people are in to."

"Not even me?"

"I'm just getting to know you, Riley. Give me some time. I'm sorry I ever doubted you."

"Just don't let it happen again," he teased.

"I won't. I promise."

"So I figured we'd pick something up and sit in the car. That way we don't need to worry about anyone overhearing the details of your counseling session."

"What makes you think I'm divulging any information about my counseling?" I taunted.

"You better, or you're buying your own lunch."

"All right, all right."

"Wanna get the old standby?"

"Sonic?"

"Of course, what else?"

"Sounds good to me. You know what I want."

"Grilled chicken sandwich with mayo but no tomato. Tator tots and a diet cherry Coke?"

"You got it."

After getting our food, he drove us to the park, where we made ourselves comfortable and unpacked our lunch.

"So what did you think of Joshua?" he asked as he removed the wrapping from his burger.

"Oooh, that looks good."

"Do you want a bite?"

"No thanks." As I unwrapped my grilled chicken sandwich, I coveted Riley's juicy burger and wished I'd gotten one for myself. "So Joshua was great, and his wife was very nice too."

"Yeah, Nicole's great," he said quickly. "Okay, you're killing me here, Smalls. Enough chitter chatter, get to the good stuff." As he took a bite of his burger, mayonnaise dripped down his chin, so I reached over and wiped it off. "Ank ou," he said with his mouth full.

"Don't mention it."

"Spill it already. I've been waiting to hear about it all morning."

"Well, this will be no shock to you, but basically I verbal diarreha'd all over them."

"You're right." He sipped his soda. "No shock there. Was there crying involved? They usually go hand-in-hand."

"No. No crying this time."

"At all?"

"Nope." I shook my head and held out the French fries so that he could help himself. He grabbed a few and put them on his lap.

"Wow. So what's their diagnosis? Is it loony bin time?"

I couldn't help but laugh. "Not quite yet, but they did suggest strapping me down at night," I teased.

"Oooh, sounds very interesting," he said with a mischievous grin.

"Mind out of the gutter, Riley Bennett."

"Was that the gutter? Sounded more like heaven to me."

"You're sick and twisted."

"I know." He laughed some more before taking another bite from his burger. "So continue."

"Oddly enough, they don't think I'm mentally unstable at all."

"I don't either."

"Yeah, but you don't know all the scoop."

"Why? Don't you trust me?"

"Of course I trust you."

He looked at me with concerned eyes. "So then what's the full scoop?"

"I talk to Jesus every night," I blurted.

"That's not strange, Charlie; I do that too."

"When you talk to him, is he standing in your room in a t-shirt and jeans?"

"Uh—"

"And does he talk back to you?"

"Well, I can't say that, no."

"I don't know if I believe he's literally standing in the room, but I do know that I see him there. As I've told you before, I have an active imagination."

"Well who knows, maybe he is there. He rose from the dead, so I guess if he wanted to show up in your room every night it wouldn't be that difficult."

"I never thought about it like that."

"So how long have you been able to see him?"

"Since the accident. More fries?"

"No thanks. So he doesn't tell you to drown puppies or anything, does he?"

"Not yet."

"Well then, I don't see the problem."

"Really?"

"I wish Jesus appeared like that to me. It sure would make life easier."

"That's kind of what Joshua and Nicole said."

"So what's he like? When you talk to him?"

"It depends on his mood."

"His mood? He has moods?"

"He's human, you know," I reminded. "Well, sort of. Well, you know what I mean."

He nodded.

"He has a great sense of humor. He's charming and caring and gentle, but sometimes he can get kind of stern. He gives good advice, and he helps me work through my problems."

"Sounds good to me." He took the last bite of burger and shoved it in his mouth.

"Yes, it's nice."

"Has he said anything about me?"

"Yes."

His eyes grew large, and he sat straight up in his seat. "He has? What?"

"I don't know if I'm supposed to divulge that kind of stuff," I teased. "Our conversations are very private."

"I call crap on that. You better enlighten me right now."

"Do you share everything with me?"

"Yes."

"Oh. All right, he said that he thought you were good for me, that we were good for each other."

"I knew I liked him!" he joked. "Maybe you should spend more time with him and see what else he has to say about us."

"I'll see what I can do, but he doesn't tell me my future or anything. Everything is day-to-day. Except for that one time…"

"He told you your future?"

"One small thing."

"What?" he asked while leaning toward me in anticipation of the news.

"He told me I wasn't going to be a nun."

"Well that's a relief; otherwise, I've wasted a lot of time and words when I'm talking to him."

"You talk to him about us?"

He shrugged. "Of course. You're a major part of my life, Charlie. It's not like I'm not gonna talk to him about you."

"Well, what does he say?"

"To keep my hands to myself."

"Yes," I added. "That sounds exactly like something he would say."

chapter 14

Between the two of us, there'd been over 730 days since Marme and I enjoyed a girls shopping extravaganza. She called it "well-needed retail therapy," and I agreed wholeheartedly.

The drive into "the city" (as she called it) was a lot of fun. We listened to the *Footloose* soundtrack and sang along to the songs. I only knew portions of the songs, but Marme, of course, knew them word for word.

The term "the city" sounded ridiculous because in this particular situation she was referring to Oklahoma City. In New York when you referred to "the city" you meant *the* city, the Big Apple. Now that was a city! Mom took me there on several mother/daughter trips before she died. She loved Broadway shows, but my dad wasn't interested in seeing them, so I became her "date."

I loved the entire experience and always looked forward to going back. For me, coming out of the subway and into the main terminal of Grand Central Station was like a scene out of a movie. There were people everywhere, and the quickness of their movements could almost put you into a catatonic state if you watched them long enough. Sadly, it didn't seem as if anyone stopped to enjoy the beauty of the massive room. I used to try to imagine what it was like in the olden days, when people's lives weren't so hurried. I bet they appreciated its grandeur. I know that I certainly loved to stand and take it all in.

In New York City nobody stood still, and if you made the mistake of remaining in one spot for any amount of time, you would be trampled.

"Moving with the crowd is a necessity, Attie," my mother told me. "Otherwise, you'll get yourself hurt or lost somewhere."

She stayed in a constant state of panic as she ensured that I was close by her side. Mom carefully watched over me due to my tendency to wander off while walking mesmerized through the city streets or buildings. There was a seductiveness to the town, and I enjoyed it as much as my mother.

Being from a small town in the middle of the country, Mom made a commitment to herself that she would expose me to more experiences than she had growing up. She planned every trip weeks in advance so as to guarantee that I would experience something new, and the weekends usually incorporated a theme that focused on museums, parks, or boroughs. One weekend was designed merely for shopping at famous stores. We spent hours in Macy's alone but hit up FAO Schwartz and walked through Tiffany's as well. Being an amateur photographer, she documented every adventure and then religiously added them to our photo albums.

One of my favorite memories was our "China Town Adventure." We originally went to take in the sights and enjoy the food and culture, but that lasted for only a short time before we found Canal Street, the famous shopping district. Within minutes we entered into a shopping frenzy. It was astonishing! Every store had mounds and mounds of merchandise, much of it faux designer items that so closely resembled the actual manufacturer that I couldn't spot the difference. The only telltale sign I found was a tag on a purse that read "Kade Spade" rather than "Kate Spade." I bought the purse anyway and figured I would simply turn the label toward my body when I carried it. We bought more on that trip than any other, and my father hadn't been happy with the amount of money that was spent.

We always capped off the weekend with a Broadway show. On one of our first trips we saw one of the last showings of *Les Miserables*, and it still remains my favorite musical of all time. I downloaded the complete symphony version from iTunes and listen to it often as I picture it scene by scene in complete detail.

I remember sitting with my mother's hand in my left hand and the playbill in my right. Within only a few notes of music I was swept away into the drama as the powerful story pierced my heart.

The story unfolded before my eyes. Jean Valjean was once a spiritually lost man whose life had been redeemed. He became very powerful but ended up finding his true purpose in life when he made an oath to a dying woman that he would raise her child as his own. His past haunted him, but eventually, at the end of the story, he revealed the truth to his daughter, and his soul was free forever. I wept through much of the story and wished I could have seen it again and again. Sharing that night with my mother was my favorite memory of her, and unbeknownst to Riley, the picture that he sketched of my mother and I was taken moments before the story came to life that evening.

Marme's voice interrupted my thoughts. "Thank you for asking me to join you, Attie. It means a lot to me."

"Of course, there isn't anyone I would rather have going with me."

She was sincerely touched by the invitation, and I was delighted that such a small request was bringing her so much joy. Being so focused on my own misery, I hadn't thought about how having me around was affecting her. I was sure that having a girl in the house made her long for Melody's company and miss her more than ever.

Marme pulled into the parking lot of the store and turning to me said in a very serious tone, "Let the games begin."

We quickly jumped out of the car and made our way inside the trendy boutique. Vibrant colors came to life all around me, and a rush ran through my body. I had seventy-five dollars to spend, and I didn't even know where to begin. As I walked through the racks of clothes, I allowed my fingers to run across the fabrics. The clothes and their different textures felt wonderful to my touch. Indeed, this was a therapy all its own.

"Oh, Attie, look at these!" In less than ninety seconds she found a pair of white linen pants and wanted me to take a look. "These would look adorable on you, with your small, cute little body. Oh gosh, you'd be smashing!"

I laughed at her excitement and then looked at the price tag. "Oh, Marme, they're great, but they're also eighty-seven dollars. That's more than I have. There's a sale rack in the back; maybe we should just start there?" I hung the pants back up and started toward the rear of the store.

"Oh no you don't, Attie Reed." She grabbed my arm and shoved the pants back into my hands. "True retail therapy cannot be done by buying items on sale."

"But Marme, I only have seventy-five dollars."

"Well..." She reached into her purse and pulled out her wallet. "I have a credit card that hasn't been used in over a year, and it's gotten very lonely in this deep, dark cavern of a purse. I'm certain that it wants to come out and play for a while."

I chuckled. "I can't ask you to do that."

"You didn't ask. I want to do it. Please let me." She was practically begging.

"Only if you promise not to get carried away."

"Define what you mean by 'carried away.'"

I hugged her. "You're too much."

"Now, let's keep looking; we've got a long way to go and a short time to get there," she said before hunting down a sales associate to have them get a dressing room ready.

Splitting up, we grabbed anything we thought might look good.

"Attie, don't just think about the pool party. You need other clothes too."

I started to fuss, but she gave me a stern look, so I closed my mouth.

"What about a bathing suit, Attie? Do you have one?"

I shook my head frantically. "No way!"

"What do you mean no way?"

I yanked down the collar of my t-shirt and pointed to my scar so she would get my point.

"So?"

"So? They're ugly. I won't walk around in a bathing suit, especially the first time I meet people."

"You aren't gonna swim or lay out all summer? Spare me. We're getting you a bathing suit. You never know when you might need one."

After several more minutes, we finally made our way to the dressing room. The saleslady was practically salivating as Marme pulled up a chair and I got busy trying on clothes. After removing an item and handing it over the door to Marme, she would put it in either the "Keep" or "No" pile. I glanced at the piles each time I showed her a new item and realized the "Keep" pile was becoming much larger than the "No" pile.

"Don't you be looking at these stacks of clothes. This is my business," she teased. "Now put on that bathing suit with the flowers on it."

"It's a bikini," I complained.

"Let me see it."

I put on the suit and looked at myself in the mirror. All I could focus on were the scars. I felt naked and uncomfortable.

"Come on out here. Let me see you."

"I don't know," I mumbled.

"Get your tiny butt out here right now," she ordered. I opened the door and she smiled up at me. "You're gorgeous. Look at that body!" I stood with my face cringing. "Yep." She nodded. "It's a keeper."

Rolling my eyes, I walked back into the stall and shut the door.

"Don't you roll your eyes at me, young lady."

"Yes, ma'am."

"You do know you're supposed to keep your underwear on when you try on bathing suits, don't you?"

"I did."

"I didn't see them."

"They're just a thong; there isn't much to see."

"Attie Reed! You wear thongs?"

"Well, yes."

"That's a little Britney Spears, don't you think?"

"Only if you make them hang out the top of your britches."

She laughed and then shivered. "If I tried to wear one of those things, it would get lost forever." I was sure she was trying to picture herself wearing one.

"I don't know. They're pretty great."

"No, thank you."

I put my clothes back on and headed out of the stall. "I'll tell you what, I won't complain about you buying all of those clothes if you'll buy one thong for yourself."

Her eyes got huge. "Do they even make them in my size?"

"What size are you?" the sales associate asked as she tried to hide a snicker.

"Gigantic," Marme replied sadly.

"Hardly! You've got a great body. I hope I look as good as you do when I'm your age."

"My age? You mean old as dirt? All right, just grab me a pair," she said to the sales associate. "The cheapest pair you've got; I don't think I'll be wearing them more than a few seconds."

The saleslady carried the pile of clothes to the checkout counter and grabbed Marme a thong on the way.

"Now, Attie, you go on and entertain yourself while I check out. You don't need to be privy to how much I spend."

I walked away but peeked back and caught her throwing several pairs of earrings and two pairs of sunglasses onto the "Keep" pile.

I wasn't certain, but I would guess that she was spending well over seven hundred dollars. Pops was going to kill her.

chapter 15

"Attie," Marme said outside my bedroom door. "The girls are here."

"Great, send them up."

"What did you decide to wear?" she asked.

"Come on in. Give me your opinion."

Opening the door, she looked in, and upon seeing me she clapped. "Oh, Attie, you're beautiful! I hoped you would wear that."

"You don't think it's too dressy for a pool party?"

"No, it's perfect."

I was wearing the white linen trousers and a lime green linen top with pale gold stitching, a high collar, and three-quarter length sleeves.

"Do you feel comfortable in it?"

"Yes."

"Does it cover everything you want covered?"

"Yes."

"What shoes are you gonna wear?" she asked.

I walked over to the closet and pulled out a pair of sandals.

"Will these do? They're all I've got."

"They'll be fine for today, but this weekend we'll go shoe shopping. What about your hair? What are you gonna do with it?"

"A ponytail I think, but where it kind of poufs a little on the top like this." I fixed it as I spoke.

"Oh, I like it like that. It's sassy. And maybe a little mascara and lip gloss," she suggested.

"Sure."

"Perfect, Attie, you're gonna look perfect. Boys are gonna be falling all over themselves to get near you."

"Hey chick-a-dee," Tammy greeted as the girls made their way into my room.

"I'll leave you girls to finish getting ready," Marme announced as she left the room.

"Look at this room! It's amazing, Attie. It's changed so much." Anne beamed.

"Don't you love it? I do. They did it on Monday while I was at work."

"How sweet is that?" Anne said softly and made a face as if she would cry.

"Look at these drawings!" Tess sounded far away in a dream state. "Aren't they amazing?"

"Where did they come from?" Anne asked.

"Riley drew them for me," I answered before thinking about it and regretted the words the moment they left my mouth.

I waited for Tammy to make a remark. "Get out!" There it was. "Move outta the way and let me see. You're hoggin' the wall, Tess."

"No, I'm not, Tammy, there's plenty of room for both of us," Tess said then sighed softly. "I'm in awe."

"Attie, that's the sweetest thing I've ever seen," Anne exclaimed.

"I couldn't thank him enough."

"You could have planted a big ole kiss on him. That would have done it," Tammy informed me.

"You think?" I asked sarcastically.

"Are you sure you don't like him? He's the sweetest thing ever." Tess was disappointed that we weren't an item.

I made a gloomy face in her direction. "Sorry, Tess, we're just friends for now."

"For now?" She lit up. "You mean maybe one day?"

"We aren't even considering it until I move out."

"So you've talked about it?" Anne asked, sitting down on the bed.

I was surprised that Tammy hadn't told them about our conversation.

"A little."

"Oh my gosh! Attie!" Anne squealed. "You two would be adorable together!"

"You would," Tess agreed.

"Well, we'll see. We've got a few more months till then, so let's not jump to any conclusions. A lot can change between now and then."

"I doubt it. You're a keeper, Attie." Tammy smiled at me. For as spunky and unconventional as she was, she had a heart of gold.

"I'll make sure I keep everyone updated, okay?"

"Oh good!" I'd made Tess's day.

"Get your suit and let's go," Anne ordered as she jumped off the bed.

"Oh, I'm not bringing a suit."

"Why?" they all asked.

"My scars, I don't want to show them off today," I explained.

"Scars?" Tess asked.

"From the accident," Anne explained before giving me a reassuring smile.

"Oh," Tess sighed softly.

"How bad can they be?" Tammy asked.

"Pretty bad." I scowled.

"Let's see 'em," she said.

I rolled my eyes and then unbuttoned my shirt and let it fall to my waist. All the girls stepped closer to me so they could get a better look.

"They aren't bad at all, Attie," Anne said reassuringly.

"No, not bad at all," Tess agreed.

I looked at Tammy and waited to hear what she would say. "You're beautiful even with the scars. And you kinda remind me of the six-million dollar woman," she added.

I laughed. "Thanks, guys, but still, I wouldn't be comfortable." I put my shirt back on and buttoned it up.

"All right, well, let's get going," Anne announced. "Cute boys are waiting."

"And Chase," Tess added.

"Chase is a cute boy, Tess," Tammy said, throwing her arms over Tess's shoulder.

"Well, I didn't mean it like that," Tess said sweetly.

They filed out of my room, and I followed them down the stairs. Walking behind Tammy, I noticed she was wearing cutoff blue jeans with holes all over them and a Grateful Dead concert t-shirt.

"I see you got dressed up, Tammy."

"Only the best for my friends."

· ·

By the time we arrived, the party was in full swing. Anne, being the social butterfly, immediately walked away and began chatting with friends. Tammy spotted the food table and made a beeline for it without even looking back, and Tess and I were left standing alone.

"How does she stay so skinny?" Tess asked, watching Tammy walk away. "If I ate like that, I'd be three hundred pounds."

"Life's not fair, Tess."

"No, it's not." She sighed in agreement.

"Do not leave me alone. I don't know anybody here."

I heard a familiar voice call my name.

"Oh no." I grabbed Tess's arm.

"What?" she asked, concerned.

"Please don't tell me that's Cooper Truman."

She shook her head and spoke softly, "I don't even know who that is."

"Hello, Attie." His voice came from directly behind me.

I rolled my eyes and turned around to face him. "Hey, Cooper, good to see you."

He gave me a hug, and it lasted way too long for it being given by someone that I hardly knew. "I'm so glad that you made it. I've been looking for you. Come on, I'll introduce you to some friends."

"Oh, I don't know, Cooper; I probably shouldn't leave my friend."

"What friend?"

"Tess..." I turned and realized that she was gone. "Uh, nobody I guess."

He grabbed my hand and started dragging me through the crowd, and as the other kids laughed and enjoyed each other's company, I frantically searched their faces for Riley's. Unfortunately, none of the faces I saw were his.

"Hey, guys," I heard Cooper say. "This is Attie. She just moved into town with her family. Her grandfather runs the veterinary clinic over on Main."

I looked at four new pairs of eyes staring at me. "Hello." I spoke softly and gave them a weak wave.

Cooper began making introductions. "This is Rick, Beth, Wes, and Tiffany."

My instincts told me that this was the dreaded "in crowd," but they were totally mismatched, and even though they weren't much taller than I was, I felt like they were looking down on me.

"Hi, Attie. I'm Tiffany," one of the girls spoke as she offered her hand for a shake. I wondered if this was the Tiffany that Riley took to prom. "So you're the girl that's living with Riley?"

"Um, with his family, yes," I answered.

"I've heard about you. Riley and I have been dating for a while."

"Really? He hasn't mentioned you." I couldn't believe the words left my mouth, but I was pleased with myself.

Yes, this was the girl, and as far as she was concerned, they were still dating. Riley might be interested in knowing that little piece of information.

"You're the girl from the accident." The boy named Wes pointed it out as if I didn't already know. "Cool."

"Yes, cool," I repeated.

Cooper and his friends chatted, and I took the opportunity to inspect Tiffany. She was the complete opposite of me, tall with an athletic build and jet-black, curly hair. Her tanned complexion caused her blue eyes to radiate. She was stunning, and I immediately wanted to hate her. I also happened to notice that unfortunately, she did have big boobs, and the revelation was very upsetting.

I turned my gaze to the other girl, Beth. Looking at her, the first question that came to mind was how she made it into the in crowd. She wasn't unattractive, but she wasn't attractive either. She was a little plain, like me, and she had a nervous little giggle. She looked friendly enough; maybe I could like her.

"Did you see what Tammy's wearing?" she asked Tiffany. "That girl is so strange."

Nope, I determined that I couldn't be her friend after all.

Wes was, well, dirty for lack of a better term. Or at least he looked like he hadn't bathed in days. His brown hair was greasy, his clothes were wrinkled, and it was obvious he didn't believe in shaving. Worse, he was eating a hot dog and talking with his mouth full. To keep from getting sick, I looked away and gave Rick the once over.

Rick was a pleasant enough looking guy and much more like Cooper. He was clean, nicely dressed, and appeared to be friendly. His personality was very outgoing, and he kept everyone in the group laughing, so he was more than likely the ringleader of the clique. He seemed nice enough, but I was sure that he probably possessed a dark side. Most members of elite cliques did.

After several moments Cooper finally excused us and pulled me toward the house. "Come on, Attie, I'll give you a tour."

I searched for one of the girls to rescue me but couldn't find one. "Maybe I should try to find my friends so they don't worry about me," I suggested.

"Oh, we'll just be a minute, Attie." He grabbed my hand and pulled me along behind him.

More than thirty minutes later, we still hadn't made it beyond the first floor. Cooper took me through every room on the first level and made sure to point out every piece of art or artifact and give its history. I didn't get to say one word, and all the excess information was nauseating. If he was trying to impress me, he was failing miserably. He talked nonstop about all the travel he'd done to Europe and how much he loved art.

"Are you an art lover, Attie?"

"Can't say that I am, no."

"Have you been exposed to much?"

"Just a few museums in New York, but that's it."

"Oh, I bet if you were exposed to it a little more you'd fall in love with it."

My mind wandered to Riley's sketches. Come to think of it, there was one type of art that I liked—Riley's.

"Attie." I heard Tammy say my name.

"Tammy!" Instant relief washed over me. "We're back here."

She made her way into the back hallway to join us. "Whatcha doin', Cooper?" she asked distrustfully.

"Hey, Tammy," Cooper said warmly. "Attie wanted a tour of the house, so I thought I'd oblige."

"Did she now? Well, Cooper," she said softly, "you have to share the new girl. Everyone wants to meet her."

"She hasn't seen the upstairs yet. We'll only be a few more minutes."

"Oh, Cooper, that's all right. I'll make sure to see it next time," I lied.

"Well…" He hesitated. "Promise?"

"Yes," I lied again.

"I guess I should probably check on the guests," he admitted.

"Yes, you probly should," Tammy replied. "I think they were running out of hot dogs, and you know how high school kids are when they run out of hot dogs."

"Okay, I guess I'll find you in a little while, Attie?"

"Looking forward to it," I lied for the third time.

Cooper walked off, and when he was out of sight Tammy stuck her finger into her mouth as if she was gagging herself.

"Tell me about it." I rolled my eyes. "How did you find me?"

"Riley sent me in after you."

"Riley? He's here?" My heart raced.

"Yep. But don't you dare tell him I told you. He'd kill me. He saw Cooper drag you in here and got worried after you'd been gone awhile, so he asked me to come in here and drag you back out."

"Did he seem jealous?"

"Oh yeah. He was totally jealous; it was awesome."

As we made our way outside I intentionally didn't look around. If Riley was watching, I didn't want him to know that I knew he was there. I did, however, notice Tiffany walking up to me.

"So, Attie, did you like the house?"

"It's very nice."

"Hey, Tiff, how's it going?"

"Hi, Tammy," Tiffany responded without even looking her direction. "So, Attie, looks like we'll be on the cheer squad together."

I gulped and then gave her a weak smile. "Great. That'll be nice." I lied again—what was this, the fourth time today already?

"I'll probably be captain this year. We vote before the first game."

"Good luck. You've got my vote," I lied for the fifth time.

"Captain? What does that mean? Like, you kick the highest?" Tammy asked dryly. "I'm underwhelmed."

Tiffany rolled her eyes, "See you around, Attie." She turned to walk off and then spoke over her shoulder. "Tell Riley to call me; he owes me a dinner."

"I will," I called back to her and then whispered in Tammy's ear, "when I wake up next to him tomorrow morning."

She laughed. "That was awesome, even if I was the only person to hear it."

"That's the most wonderfully tacky thing I've ever said," I boasted. "I'm in awe of myself."

"You should be. Did it feel good?"

I nodded my head enthusiastically.

"I've trained you well, my fine young padawan." An extremely large smile covered her face. "Pretty soon you'll even be able to say stuff like that out loud."

"Attie! Tammy!" Anne called for us to join her and Jennifer. "We got some lounge chairs."

"Thanks for deserting me, Anne," I taunted as I took a seat. "Hey, Jennifer."

"Did I desert you? I'm so sorry, Attie. I didn't realize."

"You left me to chat, Tammy left me to eat, and then Tess took off and I don't know where in the world she is."

"Oh." She looked sad. "I'm so sorry."

"I'm just teasing you; don't worry about it."

"But she was saved by Cooper, and he blessed her with a tour of his lovely home," Tammy added sarcastically.

"Ugh," Anne moaned.

"Cooper's a freak," Jennifer added.

As if he heard his name, Cooper appeared in front of me. "Hello, girls." He grinned.

"Hey, Cooper," we said flatly.

"Do you girls want to help judge the belly flop competition?"

"Are you gonna be in it?" Tammy asked.

"Of course." He nodded.

"Sure, we can do that." She tried to sound friendly but wasn't very convincing.

"Great! You'll have a blast. Now, as we each take turns, yell out your score—anything from one to ten with ten being the best."

"Thanks so much, Cooper. I don't know if we could have figured out how to do it on our own."

"Anytime." Again, Tammy's sarcasm flew right over Cooper's head, and he trotted off to join his friends.

"Maybe he'll hurt himself," Tammy mumbled.

"Tammy, be nice," Anne scolded.

The boys lined up to take their turn at being physically tortured. The first to go was the dirty boy that Cooper introduced me to.

Before he jumped, he looked over and gave Tammy a wink.

"Automatic two-point deduction for the wink," she grumbled.

His body hit the water in a slight curve, so technically it wasn't the perfect belly flop. Under normal circumstances, he would have received three sixes, but with the two-point winking penalty he got fours from everyone but Anne, who went ahead and gave him a six.

I scanned the line of willing volunteers and caught Cooper looking at me. Our eyes met, and he gave me a large smile.

"His teeth are perfect," I noted. "I wonder how much they spent
on orthodontia for teeth like that."

"Who?" Anne asked.

"Cooper."

"Well, sadly both he and his sister were born perfect. Neither
one ever experienced an awkward phase."

"Totally unfair," Tammy stated and then quickly followed by
yelling, "Seven!" I hadn't seen the boy jump, so I gave him a seven as
well. Anne gave him an eight, and Jen gave him a six.

I looked back at Cooper who now enthusiastically talked to the
boy in front of him. He was shorter than Riley but a few inches
taller than me, and he wasn't built as muscular as Riley. Cooper was
muscular in the way that rider's bodies are developed. He must have
spent a lot of time on horses.

As if she could read my mind, Tammy spoke, "He may be annoying, but that Cooper sure does have a tight butt."

"You think?" I asked.

"Oh yeah." She nodded her head.

I looked back at him. His deep blue eyes stood out against his
blonde hair, and his teeth were a brilliant white. With his tan he
looked more like a California surfer than an Okie. I could see him
fitting in nicely at Cornell; he certainly had a well-manicured look
about him.

I moved my gaze to the next flop victim, a rather large boy who
looked like he could be a lineman for the football team. As he flew
into the air, he arched his back in perfect belly flop form, and I
waited to hear the slapping noise that was certain to reverberate as
soon as his skin made contact with the surface of the water.

Smack!

There it was.

Everyone groaned in sympathy but followed with loud cheers.
As he jumped up and down in celebration, his tummy jiggled. The
girls and I gave him a sympathetic applause and then followed with

giving him tens across the board before Cooper took his spot on the diving board. As he waited at the back of the board in anticipation of a friend telling him it was time to go, he yelled to get my attention and make sure I watched his "perfect belly flop."

I gave a fake smile and nodded.

He also executed perfect form, but the splash wasn't as large as the boy who received the perfect score.

"Nine," I shouted.

"Nine," Tammy and Jen agreed.

"Ten," Anne countered.

He climbed out of the pool wearing a grin from ear to ear and his chest bright red from the impact of his skin on the surface of the water. Walking directly over to me, he took the liberty of sitting on the end of my lounge chair. "Attie, I can't believe you only gave me a nine."

"Not enough splash, Coop," I answered. "The big boy blew you away."

"Fair enough." He smiled. "I guess a nine is a pretty great score for a scrawny kid like me."

The competition continued, but Cooper didn't leave my chair. Since he wasn't leaving my chair any time soon, I figured that I might as well be nice to the boy. And actually, we carried on a fairly interesting conversation.

"Oh, I didn't tell you that my dad is a professor at Cornell. He teaches veterinary medicine," I advised.

"That's my major!"

"Really? That's what I'm going to study as well."

"You're kidding?" he asked, laughing.

"Nope. It's in my blood."

"Could your dad be one of my professors?"

"Unfortunately, he won't be there next year. He's moving back here this summer to join my Gramps's practice."

"Oh, is he?"

"If he gets here before you leave, I could introduce you. I'm sure he'd give you all kinds of good information."

"Would you really?" I didn't think it was possible, but his smile got bigger, and I was practically blinded.

"Are you going to specialize in equestrian?"

He pointed toward the stables. "Do you think I have a choice?"

"Is that not what interests you?"

"Does it matter?" he teased.

"Are you gonna answer all of her questions with a question?" Tammy interrupted.

"Is that what I'm doing?"

"Yes, it's very annoying," she informed.

"Tammy, do you say everything that comes into your mind?" he asked.

"Yes, actually I do."

"I can tell," he teased.

"Mind your own business, Tammy," I added. "So, Coop, answer my question. What type of veterinary medicine interests you?"

He shined his bright teeth at me again. "Growing up I wanted to work with zoo animals. I've been around horses my entire life; I thought a little variety would be good."

"I can understand that." I felt a little sorry for him. It was as if he was expected to fulfill his family's expectations and his interests weren't considered.

"Other than my time away for school, I'll probably never get away from this place."

"It's beautiful, Cooper. I would love it here."

He grinned. "You're welcome anytime."

I ignored the blatantly obvious invitation and kept talking. "So why Cornell?"

"It's about as far away as I can get. If I went to OSU my parents would expect me to come home every weekend. I'm ready to get away for a while."

"Oh." I nodded. "Your parents were okay with Cornell?"

"Yes, it's kind of a status thing. I know it sounds terrible, but in the circles they run in, that kind of stuff is important."

"Sorry," I said.

"Why?"

"It seems like you have a lot of expectations to meet."

He grinned at me again. "You're very perceptive."

"You ride English I assume?"

"Yes. You?"

"Western."

"Uh-oh, you're one of those," he joked.

"Yes, I am. You better watch it, Coop. Your parents find out your hob-knobbing with a girl who rides western and you could be disowned."

"Promise?" Cooper laughed before excusing himself to chase down a runaway beach ball.

As he left I saw Riley across the pool directly in front of me. Tiffany stood between us as she talked, but with his weight shifted to his left, I could see him clearly. She may have been standing there barely clothed, but he didn't seem to notice. His eyes shifted back and forth between looking at the ground and me. His arms were tightly folded across his chest, and his face wore a scowl. He looked miserable.

"She hates me," I mouthed as I pointed at Tiffany.

He laughed and nodded, which caused Tiffany to turn to find out what he was laughing at. A bitter scowl exploded onto her face the moment we made eye contact. She quickly turned back around and repositioned herself in order to block Riley's and my view of each other, but within seconds he walked away.

My heart rate increased as he somehow managed to keep his eyes on me while making his way through the crowd and finally took the spot Truman left empty.

"Having fun?" he asked.

"Oodles."

"Oozing with sarcasm, are we?"

"I've been hanging around Tammy too long."

"I hate to tell you this, Charlie, but you were sarcastic long before Tammy came along."

"You get stuck talking to Cooper Truman for thirty minutes and see how much fun you're having," Jen said.

"It's actually been an hour. I also got stuck with him in the house for thirty minutes, remember?"

"I'd rather not think about it," Tammy said, rolling her eyes.

"Oh, girls, he isn't that bad," Anne interrupted. "Attie, you and he have a lot in common."

"What?" Riley asked.

"The whole vet school thing," she answered.

"That's one thing, Anne, not a lot of things," I said.

"Still, he's nice."

"Oh, Anne," Tammy scolded. "You like everybody. Why can't you just be judgmental and hateful like the rest of us?"

"I don't like everybody," Anne clarified.

"Name one person you don't like," Tammy challenged.

It took a few moments, but Anne finally spoke. "Tiffany."

"No, Anne, I said to name a *person*."

"Oh, Tammy, be nice." I don't know why Anne bothered; she was wasting her breath. Nothing short of Jesus appearing before Tammy and telling her to be nice to Tiffany would work, and I wasn't even so sure that would do it.

"Girls sure are catty," Riley said.

"Aren't we?" Jen agreed.

I lightly kicked his shoulder. "Your girlfriend asked me to remind you that you owe her dinner."

"My girlfriend?"

"Tiffany." I lightly kicked him on the shoulder again, and as I pulled my foot away, he grabbed me by the toes and placed my foot in his lap. His fingers never broke contact with my skin.

"She's not my girlfriend," he said adamantly.

"Well, evidently she doesn't know that. She informed me that she's been dating you for a while, and I didn't get the sense she's realized you aren't dating her back."

"She knows, she just doesn't wanna admit it, and she isn't gonna concede anything to you."

"Me?"

"She sees you as competition," he pointed out.

"Ooh, there's a competition for Riley's heart," Tammy teased.

"No." He shook his head at Tammy but kept his eyes on me. "You look a little tired, Charlie, are you?"

"A little bit."

"Do you need to go home?" Anne asked. "We can take you. We just need to find Tess first."

"You want me to take you home?" he asked.

"Nobody needs to take me home. I want you guys to stay and have fun. I can stay."

"No, I don't mind," he offered. "I've had my fill anyway. This really isn't my scene."

"What is your scene, Riley?" I asked.

"Sitting on the couch watching movies."

"Sounds thrilling," Tammy said.

We ignored her.

"I am pretty tired. Are you sure you wouldn't mind leaving?"

"Positive."

"Do you girls care?" I asked. "I didn't get much sleep last night."

"No, go ahead," Anne said cheerfully. "Go home and get some rest."

He stood up and pulled me to my feet.

"Will you guys tell Tess I said good-bye and I'll see her later?"

"Sure. Hey, you have any plans for Monday during lunch? Maybe we can all get together," Anne said.

"Monday?" I couldn't hide my growing anxiety.

Anne looked surprised. "It was just a suggestion; we don't have to."

"Oh, no, Anne. I would love that. Thanks for asking. It's just Monday's the anniversary of the accident..."

Riley wrapped his arm protectively around me as the girls' eyes grew large and filled with sadness.

"...and I don't know what the day's going to be like yet."

"Oh my gosh, Attie! I'm so sorry I didn't realize."

"Don't worry about it, Anne. How could you have known? It's no big deal. If I don't have anything planned, I'll call. I'd love to go to lunch with you guys. It'll probably help."

"Good." Anne sounded hopeful.

"All right, see you guys later."

As we turned to go, I heard Riley whisper, "She'll be okay," over his shoulder. He kept his arm around my waist until we made it to the car.

"Do you think that's why your nightmares have been getting worse? Because of the anniversary?"

"I don't know, maybe." I wasn't sure of anything at the moment. Consecutive nights of hours without sleep were catching up with me, and my mind was a complete crow's nest. My thoughts were jumbled, and sentences were slow to form.

He pulled me to him, and without thinking twice I laid my head on his chest. He kissed the top of my head several times as my body relaxed into his.

"You know, one day we're gonna look back on all this and not believe we've come so far. The pain and the nightmares will be a far-off memory."

"Promise?" I asked.

"Yes."

"Well, can we stay like this until then? I don't want to move."

"Trust me. I'm game if you are. I don't wanna move either."

"Then let's not. Not right this second anyway."

He wrapped his arms more tightly around my body, and I allowed my eyes to close. We stood silent and still for several minutes, and when I opened my eyes, I caught a glimpse of Tiffany standing next to a tree watching us.

"We better get home," I whispered as I removed my head from his chest and looked up at him.

The look on his face was one I'd never seen before. Somehow I could sense the battle raging in his mind. He wanted to kiss me, that much was obvious, but he wouldn't. He wouldn't break the promise he'd made to his father no matter how much he wanted to or I secretly wished he would.

I ignored Tiffany as he rested his forehead on mine. "Riley, if we're going to leave, then you have to let go of me."

"I realize that."

"So I take it we aren't leaving then?"

"No, we are." He released his grip and reached behind me to open the car door. "Hurry and get in before I change my mind."

I laughed as I hopped in and took one last look at Tiffany before we drove away.

chapter 16

(Riley)

"Kids! We're gonna be late!" Dad yelled up to us from the bottom of the stairs.

"Come on, get your butts down here!"

"Go without us then," I yelled. "We'll meet you there!"

"No, sir! We're going as a family. Now get your butts down here!"

I knew when my dad meant business, and he meant business. "Come on, Attie, we've got to go. Dad's gonna bust a gut."

"I'm coming," she said through her bedroom door. "Go on down. I'll be right there."

I obeyed and made my way down to the foyer where Mom and Dad were both waiting.

"What in the world, son?" Dad asked.

"She's nervous; give her a second. Besides, it's best that we're a little late; otherwise, she might run into Mitchell. He does the greeting each week."

"Well, that's true. I didn't think about that." He nodded. "Molly, let's go on out to the car. Riley, go get her and bring her down this instant."

"Yes, sir."

I was nervous for Attie. Gramps called the night before to let her in on a secret. Today would mark forty years to the day that he sang in the church choir for the first time. The worship pastor decided to celebrate by asking him to sing a song at the end of service, and Gramps agreed but made the request to do a duet rather than a solo. A duet with Attie.

"What?" she shrieked over the phone when he called to ask her to sing with him. "Have you lost your mind? I haven't sung that song in years, and I haven't sung it in front of people *ever*! Gramps, don't ask me to do this!"

He asked anyway. This was his one wish, he told her. He would never ask her to do another thing for him again.

After getting off the phone, she went into a complete panic, and I joined her.

"Have I ever heard you sing?" I asked.

"I doubt it. It's not like I'm that good, and I only sang with him or my mom, and it was always in the car." She searched iTunes for the Sandi Patty song on our family computer.

"I can't even believe this song is on here; it's from the eighties, which would make it a classic in your eyes."

"I don't even know who Sandi Patty is," I admitted.

"Most kids our age don't."

After downloading the song, she spent the rest of the night practicing outside in the pasture so that none of us could hear her.

"Come on, Charlie! We've got to go!" I peeked out the door and saw my dad's scowl. "So glad we're all in such wonderful moods for church today."

I heard her footprints on the steps and turned to tell her to hurry. "Gorgeous," slipped out instead of "hurry."

Her chin dropped, and she looked at me through squinting eyes. "Nice try, Riley."

"I'm dead serious. You look amazing."

"Thank God your mom took me shoe shopping yesterday. I don't know what I would have worn on my feet."

"You could have gone barefoot," I suggested. "Personally, I love the red toenails."

"They're crimson, and no way, some of those old geezers would think I was going to hell if they knew I wore crimson polish on my toes."

"Does that make you a harlot or something?"

"Probly."

"Did you say 'probly' instead of 'probably'? Ya getting a little Okie in ya finally?" I teased.

The car horn honked.

"Jesus Christ," Dad screamed. "Get your butts out here!"

"Nice talk for Sunday morning, Dad!" I locked the door behind us. "You do look gorgeous. Everybody's gonna love you."

"I wouldn't bet on it. They're going to wish that God never gave them eardrums by the time I'm finished. Gramps is the singer in the family, not me."

I closed the car door behind her, ran around to the other side, and jumped in before Dad could leave without me.

"Sorry about the J.C. comment earlier," Dad mumbled while Mom stared at him in contempt.

"You gotta watch that stuff on Sundays, Dad. I think it's a double sin to say the Lord's name in vain on the Holy Day." I felt compelled to give him a hard time; plus I needed to keep Attie's mind occupied.

"Enough out of you, Riley."

I rolled my eyes. "Yes, sir."

"Oh, Attie, I can't wait to hear you sing!" Mom was gushing. "Your mom used to brag about your singing all the time."

Attie looked like she was about to vomit. "Did she now?"

"They should have done the duet early in the service so you could get it over with instead of having to suffer through," I said.

"Tell me about it." She started fanning herself. "I should have brought a brown paper bag to breathe in."

"Put your head between your knees," I suggested.

She did, and she stayed in that position for the rest of our drive to church.

Under normal circumstances I would have said that church service was great and the sermon powerful, but I quite honestly have no idea what happened the majority of the time because I busied myself praying for Attie not to pass out before, during, or after the song.

"Is the sanctuary always this crowded?" she whispered in my ear.

"Yes, always." I tried to assure her, but I was lying. It looked much more crowded than normal.

Anne, Tammy, Jen, Tess, and Chase were sitting directly in front of us, and they had no idea what was about to take place. I would have warned them, but I didn't wanna make Attie more nervous.

"Well, we have a very special treat for everyone here today," the pastor announced. "What a perfect day too because we seem to have a packed house. It's never this full!"

I felt Attie stare me down, but I pretended I didn't hear him comment on the size of the crowd.

"Richard?" The pastor turned to the choir and addressed Gramps. "Would you join me down here, please?"

Attie grabbed my arm and squeezed—very tightly. Her nails were digging into my skin, and I bit my bottom lip to keep from screaming out in pain.

I took in a slow deep breath and blew it out in an effort to get her to do the same. She didn't; she just looked panicked.

"Breathe," I mumbled.

"I am!" she spat back under her breath. "If I don't die of a heart attack up there, would you please remind me to kill my Gramps when this is over?"

The pastor explained to the audience the significance of the day.

I pried her fingers from my arm. "I may kill him for you."

I heard Gramps call Attie to the stage, and at least he called her Attie instead of Atticus. In front of all these people, calling her Atticus really would have ticked her off.

The gang on the row in front of us turned around and looked at Attie in complete shock. She shook her head slowly as she got up.

"Sorry for what you're about to witness," she whispered to them as she left the pew and stepped out into the aisle.

The congregation clapped for her as she made her way to the stage.

"Isn't she lovely?" Gramps gushed proudly as she joined him.

My skin felt as if it was gonna break out into hives, and I couldn't stop myself from running my fingers through my hair.

"Can you tell she can't wait to do this?" Pastor Rick teased.

The audience laughed. Attie rolled her eyes and took his microphone.

"I'm never going to forgive you for this. You know that, don't you?" she teased her Gramps.

"I'm very aware, darlin', I'm very aware." He laughed and the congregation joined. "But you're makin' me one proud grandpa."

"Aws" were heard all throughout the audience as he gave her a kiss on the cheek.

"I'm a big Sandi Patty fan," he explained. "And when Attie was a little girl, we used to listen to the same Sandi Patty cassette every time we got in the car."

Attie interrupted him. "And for those of you that don't know, a cassette is something that they used to play music on back in the olden days before we had CDs."

The crowd laughed, and she gave a big grin.

"Yes, thank you for clarifying, Attie," he teased.

"Anytime."

Gramps continued, "Our favorite, or my favorite song on the album, is a duet that Sandy did with Lionel Harris. The song's called 'More Than Wonderful.' Attie and I would sing that song together over and over again when we drove around in my car." He smiled at the memory. "One day after listening to Sandi Patty all day and singin' to the Lord, Attie turned to me and said, 'Gramps, don't you think that if I'm gonna sing songs like this to the Lord he should be in my heart so he can hear 'em better?'"

The crowd sighed and cooed while listening to the story, and a big smile spread across Attie's face.

Gramps continued, "I pulled over right there on the side of the road and prayed with her as she accepted Jesus Christ as her Lord and Savior." The audience cheered and Gramps beamed again. "It was one of the most wonderful moments in my life," he said softly.

Tears filled Gramps's eyes, and looking around I realized that most everybody in the room was getting weepy—including me.

"So thank you for indulgin' an old man and lettin' him relive a wonderful memory," Gramps added.

Attie gave her grandfather a quick kiss on the cheek. "Well, when you put it that way, how can I say no?"

The audience clapped again. They, like me, had fallen in love with the witty little blonde standing on stage.

As the music started and the choir hummed behind her, Attie got startled and giggled. She hadn't expected such a large production, but she grabbed Gramps's hand, looked into his eyes, and began to sing.

To me, her voice sounded as if an angel were singing, but afraid that I might be biased, I looked at our friends sitting in front of me to check their reaction. Their jaws were dropped. They were also blown away by Attie's voice.

Their voices were amazing separately, but when they sang together it was as if God created them to sing together. The words were powerful enough on their own, but coming out of their mouths, you could feel that everyone in the room believed that they were witnessing an amazing moment. People stood all over the auditorium with their eyes closed and their hands held high in worship, and by the time they reached the end of the song, people were clapping and shouting praises to their Lord.

Trumpets brought the song to an end, and the room erupted in cheers as Attie and her Gramps smiled at each other and took a small bow. Then, as Gramps stood back and pointed to Attie, presenting her to the audience, the congregation erupted with louder applause and cheering.

Attie shook her head in embarrassment and gave a weak smile.

"Oh my!" I heard Pastor Rick's voice over the noise. He joined them on stage, and as the clapping continued, Attie looked more and more uncomfortable. Finally, the cheers died down, and the audience sat so that Pastor Rick could speak.

"Mike," Pastor Rick said, looking over at the worship leader, "why isn't this girl in the choir?"

Mike shrugged his shoulders. "I'll get right on that," he said into his mic.

I was so proud that my heart was about to explode, and I wasn't sure whether to laugh or cry, so I did both.

"I think we need to hear that more often," Pastor Rick suggested before turning to Attie. "Are you available next week?"

The auditorium erupted again as Attie simply shrugged and looked down at her feet. She hated compliments.

Pastor Rick kept a hold of her hand and grabbed Gramps as well. "Can we all bow our heads and pray?"

I couldn't bow my head because I couldn't stop looking at Attie. I was amazed, blown away, and even crazier about her.

Midway through the prayer, I noticed her look up with a small smile on her face and glance around the room, but the smile left her face and she looked frightened. Her eyes locked in place, and I followed her gaze. She'd spotted Mitchell King, and it registered in her mind whom he was.

I nudged my dad and he looked over at me. "Attie spotted Mitchell," I whispered.

Dad's head jerked in her direction, and his face turned pale. "You get ready to go grab her as soon as Pastor finishes," he whispered back.

Her eyes, large and full of fear, left him and frantically searched the auditorium until they met mine.

I gave her a small smile and nodded. "It's all right," I mouthed.

Attie slowly nodded and didn't take her eyes off of mine until Pastor Rick finished his prayer and dismissed everyone.

Within seconds I made my way down the aisle and whisked Attie away behind the stage. She contained herself until we were alone, but eventually her body trembled, and she started to cry.

"I saw him! I saw him!" she whispered loudly.

"I know, Charlie, I know. It's all right." I rubbed her back in an effort to comfort her, but it wasn't working. She was inconsolable.

Dad came running into the room with Joshua, Nicole, and Pastor Rick. Joshua knelt down next to her.

"Attie," Joshua spoke to her. "Attie, can you hear me?"

Salvaged

She nodded.

"What happened? Can you talk to me and tell me what happened?" he asked.

Attie slowly lifted her head and looked at him.

"I saw him."

"Saw who?" he asked.

"I've seen that face every night for almost a year; I'd know it anywhere." She shook her head as if she were trying to force his picture out of her mind. "I wasn't ready. I didn't expect to see him. Why didn't someone tell me he went to church here?" She turned and looked at me. "Riley, why didn't you tell me?"

"Who was it, Attie?" Joshua asked.

She slowly turned and looked into Joshua's face.

"I saw the man that killed my mother."

167

chapter 17

Joshua joined us in the family room. "She's all right. I think that she'll be fine."

"Can I go up now?" I asked. "Can I check on her?"

I hadn't even seen Attie since church. Joshua and Nicole brought her home in their car and took her straight upstairs.

"Not right now, Riley. I want to talk to you two. I think I might want to try something tonight."

My heart started racing. "Look, we're not gonna make her sleep alone after today, are we? She'll have a really bad one tonight, I know it."

"No, Riley, I won't do that to her," Joshua answered. He turned to my dad. "Mr. Bennett, if it's all right with you, I'd like to take Riley home with me tonight and then have Nicole sleep over here. I want to get her perspective on what's going on."

"No way, I'm not doing it." I hadn't spent a night away from Attie since she arrived, and I wasn't planning on changing the routine.

"Riley," Dad scolded. "This is about Attiline, not you. If this is what we need to do to help her find out what's going on, then that's what we're gonna do."

"It's just for a night, Riley. You can come back first thing in the morning," Joshua informed. "I thought we'd make it a little less frightening for Attie and let her have a friend or two over if that's okay with you, Mr. Bennett?"

"Whatever you think; we can make it a sleepover or whatever it is they call them. A big shindig. We can celebrate her singing debut," Dad suggested.

I started to speak, but Joshua cut me off. "We can stay until it's time for them to go to bed, and then we'll head to my house. What, you don't want a boys' night out?"

"Not really," I mumbled.

"You're getting too attached," Dad said.

"I'm not too attached, Dad. I'm concerned."

"Mr. Bennett—" Joshua began.

"Tom," Dad corrected.

"Tom, I wouldn't worry about Riley and Attie being too attached right now. I think he's helping her."

I appreciated Joshua's input, and Dad looked relieved. "All right, if you say so."

Nicole and Attie made their way down the stairs, and I ran to her and gave her a hug. "Are you all right?"

"I'm fine, Riley, really."

She looked exhausted. Not so much physically, but mentally. A year of sleepless nights was draining her, and the constant turmoil had taken a toll on her body.

"Hey, Attiline, we have a great idea," Dad announced.

"You do?" Her voice sounded tired.

"Yeah, in order to celebrate your wonderful singing today, why don't you have some friends spend the night? We can have a little party!"

"Oh?" Her brow creased. "I don't know. It may not be the right night."

"I think it's the perfect night," Joshua announced. "Nicole wants to come too, and if you have a bad dream, she'll be there." He tried to sound encouraging, but she didn't seem to buy it.

"If this is some type of therapy thing, I'd prefer you just tell me that rather than try to sell it as a party."

Attie was no idiot; she could smell a rat from a mile away.

"All right, Attie," Joshua conceded. "It is. I want Nicole here with you to see what's going on. But you might as well make it as much fun as possible, get a good girls' night out of it."

"Come on, Attie," Nicole said softly as she grabbed her arm. "It'll be fun! I haven't been to a sleepover in years. Make an old woman ecstatic and let me sleep over."

Attie smirked. "All right, I guess."

"Riley's going to come to my house," Joshua explained.

Attie immediately looked concerned. "Riley won't be here?"

"It'll be okay, Charlie."

"There's a present involved," Dad taunted.

"Present?" Attie perked up. I smiled at her sudden joy. "I do love presents," she said softly.

"It's a good one, Attiline. I've been saving it for the perfect time, and this is it."

I was amazed at watching Dad with Attie. He doted on her. His love was visible and so powerful that it showed even in the way that he looked at her. In his own way, he wanted to help her.

"Well, all right," she finally conceded.

"Yay!" Nicole clapped her hands.

"Do I get to invite the girls over?" Attie asked.

"Yeah, go give them a call," Dad encouraged. "Nicole, why don't you go collect your things and head back over?"

"Yes! I'll be back in no time!" Nicole ran out the door and down the street.

I followed Attie as she went upstairs to call the girls.

"So they're kicking you out? What's all this about?"

"I'm not sure. I just told them I'd go along with it. I'm not happy about it at all." I might as well be honest with her; she would know if I was lying.

"It'll be okay," she said. "You need a good night's sleep. All this sleep deprivation can't be good for you."

"I'm getting used to it."

Out of nowhere, she clutched onto my arm. "I'm scared, Riley."

I pulled her to me and wrapped my arms snugly around her. "I know."

"I haven't spent a night without you since I got here. What if I have a really bad one tonight? I'll need you here, not Nicole."

"I wanna be here too, but they think this will end up helping you in the long run."

"You know what to do. You know how to make them stop. What if Nicole doesn't? What if she doesn't wake me up in time?"

"She will. I'll tell her what to do. Please don't worry; it'll only make things worse."

"And what about the girls? They'll hear me. They'll know."

"They'll understand."

"I guess I'll need to fill them in on my issues. That should make for quite the party."

"It won't be that bad. They're your friends, Charlie; they won't care, and they'll wanna help you—just like me."

"Nothing like sympathy friendships." She winced at her own comment. "Forget that I even said that; I'm not in a very good mood."

"Attie, we aren't your friends out of sympathy—at least I'm not. During the day, you're a very normal girl," I teased.

She giggled. "Unless I'm having a nervous breakdown or a crying fit."

"Well, yeah, other than those things."

• •

Within the hour all the girls arrived, and I got stuck carrying pillows, sleeping bags, and other items up the stairs. Attie's room filled with all things girl, and the sounds coming from downstairs resembled cackling hens.

"Riley, get down here," I heard her scream for me. "I want to open my gift!" There was excitement in her voice, and I didn't wanna make her wait any longer.

I ran down the stairs. "All right, all right. Let's get the party started."

Mom ran around in the kitchen making food for the girls with her iPod on full blast. She was in heaven; she lived for this kind of stuff.

"I can't believe you're leaving me here alone with all these girls," Dad complained.

"You should come with Riley to my house. Surely we can think of something manly to do," Joshua suggested. "You can sleep in the guest bedroom."

Dad raised an eyebrow. "Hey, that's not a bad idea."

"We can rent a shoot 'em up movie on pay-per-view or something," I added.

"I've got some cigars we can enjoy," Joshua said, sweetening the offer.

"Deal." Dad accepted immediately.

"In the meantime, give the poor girl her gift; she's about to lose it," I begged.

Dad walked into his bedroom and then came out holding two gifts that looked exactly the same. He handed one to Attie and the other to me.

"Riley gets a gift? He didn't humiliate himself in front of the entire church today. Why does he get a gift?" Attie pouted.

"Hey, I deserve a gift!" I defended. "Look at the holes in my arm." I showed everyone the claw marks. "You did that this morning before you sang."

"Well, good grief, you were making me nervous."

"I was making you nervous? Gimme a break."

"You both deserve a gift," Mom declared.

"Yeah, Charlie, we both deserve a gift."

"Shut up, Riley."

"Just open it, Attie. Let's see what it is," Anne cheered.

Attie and I looked at each other. "Ready?" I asked.

She nodded.

"Go," I ordered.

We tore into the paper.

"Cell phones!"

Everyone clapped as we tore into the boxes.

"We got you the same ones, except Attiline's is crimson and Riley, yours is silver." Dad acted as excited as we did. "I got one for all of us. We're on a family plan, so we can talk to each other as much as we want, and I also got something called unlimited texting. All our numbers are exactly the same except for the last digit."

"This is so cool, Dad!"

"Thank you! I love it!" Attie jumped into Dad's lap and gave him a kiss on the cheek before jumping onto the couch next to me. "Look, Riley, it has a camera and everything!"

Attie got busy playing with her phone and taking pictures of the girls. I grabbed it and took a picture of all the girls together so that she could put it on her home screen.

"Here, Riley," Tammy said, snatching my phone out of my hand. "Let me take a picture of you and Attie."

Attie climbed onto my lap and wrapped her arms around my neck before Tammy snapped picture after picture.

"Here you go, Riley, you've got several to choose from," she said, winking at me.

As the girls shrilled and played with the phone, I looked through the photos that Tammy had taken. They were all good, but my heart stuttered when I saw the last one. I'd imagined the moment when I drew the picture last winter. Attie smiled at me the same way she smiled at her dad. Her nose was scrunched up, and she looked blissful.

A small shiver ran up my spine as I saved it as my home screen picture.

The evening continued as we ate dinner and played a mean game of Chicken Run Dominos. Of all people, Joshua won the game and gloated about it for the rest of the evening.

"Look what I brought," Tess announced as she ran to her purse and pulled out a video. She held it up, and squealing erupted out of every person in the room without a Y chromosome. It was *Pride and Prejudice*.

"That's our sign to leave," Joshua announced as he stood up.

I couldn't have agreed more.

Dad and I loaded up our stuff and headed for the front door. When I turned around to say good-bye to Attie, she and my mom were busy reading the video cover. I left without getting a chance to talk to her.

As we walked down the street to Joshua's house, my pocket started vibrating. I quickly threw all my stuff to the ground and snatched the phone out of my pocket.

I had one new text message: "U didn't sA gdby 2 me ☹"

I replied: "U wr bZ"

I stood still and waited for her response.

"Are you coming, Riley?"

"Go ahead, Dad. I'll be right there."

I couldn't wait to get another text from Attie.

"Look at that, Joshua, he hadn't had that darned phone for an entire day, and he's already addicted to it."

My phone vibrated again: "Nvr 2 bZ 2 sA gdby ☺"

I responded: "zzz wel."

She replied: "Vry funE. C U 2moz."

Picking my stuff back up, I ran to catch up with Dad and Joshua.

"Who was that?" Dad asked.

"One of the guys," I lied. He'd flip his lid if he knew Attie and I couldn't go five minutes without talking to each other.

Dad, Joshua, and I watched the original *Terminator* and then sat on the back porch, and I watched as they smoked cigars. Time drug on until we all went our separate ways so we could get some sleep. I got the raw end of the deal and ended up on the couch.

Some time passed, so I picked up my phone to check the time. It was almost one thirty, and I hadn't fallen asleep once. I looked at our picture on the phone and wondered if she'd fallen asleep yet. Had she had a nightmare? I wanted to text her, but I was afraid I would wake her up. If they watched the movie, she wouldn't have gone to bed until at least eleven, and they more than likely talked a lot, so she was probly just now heading to bed.

I decided to go ahead and text her: "U zzz?"

In fewer than forty-five seconds my phone vibrated: "No wA"

I smiled. "U btr go 2 zzz. Dnt wnt 2 ruin xperiment."

She quickly replied: "Y U tlkn? Yr awake 2. Am I lab rat now?"

Unfortunately, yes: "Sry"

Her response: "Tnx for chekin' on me."

I responded: "☺ Go 2 zzz now!"

My heart melted as I read her reply: "I'd feel btr noing u wr hre."

I replied: "Me 2."

· ·

(Attie)

"Charlie?"

"I must be dreaming because you're not supposed to be here," I grumbled.

"You dream about me?" I could hear a smile in Riley's voice.

"Evidently."

"I thought you only had nightmares."

"My point exactly," I teased.

I heard him laugh. "You aren't asleep, silly."

Opening my eyes, I realized that Riley was sitting next to me on the floor. "Good grief, what time is it? And what's with your hair?"

"About eight o'clock." He ran his fingers through his mane. "Why, what's the matter with my hair?"

"It looks all neat."

"I got bored waiting for you to wake up and tried to fix it."

"Well, don't do it again." I signaled for him to come closer, and after he laid down on the floor and smiled over at me, I rooshed his hair with my fingers.

"Much better," I announced. "Personally, I prefer the bed head look."

"I'll keep that in mind." He messed with it some more. "It's easier like this anyway. I don't know how you girls stand doing your hair every day."

"Why do you think I wear mine in a ponytail all the time?"

"I like your hair in a ponytail."

"Thanks, such a sweet boy. So where is everyone?"

"Downstairs eating breakfast."

"How long have you been here?" I asked.

"Home or in your room?"

"Both."

"Home since about five thirty and in your room since the girls went downstairs about thirty minutes ago."

I playfully slapped his face. "You do realize you're hopeless?"

"I know." Gently picking up my hand, he kissed the inside of my wrist and then placed my hand back onto my stomach.

"I stayed up as late as I could last night but eventually fell asleep. I don't know if I had a nightmare or not. Have you heard?"

Lines formed between his eyebrows as his face grew full of concern, but he didn't speak.

"I'll take that as a yes. Was it bad?"

"Nicole said it was."

"What's going on, Riley? Why aren't they going away? I've prayed, I've begged, I don't know what else to do."

He rolled onto his back and put his head on my pillow. "I don't know. But don't worry, we'll figure it out. We'll get rid of them eventually."

"Did you get some sleep last night? Do you feel rejuvenated?" I asked.

"That would be a no and a no."

"I can't believe you aren't running for the hills by now. I am a crazy person, you know. You should turn around and walk away. Walk away as quickly as humanly possible."

"I'd much rather walk toward you than away. I'm not going anywhere. Me or my hair."

"Well then, remember that you asked for it."

"Asked for what?"

"Craziness."

"Fine. I hereby acknowledge that you've made me fully aware that with you comes a dose of craziness. I accept the challenge—look forward to it actually."

"Good grief, you are hopeless."

"I've already admitted that."

"Are you hopelessly devoted?" I teased.

Riley laughed. "That's my girl. A little *Grease* reference, eh?"

"Are you kidding? My mom loved that movie. I've seen it one hundred times."

"Yes," he added, looking over at me. "As cheesy as it sounds, I'm hopelessly devoted."

"Good."

We lay there for several more minutes before hearing someone enter the room.

"Hi, Joshua," I greeted. "Did you gather enough information to figure me out?"

He walked over and sat onto the bed. "Sadly, no."

"Well, that sucks," Riley admitted.

"Nicole said that you called out for your mom and Melody. You didn't say anything more than that. She would have had to let it continue to see if you'd say anything else, but she couldn't bring herself to let it go on."

"I've never heard her say anything else other than 'where are you?'" Riley added.

"Hmm. I don't know what's going on." I could hear the confusion in Joshua's voice. "Nicole did say that when she and the girls prayed for you that you relaxed and fell right back to sleep. You never woke up again."

"I do that a lot too," Riley informed him.

"Attie, I don't know what to tell you. I don't know why they aren't getting any better, but I won't give up if you don't," Joshua said.

"What choice do I have?" I asked. "I don't want them to continue, and it's not like I haven't tried everything I can think of to make them go away."

Joshua stood to go. "We'll talk more about this when you come over Tuesday. Don't forget we have DLT."

"DLT?" Riley asked.

Stefne Miller

"Driver's License Therapy. We're getting her a driver's license before school starts."

Riley laughed. "Well, good luck with all that."

"Thanks for the vote of confidence," I said.

"Whoa now. I wasn't laughing at the idea of you getting a license. I was laughing at the thought of 'Driver's License Therapy.' It sounded funny." His face turned toward mine. "Trust me, I have every confidence that you'll get your license."

"Nice recovery," I teased before giving my attention back to Joshua. "Hey, Josh, please tell Nicole I said thank you."

"I will. She's already at home. She left a while ago to go back to bed. She said she didn't get much sleep."

"I have that effect on people. Look at poor Riley; he looks exhausted."

"Well, Riley should have slept fine last night. So, if he didn't get any sleep, he can't blame that on you."

"I think he couldn't sleep *because* he wasn't here. He probably worried."

"Why are you two talking about me like I'm not in the room?"

"Sorry." Joshua laughed. "So why didn't you get any sleep last night?"

"Charlie got it right. I worried."

"He's a hopeless case, Josh."

"I can see that. I think you two will be keeping me pretty busy. I'll clear my calendar."

"Thanks, man."

"You're welcome. I'll see you kids later. Stay out of trouble."

I listened to his footsteps make their way down the stairs before rolling over onto my side. Riley did the same.

"I'm sorry you were so worried that you couldn't get any sleep."

"Thanks, but I wasn't totally honest with him."

"Oh?"

"It is true that I did worry about you. But I think I missed you more than worried about you. We haven't spent a night apart since you moved in, and I've gotten used to having you next to me."

"So you can't sleep with me and you can't sleep without me?"

He laughed. "Exactly."

"You do look tired."

"I am."

"I'll leave you alone so you can take a nap."

As I sat up to leave, Riley grabbed my arm. "Why don't you take a nap with me?"

"We're going to have to start getting used to sleeping apart. We can't sleep together forever."

"Why not?"

"You gonna marry me, Riley?"

His eyes widened, and his mouth opened in a slight smile. "Is that a proposal?"

"No."

The smile disappeared. "Bummer. Look, all I know is that for right now, as long as you're having the nightmares, where you sleep will be where I sleep."

"Have you forgotten that I'll be moving out at the end of summer? What if my nightmares aren't over by then?"

"I don't wanna think about that."

"Me either."

Slowly, each of the girls came up, packed up their belongings, said their good-byes, and headed home. The mood was somber due to the previous night and the knowledge that today would be an additionally difficult day.

I took a shower and got dressed before walking into Riley's room, and lying on his bed, I watched as he packed his sketching materials into their case.

"You going somewhere?"

"We're going somewhere," he informed me.

"We are?"

"Yep. Get your shoes on and let's go."

"Where are we going?" I asked as I headed toward my room.

"I'm not telling."

"Am I going to like it?"

"I sure hope so."

chapter 18

(Riley)

Attie's face went grim, and her body turned to stone.

"No, Riley. Take me home." Her head shook vigorously. "Take me home right now."

I turned to her, took her hand, and started to kiss her wrist, but she yanked it away from me.

Refusing to look at me, she stared blankly out the window. "Take me home!"

"You need to do this, Charlie. You can't move on until you do."

"I can't believe you would bring me here without asking." Anger filled her face. I was sure she felt as though she'd been sabotaged.

"I'm right here with you. You'll be all right." I got out of the car and grabbed my sketching supplies and the flowers that I'd purchased while she was in the shower.

Attie didn't move to get out of the car, so I opened the door for her.

"Riley," she whispered, "I'm not ready to do this. If you care about me at all, you'll climb back in the car and take me home."

I squatted down in front of her. "Please don't doubt my feelings for you; it's not fair. I'm trying to help." Her eyes finally met mine. "It's because I care about you that I brought you here. You've gotta understand that."

"Please, please take me home." Her hand grabbed my shirt and held it in a tight grip. "I'm begging you."

"Come on, it's time. It's time to say good-bye." As she released her grip, I turned and slowly walked away.

After several moments the door shut and footprints followed behind me as I made my way down the path to my first destination.

Attie hovered several feet away as she watched me unpack my charcoals and remove a clean piece of paper from my sketchbook. I placed the paper onto the granite and rubbed the surface. Slowly, the impression began to reveal itself.

Melody Lizbeth Bennett
May 1, 1991—June 9, 2007
Sixteen short years on earth.
An eternity in heaven.
We love and miss you.
Dad, Mom, and Riley

I carefully placed the rubbing back into my sketchbook and sat on the ground to wait for Attie to join me.

Other than the occasional sound of her footsteps, the grave-yard was completely silent. Her presence came closer and closer as I waited.

Finally, after more than half an hour, she sat down beside me.

"Are you okay?" I asked.

"I don't know."

"It took months of visiting Melody's grave before I could come and not have some sort of physical response. The first time I saw her gravestone I threw up."

Attie rested her head on my shoulder and sighed.

"Seeing her name carved in granite was a shock, and I think it confirmed that she wasn't coming home—ever. She was gone. Somehow, seeing the words in stone and the realization that her body was below my feet…I don't know, it was overwhelming."

We sat in silence for several more minutes before I spoke again.

"What are you thinking?"

"Part of me is thinking this isn't real—it isn't happening. Like, maybe it's a really bad dream and eventually I'm going to wake up and Melody and my mom will still be alive.

"Another part of me wishes it would have been me instead of them ... I would give anything for that. I look at my life and what it's become and I can't figure out why God just didn't take me instead or if he was going to take them why he didn't just take me too. Sometimes I think surviving is far worse than death would have been.

"I'm ashamed, because when I should be sitting here having memories of how wonderful they were, all I can think about is myself and how jealous I am that their pain ended instantly and mine's gone on day after day.

"They're in a happy place where they feel no pain and they never experience fear or judgment or rejection or loneliness or shame. Sometimes I want to be in that place. I want to be where they are.

"I knew every time I looked at my dad that he wished he was seeing my mother instead of me, and I know that for every moment that your mom is happy to be having girl time with me she has a million moments where she wishes Melody was here to have that time with. It's hard to know that deep down inside, whether anyone will admit it or not, they'd prefer for me to be the one in the ground. If they were honest with themselves—if you were honest with yourself, you'd agree that it would have been better for everyone if my name would have ended up being the one in stone instead of theirs."

"That's not true," I said.

"It is. No matter how much fun your mother and I have together, I can't replace what she's lost. I can't fill for her what she so desperately needs filled. I can't give my dad back the woman he loved since high school. Or you—I can't give you your sister back, and I can't replace what she was to you or the bond that you shared."

"Look at me." I pulled away from her and grabbed her shoulders. Her eyes were red and swollen, and her face was drenched in tears. "You're carrying a burden that you shouldn't. It's too much; you're killing yourself. It isn't your responsibility to try to replace your mom or Melody, and we don't have you in our lives to act as a substitute for someone else. We didn't bring you here because we were hoping that we could somehow have a knockoff version of Melody running around. We wanted you to live with us because we love you and because you're our family. Yes, we wish all of you were here, but we never wish that they were here and you weren't."

She shook her head in defiance.

"Hear me, Charlie. Do I miss my sister? Yes, desperately. But I have never looked at you and wished that I were seeing my sister instead—never.

"You're gonna have to stop beating yourself up about living, and you're gonna have to realize that it isn't your job to try to replace what's gone. It's not your responsibility to try to be everything to everyone. You can't heal us. You can't take that pain away. You can help and you can add some life and joy where otherwise there wasn't as much, but you can't make everything better. Only God can do that. You're placing expectations on yourself that just aren't fair, and you're placing thoughts and accusations on people that don't belong there.

"Your life isn't less valuable than theirs were."

"I wish I believed that," she said.

"Let it go, Charlie. Let them go and let God show you why you're still here. Let him be the one that convinces you of just how valuable you really are. No matter how crazy I am about you, I'll never be able to convince you of that. Only he can do it."

She looked over at Melody's grave for several moments before I placed my hands on either side of her face and turned her back to me. "Gosh, I wish you could see yourself the way I see you, the way my parents and your friends do. If you knew how special you really are, there's no way you'd ever doubt why you survived."

Tears filled her eyes again.

"Other than my Gramps, you're the nicest person I've ever known."

"I'm not saying all this to be nice; I'm saying it because it's true."

Gently pulling her head my direction as I leaned toward her, I bent over and kissed her on the forehead.

"I'm gonna visit your mom's grave." I stood up, collected my supplies, and handed her some flowers.

"Come meet me when you're ready."

Walking up to Mrs. Reed's headstone, I took out another clean piece of paper and made a rubbing of the granite.

Elizabeth Catherine Reed
April 12, 1970—June 9, 2007
Amazing wife to Eddie,
loving mother to Attie,
great friend to many.

After several minutes, noticing Attie standing a few feet away, I collected my supplies again. Walking up to her, I handed her the remaining flowers and noticed her face was wet with tears.

"I'll wait in the car."

She wrung her hands. "Won't you stay with me?"

I kissed her on the forehead. "No, Charlie, you need to do this alone."

I made my way to the car, put my supplies into the backseat, and then sat on the bumper waiting for Attie. My heart ached for her, and I prayed that the time spent at her mother's grave wouldn't be too painful for her to bear.

When she still hadn't returned after more than half an hour, I went to check on her and found her sitting on the ground with her cheek pressed to her mother's headstone. She'd curled in a ball as if she tried to crawl into her mother's lap. My heart broke.

"I miss her," she whispered as she heard me approach.

I sat down next to her. "I know."

Slowly, she reached out her hand, wrapped her pinkie around mine, and gave me a small smile. "Thank you for this and for being so good to me."

"You're welcome."

She closed her eyes and we sat, pinkies entwined and without speaking, until she was ready to leave.

When we stood to go, she leaned over and placed the flowers in front of the headstone. "Good-bye, Mom," she whispered. "I'll be back soon."

Visiting Mrs. Reed and Melody's graves had obviously been an emotionally draining experience for Attie. As soon as she climbed into the car, she laid back in her seat and didn't speak until we were walking through our front door.

"What are you going to do with the rubbings?" she asked.

"Follow me."

I led her into her room and removed one of the empty frames from the wall.

Hearing her make a light gasping noise, I turned to face her. "Is this all right?"

She nodded her head and smiled. "It's perfect."

Walking to the wall she removed another empty frame. We placed the charcoal rubbings into their new homes and placed them back onto the wall before standing back to admire our work.

"I don't know, Riley; the wall is still missing something."

"What?"

"It needs a picture of the two of us."

"Funny you should say that." Giving her a grin, I reached into my sketchbook and pulled out a picture I'd drawn after getting home and waiting for her to wake up that morning.

"It's us!" She grabbed it out of my hands. "And it's perfect."

"I love it," I admitted. Of course it was the picture I'd been imagining in my mind for months. "Tammy took the picture with my phone yesterday."

She smiled at it and then turned her attention to the wall and back to the picture in her hands. She glanced back and forth several times before looking at me with a shocked expression on her face.

"Charlie, what's wrong?"

She shook her head. "Nothing."

"What is it?"

"I just remembered what made my dad and I laugh when we were getting our picture taken."

The mystery was about to reveal itself, and I couldn't wait to hear. "What?"

"The photographer told my dad to take a good, long look at me."

"Why?"

"Because before long I would no longer have eyes for my dad; only a special boy would grab my attention."

chapter 19

(Attie)

I made my way into the vet clinic ready to get to work and put yesterday behind me. Finally the anniversary passed, and I'd survived what I'd feared would be my worst day since the accident.

The Bennetts kept it a very low profile evening. Marme made chicken fried steak and mashed potatoes and cream gravy, which were my favorites, and we finished the night watching *Sixteen Candles* and *The Breakfast Club*. It was Molly Ringwald night, and it felt good to see high school life through the eyes of someone different for a change.

If Riley and I had believed the nightmares would leave after visiting the graves, we'd thought wrong. Only a few hours after we fell asleep, the monsters came out of hiding.

"Gramps, I'm here!"

"Great, Atticus. I'm in the back."

I stopped by the reception desk to put my purse in the file cabinet and realized that I heard another voice. I listened carefully.

It was a male voice, and it sounded somewhat familiar, but I couldn't place it.

I grabbed Baby's sling off the back of my chair and headed toward the back.

"See here? Notice the very limited range of motion..."

There stood Cooper Truman; he wore a white lab coat and stood next to my Gramps as he worked on a Schnauzer.

As the boy noticed my arrival, a large smile formed across his face, revealing his annoyingly white teeth. They practically blinded me. "Hello, Attie!"

Frustrated by his presence, I asked the obvious question. "What are you doing here?"

"Surprise, I'm working here now—or volunteering."

I'm certain that my jaw dropped. "Pardon?" Surely I hadn't heard him correctly. God wouldn't play such a cruel practical joke on a poor soul like myself. Would he?

I looked at Gramps hoping that he would clarify the situation, but he just smiled.

"Well," Cooper said, "I took the liberty of calling your dad in Ithaca to let him know that I would be coming back to Cornell in the fall and I'm studying vet med. We got to talking, and he gave me all kinds of great information, just like you said he would."

"You called my dad? In New York?"

"Yeah, our dads know each other, so I figured why not?" He gave a shrug and waited for me to respond, but seeing as how I couldn't speak due to a case of complete shock, he continued talking without missing a beat. "While we were on the phone, he mentioned your Gramps here. Your dad said he'd give Doc a call and talk to him about letting me intern this summer."

"You talked to my dad? I haven't even talked to my dad," I whispered.

"Isn't it mind-blowing?"

"You'll be working here all summer?"

"Tuesdays and Thursdays." An obnoxious, large grin spread across his face. "So, Attie, we'll be seeing a lot of each other this summer. Isn't that great?"

"Wonderful," I lied and faked a little enthusiasm.

"I'm totally stoked about it." He was practically giddy. "This is going to be awesome!"

"Yes, it certainly will be," I lied again.

"Yeah, Princess," Gramps finally spoke, "I figured with your counselin' sessions on Tuesdays and Thursdays takin' up part of the mornin's that those might be the best days for Cooper to help out 'round here."

Was I mistaken or had my grandfather told a complete stranger that I was in counseling?

"So you don't need me on Tuesdays and Thursdays then?"

"Yeah, I still need you, Atticus. We'll just have an extra set of hands to help us out. Cooper'll be here more to watch and learn than anything."

"Oh great." I headed over to Baby's cage. Peeking in, I saw her sitting in the corner.

"Hey, Baby."

She immediately responded to my voice and limped toward me. I took her out and put her in the sling. "How'd she do this weekend, Gramps?"

"She missed you, but she did get a little better. She's a wee bit more lively."

"Are you doing better, Baby?" I asked while kissing her on the head. "That's my girl."

"Is that your dog?" Cooper asked.

"Sort of, I guess. I've kind of taken her in."

He smiled at me again. "She's very cute. I can see that she likes you."

"Atticus, could you answer that phone?"

"Sure, Gramps."

I made my way to the reception desk relieved that I was escaping to the front and away from Cooper.

After answering the phone and setting an appointment for someone, I frantically searched in my purse for my phone.

I typed in Tammy's number and a message: "OMG! UR gunA di! Cooper Truman is at my wrk 2day."

I waited for her to reply, and within seconds my phone vibrated: "W@d?"

My fingers frantically typed: "He's wurkn hre now. Tues/Thur. UGH."

The phone vibrated again: "Gt ot! Lnch 2day? Gtta get scoop!"

Of course: "Yes! 11:45?"

She replied immediately: "Pik u ^"

I rolled the chair over so that I could peek down the hall at Gramps and Cooper. Under the white coat he wore a baby blue shirt, which made his blue eyes sparkle, his tan appear darker, and his teeth whiter. Surely he had to bleach his teeth every night; nobody got teeth that white naturally.

His jeans were stonewashed just the right amount, and his shoes were the latest in fashion—well, I assumed so; I really had no idea what the latest fashion was.

As Cooper watched Gramps work on the pooch, I thought back to the conversation we had at the pool party. He was tired of horses, so I guess he found dogs a change of pace.

My vibrating phone startled me and caused Cooper to look in my direction. He caught me watching them and smiled up at me.

"Everything okay back there?" I asked so it wouldn't look like I was checking him out.

"It's great," he said proudly.

"Wonderful," I lied again and then rolled back to the desk to get my phone: "Anne n Tess cmng 2 lnch 2, K? Wnt scoop!"

"Hey, Attie."

Cooper's voice startled me, and I dropped my phone onto the desk. Looking up, I saw his smiling face peeking around the corner.

"Yeah, Coop?"

"Want to go to lunch today?"

I held up my phone. "I just accepted an invite from friends. Sorry." I tried to act apologetic.

"Gosh, you're one busy girl." He sounded disappointed. "Got plans on Thursday?"

"Uh, I don't think so."

"Great! We can go Thursday then."

"Great," I lied again in my fake enthusiastic voice as he walked away.

My phone vibrated. I looked down and saw that it was a text from Riley: "Gr8 nws. Dad z U cUd brng Baby hom w U."

How sweet was that? I responded: "Orsum! Tnx, Riley!!"

I never asked him to talk to his dad about Baby. He must have decided to do it on his own.

My phone vibrated again: "Got *Top Gun* & *Rainman* from Netflix. We on 2nite?"

Tom Cruis-a-pa-looza, huh? I responded: "Gr8."

I thought about telling Riley about Cooper being at the clinic but then thought better and figured I would save it for that night.

Vibration caught my attention again: "Pik u ^ @ 4:45. Bye. R"

At least there were two things to look forward to today: lunch with the girls and movies on the couch with Riley. No stuffy, highbrow, brown-nosing, vet wannabe was going to ruin my day.

"Excuse me, Attie?"

"Yeah, Coop?"

"Have you ever ridden a stallion?" he asked, grinning from ear to ear.

"Uh…"

"I thought maybe you could come over sometime and we could go riding. We've got extra saddles; I could teach you how to ride English."

"Oh, horseback riding? Uh, that sounds great." I shook my head. "No, I've never ridden a stallion… of any kind."

"Great! When do you think you can make it?"

"Oh, I don't know."

"Saturday?"

"Sure." What was the point in saying no? The boy was going to needle me to death until I said yes.

"It's a date!" He headed back toward the exam room.

"Uh, it's not a date," I mumbled after him. "It's technically more of a lesson."

He didn't hear a word.

The day continued on as I checked in patients, answered phones, and cleaned out cages all while "pretty boy Truman" stood back and watched Gramps work. I felt like Cinderella getting stuck doing all the grunt work while the chosen daughters lounged around. Tuesdays and Thursdays would be horrible. Cooper Truman had a dazzle about him, and Gramps was buying everything that Cooper tried to sell him. It was disgusting.

Lunchtime finally came, and Tammy and the girls waltzed into the clinic.

"Hey, Attie! Ready to go to lunch?" Tammy asked.

"Hi, girls."

"Hello, ladies!" Cooper greeted as he came to join us in the reception area.

I rolled my eyes at his fake friendliness. At least, I think it was fake.

"Fancy seeing you here. Are you the friends who stole my lunch date?" he asked.

"Oh, had you already made plans with Attie?" Anne asked.

"No, just hoping to," Cooper replied.

"How sweet," Tess said.

"We're going on Thursday instead," he announced.

"Oh great! Good for you," Tammy said in mock interest. "I betcha can't wait, Attie."

"Yes, and she's coming over on Saturday to go for a ride."

"A ride? Really?" Tammy looked at me with a cocked eyebrow and sly grin.

"Horses. We're going to ride horses," I clarified. "Cooper wants to go riding."

"I'm sure he does," Tammy replied. "You two are becoming fast friends, aren't ya?"

"Yes. Isn't it great?" Either the boy was deaf or he was a complete moron because Cooper didn't catch on to Tammy's palpable sarcasm. "Well, you ladies have a great time and bring Attie back safely."

"Oh, we'll do our best," Tammy said in a fake sappy voice as she rolled her eyes.

Cooper was oblivious that he was the butt of our joke.

"Would you like me to take Baby from you, Attie? I'll watch after her while you're gone."

"Uh, sure." I handed her over to Cooper assuming he would take her back to her cage, but he reached over and removed the sling from my shoulder and put in on himself.

"I'll be the surrogate," he said proudly.

"Great," I lied for the umpteenth time in half a day. "Let's get out of here!" I begged.

As soon as we got out of earshot, the girls broke out laughing in hysterics.

"What in all that's good and holy was that?" Anne asked.

"He's kind of stalkerish, isn't he?" Tess added.

"Oh my gosh, you guys, good grief, it's worse than you can ever imagine!" I couldn't even believe it myself.

"So what, is he working there now or something?" Tammy asked.

"Yes, twice a week!"

"He sure knows how to weasel himself in, doesn't he?" Anne replied.

"What does Riley think about that?" Tess asked softly.

"Riley doesn't know yet."

Tammy climbed into the car. "He's gonna blow a gasket."

"Oh no he won't," I said.

"Oh yes he will! You didn't see him at that party when you went into the house with Cooper. Riley was flipping out."

"Get out!" Anne screamed.

"I swear, Anne! I thought the boy was gonna come unhinged," Tammy said, laughing.

I shook my head at her. "Oh, Tammy, you're exaggerating."

"If I'm lyin' I'm dyin'! I swear, girls, it was pathetic!" Tammy couldn't contain her amusement. "I've gotta be a witness when Riley finds out about Cooper."

"Well, he's picking me up at 4:45."

Tammy pounded on the steering wheel in excitement. "I'm so there!"

"Me too!" Anne and Tess agreed.

"Want to hear the worst part?" I asked.

The girls couldn't contain their curiosity. "Yes!"

"Coop peeked around the corner and asked me if I'd ever ridden a stallion. My mind totally went to the gutter; I about died!"

Anne and Tammy started laughing, but Tess sat shaking her head. "I don't get it."

"That's why we love you, Tess," I said, giving her a playful pat on the back.

"Are you gonna tell me the joke? I don't get it," she repeated.

"Ask Chase. He'll get a jolt out of it," Tammy suggested.

"Riley's just freaking out because of the whole Melody thing," Anne said.

"What Melody thing?" I asked.

"Melody and Cooper dated for a while when she was a sophomore and he was a senior. He took her to Winter Formal, remember?"

"Shut up!" It was the loudest I'd ever heard Tess speak.

"Oh yeah," Anne continued, "Melody was crazy about him, and they were together all the time. Then rumor has it that Melody found him in his car after school one day with…none other than Tiffany Franks."

"Get out!"

"I can't believe you guys didn't know this!" Anne was excited to share such juicy gossip. "Anyway, Riley found out and knocked the soup out of him."

"He did not!" I shouted.

"He did! He punched him in the face after a basketball game. Tammy, you don't remember this? That was when Riley got suspended from school for that week."

"I didn't know that was why."

"Yep." Anne nodded with a big smile on her face.

"Oh man, that's good stuff," Tammy said with a smirk. "You couldn't pay me enough money to miss the fireworks that'll be going off at 4:45."

"You'll be disappointed, Tammy. Riley's not going to care a bit," I assured. "He'll be fine with it."

chapter 20

From behind the reception desk I looked over at the girls as they sat in the orange chairs in the waiting area. Tammy's elbows were on her knees and her chin on her fists, and Anne sat Indian style in her chair next to Tess, whose eyes were about to pop out of her head. They had invited Jen along to enjoy the show, and she sat curled up in a ball on a chair with her knees pulled up to her chest. If they'd had popcorn, they would've looked like they were watching a horror movie.

Gramps was hiding out in his office.

"Truman?" Riley's voice sounded disgusted. "What are you doing here?"

"Hello," Cooper said coldly as he kept his distance. "Didn't Attie tell you I was working here?" His eyebrows were lowered and he glared back across the room.

Riley and the girls looked at me and waited for me to respond. "I hadn't had a chance yet. I was going to tell you tonight."

Riley's face turned crimson and his jaw grew tight. He and the girls looked back at Cooper. "What do you mean you're working here now?"

"I'm doing an internship of sorts."

Riley and the girls looked back at me. "Really?"

"I didn't know until I showed up this morning. I had no idea."

Riley and the girls looked back at Cooper again. "For how long?" Riley's teeth were now clinched. "How long is this internship thing?"

"All summer." Cooper folded his arms across his chest.

"All summer?" Riley practically screamed. "How did you hear about this internship?"

"Attie's dad told me," Cooper replied as he rolled back and forth on the heels of his feet.

Riley and the girls looked back at me again. I shook my head. "I didn't know that Cooper called him."

They looked back at Cooper.

"You talked to Attie's dad? On the phone?" Riley's arms were also across his chest, but his hands were tightly gripping his upper arms.

"Yes, I picked up the phone and called him, no big deal."

Riley took a deep breath. "Do you even know him, Truman?"

"Our dads know each other. Plus, Attie told me that he would be more than happy to give me information about Cornell."

Riley and the girls turned their gaze back to me. "Did she now?"

"I briefly mentioned it at the pool party."

Riley held my gaze for a long moment. I couldn't tell what was going through his mind, but his eyes tightened in the corners, which sent a shiver down my spine.

The girls' eyes shifted back and forth between Riley and me as he glared at me. "Well, I guess I better go," Cooper announced, looking at me.

I noticed Riley turning his glare back to Cooper as he spoke.

"Attie, let me know what time you want to come over on Saturday. I'll have the cook make us some food."

Riley's head snapped back my direction, and I could see the girls recoil as if someone just got punched.

I shut my eyes and instantly started biting my thumbnail as I managed to squeak out an "All right" in Cooper's direction.

"See you Thursday, Attie," Cooper said as he walked out the door.

We all sat in silence as the girls watched Riley glare at me.

Cooper stuck his head back in the door. "Attie, go ahead and decide where you want to go to lunch on Thursday, my treat."

Riley jerked his arm in Cooper's direction as if he was about to strike him. Cooper quickly turned and walked away.

"You're going to lunch with him on Thursday?" He could barely speak. "And to his freakin' house on Saturday?"

"What was I supposed to say, Riley? He asked me."

"You could have said no! That would've covered it!"

The girls sat completely still and stared at us.

"I've got to work with the guy. I can't be a jerk."

"Well, you don't have to act like a jerk, but holy moly, you don't have to agree to go out with the guy twice in one freakin' week!" His voice became louder the more he spoke.

"Don't you get mad at me, Riley Bennett!" I shouted back. "I was being nice."

As he glared back at me, his right eye twitched. I'd never seen him angry.

"Look, he asked me if I'd ever ridden a stallion—"

"Did he now?" he practically screamed.

"He wants to go riding, that's all."

Riley's veins about popped out of his neck. "I'm sure he does!"

"That's what I said," Tammy said.

"I still don't get it," Tess said softly.

My own anger was rising. "You two stop it right now! I'm going to lunch with a coworker, and then I'm getting a riding lesson—an English-style horseback riding lesson." I spoke slowly and clearly so there was no confusion. "It's no big deal."

"No big deal?" He started pacing and opening and closing his fists. "It's no big deal?"

I glanced over at the girls. They were in awe of the spectacle. I then noticed that Gramps was peeking his head through the door.

"Good grief, Riley, you don't get to be mad. It's not like you and I are dating or anything." I immediately regretted saying the words.

He spun around to face me. He looked devastated but angry. "You're right, Attie."

I gulped. It stung to hear him call me Attie.

"You're right; we aren't dating." He shook his head as he continued to glare at me. "You can do whatever the heck you want with whoever you wanna do it with, and I can't say a thing."

"Riley—"

He cut me off. "I'm so glad you spelled things out for me. I guess I'm fortunate to know where I stand."

The girls loudly inhaled.

"That's not what I meant! You're misunderstanding my words."

"I'm not misunderstanding anything." His voice was cold. We stared at each other for a moment before he spoke again. "Let's go." He turned and walked toward the door.

The girls stood up.

"No," I said softly.

He spun back around and walked toward me.

The girls sat back down.

His eyes were dark. "What do you mean 'no'?"

"I don't want to go with you if you're angry like this."

"Come get in the car, Attie," he ordered.

"No," I shouted back.

"How are you gonna get home?"

Tammy quickly stood up. "I'll take her." Riley glared over at her, and she sat back down.

"Yes. Tammy will take me."

He stood glaring at me for several more seconds before he spun around and stomped out of the clinic. The girls finally let out the breath they inhaled earlier.

"Okay, I'd say that went well," Tammy said sarcastically.

"Well, we said we wanted a show." Tess looked incredibly sad. "I guess we got one."

"Oh my gosh, I've never seen him that angry," Anne said, shaking her head slowly.

I immediately started crying. "He had no right to talk to me like that."

"No," Jen agreed. "No, he didn't. Jerk."

"He's hurt, Jen," I said. "I've hurt him."

The girls tried to comfort me, but it was useless. I was inconsolable. Nobody had ever talked to me that way, and the fact that Riley was the first to do it was beyond painful. They accompanied me to the car, and Tammy drove me home. Riley hadn't made it home yet when she dropped me off, so I went straight up to my room and shut the door. I surmised that there would be no Tom Cruise-a-pa-looza tonight.

Three hours passed before I heard him pull into the driveway. It took several minutes, but I heard him make his way up the stairs. I could hear the crackling of grocery bags as he walked.

Sitting on my bed, I waited.

"Here." I looked over and saw him holding Baby out to me. "You forgot her." His voice was as cold and detached as it was earlier in the day.

"How did you know?" I got up and gently took her from him.

"I went by the clinic to apologize to your Gramps and saw her there." He wouldn't look at me.

"Thank you," I whispered.

He set the bags down. "I got her some food, bowls, toys, 'n' stuff." He turned to go. "Oh, and a collar with a name tag on it."

"Riley?"

He walked into his room and slammed the door.

My heart sank. I wasn't sure what to do; I'd never been in a fight with someone like this before. For several minutes I debated charging into Riley's room and demanding that he speak to me but decided it probably wasn't a good idea. I put my ear buds in and listened to some music in an effort to take my mind off of the look that was plastered on Riley's face when I reminded him that we weren't dating. I badly hurt him.

After playing with Baby for about an hour, I headed down the stairs and outside so that Baby could go to the bathroom.

"Go potty, Baby. You go potty for Mommy," I encouraged.

I stood and watched for her to do her deed as Third Day played on my iPod. It was very warm outside and smelled like fresh cut grass. Riley must have mown the lawn while I was at work.

"Look at that big girl! Good girl, Baby, you went potty like a big girl!" Baby shook her tail as she limped toward me. "You're a rock star." I picked her up and kissed her on the head. Turning to go back inside, I spotted Riley sitting motionless on the porch swing.

I yanked out my ear buds and turned off the iPod before starting up the porch steps. "Sorry, I didn't know you were out here."

He shrugged. His eyes were dark and sad.

I stood looking at him and hoped that he would talk to me so that I could explain, but when I realized he wasn't going to say anything, I started to go inside.

"Do you like him, Charlie?"

"No."

I turned toward him as he jumped out of the swing and walked toward me.

Planting my feet on the ground, I stood and waited for his anger to pour out over me.

"You're going out with him twice in one week for cryin' out loud." His jaw clinched and he sounded angry, but he didn't raise his voice.

"I'm not, Riley. I'm not going 'out' with him."

He closed his eyes and shook his head as he stood within inches of me. His face wore a pained grimace. "I bet he thinks you are," he said quietly.

"Why would he think that?"

Opening his eyes, he looked back at me. "Because he asked you out twice and you said yes twice, that's why." He rolled his eyes as if he couldn't believe my complete lack in understanding the male mind.

"Oh," I whispered.

"My gosh, Charlie, you and I haven't even gone out on a date yet." He practically whimpered as he stared blankly in my direction. "I'm trying to do the right thing by waiting, and this other guy swoops in and asks you out. Twice. And you said yes. Twice." He put his hands over his stomach and closed his eyes. "The thought of it makes me sick."

"Riley, I..."

What could I say? He was upset, sick even, at the thought of me going out with another boy. Part of me was elated at the idea that he could be so jealous, but the other part of me felt guilty. I hadn't given his feelings any consideration at all.

He turned and walked away from me making his way down the porch steps and into the grass as I stood watching him.

He turned and looked at me. "What if he tries to kiss you?"

The thought disturbed me. "He won't." I hoped he wouldn't.

Riley threw his hands on his hips and tilted his head as he looked at me like I didn't have a clue what I was saying. He spoke slowly. "What if he does?"

My mind raced around the idea of Cooper trying to kiss me, and I immediately felt nauseated.

He threw his hands up in the air and started pacing. "Seriously," he said with what sounded like a growl. "You want your first kiss to be with Cooper Truman?"

"No!" I ran down the porch steps and onto the lawn.

"Well, it could happen, you know!" His pacing became hurried. "He could help you off a horse and then kiss you. Or he could have his cook make some picnic lunch, take you to some romantic spot on his ranch, and then try to kiss you." The words were flying out of his mouth, and his pace quickened. His hands were tucked tightly into fists. "There are tons of different scenarios, and I'm sure he's thinking of all of them. I know I sure as heck am."

He turned and started walking toward the side of the house.

I set Baby down and started chasing after him. "Riley?"

He spun around, grabbed my hand in his, and then turned and continued walking.

"Riley!"

He pulled me along behind him. "Shhh!"

He walked so fast that I had a difficult time keeping up. "Riley, slow down, I'm—"

He dropped my hand and swung around. Wrapping his right arm around my waist, he pulled me close to him.

"I'd planned on giving you your first kiss." He spoke in a whisper as his left hand tenderly wrapped around the back of my neck.

"Oh?" I muttered.

He brought his face to mine, and when our lips made contact, I thought my heart might explode. His lips were sweet and his touch was gentle. After only a few moments, he pulled his face away from mine but kept his hands firmly in place.

I practically whimpered as he pulled away. I wanted him to stay just where he was.

Opening my eyes I could see him in the light of the patio, gazing at me with a large grin on his face. I weakly smiled back at him, and before I knew it, both of my cheeks were in his hands and he pulled me to him once more. Our lips met over and over again. Although he was sweet, the kiss was forceful. When our lips parted, he hugged me tightly to him.

After several moments, I stepped back a bit. My body felt weak.

"Riley—"

Before I could get another word out, he pulled me to him and kissed me again. When he let me go, my knees were wobbling, and I stumbled.

"See if Truman can get that reaction out of you." He grinned and then made his way toward the house. "Come on, Baby."

chapter 21

Once Riley made it inside, I allowed myself to fall to the ground. I lay there thinking about what had just happened. My heart was thudding with excitement.

Giggles overcame my body. I was beyond thrilled to have finally been kissed, and the fact that it happened before my seventeenth birthday and with Riley Bennett made it even better. I would have been more than willing to wait until the end of the summer, but I was glad that he hadn't held out any longer. He certainly knew what he was doing; evidently, he'd had a lot of practice. I, on the other hand, hadn't had any practice, and since he didn't comment in any way, I didn't know what he thought about the experience. Walking off like that was plain cruel.

"Attiline!" I heard Pops's voice. "Movie's about to start."

"All right, I'll be right in!"

Evidently, Cruise-a-pa-looza was back on.

The closer I got to the house, the more my heart raced. I didn't have any idea how to act around Riley. I could feel my cheeks begin to warm, and I assumed that I was blushing. Luckily, the lights were already off. Unluckily, the only available seat was next to Riley on the couch. He didn't look up at me, but a large grin was plastered on his face. Baby looked very content curled up in a ball on his lap.

I quickly took my spot and looked toward the television hoping that the movie would start immediately.

"Attiline, we decided to watch *Top Gun* first. Since it's so late, we need to save *Rainman* for another night."

"Maybe we can watch it with *Cocktail* some night," Riley suggested.

"Ooh, that's a good one!" his mom replied. "I love *Cocktail*. I need to add that 'Kokomo' song to my iTunes. Riley, remember to add that one."

"Yes, ma'am."

For the first time the couch felt very, very cramped. We both tucked our legs up onto the couch, and our feet were practically touching. I contemplated placing my feet back onto the floor but decided it would make me look like a wimp, so I left them right where they were.

As the movie started I settled in and tried to ignore Riley, but it was impossible. I tried to think of a way to look in his direction without it being obvious that I was trying to look at him.

"Baby," I whispered, looking over at her. "Come here, Baby." I patted my leg in an attempt to have her join me, but she refused. She was content on Riley's lap.

Glancing up at Riley, our eyes met. His face was blank.

"What?" I whispered.

A small, sly grin formed on his face. "Thinking."

"About what?"

He looked downright spectacular sitting there, but his self-confidence was becoming annoying.

"What do you think?" His grin grew slightly, and my face felt hot. "You're blushing."

"How do you know? It's dark."

"It's not that dark."

"You're downright cruel."

"Why?"

"Leaving me out there like that."

His face turned serious, and he looked down at Baby. "I had to."

"Why?"

I could see a mischievous grin creep back onto his face, and my cheeks grew hotter. "Why do you think?"

"You're killing me."

He took delight in my misery. "Welcome to my world."

"Shhh!" Pops scolded us without looking back in our direction.

I leaned toward Riley so I could speak more quietly. "And what world is that?"

He leaned to within inches of my face and gazed at me. Parents or no parents, I wanted him to kiss me right then and there, and he looked like he wanted to kiss me as well.

"The world of wanting something you can't have."

His eyes remained locked on mine as I felt his hand slowly place itself on my thigh. Although it sent a rush up my spine, I tried not to react. He held my stare for a moment longer and then removed his hand.

"Butthead," I whispered back.

With a large grin on his face and looking very content with himself, he turned and watched the movie.

I was not content. He had me right where he wanted me, and I wasn't interested in having him think he had me figured out so quickly. He still hadn't apologized for the way he behaved, and until he did he wouldn't get any more affection shown in his direction—physical or not. I pulled my legs closer to my body, set my jaw, and watched the movie. I wasn't going to let Riley Bennett torture me. This was war.

When the movie ended, I gave an excuse to leave and quickly made my way up the stairs. As I threw myself onto the bed, I heard Riley's voice outside in the front yard. I moved the curtain back slightly and watched as he encouraged Baby to do her business.

Anne was right; he was adorable. Gorgeous actually.

I liked being able to study the way he looked and the way he moved. He carried himself in a very self-confident way, but there wasn't arrogance about him at all. It was as if he wasn't aware or concerned at all about what other people thought of him.

I forced myself to get ready for bed. As I brushed my teeth, I wondered if he would still sleep next to me or go back to his room. I figured that it would depend on his reaction to the kiss. If it hadn't had any effect on him, he should be able to sleep next to me without any problem. If the kiss had affected him the way it had me, there would be no way he would be able to trust himself lying next to me on the floor every night. I didn't know which sounded better, for him to remain sleeping next to me or to have had him enjoy the kiss enough that he now needed to keep his distance.

When I walked out of the bathroom, I got my answer. Two sleeping bags were unrolled on my floor, and Riley sat on my bed with Baby. They were waiting for me, and I was disappointed. Evidently the kiss didn't have any effect on him at all.

"I wondered where you would be sleeping tonight."

He frowned. "What? You don't want me to sleep next to you anymore?"

"I didn't say that. I just didn't know what you would be thinking, what you were feeling about today. Maybe your feelings have changed."

"You're not gonna run me off that easy."

I sat down on top of my sleeping bag and clasped my hands to ensure that I wouldn't fidget. Looking up at him, I realized I needed to stand my ground and not let him win the battle by giving in too soon. Regardless of how great he looked, the fact still remained that he needed to apologize for his behavior.

His soft eyes looked down at me for several seconds. "We need to talk," he said.

"We do?"

"Yes." He stood up and placed Baby in her crate before joining me on the floor. "It's about what happened outside."

"I figured as much."

"You know that can't happen again—"

"I understand that it didn't mean anything to you; it's okay."

"—I mean not for a while anyway."

"What?" we asked each other simultaneously.

"I said we couldn't kiss like that again," he answered.

"Okay." I shrugged in an attempt to act like it wasn't a big deal. I didn't want him to know that I was disappointed by his news.

"So you're okay with that?" he asked bitterly.

"Yes. Aren't you?"

"No." He ran his fingers through his tousled hair. "No, I'm not okay with that."

"Oh." I was relieved. Truth was, he was just as tortured as I was.

"What? Why did you say that like that?"

"Say what like what?"

We weren't making any sense.

"Oh." He repeated the word I'd used. "Like you're confused or something."

"I am confused." I owned up to my own stupidity.

His forehead heavily creased. "About what exactly?"

"Why isn't it okay that you can't kiss me? It isn't as if you've never kissed a girl before. Obviously you have." He rolled his eyes and messed with his hair again. "There are plenty of other girls out there that would kiss you if they got the chance. I won't be moving out for over two months. You could go out with sixty-five girls between now and then. You could kiss a different girl every night if you wanted to. Heck, if you threw in lunch dates, you could kiss over a hundred and twenty girls between now and then."

"Thanks for the suggestion," he said sarcastically. "I wonder why I hadn't thought of that."

"You're welcome."

"Seriously, you think my problem is that I wanted to kiss someone?"

"Well, yes." It made absolute sense to me.

"So you think this is about some pent-up physical desire that I needed to let out on someone? On anyone?"

"Isn't it?"

"Argh!" He lay down on the floor and placed his clinched fists over his eyes.

"What?"

"You're so dang frustrating! I swear it's like you don't get it."

"I don't." I didn't get it. I was being honest.

A distressed laugh escaped his lips. "How many times, in how many different ways, do I need to tell you that I like you? I...like...you. Riley likes Attie. Do you not get that?"

"Uh, I guess not?" I asked a question more than made a statement. It was nice to hear that he liked me, but it wasn't believable for some reason.

"Why?" He took his fists off his eyes and looked up at me. "Why is that so hard for you to believe?"

"Because." I waved my hand out in the air in front of him as if I were showing off merchandise on *The Price is Right*. "You're you." I then waved my hand in front of myself. "And I'm me. Just me."

He bolted to sitting up again. "What does that mean, 'Just me'?"

"It means that you're you and I'm me."

"Yeah, we've covered that already. Could you clarify *a lot* more?"

"You've kissed girls like Tiffany Franks for crying out loud ... freakin' smokin' hot swimsuit supermodel hussy."

"Whoa! Tiffany Franks? What does Tiffany have to do with us? And she is not smokin' hot by the way."

"Oh yes, she is." I shook my head in disgust. "Never mind. I can't explain it to you."

"Try." He sat cross-legged with his elbows on his knees and leaned toward me.

"Why did you kiss me tonight, Riley? If you didn't need to kiss *somebody*, then why did you do it? Why tonight?"

"Whaddya mean?" He shook his head as his eyes squinted and his brow creased.

"I mean why did you kiss me? Out of competition? Because you didn't want Cooper to kiss me first?"

Hiding half of his face with his hand, he sighed heavily. "Maybe a little."

"A little or totally?"

"A little bit, Charlie. I mostly kissed you because I wanted to. The fear that Cooper might get to it first is what threw me over the edge and actually made me do it, but I've wanted to for a while now."

"I see." I rolled my eyes and lay down.

"Why are you rolling your eyes?"

"Because this is a game to you."

"It's not a game. I told you that. I thought we already had that conversation."

"It is a game, Riley! Because some other guy asked me out, Cooper specifically, you came in to stake your claim. That kiss was nothing more than a symbol of you trying to win a battle with Cooper Truman. Probably some type of retribution for the way he treated Melody."

He shook his head vigorously. "That is not true; you can't say that."

"Isn't it?"

"No. I promise that's not true."

"Yeah right."

"Argh." He threw clinched fists into the air. "You're so darned frustrating!" His elbows fell back onto his knees, and he buried his face in his hands.

"I know, you already told me." I sat up and then grabbed his wrists to move his hands away from his eyes. "What?"

His face wore a sad scowl, but he talked gently. "As completely stuck up as it sounds, yes, I probly could call up any girl and get her to go out with me. She would probly kiss me and just about anything else I wanted to do with her. But that's not what I wanted. I didn't wanna kiss just any girl; I wanted to kiss you. I'd planned to wait. I thought there would be time." His face turned pale, and he looked sick again. "I never dreamed that some other guy would come along and ask you out."

"Thank you! You're making my point for me."

"What point am I making for *you?*"

"That you didn't think that somebody else would want me. Even you don't think I'm pretty enough or sexy enough or whatever enough for someone to ask me out."

He shook his head as if he'd been given a small electrical shock and threw his arms into the air again before slapping his hands onto his face. "What? That's not at all what I was saying." His voice sounded exasperated. "I'm crazy about you, Charlie, but I swear you've lost your everlastin' mind."

"You're just now figuring that out?"

He drug his hands down his face before shoving them into his moppy hair. Looking up at the ceiling in a daze, he talked to himself out loud. "Am I speaking French here and don't know it? How did me saying I wanted to kiss her turn into her believing I don't think she's pretty? Somebody, please help me get through to this girl." He covered his face with his hands again and took a deep breath. "Don't take this the wrong way, but sometimes you can be a total moron."

"I already know that."

We sat in complete silence disgusted with each other and unsure of what else we could say.

Finally he spoke. "Okay, give me your hands."

"What?"

"Give me your hands. We're gonna try something."

"What?"

"A technique we learned in counseling. It's a way to communicate clearly with someone that you're in a relationship with. We may not officially be in a relationship, but we're on totally different planets right now, and we need to figure out a way to understand each other." He held his hands out in front of me, palms up, and spoke in an encouraging voice. "Come on, give me your hands."

I slowly laid my hands on top of his, and he wrapped his fingers around them.

"We're supposed to look at each other when you do this."

"Oh, Riley, do we have to?"

"Yes. Why can't you look at me?" His voice sounded perturbed.

"It's embarrassing."

"It's embarrassing to look at me?" Now his voice sounded confused.

"Well, it's uncomfortable."

"You'll get used to it. Come on, look at me."

I could feel my face scrunch up and my bottom lip protrude. "I don't want to."

"You can kiss me, but you can't look at me?"

"If I look at you, I'll want to kiss you."

He chuckled. "Well, I won't let you. Now come on, look at me."

I shook my head.

"Please don't make me beg."

Feeling sorry for him, I finally gave in, but it was painful. I'd never sat and looked at someone like that before, and I'm certain it was the most uncomfortable thing I'd ever done.

"Okay," Riley began. "What I hear you saying is that you don't believe that I think you're pretty. And, since I've been out with people who you think are prettier than you, I couldn't have wanted to kiss you as much as I just wanted to kiss anyone. Is that right?"

"I think so." Evidently he was a good listener. "But you forgot the Cooper part."

"All right, then what I also hear you saying is that you believe that the main reason that I kissed you was because I wanted to beat Cooper to the punch and somehow punish him for how he treated Melody. Is that right?"

"Yes."

"All right, your turn."

He gave my hands a small squeeze.

"My turn to what?"

"Your turn to tell me what you heard me say to you."

"I already told you what I heard you say to me."

"Humor me please." I rolled my eyes, and he responded by squeezing my hands more firmly. "You can do it," he encouraged.

"Do I have to say the 'what I hear you saying' part?"

"Yes."

"Why?"

"Because that's how it's done. Just do it for cryin' out loud."

"All right." Gritting my teeth, I spoke slowly. "What I hear you saying is…"

He raised his eyebrows and looked at me intensely, willing me to speak.

"…you like me. God knows why, but you like me."

"You can't throw in your own comments. Only repeat back what you actually heard me say."

"Sorry."

"Start over," he instructed.

I let out a heavy sigh. "Okay, what I hear you saying is that you like me and you wanted to kiss me because you were afraid that Cooper might do it first and that you could have any girl you want, but you don't actually want any of them."

"Okay, now you ask me if that was correct."

"Is that correct?"

"No, not even close. You don't listen very well." He sounded exasperated again.

"Well, maybe you don't explain very well."

"Okay, now I get to clarify," he explained. "I'll talk slowly so the dense girl in the room can completely understand."

"I doubt that insults are an approved part of the technique," I whimpered.

"I'm completely teasing, but you're right. I'm sorry." His thumbs sweetly rubbed the tops of my hands.

My heart beat wildly. I needed to talk so that I could expel some of the energy that was building in my body. "When do I get to clarify?" I asked.

"You don't need to clarify; I got it right, and you said I understood you correctly."

"But I want to get to clarify."

"You can clarify later; let me clarify first since I actually have stuff to clarify."

"All right," I conceded.

He rolled his eyes at me. "Well crap, now I can't remember what I needed to clarify. Tell me again."

"Riley!"

"No, no, I got it. I got it, I remember." He took another deep breath. "You were right about the fact that I said I like you. You were not right about the Cooper part. What I was trying to say was that I already wanted to kiss you and the fear that Cooper might do it first is what caused me to break my promise to myself. I wanted to kiss you."

"You said that already."

"Shush, you have to be silent during my clarification."

"Sorry."

He continued, "I wanted to kiss you anyway. Fear and desire got mixed in together with a little amount of losing my mind, and what it added up to was me kissing you tonight. It wasn't a competitive thing as much as it was a fear that I would lose you if I didn't act fast. I'm afraid that while I'm sitting around waiting for you to move out, Cooper or someone else might woo you away.

"In my strange and moronic male mind, I thought that by kissing you it would make it darned near impossible for you to like anyone else. At least until I can compete on a level playing field anyway. If other guys are taking you out and kissing you and I can't do the same because of some promise I made to myself, well then I'll probly lose you, and I'm not okay with that. Does that sound reasonable?"

"I think so."

"Okay, so what did you hear me say?" he asked.

"You don't want … what I hear you saying is that you don't want someone else to come in and date me before you have the chance to date me too."

"Right."

"But I don't feel like I'd be dating Cooper, I …"

"Please, one thing at a time. I'm not done clarifying yet."

"Sorry, continue."

"About other girls, I was making the point that I could have just about any girl, but I don't want any other girl. I want you. I didn't kiss you out of a desire to kiss someone; I kissed you out of a desire to kiss you. You specifically."

"Okay, what I hear you saying is that you didn't want to kiss anyone but me."

"Yes. I didn't and I don't wanna kiss anyone but you." He paused to let the statement sink into my brain before he continued.

"Lastly, this whole pretty versus not pretty or who is or who isn't pretty, it's silly. I can honestly say that you're the prettiest girl I've ever known, and nobody comes close as far as I'm concerned."

I rolled my eyes and felt my face turn hot.

"Charlie, I'm serious. You may not see it, but I do."

He stopped and waited for me to respond. "Is this necessary?" I complained.

"Yes."

"What I hear you saying is that you … think that I'm … pretty." I spit out the word and then covered my face with my hands.

"And?"

"Don't make me say any more; it's horribly embarrassing."

"Hey, I admitted that most the girls at my school wanna go out with me. Now that's pretty embarrassing."

"Can I keep my face covered when I say it?"

I heard him laugh. "I guess so."

I talked quickly from under my hands. "What I hear you saying is that you think I'm the prettiest girl you know."

"Why is that so bad to say?"

"I don't know. It just is." This was now beyond uncomfortable. It was actually physically painful.

"You're hot, totally hot. I bet all the guys think so."

"Stop it, Riley."

"You've lived here less than a month and two guys are already after you. That's got to say something."

"Enough, please."

"All right, I'll stop. It's true though." He laughed as he gently removed my hands from my face and held them again. "Okay, you were trying to say something about Cooper."

"I was trying to say that I don't see it as going out with Cooper. The thought never crossed my mind, so I never dreamed that's the way he saw it. I mean, he hardly knows me; how can he want to ask me out that fast?"

"I wanted to ask you after only seeing your picture."

"Riley," I moaned.

"I'm serious." The sound in his voice confirmed his statement. "That's why boys ask girls out. They like something about them, and they wanna spend more time with them to find out if there are more things about them to like. You don't have to be totally in love with someone before going out with them; you just have to want to get to know them better. That's the point of dating."

"I wouldn't know that. Nobody's ever asked me out before." I felt like an idiot admitting the fact that nobody had ever been interested enough to ask me out on a date.

"I asked you out, sorta."

"I know, but you asked me out after you told me you liked me. Cooper hasn't said anything like that. I think he just wants to be friends. I'm someone to hang out with."

"Have you ever seen the movie *When Harry Met Sally?*"

"No. Good grief, what are you, the walking movie encyclopedia?"

"No, seriously. I'm ordering it tonight. It'll give you a lot of insight into the male mind."

"That sounds scary. Is it a horror movie?"

"Ha, ha."

"Are we done with this whole thing now?"

"Not quite." He grabbed my hands tightly so that I wouldn't pull them away.

"Oh, all right." I was growing more annoyed with the entire process and wanted it to end.

"I wanna apologize for the way I acted today."

"You do?" Oh no, as if I weren't weak enough as it was, now he was apologizing, which meant my little war would have to end immediately.

"Yes. It was uncalled for, and I never should have raised my voice to you like that. I'm sorry."

His voice sounded so loving that it made my heart start melting.

"I was excited to see you because I hadn't seen you all day. So when I walked in there and saw you talking to Truman, I freaked out a little."

I glared at him.

"Okay, I freaked out a lot," he admitted calmly. "It's obvious that I don't like the guy anyway, but when he mentioned you going to his house on Saturday and everything, I about lost my mind. I got angry and scared, and I took it out on you. I shouldn't have. I'm really, really sorry."

"Thank you for apologizing, Riley. That means a lot to me."

"You're welcome. I've already apologized to your Gramps, but I still need to apologize to the girls."

"You don't need to apologize to them; they loved every minute of it." I thought of them sitting at the clinic completely enthralled in the action.

He gave me a small grin. "No, I do need to apologize. I don't want them to think that I believe it's okay for me to talk to you like that."

I looked down and watched as he stroked the top of my hands with his thumbs.

"How can I resist you when you're so darned sweet?"

"Why would you be trying to resist me?"

"Isn't that what we're doing here? Trying to stay away from each other until I move out?"

"I knew I was trying to resist you. Do you have to make yourself resist me?" He sounded hopeful.

"I'll never tell," I teased.

"Uh-huh. Interesting." He winked at me. "There's one more thing to say, and then I'm done and we can go to sleep—or try to anyway."

"Go for it."

"I want you to know that no matter what the reasons were behind that kiss tonight, I've never felt like that before."

"What do you mean?"

"I mean, I've kissed a few girls..."

I raised my eyebrows at him.

"Okay, more than a few, but that's beside the point. What I mean is that I've never felt the way I felt when I kissed you. With you it was like my whole heart was involved. It's the most amazing kiss I've ever had."

I yanked my hands out of his and covered my face in embarrassment. "Get out! You're so full of it."

"No, I'm not, I'm totally serious. I had to walk away or I could have been there doing that all night, I swear. I've never felt like that before."

By the temperature of my cheeks, I knew that I was turning crimson. "Well, unfortunately, if I tell you it was great for me, it won't matter because I don't have anything to compare it to."

"But was it?" His voice sounded hopeful again.

"Yes."

"Do you wanna do it again?"

"Oh yes."

He laughed. "Let's hope that the rest of the summer flies by or your dad decides to move back early."

"I'll keep my fingers crossed."

chapter 22

Cooper and I made our way through the buffet and then took a seat at a table. I'd begged Gramps to join us, but he refused. I was stuck having a one-on-one lunch with Cooper Truman, and I wasn't looking forward to an hour-long conversation. I planned on staying as far away as possible from any personal discussions, so I made sure to start the conversation.

"So, Coop, tell me all about how you got into Cornell and your school plans. I'm very curious seeing as how we're sort of on the same path."

He smiled at me. "No small talk? You get straight to the point."

"Sorry, I don't know anyone else that's close to my age and is doing what I want to do. We can have small talk if you would prefer."

"No, I want to talk about whatever you want to talk about."

"Thanks." He seemed genuine, but I was cautious. "So school?"

"Well, I've been planning on being a veterinarian for years, so all of my schooling has been in preparation to get in and out of undergrad as soon as possible. I attended UCO in Edmond the summer before and during my senior year of high school."

"Really? Did you CLEP out of school classes or what?" I was intrigued and cut into my chicken fried steak while I listened.

"Yes. I went all AP during high school and then CLEPed out of every class I could—I think about thirty hours. As I said, during the summer and at nights, I took college courses at UCO. Cornell will let you transfer up to sixty hours, so I cut two years off my undergrad while I was still here and started up there as a junior."

"So this fall you're already going to be a senior?"

"Yes, and you can apply for Cornell vet school in the spring of your sophomore year, so that's what I did. I got accepted to early admissions into the DVM program. I'll actually start vet school this year."

"So you'll finish three years earlier than most?"

"That's the plan."

"That's amazing. How would I do it if I wanted to?"

"Cornell, or any vet school, wants you to focus on science and chemistry, so I took every science class in high school and my year at UCO but then tested out of English composition, English lit, economics, Spanish, and stuff like that."

My curiosity was growing. "How did you prepare for the tests?"

"Have you gone AP through school?"

"Yes."

"Then you shouldn't have any problem. But they have study guides just in case you need them."

"Great, thanks for the information. You could be saving me a lot of time. Not as much as you of course, but some anyway."

"I can take you up to UCO one day if you'd like, that way you can get all the information you need. It's so close by. It only took me about twenty minutes to get to class every day."

I noticed he hadn't touched his food.

"That sounds great. I would appreciate that." My mind was spinning with all the new possibilities that lay ahead of me.

He folded his arms onto the table and stared at me. "Where do you want to go to school?"

"You eat, Cooper. I'll talk if you eat. We can't have you passing out during the middle of a surgery or anything."

"Deal." He cut open his potato and smothered it in butter and sour cream.

"I was thinking I would go to UCO for my undergrad and then try to get into OSU for vet school. My Gramps knows a lot of people up there, so hopefully I won't have much trouble. Plus, I've always done very well in school."

"You never considered Cornell? I would think that would be your first choice seeing as how your dad teaches there and you lived there for so long."

"You think I would go for which, undergrad or vet school?"

"Both."

Actually, I hadn't thought about it at all. "Well, my dad's moving back here at the end of the summer, so he won't be there anymore."

Cooper took a bite of his potato and then placed his fork onto his plate. His manners were impeccable.

"Plus, I don't fit in with that type."

"What type is that?"

"The English riding type," I teased.

"Oh yes, that type—don't you hate them?" I found Cooper's sense of humor surprising.

"I'm not cut out for that kind of life. I'm more your plain, lower-income type. I don't think I would fit in."

"You'd be surprised, Attie; not everybody up there is highbrow. I don't think I am. My parents are the ones with the money, not me."

"Are you being humble, Coop?"

"Not so much humble as honest." He blushed and looked down at his baked potato. "I try not to get into all that stuff. I go to class, go home, study, and repeat it all the next day."

"Sounds exciting, or not."

"You can live through anything if you know it isn't going to last forever." He looked back up at me. "Would you not agree?"

"Yes, I guess I would."

Fidgeting a bit, he grabbed his soda and took a sip. "I didn't want to bring it up, but . . ." He shrugged.

"Go ahead, you can ask."

"How are you doing? I know you've been through a lot over the last year."

"Oh, I just try to make it day by day. Not much else I can do."

"I can see that. Not see it physically necessarily," he clarified quickly, "just, well, I understand what you're saying." He shook his head in embarrassment. "I'm not making any sense, am I? I'm not good with this type of thing."

"What type of thing?"

"You know, emotions. We aren't very emotional in my family. We don't talk about them, and we certainly don't show them."

"Then you better stay away from me because I'm one big emotional mess. That's about all I know how to be—emotional."

"I'm not scared; I find it intriguing." His eyes blazed as he looked at me.

Uh oh, there it was, the "I-can-dazzle-everyone" look.

I became uncomfortable and looked down at the table.

"What do you like to do?" he asked.

"I like to hang around my friends and have fun, not be so serious all the time. For the last year, my life has been nothing but serious. I think I needed to relax and enjoy things for a while. I mean, God spared my life for some reason; it wouldn't be wise not to make the most of it."

"I would agree with that."

"You know, Cooper, I don't know much, but one thing I'm certain of is that we don't know when our time is up down here. I would hate to think that you missed out on fun because you had to prove yourself to someone."

"You think that's what I'm doing? Trying to prove myself?"

"Honestly?" I asked.

"Yes."

"Yes, I do."

"Interesting. You've known me all of a few hours and you've got me figured out," he said with sarcasm.

"I'd rather try to figure you out than myself. We've all got issues, I can tell you that, and I'd much rather focus on somebody else's."

"Sure, you can focus on me anytime."

We continued talking as Cooper finished his baked potato. It struck me how different he was than what I thought he would be. I'd definitely judged him wrongly, and so had Riley.

"Well, do you think we should head back to the clinic to check on Gramps?"

"Sure," he agreed and then reached for his wallet. "Thanks for coming with me to lunch today. I enjoyed it."

"No, Coop, thank you. I learned a lot, and you gave me some stuff to look into."

He grabbed the check and laid down some cash.

"What's my part?" I asked.

"I've got it, Attie. I'm the one that invited you to lunch, remember?"

"No way, you're not going to pay for my lunch. You gave me a freakin' college counseling session. I should buy your lunch."

"No, ma'am, I enjoyed myself." He grabbed the bill before I could reach it with my hand. "Honestly, I had a great time."

"Let's just split the bill and call it even then," I insisted.

"All right, if we must."

I tried to lighten the mood again. "You can go spend your parents' money on someone else."

He wasn't pleased about the fact that I was paying for my own meal, but there was no way that I was going to let him think this was a date—not after everything that Riley said.

We made our way out of the restaurant and toward his car.

"When do you leave for school?"

"Mid-August."

"Are you looking forward to it?

"Not as much as I'm looking forward to the rest of this summer." He winked at me as he opened my car door, but I again pretended not to notice.

"Can I be honest with you?" I asked as he buckled himself in.

"Sure."

"I'm very surprised that this is your car."

He laughed out loud and then turned to face me. "I've got to hear this. Why are you surprised?"

I could feel my cheeks blush. "I'm sorry, sometimes I speak before I think. It tends to get me in trouble."

"Nothing to be sorry about, Attie. I think it's charming." His bright white teeth were glaring at me. "So tell me, why are you so surprised?"

"It's an older car. It's falling apart actually. I figured you'd drive some expensive sports car or something."

He smirked. "Like I said, it's my parents' money, not mine. I had to work in the stables to earn the money to buy this car."

"Really?" It surprised me that Cooper had to work for anything.

"Oh yes! A little ironic, don't you think?"

"What?"

"The fact that I had to shovel a bunch of crap to get enough money to buy a piece of crap car." He laughed again and then turned to start the engine.

"Why yes, it is a bit ironic now that you mention it."

"They did get me a nicer car when I went off to school. I leave it up there and drive this one when I'm home."

"What's the other one?"

He shook his head, and I could see his face turning red.

"What is it, Coop? You've got to tell me."

"A Hummer," he mumbled.

"A Hummer? Good grief!"

"It's all for show. The car wasn't so much for me as it was for everyone else to see me in it. It was all their idea. I would have been more than happy to take this clunker up there with me."

"Well, I guess you've got to play the game, right? But if I had to play along, I'd take a Hummer; they seem kind of cool. Even I couldn't get hurt in one of those things."

"I'll remember that during Christmas break," he said, looking over at me. "I'll bring it home and make sure you get to take it out for a spin."

I worried that he would think that I wanted to spend more time with him. "Oh, don't worry about it. I was saying it would be fun; that's all."

"No, Attie, it's a date. I would love to let someone take a ride that would appreciate and enjoy it. For everyone up at school, it's just another car. There isn't anything special about it."

"I'll look forward to it then."

Part of me did look forward to it, but the other part of me felt guilty for the fact that Cooper wanted to spend more time with me.

Cooper Truman was a nice boy. I enjoyed his company and was thankful to be his friend. I just wasn't sure what Riley would think about it.

chapter 23

"What do you want to be when you grow up?"

"When I grow up?" Riley asked, laughing. "What are we, five?"

My head rested on one of the arm rails of the porch swing as my legs were draped across Riley's. "You know what I mean. What are your plans?"

He let out a deep sigh. "I don't know for sure. I've tossed around some ideas, but I haven't made my mind up yet."

"So there isn't something that you've always wanted to be?"

"No," he said as he reached for a blackberry sitting in a bowl on my stomach. "Not realistically anyway."

"What do you mean 'realistically'?"

"The only two things I enjoy are drawing and football, but I'm not good enough at either one to make a living doing it, so ... "

"So?"

"I'm waiting until something clicks in me, something that says, 'That's what I wanna do for the next fifty years of my life.'"

I watched as his foot pushed off the ground causing the swing to sway. "Are you a good student; I mean, do you want to go to college?"

"Yeah, I'm a good student, not straight As or anything, but I do pretty well."

"And college?"

"I wanna go, but I don't wanna go far away. I think I'd be content living right here and going to UCO."

"That would probably make your mom happy."

"No doubt."

I took in a deep breath and closed my eyes.

"You know, I wish I were more like you, Charlie. I wish that I always knew what I wanted to be, but I never have."

"I think you should be a police officer or an attorney or a doctor or something," I offered.

"Why do you think that?"

"You like to protect people, take care of them."

"No, I don't," he replied.

My eyes flew open. "Riley! Yes, you do. Look at how patient you are with me; not everyone could do that. Even my dad, who I believe is a great guy, couldn't deal with my issues. You have a heart of gold."

"Nah, I just have a heart of gold for you," he teased. "When I got in all that trouble a few years ago, I thought of doing something in criminal justice, something to help kids that are in trouble."

"You got in trouble?"

He acted surprised. "You didn't know that?"

"I heard you punched Cooper."

"That isn't the half of it. I was a mess, an absolute nightmare to my parents." He looked down at me with a guilty face. "Oh, sorry I said I was a nightmare."

"I didn't even notice. You're being paranoid."

He smiled down at me and then continued. "I lost total control my sophomore year. I hung out with the wrong kids and got into a lot of trouble. I even spent a night in jail."

I bolted upright and sat cross-legged facing him.

"You were in the pokey?"

He chuckled. "Yes, Charlie, I was in the 'pokey.' I got drunk one night and stole some Cheetos from a gas station."

"Good grief, Cheetos? Seriously, Riley?"

"I know, ludicrous isn't it?" He rolled his eyes. "Anyway, the kid behind the counter knew who I was and called the cops. Yada, yada,

yada, my dad wouldn't come bail me out, so I spent the night with a bunch of drunks in the holding tank."

"Ew, what was that like?"

"Everything you can imagine. It sure taught me a lesson. I even ended up having to do community service. I felt like a total heel."

"What was your community service?"

"Picking up trash. I had to wear one of those stupid orange vests and everything."

I gave him a small pat on the shoulder. "Wow, that's embarrassing."

"No, what embarrassed me was Mom showing up to take pictures."

"She didn't?" I started laughing at him.

"Oh yes, she said she wanted to document my life of crime. I'll have to show you the pictures sometime."

"That sounds like something she would do." I lay back down and put my legs back over Riley's. "I can't wait to see the photos. Maybe you can sketch one and put it on my wall."

"No, thank you." He shook his head and laughed. "What can I say? Mom lives to humiliate me."

"So what did your parents do? Did they freak?"

"Mom was a blubbering mess for several days, and my dad sat me down and gave me a stern talking to."

"What did he say?"

"He said that the way I was acting wasn't me. It wasn't who I was or how he raised me. The drinking was one issue, but the stealing was the thing that most disappointed him. They didn't raise me to be dishonest or untrustworthy."

"Did they punish you?"

"Oh yeah, I was grounded. But you know, it wasn't the punishment that was the worst part."

I found his honesty very attractive. "What was?"

"The fact that they were disappointed in me. They've always been great parents, but I'd treated them like dirt. They were hurt and disappointed in me. I hated it."

"Nothing like having a conscience, huh?"

"Tell me about it," he mumbled.

"So what made you change? Just the fact that they were disappointed in you?"

"No, I was grounded for three months, and the only places I was allowed to go were school and church. That's when I ended up becoming a Christian, and my life pretty much changed immediately after that. Melody became a Christian about a month after me and then she died a month after that."

"Then it was all worth it. Who would have thought that getting drunk, stealing Cheetos, and spending a night in the pokey would end up helping to save Melody's soul? And just in time."

His eyebrows rose, causing lines to fill his forehead. "I've never thought about it like that. I guess that God can use our issues to bring change in other people."

"I hope so. I have a lot of issues, so they better be good for something."

He doubled up laughing. "You crack me up."

"Well, I'm glad my misery amuses you."

"Me too." He picked up one of my hands and slowly kissed me on the inside of my wrist.

"I can't believe you were such a bad boy, spending the night in the pokey and everything."

A sly grin spread across his face. "Do you like bad boys?"

"Not if they're still bad boys. I've got enough problems to deal with."

"Good thing I'm an angel now."

"Well, I wouldn't say that," I joked.

"You're right. Not quite an angel, but I'm trying hard to be good."

"You're a good boy, Riley. A great boy."

We stayed on the swing for several more minutes until the sun completely set and it was pitch dark outside.

"All right, it's time," he announced.

"Time for what?"

"You'll see; wait right here." As I got out of the swing, he ran inside and returned with two empty mayonnaise jars.

"No more fun and games like when we were kids. This time, it's war."

"Oh?" I rubbed my hands together in preparation for a battle.

"Yep, we have thirty minutes," he explained as he set his watch. "When this thing goes off, the person who caught the most fireflies wins."

"You're on. What's the prize?"

"The person who wins gets to choose the theme for a week of movie nights."

"That's not a prize for you; you already choose every time."

"Well then, if you want me to watch any of your dumb chick flicks, you better get busy."

I grabbed a jar out of his hands and was off the porch and running toward the backyard before he even finished his sentence.

After our battle, we walked inside to announce the victor.

"Well, Marme, I just got us a week of chick flicks, so start making up your wish list so Riley can order them from Netflix."

"Awesome!" she squealed.

"Riley, what did you do?" Pops whimpered.

"Riley lost a bet, so I get to choose the movies for the next week. It's going to be chick flick mania around here."

"Son, what in the world? How could you risk something like that without clearing it through me?"

"I didn't think she had a chance. She's a lot faster than I thought. She's like the freakin' firefly whisperer or something."

I hopped around the kitchen showing off my jar of light.

"Don't rub it in, Charlie; be a good sport."

"Heck no, I never win anything, and this feels good!"

"We have to start with *Pride and Prejudice* and then maybe do *A Walk to Remember*," Marme announced.

"Oh Lord, this is gonna be worse than I thought." Riley flung himself onto the couch.

"Riley," I said as I sat next to him, "don't you want to better understand the female mind?"

"Is that even possible?" he asked, looking at his father.

"No," Pops spat. "Heck no, it's not possible."

"Relax, boys, it won't be that bad. We'll go easy on you," I offered.

"Yeah right," Riley moaned as he got up to put in the newest DVD.

"What's showing tonight?" I asked.

"We're watching *Beverly Hills Cop* and *Coming to America.*"

"Oooh, Thomas, do you remember the song that Eddie Murphy sang?" Marme asked.

"No."

"Riley, jot that one down; I need to add it to my iTunes."

"What's it called?"

She started singing the song. "My girl wants to party all the time, party all the time, party all the ti-ime."

He rolled his eyes at her. "Mom, seriously, stop."

"It's a good song, Riley; wait until you hear it."

"I'll load it on there if you'll promise to stop singing it so we can watch the movie."

"You're no fun," she pouted. "He's not any fun, is he, Attie?"

"Nope. No fun at all, and he's also a sore loser."

"You're a poor winner—you rub it in."

"Poor baby, got his butt kicked by a girl," I sang.

"Again," Pops added. "It's becoming a regular event around here."

• •

The doorbell rang at ten o'clock sharp the next morning. I started to run to answer it, but Riley beat me to it. As I finished getting ready, I could hear the conversation from my room.

"Hey, Riley!"

"Chase, what are you doing here, bud?" Riley asked.

I smiled as I waited for Chase to respond.

"Attie invited me to go horseback riding at Cooper's with her today."

"Really? She invited you along?"

"Yeah, wasn't that nice?" Chase sounded pleased. He had no idea that I had ulterior motives when I suggested he tag along.

"Yes, it was nice," Riley agreed. "Well, come on in; I'll go get her. Dad, keep Chase company while I get Attie."

Hearing Riley's footsteps running up the stairs, I waited for him to enter my room. He had a huge grin on his face as he walked through my door. "You invited Chase to go with you?"

"Chase loves horseback riding. I thought he would enjoy it."

As he walked closer to me, his grin somehow grew larger. "Is that the only reason you invited him?"

"Well,"—I shrugged—"I wouldn't want Cooper to get the wrong idea. I mean, it's not like it's a date or anything."

He grabbed me and gave me a hug as he picked me up off the floor. "Thank you, Charlie; you don't know how much this means to me."

"Yes, I do." I wrapped my hands around his neck and looked down at him. "Besides, you were my first kiss, Riley. I'll be darned if you aren't going to be my first date too."

He lovingly gazed up at me. "I'm so crazy about you."

"I know."

"I swear, if I could kiss you right now, I would."

"If you could kiss me right now, I'd let you."

He slowly lowered me to the ground and then gently grabbed my hands and kissed the inside of each of my wrists.

"That'll have to do for now," he said miserably.

I could feel my face blush. "I'm starting to like it when you do that."

"Then I'll do it more often."

• • • • • • • • • • • • • • • • • • • •

After bringing Chase along with me to horseback riding, Cooper got the point that I wasn't interested in a summer fling. We worked alongside each other every Tuesday and Thursday thoroughly enjoying each other's company, but he never asked me out again. We did continue going to lunch once a week as he helped me prepare for CLEP testing. We also spent a day at UCO getting all of the necessary enrollment information together. He became a very good friend, and I enjoyed spending time with him. I never brought him up to Riley, and I never talked about Riley with him. I believe that they both preferred it that way.

chapter 24

Summer quickly passed, and Riley and I spent almost every night watching movies with his parents followed by camping out on my bedroom floor. I still experienced nightmares almost every night, but Riley learned to calm me so that we were both able to fall back to sleep within a matter of minutes.

Cheerleading practice began, and if it hadn't been for Anne and Jennifer, it would have been the worst two hours of each and every day. Most of the senior girls wanted nothing to do with me, and Tiffany managed to make it the entire summer's worth of practices without so much as saying hello. I wished that I'd stuck with my initial gut reaction to have Mr. Bennett get me completely off the cheer squad. Surely living with the school principal had to have *some* advantages.

After my first counseling session with Joshua and Nicole, every session also became "driver's license therapy," or "DLT" for short. They were set on me getting my license before school started.

The first DLT session was spent with me sitting in the driver's seat of Joshua's old Honda. He sat in the passenger seat, and Nicole sat behind him in the backseat. All we did was pray. I never even got to start the engine.

During the second and third sessions, I got to stick the key in the ignition and turn it on. The rest of the time we prayed while a Chris Tomlin CD played in the background.

The following week we focused on getting in the car, turning on the ignition, and doing visualization techniques. Or, as Joshua called them, DLT-VT (for some reason he was into titles). I closed my eyes as Joshua took me through different driving scenarios, and I would respond with acting out the appropriate behavior. In a typical session, you might have heard the following:

Joshua: (speaking slowly) "You're driving down the street, and a stop sign is coming up in twenty feet."

Me: I would tap the brake to slow down.

Joshua: "You're six feet from the stop sign and have decided to turn left."

Me: I would turn on my blinker and slowly apply steady pressure to the break.

By the middle of June, we moved on to DLT-Advanced Visualization Therapy. DLT-AVT was similar to the regular visualization except that Joshua would suddenly scream some action as it could possibly happen if I ever actually left the driveway.

Joshua: "You're driving through an intersection, and someone just ran a red light!"

Me: I would calmly but firmly press the brake.

Unfortunately, I almost failed one DLT-AVT session.

Joshua: "We're driving past Mr. Hendricks's house, and his dog just ran into the street in front of your car!"

Me: I swerved to miss it by yanking the steering wheel to the right.

Joshua: "No, Attie, you never swerve like that. You could roll the car or get out of control and crash. Your life is much more valuable than a dog's."

Me: "Is it necessary to hit the dog?"

Nicole: "You didn't tell the future vet to hit the dog, did you?"

Joshua: "Nicole! Would you rather she hurt herself and save the dog? Isn't that the point of DLT? To save her life and the life of other human beings? Seriously, this could set us back a few sessions."

Nicole: "No! Attie, next time, you hit the dang dog, do you hear me?"

Me: "Yes."

Nicole: "See, Joshua, next time she's gonna hit the dog. Aren't you, Attie? You're gonna hit the dog?"

Me: "Yes! I'll take the dog out!"

Nicole: "Thank God. We're *not* adding more sessions! If we don't eventually get out of this driveway, I'm going to lose my mind."

Me: "I know a good therapist."

Joshua: "Very funny, Attie. I'm trying to be thorough, Nicole!"

Nicole: "No, you want to be able to say 'DLT-AVT' some more!"

And with that, DLT-AVT sessions were over.

The third week of June we actually got out and drove. Of course Joshua drove the car to a remote location and then let me take over, but at least we were moving.

The first week of July I got to drive on city streets, and by the third week I was on the highway and was allowed to turn the music up beyond a whisper.

On the fourth Tuesday of July, Nicole finally took me to take my driver's test.

• •

(Riley)

We brought every extra chair and lawn chair into the family room so that we could wait for Attie to get back from taking her driver's test. Anne, Tammy, Tess, Chase, Matt, Curt, Gramps, Joshua, my parents, and I all started praying when Nicole called to announce that Attie had "gone into the building."

"Do you suppose that God has ever heard so many prayers for one poor child to get her driver's license?" Gramps asked when we were finished.

"I couldn't imagine it," Dad replied.

I paced, Joshua was biting his fingernails, and Anne knelt praying in the corner.

"I've gotta leave the room. You people are freaking me out!" Tammy announced. "She might as well be having a baby!"

"I'm a nervous wreck," Tess said as she rocked back and forth in her chair.

Finally we heard the car pull into the driveway. Everyone jumped up and looked at the front door in anticipation. We held our breath.

The door opened, Nicole walked in, and I noticed that her eyes were red. She'd been crying. The air left the room, and our hearts broke.

"Where is she?" Joshua asked.

"Composing herself. She'll be right in." Nicole cried and walked into Joshua's arms.

We all looked back at the door and prepared ourselves to comfort Attie after she failed for the fourth time. I could hear her footsteps make their way slowly up the patio stairs, and I waited to see her face. But instead of walking into the room, she merely stuck her arm inside the door, and in her hand she held a driver's license.

The room exploded in screams and cheers.

Attie ran into the room. "I'm a licensed driver!"

"Watch out, world," Dad yelled.

She wore the largest smile I'd ever seen. The girls ran to her, and they all jumped around in circles and took turns looking at her driver's license picture.

"Thank you, Jesus! Thank you, Jesus!" Gramps waved his hands in the air.

I looked over and saw Joshua on his knees crying. I didn't know if he was crying out of happiness for Attie or out of relief for not having to continue DLT sessions. I assumed it was probably a combination of both.

Nicole sat next to him laughing. "I fooled you! I fooled you!"

After a long celebration of hugs all around, Mom brought out a celebratory cake. The cake decorator had drawn a blonde cartoon character with car keys in her hand sitting in a tank. Attie's favorite part was the angel's wings coming out of the roof.

Chase, our official photographer, made sure to document the entire event, and we all sat and ate cake as Nicole shared the journal entries she made after every DLT session. By the time she finished, Attie and Joshua were bright red, and the rest of us were in stitches.

"I can't believe you agreed to kill the dog, Attie," Tess teased.

"I was willing to do anything not to have to add Advanced Visualization sessions," Attie said, giggling.

Gramps stood up and quieted the crowd. "I'd like to lead a prayer in thanksgiving," he requested.

Everyone got serious and bowed their head.

"Dear Lord, Heavenly Father. It's about time. Amen."

"Amen!" everyone shouted.

I hadn't ever seen Attie as joyful as she was that day. There were no signs of the girl who moved in almost three months before. She'd turned the corner and was enjoying life again.

"Okay, Attie, are you ready for your present?" Gramps asked.

"Yes!" she squealed. "I love presents!"

"Riley?" Gramps looked at me, and I got up and grabbed her hand.

"Are you my present, Riley?" she whispered while squeezing my hand.

"I wish," I mumbled under my breath.

"Everybody out the back door," Gramps ordered.

Friends filed out, and Attie went to follow them, but I gently kept hold of her hand to keep her back.

"Just wait," I whispered.

After a few minutes Gramps told me to go ahead and bring her out. She closed her eyes, and I led her through the kitchen and out the back door to the patio.

"Now, stay right here, and don't open your eyes 'til we tell you to." I ran to join the others.

"Okay, open them," Gramps yelled.

She opened her eyes.

"Surprise!"

Her jaw dropped, and she didn't move a muscle.

"It's a miracle!" Tammy yelled. "She's speechless!"

"Is it mine?"

"Yes," her Gramps told her as he walked up to her and gave her a kiss on the cheek.

"Gramps, it's brand new. It's too much!"

"What else do I get to spend my money on? Let me spoil you a little."

"What kind is it?

"It's a Toyota Sequoia, and it seats eight people. I thought it would be good for driving all your friends around."

"Good grief, it's huge!" Attie screamed.

"Well, it can certainly withstand a pounding if it needs to," Dad told her.

"Go check her out!" Gramps ordered.

Attie ran around and climbed into the driver's side. She was in awe. Matt, Curt, and Chase all jumped into the row of seats in the back, the girls got in the middle row, and I got in the passenger seat.

"Oh look, it has a butt warmer!" she gushed. "I've always wanted a butt warmer."

"I think the correct term is heated seats," Chase corrected.

"I don't care what you call them; I just like my butt to be warm."

"Take her for a spin!" Dad yelled.

Without thinking, I snapped my head around and looked at everyone else in the car. They all looked slightly afraid, and Attie noticed.

"Hey, I'm a good driver!" she shouted.

"Yes, I'm an excellent driver," Tammy said in her best *Rainman* impression.

"See, Charlie, even Tammy knows *Rainman*."

"I already told you I'd watch it, Riley," she snapped back. "All right, everyone, you ready?"

"Hold on!" Matt yelled as he clutched the seat in front of him.

"Enough from the peanut gallery," I yelled back. "You'll make her nervous, and then we'll really be in trouble."

We were all excited for Attie but a little nervous for ourselves. I could hear people snapping seatbelts in place and preparing for the ride. Chase passed me the camera, and I took pictures of everyone in the back. They posed and acted out various scenarios. In one particular pose, everyone acted like they were terrified. In another, everyone's arms were raised in the air as if they were on a roller coaster. I couldn't wait to get the pictures developed.

"Let's get the show on the road," Tammy ordered.

Everyone not going in the car with us walked around to the front of the house so they could see us as we drove by.

Attie carefully put the car in drive and started toward the driveway.

"I'm ruining your dad's grass, Riley; he's going to kill me."

"Hey, he's the one that parked it there. What else can you do? Just go slow."

She did.

"Okay, maybe not that slow," I corrected.

She sped up little.

As we drove past the patio, everyone started cheering, and Chase snapped photos of the waving family members and friends. Attie slowly made her way down the driveway, turned on her blinker, and made her way onto the street. As soon as she officially exited out of the driveway, we all started clapping.

Attie drove us around the neighborhood several times and honked at everyone on the patio every time we passed the house. Granted, she never drove over twenty miles an hour, but she did great.

"Do you think you can handle a Sonic run?" I asked.

She bit her thumbnail and then smiled over at me. "I think so."

We drove by the house so we could tell everyone where we were going and get money from Dad, and then Attie drove her new car down to the Sonic.

Sitting in the car talking, we drank our Route 44s and planned our first road trip. Everyone agreed that we needed to float the Illinois River and go camping, so we put Chase and Tess in charge of planning the event.

Once we made it back home, everyone took turns riding around the neighborhood, and then we sat on the patio and watched as everyone said good-bye and drove away.

• •

(Attie)

"Wanna go to the drive-in?" Riley asked. "There's a showing tonight."

"I thought you weren't going to ask me out until I was out of your house? Wouldn't that be considered a date?"

"No," he said quickly and firmly.

"It wouldn't?"

"No, because there will be no touching involved."

"Oh?"

"You sound disappointed."

I felt my face blush. "Do I?"

"Yeah, I think you did. I love it. Come on, let's go," he begged.

"You know as well as I do that I can't say no to you."

"Really? Well then, maybe there will be some touching going on," he taunted.

I gave him a playful glare before punching his shoulder.

"One can always hope," he added.

I waited on the patio while he grabbed a couple of blankets, pillows, bottled waters, and snacks, and although it wasn't actually a date, I couldn't wait to spend time with Riley alone.

We got there early enough to park on the front row and get ourselves situated. Folding down the backseats, we lay on our backs and propped ourselves up with the pillows.

"This is so comfy. If my Gramps had realized that this car gave me the ability to fold down the seats and lay down in the back with a boy, he wouldn't have gotten it."

"He wouldn't care if he knew it was me. He loves and trusts me."

"He doesn't know you well enough." I laughed. "Good thing he can't read minds."

"That's the truth."

As we waited for it to get dark, we watched as other cars filled the vacant spots and children ran around playing on the field below the movie screen. I remembered when Riley, Melody, and I were little and our parents used to bring us to the same drive-in. When very young, we would play in the field just like the kids did tonight, and the older we got, our parents let us lay on a blanket and watch the movie in the grass instead of in the car with the adults. We felt so grown-up and independent. I couldn't wait until I was old enough to drive my own car to the movie and leave my parents behind.

Now I'd have given anything to stay with them in the car a little bit longer and not been in such a rush to spend time away from them. Had I known then what I knew now...

"I haven't gotten to congratulate you on your success today," Riley said, interrupting my thoughts.

"You haven't?"

"No." He reached into a bag and pulled out a gift. "Congratulations," he said, handing it to me.

"I get another gift!" I snatched the box out of his hands. "Oh, Riley, you didn't have to get me a gift."

He sat up. "It's not much, trust me."

I carefully peeled the wrapping off and opened the box. "Key rings!"

"Okay, now I need to explain why there are two." He gently took the box away from me.

"All right."

Pulling the first one out, he showed it to me. It was a circle made out of silver.

"This one has your initials on it. See?"

"Yes, it's beautiful." I took it from his hand, placed it in my palm, and looked at it closely. I traced the engraved initials with my finger and then looked back at him.

"I love it. So what's the other one?" I asked, trying to peek into the box.

He grinned at me and then pulled out the second keychain. It was a silver heart. "This one has your initials on one side,"—he turned it over—"and mine on the other. You don't get to use this one until we're officially dating."

For some reason I was surprised that he was still interested in dating me.

"What?"

"Good grief, Riley, you still want to go out with me after all this time? I thought for sure you'd be sick of me by now."

I lay down on my side and looked over at him.

He turned to face me. "Yes, I still wanna go out with you. I'm not anywhere near sick of you. Why is that so hard for you to believe? I don't think I'll ever understand why you constantly doubt how special you are."

"I don't know; I just do."

"You're a keeper, Charlie. You might not realize it, but I sure do."

"We'll see, Riley Bennett. The summer isn't over yet."

"You haven't seen anything yet."

"No?"

"Not even close."

chapter 25

"All right, let's get this road trip started!" Tammy yelled.

"You're driving, right, Riley?" I asked.

"Do you want me to?"

"Yes. I don't trust myself pulling that trailer thing behind us."

He laughed as I handed him the car keys. "I think I drive your car more than you do."

"Don't worry about it. Gramps said that you were covered on his insurance. You can drive, and I'll be in charge of the entertainment."

He cocked an eyebrow. "Entertainment?"

"The music. You can't have a road trip without good music. Isn't that part of the fun?"

"It depends on the music," Tammy interjected.

"I brought all kinds. Hopefully everyone will be pleased."

We said our good-byes to Riley's parents and piled into the car. Anne, Curt, and Matt sat in the back row, and Tess, Tammy, and Chase sat in the middle. Riley apparently didn't trust my ability to give good directions because he asked Chase to sit directly behind him and handed him the directions.

I pushed out my bottom lip and tried to make sad eyes. "I don't get to give you directions?"

"I didn't figure you could do entertainment and directions at once."

"Hmm, good call. You know me well," I admitted.

"I know." He gave me a large grin. "Shall we go?"

"Yes, sir."

As Riley started the car, I began the entertainment portion of our trip. "Let's Go Crazy" by Prince was the first song that I chose to play.

Chase screamed at Riley over the music. "Take I-35 south. We're gonna go past Tinker Air Force Base and then stay on I-40 east until we get to 69 north."

"Gotcha." Riley had already settled in and was heading toward the highway as the rest of us bobbed our heads to the music. Curt and Matt played air guitar as the song came to an end. I followed up the awesome pop song with a classic country hit, "She Thinks My Tractor's Sexy" by Kenny Chesney.

We spent the first half of the drive listening to songs from all different decades and genres. "Bad Medicine" by Bon Jovi got the best reaction from the crowd, so we played it three times in a row, and in general, hair bands from the eighties got the most requests.

After about an hour and a half of driving, Anne decided to start a game of "Let's Get to Know Each Other."

"Okay, first question. Is everyone ready?" she asked.

Riley and I rolled our eyes at each other. "Yes," we answered not so eagerly.

"Just answer if you want to. No pressure or anything. Okay, here goes. What's your favorite thing to do?"

Curt spoke first. "Playing basketball with my friends and kissing."

"Kissing the boys you play basketball with or kissing in general?" Tammy asked.

"Kissing hot girls. Any hot girl," Curt answered, laughing. "It's fun."

"I like to mow the yard," Tess added, "and work in the flowerbeds."

"You have got to be kidding?" Tammy asked with a look of disgust on her face.

"Be nice, Tammy," Anne ordered. "Okay, next question. What's the strangest thing you've ever done?"

"I wear black on the anniversary of Elvis's death," Tess admitted.

"You do or you did once?" Anne asked.

"I do, every year," Tess clarified.

"Good grief. I've never heard of such a thing. He died way before we were alive. Why would you do that?" I asked.

"My grandmother is a big fan. We listen to him all the time. I was kind of raised to be obsessed with him."

Tammy leaned up and looked over at her. "So you up and decided to wear black on the day he died?"

"Uh-huh. It's a respect thing. I like to honor his memory." Tess nodded. "You wanted something strange about me; you got it."

"Well, that'll do it," Anne admitted. "Attie, can you think of anything?"

I responded without thinking through my answer. "I ran away to New York City for two weeks."

"What?" Riley practically screamed. "You ran away? When?"

"In March." I realized I'd opened a can of worms I hadn't intended. "Watch the road, Riley."

"Where did you stay while you were there?" Tammy asked.

"I slept on some guy's couch. I think he was the big brother of some girl in one of my classes or something like that. I didn't really know him; he just let me sleep there."

"You lived with a complete stranger?" Curt yelled from the back row. "How cool is that?"

Riley looked at him through the rearview mirror. "Not cool at all." He shook his head in disgust.

"It wasn't a big deal, Riley. I wasn't in any danger."

"What did you do with all of your time?" Tammy asked.

"I mostly wandered around the city. It was a learning experience if nothing else. Next person, please."

"Who can beat that story?" Matt complained.

"Okay, then here is the next question," Anne said. "Which do you prefer, Kraft Macaroni and Cheese or Velveeta Shells and Cheese?"

Everyone answered Kraft except for Tess, who preferred Velveeta.

"Okay, Tess, why the Velveeta?" I asked.

"The cheese is creamy in Velveeta, and Kraft is that yucky powder stuff that you have to stir and stir to dissolve. It's not even real cheese. I can't believe I even have to explain it to all of you people."

"Velveeta's not real either," Anne added.

"Well, it looks more real than Kraft."

"Okay then, Tess, what's your favorite book?" Anne prodded.

"Any of the *Twilight* books," she answered.

"Are those the vampire books I've heard so much about?" Tammy asked.

"Yes, they're awesome!"

"All the girls at school in New York were into them," I said. "At first I tried to figure out who this Edward guy was that everyone was talking about. I thought he was a student at the school. Someone finally told me that Edward was a vampire in the books."

"My mom won't let me read those," Anne said. "She doesn't like that they're about vampires."

Tess looked stumped. "Oh?"

"Yeah. She's afraid that they glamorize evil or something like that."

"Um, I guess I can sorta see that," Tess considered. "But these vampires are good. They don't kill people or anything."

"Are there such things as good vampires?" Anne asked.

"In this story there are," Tess clarified. "But I guess I can see your mom's point a little bit."

"I'd like to read the books to see what all the excitement is about," I added. "I hear they're good."

"I read them to you," Riley informed me.

"When?"

"When you were asleep in the hospital."

"You did? You visited me in the hospital?"

"Yeah, they're pretty good books. I mean, for girls' stuff they're not bad. You should read them now that you're awake."

"I will. I didn't know you were at the hospital with me. How did I not know that?" Riley and I were now having a private conversation as the others continued the game.

"You were asleep. How could you have known?"

"Asleep is a funny way of saying 'in a coma.' A little less disturbing?"

"Personally, I choose to say you were sleeping." He briefly looked my direction and gave me a wink. "One of my parents or I were always there until they moved you to New York. We didn't want you to be alone."

"I thought I was all alone the entire time."

"Nope."

"Maybe that's where I got accustomed to having you near me when I slept."

"Maybe." He nodded slightly. "I hadn't thought about it."

"No wonder your voice was so familiar to me."

"What do you mean?" he asked.

"I mean, the night of my first nightmare here. Without even opening my eyes, I knew it was you who was talking to me. I recognized your voice, but I wasn't sure why."

"Well, those books are about five hundred pages each, so you heard my voice a lot."

"I can't believe you did that. No normal teenage boy would sit in a hospital room with some dumb girl in a coma and read to her."

"Sure they would." He shrugged. "I didn't mind."

"Other than football practice, we never saw Riley last summer," Matt added from the backseat. "He was either heading to or coming back from the hospital."

Tess sat in a trance. "That's the sweetest thing I've ever heard."

"It's sweet." Anne cried. She was a crier like me.

"Everybody shush," Riley ordered. "It's not a big deal; any of you would have done the same freakin' thing."

"No," Matt admitted. "I hate to say it, but I don't know that I would."

"I hope we all would if we were in that situation." Tammy became serious. "That's a big deal, guys. Here Attie thought she'd been left all alone, but Riley's family was there the entire time. It's amazing."

"Oh, Charlie, please don't cry; it isn't that big of a deal."

"It is a big deal. I can't even tell you what it means to me to know you guys were there." I looked out the window trying to hide my tears. "I wish my dad would have left me here. Whether I was awake or not, he didn't visit me once." I talked more to myself than to Riley.

The car grew silent.

"Well, thanks a lot, Debbie Downer," Curt complained.

"I know, I'm sorry." I wiped away my tears and took a deep breath. "Okay, Anne, next question."

"All right, let's lighten it up a bit. What's your most embarrassing moment?"

Tammy went first. "My freshman year I was on the pom squad at my old school. We had a huge pep rally, and after our performance one of the girls on my team came over and asked me why I wasn't wearing my bloomers."

"Cool, I bet there was extra excitement during that pep rally," Matt said.

Tess offered to go next. "Well, mine is sorta like Tammy's."

"Yours isn't a thing like Tammy's," Chase corrected.

"You hush, Chase! It sorta is. I was walking down the hall last year, and Jason Cleaver slipped on something…"

Chase was already laughing. He'd obviously witnessed the embarrassing moment live.

She continued. "Anyway, he reached out to grab something to keep himself from falling, and somehow he got the waist of the back of my jeans. Instead of keeping himself up, he ripped the back of my jeans completely off of me. The two halves totally ripped apart, and I was left standing there with no pants on. It was horrible."

The entire car filled with laughter. Personally, I laughed so hard I thought I was going to wet my pants.

"Chase just stood there laughing at me. He didn't even try to help."

"I was in shock!" Chase attempted to defend himself. "I didn't know what to do."

"You could have given me a jacket or something. I ran off to the bathroom and waited until someone brought me some clothes. It was the most horrible and frightening experience of my life."

"I guess now we know why our parents tell us to make sure to always wear clean underwear," Tammy said dryly.

After several minutes of hysterics, everyone calmed down enough for the next person to share their story.

"I'll give Riley's!" Curt announced.

Riley rolled his eyes. "I'm sure you will."

"When we were in middle school, sixth grade, Riley used to pretend that he was sick all the time so he wouldn't have to go to school. One day he really was sick, but his parents didn't believe him, so they made him go to school anyway." Curt's voice grew louder and more excited as he told the story.

"Close your ears, Charlie," Riley suggested. "You'll never look at me the same after you hear this."

"Sorry, Riley, I can't wait to hear it." I urged Curt to continue.

"Well, right in the middle of third hour, Riley got diarrhea all over himself."

"I remember that!" Anne said.

I failed miserably at being sympathetic. "Oh, Riley, that's so pathetic."

Riley tried to stay focused on driving as he laughed at the memory. "I did; I crapped all over myself. It was completely disgusting."

"No, what made it worse was Sheila Bright," Matt added to the story. "She was sitting next to him, and she got so grossed out that she puked all over the floor!"

Curt continued, but he was laughing so hard that he could barely speak. "Half the class started dry heaving and stuff. It was nasty. Everyone practically trampled each other trying to get out of the room."

Riley finished giving the account of events. "Everyone including the teacher—"

"Mr. Bell," Anne interjected.

"Yeah, Mr. Bell. They all left Sheila and me standing there in the room all by ourselves. I was standing there with crap running down my legs, and Sheila had puke all down the front of her clothes and in her shoes. We both started crying. It was horrible."

"What did you do?" I asked.

"I don't remember. I think I was so traumatized that I went into shock. I honestly don't remember anything else."

I gave him a pat on the shoulder. "Poor Riley."

"I came home and begged my dad to let me change schools. Of course he said no and made me march back the very next day. When I got there, someone had taped diapers all over the front of my locker."

"We never did figure out who did that."

"You shut up, Curt," Riley shouted. "I know for a fact it was you."

Curt laughed. "That's what friends are for, Riley. We're there to keep you grounded."

chapter 26

After losing and regaining the nerve several times, I decided to wear the bikini that Marme bought me. I reasoned that it might as well get some use. Plus, everyone was going to see my scars soon enough anyway; there would be no hiding them in my cheer uniform.

The girls and I took turns changing clothes in the car. As three girls held up blankets, the other fumbled around and put her bathing suit on.

After we piled out of the car, I noticed Riley give a double take in my direction. His shoulders straightened and his chest puffed out as his mouth hung open in a large smile. Feeling myself begin to blush, I threw shorts on over my bikini bottoms and then put on my old sneakers.

Riley joined me on the rear bumper of the car. "Dang, you look remarkable."

I playfully pushed him away. "Whatever."

"Seriously, your body's amazing."

"Riley," I scolded.

He leaned toward me and spoke softly into my ear. "Surely you didn't think you'd be able to wear that and it wouldn't get my attention." His breath was warm on my face, and I could smell his cologne. My mind blurred.

"It's just a bathing suit; everyone wears them. Besides, your mom picked it out."

He sat back and looked at me with a devious grin. "My mom?"

"Yes."

"Sweet! Remind me to thank her later." He chuckled, got up, and walked away, but before he made it too far, I jumped onto his back and wrapped my legs around his waist. "Keep your eyes to yourself, Riley Bennett," I teased into his ear.

"You're smoke, Charlie. I'm not gonna be able to keep my eyes off of you."

I jumped off his back. "Flattery will get you nowhere."

"Flattery?" He turned to face me. "You think I'm trying to flatter you? I have a hard enough time controlling myself around you when you're completely clothed."

He grabbed me by the waist, pulled me to him, and for the first time in my life, a boy's hands were touching my bare back. His warm touch and fiery gaze caused my heart to race, and I instinctively pressed my body completely against his as a gentle moan escaped his lips.

He placed his cheek against the side of my head. "You're killing me here, Charlie."

That made two of us.

His fingers skimmed the surface of my skin. "I can't take my hands off of you." His confession was pained. "You feel amazing."

I could feel his heart beating through his chest. "Riley..."

"Say something to make me walk away."

"I don't want to."

The skin of his cheek gently skimmed mine as he spoke. "We can't do this. I can't. You're gonna have to make me walk away."

"No. I want you to kiss me again."

He pulled away from me and shoved his hands into his pockets. "No, Charlie."

I stepped toward him, but he backed away. "You don't want to kiss me again?"

"Shhh." He looked around to make sure nobody was paying attention and then walked around to the side of the car farthest away from our friends. I followed. "Of course I want to, but we can't do this." He was practically crying. "I promised myself and my dad that I wouldn't do this. You have to help me keep that promise."

"Oh, all right!" I kicked the car tire, threw my back against the side of the car, and crossed my arms across my stomach.

"Don't start a temper tantrum here, Charlie."

"Fine!"

Removing his hands from his pockets, he clasped them behind his head and started pacing. "Remind me, when does your dad get here?"

"Two weeks," I grumbled.

He kicked the dirt before throwing his hands on his waist and turning to face me. "This is freakin' agony."

"Who's throwing the temper tantrum now?" I asked. "I just wanted you to kiss me for my birthday. That's all."

"Your birthday?"

I shook my head. "It's stupid, I know. So shoot me."

"No. I mean, when's your birthday?"

"Tomorrow."

"Tomorrow?" he shouted. "You didn't tell me your birthday was tomorrow." His pacing quickened. "I'm such a jerk. How did I not know your birthday was tomorrow?"

"So."

"I didn't get you anything. You love presents, and I don't even have anything to give you on your birthday." He slapped himself in the head. "I'm such a heel."

"I told you what I want."

His swift movement stopped, and he turned to look at me at me again. "What? You want me to kiss you?"

"Yes."

"For your birthday present?" His voice was like ice.

"Yes."

"That's not fair. I'll give you anything but that."

"Why?"

"Because to give you what you want requires me to break a promise. It's not fair."

My heart sank. "Oh."

He walked over to me and grabbed my hands. "You have no idea how hard this is for me. Please, please help me make it two more weeks."

I felt my face scrunch. My disappointment was growing, but I bit my thumbnail so that I wouldn't say anything I might regret later.

"Please. In two weeks I'll kiss you like crazy, I promise. You'll probly have to peel me off of you. But for right now, no matter what I say or do, you have to keep me from kissing you—or doing anything for that matter."

I started coming to my senses. "You're right."

"I am? No. Right, I am, I'm right." He rolled his eyes.

"At least I got kissed once before I turned seventeen. It's a good thing you're so darned noble."

He wrapped his arms around my neck and hugged me close to him. "It's too bad you're so darned irresistible." He slowly kissed me on the tip of the nose and then pressed his forehead to mine. "In two weeks I won't mind that you're so alluring. At least, I won't mind as much."

"I'll do better next time. I won't give in."

"Hopefully there won't be a next time. It's all too much." He kissed me on the forehead again. "Now let's go have some fun and forget about all of this. All right?"

"All right."

"Make sure you wear lots of sunscreen. You haven't been out in the sun for a while."

"Yes, sir."

• •

With camp settled and kayaks rented, we finally made our way onto the water. We took the "Round-the-Mountain-Trip," which lasted about seven hours, and divided up into four kayaks so we could switch riders and all have the opportunity to share kayaks with each other. The scenery was beautiful, and other than the boys tipping the kayaks over on several occasions, the journey was very peaceful. We all stayed close together, and our conversations flowed right along with the water. With each passing moment I was crazier about my new friends. They were true and genuine people who weren't trying to put on a show for anyone. Everyone was free to be themselves, and I felt more comfortable with this group than I had with any other.

At one point when Tess and I were sharing a kayak, Curt tipped us over, and somehow I got caught under the water with the kayak on top of me. I flailed around until a pair of arms grabbed hold of me and pulled me out from under the boat. Coughing and sputtering, I looked up through the mat of hair that stuck to my face and realized that my rescuer was Riley—of course.

"Are you my very own personal lifeguard?" I dunked my head into the water so that the hair would unstick itself from my face.

"I'm on duty twenty-four/seven." He picked me up and tossed me back onto the upright kayak. "Now stay put. I don't wanna chase you down the river."

"Tell your boys to quit tipping my kayak and that shouldn't be a problem."

"Will do." He waded over to the kayak he was sharing with Anne and hopped in.

"Is that a snake?" she asked him as she pointed at a tree.

"Probly. They're everywhere." His voice was calm.

"What!" She shrieked. "We've been on this water for five hours, and nobody told me there are snakes in the trees!"

I frantically looked around at the trees surrounding me.

"They're in the water too." Curt laughed.

"What?" I screamed as I grasped onto the sides of the boat.

"Relax. They stay away from humans," Chase said before shooting Curt an evil glare.

"What? It's true," Curt said back to Chase.

"It may be true," Chase was talking slowly and quietly, "but you don't always have to share everything you know."

"Oh yes, he does," Tammy added from the seat she occupied in the kayak with Curt. "If my life's in danger, I need to know it."

Chase looked over at Tammy. "Your life is not in danger. There are hundreds of people on this river today. The snakes are hiding away. Plus, it's too hot for them to be out and about."

"Yeah, they wait until dark to come out," Matt added as he gave an evil laugh.

"Matt!" Chase scolded. "Enough, you guys are gonna have these girls scared to death."

"I'm already there," I admitted.

"Me too," Anne and Tammy added.

"You girls are fine, I promise." Chase glanced at each of us. "Let's enjoy the rest of the river, all right?"

We all agreed and tried to push the thought of snakes in trees out of our minds. I glanced over at Riley and caught him smirking at me. When he realized I caught him, he shrugged his shoulders and then put his oar in the water and paddled.

After seven long hours, our float trip finally ended. It was a long seven hours, and I was exhausted. My muscles hadn't ever had such a workout and were already starting to ache. I never dreamed that floating down a river could be so much work. I envisioned that we would sit back and relax as the boat drifted down the waterway, but that wasn't quite how it happened. The kayak drug on the river bottom several times, so we would get out and push the boat until the water was deep enough to float again. All in all, it was a good workout. I looked forward to doing it again the next day but wasn't looking forward to the hike that we planned for later this evening. I was tired enough as it was and could only think of resting.

chapter 27

(Riley)

"So, Riley, I hear Tiffany's pretty upset with you," Matt informed me.

"Me, why?"

"You haven't called her or anything in a while. I guess she was under the impression that you two were an item."

"Well, she's delusional then because I never said we were."

"Didn't you guys date pretty hot and heavy there for a while?" Curt asked.

"Hot and heavy petting maybe." Matt laughed.

I ignored him. "We went out a handful of times before prom and then twice after. It wasn't any big deal. I wasn't that into her; it was just kinda convenient." I didn't like the word *convenient* as it left my mouth. It sounded cheap.

"Yeah, Curt, now he's got Attie in the room with him every night. Talk about convenient."

"That's a lot different," I tried to correct him.

Matt grinned at Curt. "Sure it is."

Chase didn't say anything as he sat looking down at his shoes.

"Come on, Riley." Curt laughed. "You've got a sixteen-year-old girl living in your house, sleeping next to you every night, and you're trying to convince us that you don't have a little fun? We know you better than that, my friend."

"I would think it would be nearly impossible to control—with her walking around in a towel or nightie," Matt said.

"I'd have done it in every room by now," Curt added. "Not that you'd tell us if you did."

"Shut up, Curt," I snapped. "Look, I'm not gonna tell you again that it isn't like that; now drop it."

"Yet, you mean, right," Matt chided. "It isn't like that *yet*."

"Just give him time, Matt. Give him time. He'll get 'er done," Curt continued.

I stood to walk off and told Chase that I was gonna check on Attie.

"Ooh, Riley, save me, I can't sleep," Matt teased in a girl's voice.

"I'm sorry I even told you," I shouted.

"Dude, we were just fooling around; lighten up," Curt pouted.

"I don't see that topic as funny," Chase said without looking up. Matt became angry. "It was a joke, Chase."

"And I'm saying it wasn't funny," Chase said as he got up. I gave him a grateful smile, and he shrugged before walking toward his tent.

• •

Still wearing her swimsuit, Attie was lying in our tent on top of her sleeping bag.

"Whaddya doing, Riley?" she whispered without opening her eyes.

"Looking at you," I said as I lay down next to her.

She smiled, but her eyes remained closed. "Enjoying the scenery?"

"It's by far the prettiest I've seen all day. You're perfection personified."

"Hmm, good line."

"I think I heard it in a movie."

"I'm sure you did."

"Go to sleep, Charlie. I'll stay; you don't need to worry."

"Thank you."

The small bathing suit didn't hide her scars, and I was proud of her for wearing it. For me, it was confirmation about the comfort level that she felt with her new group of friends. The raised lines were pinker, more sunburned than the rest of her body due to their first real exposure to the outside world. A thick scar ran from her belly button up to just below her ribcage, and then another one started what looked to be between her breasts and up to the bottom of her throat. There was also a scar from the tube they stuck into her neck. Her left arm, the one closest to me, sustained the most damage. It was the arm that kept her pinned into the car. There were several small scars, but the largest ran down the outside of her tricep. She tucked the other arm behind her head so I couldn't see how much damage it suffered.

As if I held a piece of charcoal in my fingers ready to sketch, I reached over and traced one of the small scars near her shoulder. I imagined myself drawing her, battle scars and all.

The small raised lines were fascinating to me. They were a reminder of all she'd gone through before she walked back into my life three months before. She'd fought back and won, and added to all of the other amazing things about her, the scars made her more beautiful.

The more my fingers traced her skin, the faster my heart beat. Touching her in that way was euphoric. I'd hugged her close to me during her nightmares and held her hand briefly, but aside from earlier in the day, I'd never touched her like this. She lay there completely trusting and vulnerable.

"You better be careful, Riley Bennett," she whispered while smiling out of the corner of her mouth. Her eyes were still closed.

"What?" I teased back. "I'm sketching; leave me alone."

"Sketching?"

"In my head. I'm memorizing so I can recreate it later. If you don't hush, I'll have to start all over again."

"Hmm."

Without thinking, I bent down and softly kissed a scar on her shoulder. As soon as my lips touched her skin, my mind went blank.

"Riley." She gave me a small warning. "You told me not to let you do anything like this. You're playing with fire."

My lips were warm. "Tell me about it."

I slowly kissed each scar while my left hand made its way to her stomach. As soon as my fingers touched her skin, she shivered, and feeling her respond to my touch in that way thrilled me. It was electrifying.

The fingertip of my ring finger slowly circled her belly button, and then, when it found the beginning of the scar, it traveled up her body. As my fingers explored, my lips made their way to her neck.

"Riley, you better stop."

I ignored her.

My fingers left her skin and immediately felt cold but warmed again as soon as they found the skin just below her neck. My fingers and lips were close to concentrating on the same point on her body as my blood inched closer to its boiling point.

"Riley," she said more sternly, "really, Riley, stop. You said yourself that we can't do this."

"Okay, I'll stop," I whispered into the curve of her neck but didn't follow through. My fingers now followed the scar's trail south, and just as my fingers felt like they were about to burst into flames, my palm accidentally grazed her chest.

"Riley!" she yelled while hitting my hand away and sitting up. "What are you doing?"

"Just playing a little, having some fun." I tried to pull her back onto the ground.

"Don't touch me."

"What's the big deal, Attie? You need to learn how to have some fun."

"Fun? That kind of fun?" she asked.

I grinned and rubbed her shoulder. "Why not? I was enjoying it, and I think you were too."

She pulled her shoulder away. "I knew it!" she yelled, sounding hurt.

"Knew what?"

"I would become another game. The true player just showed his cards."

"Relax, Attie, it's not like I was tearing your clothes off or anything. God, lighten up! I was touching you; that's it."

"Really?" she yelled as she pulled a pair of shorts on over her bathing suit. "If I would have let you continue, would you have, or would you have stopped on your own?" She threw on a shirt and glared over at me.

"I would have stopped."

"You're sure of that?" Her stare made me uncomfortable, so I looked away. "I'm such an idiot. I allowed you to sleep next to me for months, believing you cared about me. What? You were getting me right where you wanted me? Buttering me up, winning me over? Conquer the virgin?" The look on her face was one of betrayal. "Guess what? Game over, and I lost."

Her words stung.

"Charlie," I said softly.

"Don't call me that. Don't you dare call me that," she exclaimed before crawling out of the tent.

My anger turned to grief as I realized I'd hurt her. I betrayed her trust, and worse, I tried to make her feel bad for not letting me have my way with her.

I looked toward the opening of the tent and saw her shoes sitting just inside the flap; she hadn't taken them with her when she ran out. Crawling over, I grabbed them and then made my way out of the tent after her.

Tammy, Tess, and Anne turned to look at me.

"What did you do?" Anne asked in an accusatory tone.

"We had a little disagreement; that's all."

"It didn't look little to me," Tammy said.

Just then Chase came into view. "I didn't see her. Are you sure she ran that way?"

The girls nodded.

"She couldn't have gone far. I've got her shoes." I knew it sounded stupid as soon as the words left my mouth.

"I doubt she was thinking about shoes," Chase said bluntly. "Dude, she's gone."

Angry, I yelled her name and insisted that she return.

"Yeah, that's gonna draw her back," Tammy said as she walked my direction. "I wanna know what you did."

All eyes were on me, and their knowing stares caused shame to overtake me. I slapped my hands over my eyes. "I hurt her."

"What did you do?" Tammy yelled.

"I got a little carried away. I think I scared her."

"Riley!" Anne screamed.

I lowered my hands and looked back at Tammy. "I was mean to her. I told her that she needed to lighten up and learn how to have fun."

Tammy's hand reached my face, and my cheek instantly stung. "I'm sorry."

"Why are you apologizing to me?" she screamed. "You need to apologize to Attie."

She started to say more, but Anne stopped her. "That's enough, Tammy."

"I will, Tammy, I will apologize. I'll never treat her like that again; I give you my word. I don't know what came over me."

"I have a few ideas," she replied, her voice still cold.

"Tammy, please," Tess said. "This isn't helping; he feels horrible. Look at him."

Tammy didn't budge. "Oh, I am."

"I'm sorry." I wanted her to believe me. I was sorrier than she could ever know.

Her face softened. "You better go find her. It's gonna get dark before long." Turning, she marched toward her tent and ducked inside before I could say another word.

Chase was packing two backpacks with water, snacks, and a blanket. He threw Matt a walkie-talkie. "Matt, you and Curt stay here with the girls. Radio us if she comes back. Riley, put her shoes in this bag," he said, throwing the pack at me and then turning to Tess. "Go get her jacket."

She ran into the tent and quickly returned with Attie's OU sweatshirt. Chase shoved it into the pack and zipped it up. Grabbing the compass and two flashlights, he looked at me. "Let's go."

• •

(Attie)

My mind was void of thought. All I could do was watch my feet as they took each step. My pace was quick and frantic, and I realized I was trying to run, run away. I wanted to escape.

My feet froze just as my next step would have taken me off a ledge and several feet into the river. The water flowing below me was mesmerizing.

I spotted an insect as it fell into the water. It moved with the current as if it understood that the force propelling it forward was more powerful than it was. The bug had realized its fate and wasn't trying to fight back. To fight the surge would have been useless and exhausting, more than something its size could muster.

I felt compassion for the insignificant creature.

But as quickly as it started, the struggle was over. The current had somehow carried the bug against a rock onto the bank of the river, and after a small rest, as if it realized that it was on a firm foundation, it went on with its journey.

Maybe it hadn't been so insignificant after all.

Goose bumps covered my body as I felt someone walk up and stand next to me.

• •

(Riley)

An hour rushed by, and the more we searched, the more frantic I became.

We called for Attie over and over again, but her voice never called back. Each time her name left my lips, I thought of the look on her face before she left the tent.

"Oh God," I cried out, "I'm sorry. I'm so sorry. Please keep her safe. Please, please keep her safe."

Of all people, I, the person she called her best friend, hurt her, and if my immaturity ended up causing her even more pain, I wouldn't be able to forgive myself.

Chase grabbed my shoulder. "You need to calm down. It's gonna be okay. We'll find her, you'll work it out, and everything will be fine."

"I can't believe I hurt her. I promised her that I wouldn't hurt her again."

"I know." He turned to continue walking but then changed direction and walked directly up to me. "I'm your friend, Riley, but I'm telling you right now, you hurt her like that again and it won't be Tammy hitting you. Do you understand?"

"Yes," I whispered.

"Let's go." He walked off again.

I'd been to the river dozens of times, but nothing that we passed looked familiar. Attie had never been here, and more than likely, she was terrified. She probably didn't even think that I was looking for her.

Another hour passed, and we still hadn't seen any sign of her. The forest grew darker, and with no city lights to illuminate the night sky, I realized the chances of finding her were miniscule.

"Did you hear that?" Chase whispered.

"What?"

"Shhh, listen."

I stood still and concentrated on hearing the sounds around me, but other than grasshoppers chirping, there was no sound.

"I'm almost positive I heard a girl's voice scream 'stop.'"

Every hair on my body stood on end, and my bones rattled. My stomach seized just before I vomited.

I'd never been more fearful of the unknown in my life. What if someone was hurting her?

Chase pointed to our right. "It came from that direction."

"Charlie!" I screamed while hunching over as my stomach continued to contract. "Charlie!"

"We have to keep walking."

"I can't move, Chase. I swear to God I can't move."

"You have to." Kneeling down next to me, he squeezed my shoulder. "She needs you. You've got to pull yourself together."

My body went numb, but I soon followed the sound of his footprints in front of me.

After several minutes, Chase stopped and grabbed me. I followed his gaze to the ground. There on a rock was a red footprint.

"Blood," he announced. "Riley, she's hurt."

The dizziness became overpowering, my vision turned spotty, and my mouth watered. I was about to vomit again.

. . . .

(Attie)

Jesus spoke from beside me. "Are we going to talk about this?"

Anger consumed my body, and I felt like being pigheaded. "About what?"

"About what happened with Riley?"

"He was being a jerk. Period, end of story. He isn't any different than the rest of them."

"Well, that's a mighty big statement coming from someone who has no idea what they're talking about." Jesus's words were sharp and crisp in my ears, but I pretended not to hear.

"It's like nobody has morals anymore," I yelled back. "Boys are all about getting laid."

"Hey!" Jesus shouted, causing me to flinch. "You don't get to make that judgment about people, and certainly not about Riley."

My body stood still, but I turned my face away from His voice.

"Since when did I give you permission to judge others? To assume you know the condition of their heart?" His arms folded across his chest. "Tell me, Attie, who are you to judge?"

I started to defend myself. "I'm not judging Riley! I'm hurt by what he did, what he was thinking."

"So you're a mind reader now? You have no clue. You don't know what Riley was thinking."

"I can assume." I sounded full of myself but didn't care.

"No, you can't."

My jaw went firm; I turned my head and glared at the Lord.

"You can be angry with me all you want, but you don't get to win this one. You're not right."

I looked away again and rolled my eyes.

Jesus continued, "Have you ever thought about what it is like to be Riley? To be a boy his age that's trying to do the right thing, to make moral choices? To follow the demands that I've placed on him? He's a boy who is trying his hardest to remain pure, but you know what, Attie? The odds are against him."

I glanced at him out of the corner of my eyes and then looked away again.

"Society today has made it virtually impossible for him. Sex is everywhere. What was created to be something loving between a husband and wife has now become defiled and thrown in his face on a regular basis. It's in almost every movie, television show, and commercial he sees. It is in almost every magazine advertisement or article, it is sung about in songs, made fun of and cheapened in jokes, and written about on practically every bathroom stall he enters. The Internet is a trap because access to pornography is at his fingertips, and he can't even go to the mall without walking past Victoria's Secret and the large posters of women in nothing but a bra and underwear.

"Have you ever been in a locker room with fifty other teenage boys, Attie? Had to sit and listen to everyone's sex stories and wonder what you're missing out on? Question whether or not it's worth the struggle? To have your friends not only encourage you to have sex but badger you when you don't? Have you walked in those shoes, Attie?"

"No," I muttered.

There was more. "His behavior up to this point has been exemplary. I've been proud of his commitment. Then he plans this trip ... for you. He wanted to show you a good time, give you a new experience, and relax and enjoy himself as well. But all of a sudden, the girl he's passionate about, whom he's been fighting a physical desire for, walks into his arms barely dressed."

I snapped my head around to look at Jesus. I was fuming. "So you're telling me this is my fault?"

"No, Attie. Riley is responsible for his own thoughts and actions. I'm disappointed in him and am dealing with him about it right now. I'll handle him, and he's very open to my correction. But you didn't help."

I rolled my eyes and turned away from him again. "Spare me."

"No, thank you, I don't think I will," he replied. "I won't be sparing you at all.

"You're so hopeful for your own Mr. Darcy, your fantasy life, that you can't even handle reality when it slaps you in the face.

"How easy do you think it would have been for your Mr. Darcy to stay noble and pure if he lived today? If Elizabeth made suggestive and flirty jokes, touched him seductively, and dressed in clothes that left little to imagination?

"You don't get to have it both ways, Attie. You can't expect Riley, or anybody, to resist constant temptation like that. You've set your expectations at an impossible level, and you're not being fair."

"So what, I'm supposed to dress like a nun?"

"No. But if you care about him, about being a friend, you can stop judging him and try to make it a little easier for him. He's helping you fight your battle; shouldn't you return the favor?"

My shoulders slumped. "It isn't my responsibility to help Riley through his lust issues."

"No, it's not," Jesus agreed with me. "That's my job. What I'm asking—no, telling you to do is have some grace. Let me deal with Riley and his demons. You've got plenty of your own demons to confront."

"What?" I turned to face him. "My own demons? I don't even know what you're talking about."

"Oh really?" He became rigid, and the corners of his eyes tightened. "So you're going to sit up there on your high horse and look down at everyone else and their issues? I don't think so.

"People are screwed up, Attie. That's why I came to save them, to save their souls. People are stubborn, prideful, envious, lustful, unloving, uncaring, self-serving…well, I could go on for hours, but I believe you get the point.

"Everyone sins. Everyone messes up, and everyone you know and love will hurt and disappoint you at some point—possibly multiple times.

"And guess what, Attie? Newsflash, you're human as well, which means that *you* are all those things and *you* will hurt and disappoint people as well. So you better start learning how to give some grace and forgive people because one day you're going to need them to do the same for you."

"I do give grace! I do forgive! You can't tell me I don't!"

"Really?" he asked.

I stood my ground. "Yes."

He gave me a disgusted laugh and shook his head. "It's no wonder you have nightmares."

"What?"

"You're being eaten up by your own demons. *They* haunt you, not memories."

My body started shaking. "I thought you knew everything; you don't know anything!" I said before starting to walk away.

"What about unforgiveness, Attie?" he called after me. "We can start there; it seems to be the biggest demon you've got."

"No!" I screamed over my shoulder as I continued to walk away from him.

"Don't you take another step," he ordered.

I stopped. My breathing was labored, and my shoulders were heaving. My jaw tightened as I slowly turned to face him. It was as if I could no longer control my body; I could feel the evil way in which I looked at him but couldn't stop.

"What about the man who hit the car? Mitchell, are you going to forgive him?"

It felt as though I'd been slapped.

"Or your mom? Are you going to forgive her for not paying attention?"

Tears welled up in my eyes, and I shook my head. "Don't."

"Or Melody for distracting her?"

A groan left my body as the tears overflowed.

"Or yourself? Are you going to forgive yourself for surviving?"

My entire body trembled. "Don't," I pled. "Please don't."

"What about your dad, Attie?"

My fists clutched as I lunged toward him. "Don't you bring my dad into this!"

"Are you going to forgive him for not being there for you in the hospital? For deserting you when you needed him most?"

I covered my ears with my hands. "Stop!" I screamed. "Don't say it! Please don't say it!"

"Are you going to forgive your dad for shipping you back to Oklahoma—"

I shook my head back and forth. "Please don't do this!"

"—for sending you here so he wouldn't have to see your face every day and be reminded of your mother?"

My legs went numb, and I fell to the ground. "Why are you doing this to me? Why are you trying to hurt me?"

Wailing, my cries were uncontrollable, and I felt as if I were going to die from the pain. I wanted to die and escape the grief.

Jesus slowly sat down next to me. "I'm not trying to hurt you, Attie." His voice became gentle. "But you can't fight an enemy that you aren't willing to look at."

He sat silent for a few moments before continuing. "Riley's presence only seems to keep them away, but the demons are still there. They're patiently waiting; they know that he won't be able to protect you forever. Besides, Riley can't fight your demons for you any more than you can fight his for him."

I hunched over into a ball and wept.

"Attie, you won't find peace until you fight this battle."

"I'm tired. I don't have the strength to fight anymore."

"I'll give you the strength."

"I don't know how to do this."

"I do."

. . . .

(Riley)

"Riley, I saw her. She's through those trees in the clearing." Bringing the walkie-talkie to his mouth, Chase spoke into it, "We found her."

I turned in the right direction but couldn't make my feet move. I'd searched for Attie for more than two hours, but now that I knew that she was nearby, I was terrified to see her.

Composing myself, I made my way to the clearing and found Attie standing on a large rock with her back to me.

"Charlie?" My fears escalated as soon as she turned around. "You're bleeding; you're hurt." I walked toward her, but scared that she might run off again, I stopped myself.

"I'm all right," she insisted. "They're just scrapes; that's all." Concern filled her face. "Riley, you're shaking … and have you been crying? Are you all right?"

I inched closer to her. "We've been looking for you for hours. I … I … was scared to death."

"I shouldn't have taken off like that." Her voice was weak. "I'm sorry I worried you."

"No, I'm sorry," I whispered. Beginning to reach out to her, I stopped myself again. "Please forgive me, Charlie."

Attie started to cry and stumbled toward me with outstretched arms. As if given permission, I ran to her, pulled her close, and gently wrapped my arms around her.

"I can't believe you came looking for me," she whispered.

"Of course I did."

"Not everyone would do that; thank you."

A small laugh escaped my throat. "You're thanking me? It's my fault you're out here."

"And if you hadn't felt like it was your fault? What then?"

"I still would've been out here looking for you. Don't think you can run off and I'm not gonna come after you. I'm practically obsessed, remember?" Tightening my arms around her, I kissed the top of her head again and again.

"Riley?"

"Yes?"

"You're hurting me."

"I know; it won't happen again."

"No. I mean, right now. My cuts, you're hurting me."

I dropped my arms. "I'm sorry."

"I think I just need to sit down for a second."

I helped her to the ground and then sat down. Looking over my shoulder, I watched as Chase sat down a bit of a distance away.

I looked back at Attie and cringed. "Your poor face," I said, reaching over and gently touching her chin. Small cuts covered her face, and blood had dried as it ran from each injury. "What were you thinking running off like that? What if we couldn't have found you?"

"I don't think I *was* thinking—not about that anyway."

"What were you thinking about?"

"What a jerk you were."

"That makes two of us. That's all I've thought about since you ran out of the tent."

"Thanks again for looking for me. I honestly didn't expect you to come after me, especially after the things I said to you."

"I acted completely inappropriately and caught you completely off guard; of course you acted the way you did. It makes me sick to think that I made you doubt how I feel about you or that I planned what happened. This isn't a game for me, I promise."

"I hate to interrupt, guys," Chase said, walking up behind us, "but it's starting to get dark. Attie, what did you do to yourself?" he asked, squatting down next to her.

"I wasn't paying any attention to what I was doing. I guess I was running into branches, and honestly, I never realized I didn't have shoes on until now."

He looked at her feet and winced. "They're cut up. We'll have to take turns carrying you."

"Good grief, you guys do not have to carry me. I'm the moron who ran off without shoes on. Let me suffer the consequences."

"No," Chase and I answered simultaneously.

"It's about to get late; we better go ahead and head back to camp. We can clean you up when we get there."

I still hadn't completely composed myself, and I was filled with the guilt of knowing that I'd caused her emotional and physical pain.

"Riley," Chase said, putting his hand on my shoulder, "she's all right; everything's okay. You need to snap out of it so we can get back to camp."

I sat in a daze until Attie's voice broke through. "Riley? I'm not upset with you. Don't feel guilty; it was me that overreacted."

My eyes found her face as she smiled at me.

I stood. "We can talk about it later. Let's get you back to camp."

chapter 28

"Oh, Attie, are you all right?" Tess cried.

"I'm fine. I look worse than I feel."

Tess shook her head. "I'm not buying it."

"Where did we put the first aid kit, Tess?" Chase asked.

"I think it's on the floorboard of the car."

Matt ran toward the car. "I'll get it."

"Actually, Matt, will you lie the seats down in the back?" Chase asked. "We'll be able to see better if we clean her up in there."

Although I didn't wanna let go of her, I placed Attie into the car. She'd been on my back since we left the rock, so I hadn't seen her face in over an hour. Upon seeing her, I started crying again. Her feet were badly cut up, and her face was starting to swell.

Chase grabbed my arm. "Okay, why don't you girls get her cleaned up? I need to talk to Riley."

The girls filed into the car as I followed Chase out by the river.

"Thanks for everything, Chase." We sat down on the edge of the water. "I don't know what I would have done if you hadn't been here. I don't think I would have been able to find her on my own. Actually, I know I wouldn't."

"Sure."

As we sat watching the water, I could hear the girls' voices coming from the car but wasn't able to understand what they were saying. Matt and Curt were arguing over a game of dominos.

"You think I'm a total jerk, don't you?" I asked over the sound of the river.

"Nah, dude. Trust me, you aren't the only guy who ever messed up and treated a girl like that. We've all done it, but I'll still hit you if you do it again."

"It won't happen again," I assured him.

"I know," he said, nodding his head. "But here's my question. Why do you let the guys say those things about her? My friends would never talk about Tess like that. I wouldn't allow it."

I was stunned.

"You're setting yourself up for frustration if you let them harass you like that all the time. Either they don't know you as well as they think they do, or you've changed and they haven't realized it. Either way, you've got to put a stop to it. If you let them talk about her like that, they're gonna think she's just another girl you're fooling around with."

"That's not the case."

"I know that, but I don't think they do. Is that the kind of girl you want them to think she is? You want them thinking about Attie what they think about Tiffany or some of the other girls around the school?"

The thought of it made my skin crawl. "No."

"Well, you're letting them."

"I hadn't ever thought about it."

"Look, doing the right thing is hard enough as it is. Hanging around people who constantly try to bring you down or encourage you to do things you know you shouldn't doesn't seem very beneficial to me."

"They've been my friends for a long time, Chase. I can't cut them off because they don't see things the way I do."

"Okay, so don't cut them off, but you can at least ask them to respect your choices. If they can't do that, then what kind of friends are they? Iron sharpens iron, and those guys are wearing you down, so I'd venture to guess they aren't iron."

I nodded. "I see that now."

We sat as I processed all that Chase said. I couldn't blame my friends for the way I behaved, but the constant taunting didn't help my resolve. I needed to make sure they realized that Attie was different. She was important to me. If they couldn't change the way they talked about her, I would be forced to choose, and they would lose.

He stood and threw a rock into the river. "Should we go check on Attie?"

"Yep."

"No more crying, okay?" Chase teased.

"I'm not making any promises. The girl brings it out in me."

. . . .

Anne and Tess were cleaning Attie's cuts with disinfectant, and Tammy followed behind them blowing on the wounds to try to keep them from stinging.

"I'm about to hyperventilate," Tammy said, breathless. "I need to clean, and somebody else needs to blow."

Anne raised her hand. "I'll blow."

"This whole thing blows if you ask me," Tess mumbled.

"I couldn't agree more," I interrupted. "Wonder what kind of jerk could have caused all this."

"A big one," Tammy answered.

"Tammy," Anne scolded.

"Well, he asked."

"She's right, Anne; I did ask."

Anne handed me some disinfectant. "We haven't started on her feet yet. Why don't you?"

Chase brought me some bottled water and then stood with the lantern so that I could see while I washed her feet. No matter how gentle I was, it caused Attie pain. Her feet were badly torn up, and some of the spots were puncture wounds rather than cuts.

"Attie," Chase said, "when we get you home, you probly need to get a tetanus shot."

"Oh no," she moaned. "I hate shots."

"Make Riley go and hold your hand," Tammy suggested. "I can go too and kick him in the shin if that'll make you feel better."

"You already slapped me, Tammy; how much more damage are you wanting to do?"

"As much as you deserve."

"You slapped him?" Attie sounded shocked. "Awesome."

"It felt good," Tammy admitted.

"Speak for yourself," I mumbled.

"No more beating up on Riley. I think he's beating himself up enough as it is," Anne said in her protective manner.

I smiled up at her. "Thank you, Anne."

"Sure."

"Blow, Anne, blow!" Attie scrunched her face in pain. "You're not blowing!"

"Oh, I'm sorry," Anne cried and then started frantically blowing on Attie's skin.

Attie sat up. "Riley, don't do the disinfectant yet. I can only handle a little at a time. I'm a wimp, remember?"

"I think we're about done with this part," Tess informed her.

"Thank God." Attie sighed and then laid back and closed her eyes. "I want to take a break for a minute."

The car went silent, and I focused on Attie's crimson toenails as we waited for her to tell us she was ready for round two.

"All right," she said. "Let's do it."

Tammy and Tess held her hands, and Anne stroked her forehead, but as soon as the disinfectant touched one of her wounds, Attie's foot jerked.

"No more kicking me in the face, Charlie."

"You kicked him in the face?" Tammy asked.

"Oh yeah. She about knocked me unconscious."

Attie told the story as I cleaned each wound. I then went on to apply disinfectant and made sure to blow on each one for several seconds in order to lessen the pain. Finally wrapping her feet in gauze, everyone clapped as I announced that I was finished.

"No more running through forests, Attie," Tammy scolded. "And no more being a butthead, Riley."

"Yes, ma'am," we said simultaneously.

"Okay, let's allow her to get some rest," Anne suggested. "Are you guys going to sleep in here?" she asked, looking at me.

"Attie can sleep here. I'll sleep in the tent."

"I'll sleep in here with you, Attie," Anne offered. "I'll get our stuff out of the tent. Come on, Tammy."

"You could have stayed with me, Riley. I trust you. Besides, you aren't going to want to make out with a girl who looks the way I do right now."

"I would if the girl was you. It's just you, Charlie. I'll take you in any way, shape, or form."

"We'll see about that; the summer isn't over yet."

"Would you please stop saying that?"

"Riley—"

"No, don't even go there. Nothing's changed; my feelings for you haven't and won't change."

Anne and Tammy returned with sleeping bags and pillows.

"Hey, Anne, can you help Attie get everything set up while I talk to Riley a minute?" Tammy asked.

"It depends," Anne answered. "You aren't going to beat him up, are you?"

"I won't lay a hand on him, I promise."

"Then yes, you two go ahead."

I climbed out of the car, and we made our way to the front bumper.

"Look," Tammy whispered, "you know I'm angry about what took place."

"Yeah, and I'm even more angry with myself."

"I believe that. I just wanna shed a little light on the situation."

"Please do. I need all the help I can get."

"Ya aren't fooling anyone."

"What?"

"This whole idea that you aren't gonna be 'romantically involved' until the end of summer is completely ludicrous, and it isn't working."

"Amen."

"I respect your choices, Riley, I do. I appreciate them. You don't wanna put yourself in a situation where you feel like you can't control yourself and you might do something that you would regret. So you avoid all physical contact, and she avoids telling you how she really feels."

"Yes."

"Well, how's that workin' for ya?"

"Not very well."

"Not at all. You freakin' woulda ripped her clothes off today if she'd a let ya."

"True. Are you trying to help?"

"Think of it this way," she said, ignoring me. "A two-liter of Dr Pepper."

"A two-liter of Dr Pepper?"

"Work with me here, Riley. If it's been shaken and you open it all at once, what happens?"

"It explodes."

"Exactly. So how do you keep it from exploding?"

I pictured it in my head. For some reason, more than any other soda, Dr Pepper always exploded when you opened it. "Open it a little at a time and let the bubbles out."

"Yes. Okay now, follow me here; you and Attie are bottles of Dr Pepper. All the time you spend together and the way you feel about each other is shaking your bottle."

I started laughing at the analogy but caught her glaring at me. "Sorry. Go on."

"You weren't opening the bottle and letting any bubbles out, so the pressure kept building to the point that you exploded. You'd never touched her like that before, so when your pressure point was at its max and you touched her, you literally exploded."

"I see what you're saying."

"Trust me; I'm not suggestin' that you guys mug all over each other all the time. You need to respect some boundaries—lots of boundaries. But dear Lord, there isn't anything wrong with showing each other a little bit of affection. Let some of the air out of the bottle so ya aren't so dang explosive. You can be intimate and physical without being sexual. Focus on ways of doing that instead of trying to avoid each other altogether."

"As weird as it sounds, that makes a lot of sense. I was being respectful of her and my parents. I wanna be there when she needs me at night without her worrying that I'm gonna try to make a move on her."

"That's sorta my point, Riley. I can't imagine many things more intimate than holding someone you care about while they're hurting. You aren't gonna be thinking of making out with her in those times. It's an intimate moment, but it isn't sexual in nature, and you've grown closer through that type of intimacy than you ever could by having sex."

"True."

"You two need to sit down and think of ways to be together without 'being together.' You know what I mean?"

"Yes."

"Seriously, Riley, all this 'we're not an item' stuff is driving everyone bonkers. I don't even think your parents are buying it at this point. They would have to be blind not to see the sparks."

"We're that bad?"

"Yes."

"You know, you're pretty good at this advice thing, Tammy."

"You aren't the only person who's been in counseling. We've all got issues."

"Well, that's a relief. Thanks."

"Sure. But know this, you act inappropriately and I will kick your butt."

"I'm sure you will. You and Chase both."

Anne came around the corner. "She's fighting falling asleep until you get there, Riley. She wanted to talk to you before she fell asleep."

"I'm going right now." I gave Tammy a kiss on the cheek. "You're the best, but I'll never look at a bottle of Dr Pepper the same again."

"You guys talked about Dr Pepper?" I heard Anne ask as I ran past her.

I climbed into the back of the car and lay down next to Attie. "I'm here. I'll stay until you fall asleep."

She started mumbling. "No, I want to talk to you. I want to make sure you're all right. I don't want you upset with me for overreacting."

"I'm all right. I'm not upset with you; how could I be?"

"But—"

"Go to sleep, Charlie, we can talk about this tomorrow."

Her eyes shut and then quickly opened again. "Do you really think you'll still want to go out with me?"

"More than ever."

• •

"What's the matter, Tammy?"

"That's the worst night's sleep I've ever had." She sat in her chair curled up in a ball. Part of her hair was hidden beneath a yellow bandana; the rest was sticking out every which way. "I can't even believe I agreed to this."

"Sorry," I sympathized with her. "Camping not your thing?"

"Holiday Inn isn't even my thing."

"You and Attie have that in common." I laughed and then looked around at everyone.

"She's with Anne. They're in the tent talking." She patted the empty seat next to her. "Cop a squat."

Matt and Curt joined in the cooking extravaganza, and I watched as Matt destroyed three eggs in the process of trying to crack them open.

Chase had the patience of a saint. "Heck, man, we'll just make scrambled eggs. It'll be easier. Just crack them open and throw them in this cup; then mix it up real good and toss it in the pan. I'll take care of the rest."

Tess kept glancing over at Matt, ready to take over the egg cracking duties if necessary, but she stood back and let him struggle through.

"Just be careful not to get shells in there, Matt," she told him.

"Okay," Matt replied as he concentrated on his duty.

Anxious to see Attie, I looked toward the tent.

"Riley," Tammy whispered, "be prepared. She looks worse today, so don't freak out or anything when you see her. You're probly gonna cry again, so ya may wanna do it now so ya don't cry in front of her."

"I'm not gonna cry again. I'll be good." I tried to assure her that I could keep from becoming emotional, but I didn't even believe myself, and before I knew it tears were welling up in my eyes.

"I knew it." Tammy snickered as she reached over and squeezed my hand.

I was disgusted with myself. "I've become a complete bawl bag."

"You're in love. We all act like complete idiots when we're in love. My brother's girlfriend loves Neil Diamond, and now he listens to him all the time. I'd much rather have him walk around crying instead of listening to 'Love on the Rocks'."

"Well, Tammy, I hate to tell you this, but I like Neil Diamond too."

"You cry *and* listen to Neil Diamond? Then, Riley, you are in fact a hopeless case."

"Come on, Tammy; have you not seen *The Jazz Singer*? It's a great movie."

"Riley, the man has sideburns that reach his jawline!"

"You're thinking of fat Elvis. I don't think Neil Diamond had sideburns like that."

"He was around in the seventies, wasn't he?"

"Yeah."

"Then he had the sideburns."

"I'm Netflix'n the movie, Tammy, and we're watching it together. If he has sideburns in the movie, I'll buy you a Route 44. Deal?"

"You're on." She reached out and shook my hand. "I'll take a Diet Coke."

"What, no Dr Pepper?"

"Nah, goes straight to my thighs."

"Breakfast is ready!" Curt announced.

"Dude, why did you get to announce it?" Matt asked. "You didn't do anything but pour coffee."

As the two of them began throwing a barrage of insults at each other, I noticed that Anne and Attie were coming out of the tent. Tammy was right—Attie's face had swollen during the night, and a yellow tinge surrounded each wound. With her feet still wrapped in gauze, she wobbled on her heels in an awkward attempt at walking.

Jumping up, I ran to her.

"Hey, Riley," she said with a large grin.

"I'll get her, Anne." I reached over and scooped Attie up in my arms.

"My hero," she teased. "All you need now is the helmet and shoulder pads."

"No, Charlie, I think you need the helmet and shoulder pads, or at least you did yesterday. You're lucky you didn't lose an eye or something."

"Stop torturing yourself. I'm fine."

I placed her in the chair next to Tammy. "Hey, chick," Tammy greeted.

Tess handed her a plate of food and cup of orange juice.

"Thanks." She took a sip and then instantly brought her fingers to her lip and winced.

"Are you all right?" Tess sounded panicked.

"It's the juice. It stung a cut on my lip; that's all."

I felt like a bigger jerk with every passing second.

"So what are the plans today, guys?" Curt asked.

"Well, we planned on hiking, but..." Matt's voice trailed off as he looked toward Attie's feet.

"You guys go ahead; don't miss out because of me. I brought a book. I can hang out, relax, and read."

All three girls offered to stay, but Attie refused their offers.

"I'm staying," I announced. "I wanted to talk to her anyway."

"No. Good grief, we live together; we'll have plenty of time to talk."

I wasn't sure if she wanted to avoid an inevitable, uncomfortable conversation or she didn't want me to miss out on the fun. "No use in arguing, Charlie; I'm not going."

She rolled her eyes at me. "You sure are stubborn."

"Not as stubborn as you," I corrected as Chase planned the day.

"We can hike for a few hours, and then this afternoon we can go out in the boats again," he said. "Attie doesn't need to walk to do that."

"Thanks, Chase," Attie said.

"Hey, everyone, guess what today is."

"Riley, don't you dare," Attie whispered under her breath.

"What day is it?" Anne asked.

"It's Attie's seventeenth birthday."

"What?" Tammy screamed. "It's your birthday? Why didn't you tell us?"

Attie shrugged as her face turned red.

"What do you want for your birthday? Tess asked.

"Umm…" She glanced over at me and grinned but then looked away. "Um, a tetanus shot maybe."

"Really, Attie, what do you want?" Tess asked again.

"I don't need anything. Honestly, being here with all of you is present enough. I'm having the time of my life."

"Well then, you've got some pretty low standards for fun," Tammy quipped.

"No doubt," Curt said.

"But there is a problem," Attie announced.

Everyone's eyes were drawn to her as they waited for her to continue.

"I have to go to the bathroom. I've been holding it since I got here, and I can't wait anymore."

Chase stood with his mouth hanging open. "You haven't gone to the bathroom in a day?"

"I was a little preoccupied," she snapped.

"I need to go too," Anne announced.

"Me three," Tammy added.

Chase evidently hadn't been camping with three princesses before. "You've got to be kidding me?"

"I'll take them, Chase," Tess announced. "It's time for a lesson in peeing in the woods."

"I can't even begin to tell you how much I don't want to do this." Attie almost cried at the thought. "I've never missed a toilet so much in my entire life."

"Oh, come on. It's not that bad. You just have to watch out for the snakes."

"Snakes?" The girls sounded terrified.

"Oh, you don't have to worry," Tess said. "They're more afraid of you than you are of them."

"Sounds like a load of hog wash to me," Tammy said, yanking the bandana off of her head.

"Why didn't anybody mention this part when we were planning the trip?" Anne asked.

Chase laughed. "I assumed you would know that there aren't any bathrooms out in the woods."

"My mind never went there."

"Well, let's get it over with," Tammy said, standing and grabbing one of Attie's arms. "Somebody get the other side."

"I'll do it, Tess; you be on the lookout for snakes," Anne commanded as she took Attie's arm and they headed toward the trees.

The guys and I were practically rolling on the ground laughing at the sounds that were coming out of the woods. I wished I could have recorded it and played it back for the girls when they could have a sense of humor about it. There were mixtures of screams, cries, and giggles. Oddly enough, I think the girls were enjoying themselves.

After the bathroom adventure, everyone got dressed and took off on their hiking expedition. They left us sitting by the river in separate chairs with our feet propped up on a single chair in front of us. I focused on her crimson toenails.

"I guess I should go ahead and start," I announced.

"You don't need to do this. I'm fine. I've moved on."

"I haven't, so indulge me and allow me get this off of my chest."

"Riley, you don't have to do this—"

"Charlie, please."

"All right."

"I don't know what got into me yesterday. I mean, I do, but I don't know how I let myself get out of control like that. You told me to stop more than once, and I ignored you. I can't even begin to justify that." Just saying it made me sick to my stomach.

Attie sat in silence as she looked out at the water.

"I think I set some darned near impossible expectations on myself. I don't think I realized how difficult it would be to be around you all the time and never get to so much as hold your hand. I don't wanna sound like a total pervert or anything, but it's nearly impossible for me to be near you and not want to touch you. A hundred times a day I catch myself about to reach for you."

She remained silent, her face was blank, and she bit on her thumbnail as I continued.

"So, yesterday when you were laying there in your bathing suit and I was that close to you with all of your exposed skin…well, I lost my mind. My fingers touched you, and it gave me a rush. I didn't want the feeling to stop. I liked it."

My anxiety reduced as she finally spoke. "I liked it too, Riley. I could have put up more of a fight. I could have stopped you earlier if I would have wanted to. Heck, I'd even tried to get you to kiss me a few hours before. I wanted you to touch me as much you wanted to."

It felt good to hear her admission. "You did?"

"Yes."

She continued, "It didn't help that I was barely clothed, I realize that." She nodded as she spoke, but her eyes were still on the water in front of her. "I did a lot of thinking on my excursion yesterday. I carry as much responsibility for this as you do. I know how you feel about me, and I was foolish to think that I could be dressed that way and talk like that while you were lying there next to me. I flirted and made no attempt to make the situation easier on you." She shrugged. "I don't know where this leaves us. I really don't."

"What do you mean?"

"It's possible that we just aren't meant to be."

"No, it isn't. Don't even say that."

"Well, maybe we should stay away from each other for a while, keep a distance. You want to fulfill the promise that you made to yourself and your dad, and I'm not doing a very good job at making it easier for you. We only have a couple of weeks left until I move out; maybe we should let things cool off and then see where we stand. Maybe if we spend some time apart you'll get some clarity about the situation."

I shook my head. "Okay, this is not the direction I was hoping this conversation would go. I don't like your plan at all; I hate it actually."

"Well, what did you have in mind?"

"Honestly?"

"Of course."

"I wanna admit to everyone that I'm crazy about you and put an end to all this suffering right now. I don't think anyone's fooled anyway." I recalled my conversation with Tammy. "I need to sit down with Dad, tell him what's going on, and that he can trust me with you."

She was silent again.

"I'm willing to do it, to have the conversation as soon as we get home. But I'm at a point where I need to know something."

"What?"

My heart raced as I got nervous. "There's no secret to how I feel about you. You've known for months, and I've told you on more than one occasion. But you've never told me how you feel."

As she continued to sit in silence, I felt like I was being tortured.

"Do you like me, Charlie, as more than a friend? I really need to know."

After what felt like hours, her mouth finally opened, and she spoke. "I hate when I wake up in the morning and you've already left for the gym or to practice because I know that I won't get to see you until late in the day.

"And if I've been away from you for any amount of time and I hear your voice, my heart starts to race.

"When you grab my hand to lead me somewhere, I always wish you wouldn't let go, and I refuse to even think about the day that I'll be moving out of your house because it makes me miserable knowing that you won't be within a one hundred-foot radius of me on a regular basis."

She paused and I remained silent. I wanted to hear her say more. These were the words that I'd been hoping to hear all summer, the words I wanted to hear from her all my life.

She continued in a whisper. "I was hoping that you would kiss me while I was lying in that tent yesterday; in a weird way I don't want my nightmares to end because I don't want you to stop sleeping next to me, and I'm freaked out that I haven't even started my senior year yet and I feel all these things for a boy.

"So, all in all, I would say I'm head over heels. Whaddya have to say about that?"

I grinned at her. "I'd say that you've made me the happiest boy in the world."

She looked at me with a scowl. "Didn't I just complicate your life even more?"

"I'm more than willing to have that type of complication in my life, Charlie. I look forward to it."

Eventually, a smile replaced her frown, and even with the cuts she was the most beautiful I'd ever seen her.

"I'll talk to Dad when we get home or the first time I get a chance. So, until then, we need to try to go ahead and follow the same rules we were before."

"Sounds fair enough."

"I am gonna give in on one part though."

"What part is that?" she asked, raising an eyebrow. "My birthday kiss?"

"No." I laughed.

"Bummer."

"I'd like to hold your hand," I requested.

She smiled and held her hand out to me.

chapter 29

(Attie)

Riley held my hand as we pulled into the driveway. Giving it one last squeeze, he grinned before easing out of the seat and making his way to my side of the car.

Getting out, I slid out of the way so he could close the door. Leaning against the car, I waited to see what he would do. The day was almost over, and my birthday wish still hadn't come true. Even though he swore he wouldn't kiss me again until he spoke to Pops, I was still holding out hope that he wouldn't allow himself to disappoint me on my birthday.

He leaned against the car with one hand and then gently placed the other hand just below my neck, flat against my sternum. As he slowly leaned in I closed my eyes but was disappointed when I felt his lips kiss the tip of my nose. It lasted only a second before he pulled away, but I understood in that short moment that Riley was battling two desires: to either kiss me or honor the commitment he made to himself and not pursue anything until I'd moved out of his home. Of course, he'd already breached the agreement during the camping trip, but I didn't want to bring the incident up again.

I was disappointed when he grabbed my hand and led me toward the house. I was aware that once we made it inside, there was no chance he would kiss me tonight. My heart sank, but I followed his lead. The fulfillment of my birthday wish would have to wait for two more weeks.

The closer we got to the house, the faster he walked. Trying to keep up, I walked carefully on my sore feet. He wanted to get me inside before he changed his mind and gave in, but just before reaching the porch steps, he veered off course. We were no longer heading into the house but around the side instead. I smiled, knowing what would happen, and as soon as we were out of sight, Riley turned and pulled me close to him.

"Happy birthday," he whispered before kissing me delicately for a moment and then hugging me tightly to him.

Placing his cheek against mine, he spoke quietly into my ear. "I think I'm in love with you, Charlie, and I have been for our entire lives."

It was the most wonderful proclamation anyone ever made to me, and I felt like the most special girl in the world. Not only was Riley Bennett choosing me, but I was his first and only choice.

I started to reply, to tell him how I felt about him, but a light caught our attention. I turned to see where it was coming from but was blinded. I felt Riley protectively shield my eyes and pull my head to his chest.

"Hello?" Riley called out. "Who's there?"

"Hey, Riley…and Attie." I heard a girl's voice. "Did I interrupt something?"

"Turn the lights off, Tiffany," Riley snapped.

The night went black, and it took a few moments before my eyes readjusted to the darkness. I glanced up at Riley. His jaw locked and his eyes glared toward Tiffany. "Riley?"

He looked down at me, his face immediately softening. "Go on inside, Charlie; I've got some business to take care of."

"But—"

"It's okay; I'll be right behind you. No big deal."

As I turned to go he grabbed my hand, pulled me to him, and quickly kissed me again. "I'll only be a minute. Go on inside."

As swiftly as possible, I made my way inside and up to my room.

(Riley)

"What are you doing here, Tiffany?"

"What am I doing here?" she asked, walking toward me. "I just came by to talk. The real question is what are you doing, Riley? Playing house with your summer guest?"

I was silent.

"Enjoying a summer fling? Pretty easy bait, don't you think? Let me guess, she's sleeping in the room next to yours? I would know. I've had a nice visit to your room a time or two."

I remained silent and still as my anger rose.

"Come on," she urged while putting her hand on my arm. "Summer's over, and it's time for the fun and games to end. The little prude isn't going to give you what you want anyway."

"Since when do you know what I want?"

"Oh, I don't know, I remember being pretty good at making you happy," she whispered as she untucked my shirt from my jeans. "You can have a lot more fun with me. Do you remember how much fun we used to have?"

"I think I'll pass," I said firmly while grabbing her hands and throwing them to her side. "We kissed a few times; don't try to make it sound like we did more than that."

"We had fun together, though, didn't we?"

"Look, I guess our wires got crossed, and I take full responsibility for that. I wanted to avoid an argument, and I thought that if I didn't call you over several months that you would realize I wasn't interested in seeing you. Evidently, I should have been more forthright."

She looked hurt for an instant, but then her face turned cold. "You like this girl, Riley? Come on, you can't be serious."

"It's none of your business, Tiffany."

"She's plain, boring, and a religious freak," Tiffany spat.

"Enough!" I grabbed her arm and drug her to the car. "I think you should go now."

"She isn't even your type," she argued.

My anger getting the best of me, I opened the car and shoved her in. "She's exactly my type. Now get off my property!" I slammed the car door and stood glaring at her.

Tiffany threw the car in reverse and peeled away as I ran back toward the house. Dad was standing in the entryway as I made my way inside. "What was that?

My teeth were clenched. "Tiffany, it's not a big deal." I turned and started up the stairs.

"Then what is it?" he yelled after me.

"Closure."

· ·

When I reached Attie's room, she was sitting on her bed looking out the window.

"Charlie?"

She turned to look at me, and I gave her a reassuring grin. "Everything's fine. I'm gonna run change clothes and I'll be right back. Okay?"

She nodded and then turned and looked out the window.

I walked into my room, slammed the door, ripped my jeans off, and threw them into the closet. The most incredible night of my life had been sabotaged, and somehow I needed to salvage it.

Pulling on sweatpants, I made my way back to Attie's room.

"Are you okay?" she asked with a small, weak smile on her face.

"Perfect." I joined her sitting on the bed and leaned over to kiss her on the forehead. "Just a little unfinished business, that's all."

"You know, Riley, you don't have to cut things off with her because of me."

I was shocked at her response. "What?"

"We're in high school; nothing has to be exclusive. There's no sense in missing out."

"Do you not remember what I said to you out there? I told you that I thought I might be in love with you."

"I remember, but I also realize that you lived a life before I showed up, and I don't want you to have to change because of me. You give up a lot by being with someone like me."

"Someone like you?"

"Plain, boring, and a religious freak."

"You heard that?"

"I wasn't eavesdropping; you were yelling at each other. It was kind of hard not to hear." She turned away from me and looked out the window again. "Riley, she was right."

"No, she wasn't." I shook my head in frustration.

I couldn't believe we were about to have this discussion. Attie was about to break things off with me before we officially got started. My chest ached.

"How did we get to this place? From what we shared on the camping trip and just now outside to this?" I knew I was whimpering, but I didn't care. Attie was the most important thing to me right then, and I wasn't gonna let the night change course in such a drastic way.

"It's called waking up to reality." She looked back at me. "School starts in a little over a week, and I'll be moving out. You'll go back to being the popular, handsome jock, and I ... well, I don't know what I'll be."

I gave her a grin and grabbed her hands. "You'll be my girlfriend. At least I hope so."

"No," she said, pulling her hands away from mine. "I can't be the reason you change and then miss out on stuff. It'll make both of us miserable. We're great together, Riley; honestly we are. But I don't know if we can work outside the confines of our little world. Out there, I don't know if we make sense."

"We make perfect sense. Charlie, please don't do this." I stood and began to pace. "I'm not changing for you. I'm changing for me and because I believe that's what God wants me to do. A lot of my transformation started long before you arrived. You just made me wanna complete the transition a lot faster. The things that someone like Tiffany offers just don't appeal to me."

Her face turned cloudy and revealed her thoughts. I knew I needed to address her concerns. "What happened yesterday—"

"We don't have to go back to that."

"Yes, we do, because I wanna make sure you understand where I'm coming from and what I feel for you." I put my head in my hands and tried to think, praying that God would give me the words I needed to say.

She sat waiting for my explanation.

I took a deep breath and began. "I'm attracted to you emotionally first and foremost. I'm crazy about your personality. You're spunky, witty and pigheaded, kind, and sensitive. Dramatic and even manic sometimes, but I love that about you.

"We laugh all the time, and unfortunately you make me cry—a lot. The impact you have on me isn't like any other person I've ever been with. You bring out the best in me, and I'm not willing to give that up, to give *you* up so that I can have a physical relationship with someone else. To use one of your words, that would be nonsensical. I'm willing and I wanna abstain from a physical relationship with you as long as I have to in order to keep the emotional and spiritual bond that we have. It's that important to me. *You're* that important to me."

She interrupted. "No, Riley. This isn't about waiting for as long as you need to or waiting until I'm ready. Until I get married, I won't ever be ready. Unless by some miracle we end up married someday, we will never have a sexual relationship; do you grasp that? Do you realize that's what you're giving up for as long as you're with me?"

"Yes, I do. I want the same thing. I know it's strange to hear that come out of a guy's mouth, but I believe that's what I'm called to, just as much as you are. It's not as if God holds females to a different standard than males. We're all held to the same principles.

"It won't be easy, and there are times when I'm not thrilled about this particular condition being placed on me. By God, not you, by the way. But it has been, and I'll have to learn how to deal with it. I can guarantee you that I'll mess up every once in a while, but I won't hurt you again like I did yesterday.

"We'll just have to make sure that we don't put ourselves in situations where we could get carried away, or *I* can get carried away like that again.

"And you're right, I did have a life before you, but it wasn't the life that I wanted for myself, and it's a life that won't be hard for me to leave behind.

"We are in high school, Charlie, and I guess we won't be exclusive if you don't wanna be, but I only wanna be with you. I want you to be my girlfriend. I want everyone to know that there isn't anyone else that I wanna be with.

"I wasn't lying when I said that I believe I've loved you your entire life. When I look back over our lives together, it's totally obvious. You're important to me, you always have been, and I'm not interested in letting you go."

She brought her thumb to her mouth and started chewing on her nail.

"Why don't you tell me what's really going on?"

"I just did."

"You told me some of it, but I think you're still keeping something hidden."

"Not intentionally."

"Why are you so hesitant to believe that could I love you?"

Tears poured down her face.

"Talk to me, Charlie; what's going on inside that head of yours?"

"I just don't see myself as someone that's loveable."

"Why?"

"I don't know. Trust me, when I say it out loud I realize how ridiculous it sounds, but it's how I feel and I don't know why. It's not like I grew up in a house that lacked love or anything. My parents loved me completely and unconditionally, until... I don't know. I don't know why it's so hard for me; I just know it is."

"Charlie, you're loved like crazy, do you realize that? Gramps, my mom and dad, our friends, Joshua and Nicole, me, your dad—"

She gave a doubtful huff. "I don't know about that last one."

"He loves you. He'll be here next week, and you two can get back to working on your relationship. I'm sure he's healed a lot since you left."

She was nodding as I spoke, but I don't think she believed me. "He loves you, Charlie."

"I wish I could believe that as much as you do."

"Look, if it'll make you feel better, I won't speak for anyone else, I'll just speak for myself. I'm not giving up on us because you can't accept how I feel about you. I'll let my actions speak for themselves, and eventually you'll come around—I know you will. I'm not letting you go."

"I don't want you to let me go, not if you don't want to."

"I don't want to." My body finally relaxed. "I won't. I won't let you go."

"I don't want to be with anyone else either, Riley."

"Thank God," I whispered as I sat down on the floor and looked up at her. "So you'll officially be my girlfriend then? When I ask you and once you've moved out, I mean."

"Of course," she said, crawling into my lap.

It felt good to hold her again.

"Charlie?"

"Hmm?"

"You know that I can't sleep beside you anymore, right?"

She shook her head. "I've realized that."

"We're on a whole 'nother level now, and I don't wanna subject myself to that kind of torture."

"You aren't the only one." She laughed. "If I had my way, we'd be continuing what we started outside."

I grinned. "It won't be long and I'll be able to kiss you again."

"Maybe I can talk my dad into moving here a few days earlier."

"I wish!"

• •

I sat with Attie until she fell asleep and then went to go to sleep in my own bed for the first time since she moved into our home.

She had a small nightmare, but I was able to help her get back to sleep within just a few minutes, and I returned to my room, where I tossed and turned most of the night.

The last time I looked at the clock it was 4:07 a.m.

chapter 30

(Attie)

I opened my eyes and realized that I was lying in a hospital bed. Placing my hands on my face, I found tubes going into my nose, and when I looked down I saw an IV in the top of my hand.

"Hello?" I tried to speak, but my voice didn't work. I realized that there was a tube down my throat.

"Hello," I screamed inside my head. "Is anyone there?"

There was nobody else in the room. I was alone.

"Dad," I tried to yell, "where are you?"

I was frantic.

"Attie," a gentle voice spoke. "You're safe; I'm here."

"Jesus?" I would recognize his voice anywhere.

"Look at me, Attie," he commanded.

I focused my eyes and found him. We were back in the black vastness standing on steppingstones, and he wore a large grin on his face.

"Turn around, Attie."

I obeyed. Turning, I saw several steppingstones behind me.

"Look how well you've done on our journey so far. Every time I took a step, you were right behind me. Faithfully behind me."

I turned back to him. "It was painful, but it feels good now."

"Good." He smiled. "Attie, it's time for you to take another step."

"Okay."

I waited for him to move onto the stone in front of him so that I could step onto the one he currently occupied.

"No, Attie, this time I'm going to share this step with you."

I shrugged and stepped to join him.

He held out his arms, making room for me. It was a tight squeeze; we both barely fit on the stone. He wrapped his arms firmly around me.

"Attie, this step will be different than the others, but I want you to remember that I'm on this step with you and my arms are holding you tightly to me. You're safe, and you'll be okay."

"I'm scared."

He held me tighter. "I'm here, Attie; you're not alone."

. . . .

I woke to shouting.

Jumping out of bed, I ran to the stairs and found Riley standing on the top step.

"What's the matter?" I asked.

"I'm not sure," he said, concerned. "I've never heard Dad yell like that."

As he slammed the phone down, Pops noticed us watching him. "Why don't you kids get dressed and meet me in the kitchen. Wait, Attiline, what happened to your face?"

"Uh, I fell into a thorn bush. It looks worse than it is." I hated lying to him.

"You sure you're okay?"

"Yes, sir."

"All right, well get dressed and meet me in the kitchen."

"Do you think Tiffany ratted on us?" I whispered as we walked back to our rooms.

"I don't know, maybe. But just in case, let me handle it okay? We were gonna have this talk anyway, so I was already prepared. It'll be fine."

I nodded my head.

"It's gonna be all right." He kissed my nose and then smirked at me. "I can handle him."

We quickly got dressed and then met back on the landing before making our way downstairs. He held my hand until his dad could have seen us and then gently brought my hand to his face and kissed the inside of my wrist before letting me go.

Riley was a few steps in front of me as we walked into the kitchen.

"Have a seat," Pops instructed quietly.

I looked over at Marme; she was standing at the sink talking on the phone. After finishing her conversation, she hung up the phone and remained standing at the sink staring blankly out the window.

Riley grabbed my hand under the table. "Dad," he began.

His father cut him off. "Son, you need to sit there and be quiet for a minute."

As Pops turned to face me, I noticed that his hands were trembling. Riley must have noticed as well because he squeezed my hand under the table.

"What is it?" I asked.

"Attiline..." His voice shook, which caused my heart to race. "Attiline, your dad called this morning."

"He did? I wish you would have woken me up. I would have loved to talk to him."

"I know you would have."

"Did he call to talk to me?"

"I don't think so."

"He took the time to call but didn't want to talk to me?"

"Attiline... he wanted me to let you know that he won't be here next week after all."

"Oh, okay. Well, when's he coming?"

"He isn't." His voice cracked. "He's not coming."

"What do you mean he's not coming?"

"He's not coming to Oklahoma," he clarified.

"So I'm moving back to New York?" I looked over at Riley. His mouth hung open, and his eyes were wide. "I don't want to move back to New York. I want to stay here."

"No," Pops answered. I looked back at him. He looked as if he were in physical pain. "You're not going back to New York."

"Wait, I'm confused. He's not coming here and I'm not going there? What are we doing?"

I heard Marme begin to cry. Looking over at her and seeing her in a stage of complete grief, reality hit, and it was as if a mountain had caved in over me.

My body shook as I remembered the words of Jesus two days before.

"Are you going to forgive your dad for shipping you off to Oklahoma so he wouldn't have to see your face? The face that reminds him of your mother."

Tears filled my eyes. "He's not coming here and he doesn't want me there?"

Riley squeezed my hand more firmly.

Pops shook his head.

"But the house, we're supposed to close on the house next week."

"He never bought the house. He wasn't honest with you."

My body went numb. "He never actually planned on coming? He knew all along that he was sending me here and he would never be coming?"

"Correct."

I panicked. "Did Gramps know? Did you know? Riley?"

"No, we're just as shocked as you. Your Gramps is devastated and very angry with his son. Riley and I had no idea."

"He's throwing me out."

"He's not ready. He says it's too painful for him to see you right now."

"Why did he tell you and not me?"

"I don't think he could bring himself to tell you himself."

I sat in silence. Feeling lightheaded, I tried to stabilize myself by searching the room for something to focus on. My eyes rested on an apple that sat on the counter.

"I'm so sorry, Attiline."

"He doesn't want me." The apple began to look fuzzy.

"He loves you; he just can't do it right now."

"He's my dad; what do you mean he can't do it right now? That's what dads do, they're supposed to do it, and they're supposed to be there."

"I know. I can't defend him; I can't."

Riley laid his head onto the table, and I sat stunned. We sat in silence for several minutes.

I couldn't move. The accident had ripped my entire family away from me. Even the person who didn't die was now gone.

"So I'm alone then."

Riley sat up and leaned toward me. "You're not alone."

"No, you're not alone," Pops said softly. "We're here. We're all here for you."

"What am I going to do? Where am I going to live? He's just leaving me here to fend for myself."

"You'll live with us, of course," Pops answered. "We're your family too, and we want you. We want you here with us."

Baby caught my attention as she scurried through the kitchen. She'd been trash, deemed worthless and thrown out, just like me. We'd been unwanted and thrown out like garbage.

"He's throwing me out like trash," I screamed.

"No, Attiline, he's not. He's hurting. He doesn't realize what he's doing." Pops tried to explain, but there was nothing he could say to excuse my father. There was nothing that could justify him throwing me away.

"No!" I screamed. "He's deserting me; he's leaving me alone just like in the hospital! He's left me all alone!"

I let go of Riley's hand and stood.

"Charlie..."

"My dad is making the choice not to be with me." My body trembled and I felt faint. I looked down at Riley, who looked back up at me; his face was full of tenderness. "My own father doesn't even want me, Riley."

He stood and pulled me to him. "Don't say that."

"He doesn't, Riley; he doesn't want me." The words practically stuck in my dry throat.

My legs gave out, and I fell against him.

"We want you. We love you." Riley pulled me closer to him and whispered in my ear, "I want you here, Charlie. *I* love you."

"No." I shoved away from him. "I knew it."

"Knew what?" he asked.

"My own father doesn't love me, Riley ... how can anyone else?"

"That's not true."

"He's throwing me out like trash. My daddy doesn't even want me."

• •

(Riley)

Attie pulled away from me and ran out the kitchen door and into the backyard as Joshua came running through the front door. He must have been whom Mom was talking to on the phone. He ran past me, and I followed him with Nicole not far behind.

Attie stood expressionless in the tall grass; her eyes were cold and lifeless and her skin practically transparent.

I'd wondered during many long nights if she would ever experience so much pain that she would emotionally shut down forever. I was afraid that she'd just reached that point.

"Attie," Joshua spoke calmly.

Without speaking or looking at him, Attie held out her hand as if to keep him at a distance. He stopped walking toward her and stood still. I could hear my parents running toward us as Nicole prayed quietly.

"Attie, talk to me. Tell me what you're feeling," Joshua asked.

"I feel like I should have died." Her voice was distant. "I might as well have."

My heart shattered. All the progress she'd made over the summer had floated away in the Oklahoma breeze.

"What does it say about a person," she continued, "when they aren't even loveable enough for their own parent to want to be with them? When their own parent can't even love them?"

"It doesn't say anything at all about you," Joshua responded. "This is about your father and his problems, not you. You're worthy to be loved, Attie. You are loved."

She let out a bitter laugh and then turned silent and still.

A hush fell over the pasture. There was no sound, and the hairs on the back of my neck stood up. I was terrified for her.

In what seemed like slow motion and without turning around, Joshua reached back as Nicole slowly walked up to him, pulled out a syringe, and handed it to him. He pulled off the protective cap, handed the cap back to his wife, and then she fell to her knees and began praying.

I could see Joshua's mouth moving; he was talking to Attie as he slowly started walking toward her. Nicole's lips were moving. I knew she was praying out loud, but I couldn't hear sound. Out of my five senses, the only one that worked was my sight.

I watched completely helpless as Attie screamed. Her head shook, and her arms violently thrashed around in the air. Thankfully, I couldn't hear her cries. I couldn't have borne to hear her cry out in pain.

Joshua motioned for Dad to join him, which he did, and the two of them quickly approached Attie. Before she had the chance to react, Dad held her tightly in his arms, and Joshua injected her with the syringe. She stood wailing with my dad holding her until she went limp. Joshua and Dad caught her as she fell to the ground. For the time being, they ended her pain.

Joshua picked her up and carried her inside with Nicole and Mom a few steps behind. Dad and I were left alone in the pasture.

Unable to move my legs, I fell to the ground. I wanted to chase after her, to tell her everything was going to be all right, but I wasn't even sure if that was true. There was a possibility that things would never be all right again.

Dad sat down next to me and putting his arms around me pulled me to his chest as I cried.

"It's okay, buddy, let it out," he encouraged. "Let it all out."

After several minutes I finally regained my composure. "I don't know what to say to her anymore, Dad. I can't rationalize any of this crap. How much does one person have to take?"

"I don't know; I can't answer that."

"Where is God, and why isn't he helping her? I don't see him at work at all."

"Be careful going down that road, son."

"Why? It's what I'm thinking. Isn't he all-knowing? Doesn't he already know my thoughts anyway?"

"Yes."

"I'm angry with him, and he knows it; no sense in pretending that I'm not."

"I guess I'm angry with him too."

"Where is he? Why doesn't he do something? Why aren't we seeing him at work here? He could have made her dad come back."

"God gave us free will, Riley. You have to know that God doesn't want any of this for Attiline. He wanted her dad to come back, but Eddie chose not to."

"God could have changed his heart, softened it toward her or something."

"If God made us do things, what would be the point in having us at all? If you knew that I only loved you because I didn't have a choice, I had to, would that mean anything to you? Would you feel loved at all?"

"I guess not."

"Free will is wonderful and horrible at the same time. Unfortunately, we make poor choices and end up hurting not only ourselves but those around us as well. Yes, God could have made Eddie come home, but I'll bet that Attiline would only want him here if he wanted to be. There'd be no joy for her otherwise.

"It's the fact that love is a choice that makes it so special. Choosing to love someone, regardless of our circumstances, is what makes love worthwhile."

"I do love her."

"I know."

"No, you don't. I mean, I'm in love with her. I was gonna talk to you today, to tell you and to ask for your permission to date her."

"Riley, give me some credit; I'm not a complete idiot. You think I didn't know you two were crazy about each other?"

I sat up and looked at him. He was laughing and shaking his head at me. "I can't believe you lasted this long."

"You know?"

"Who doesn't?"

"Mom even knows?"

"Your mom saw it the night Attiline got here. We knew it would only be a matter of time."

I shook my head. "Unbelievable."

"You two have been close your entire lives; you share a very special bond. Nobody's surprised here."

"Well, what do we do now? We waited all summer for her to move out of the house so we could go out on a date; now she's not moving out at all."

Dad was laughing at me again. "You're joking, right?"

"Whaddya mean?"

"This entire summer has been one long date. You've hardly been apart."

"Well, that may be true." I had to concede that fact, in anyone else's book, what we'd been doing all summer *was* dating. "Okay, let me clarify. I meant that we waited to officially date, to allow ourselves to … oh forget it."

"I know what you're saying; I understand." He gave me a pat on the back and then left his hand on my shoulder. "Look, in a couple of days, when she's feeling better, the four of us need to sit down and come to some sorta agreement, an understanding. I trust you two; you've proven yourselves trustworthy all summer. We just need to sit down and talk it through."

"Really? You're okay with this?"

"I'm okay as long as there are some boundaries in place, but let's talk more about it later."

"Okay, thanks, Dad. I feel much better getting it all out there in the open."

"Well, evidently you two are the only people in town who don't think it's already been out in the open." He laughed again but soon turned serious. "But Riley, if this goes badly and you two break up—"

"I know, Dad."

"You're gonna have to move out. I'm pretty sure that we like Attiline more than you."

We laughed together. "I can't blame you for that."

"Should we go inside and see how she's doing?" he asked.

We made our way inside and found everyone but Attie sitting in the family room.

"I put her upstairs in her bed," Joshua informed.

I started to make my way up the stairs. "I'm gonna check on her; she needs me."

"She's out like a light, Riley," Joshua said. "She won't even know you're there."

"You're wrong, Joshua," I replied. "She'll know."

chapter 31

(Attie)

There was a small knock on my bedroom door.

"Attiline, can I come in? I've brought you some food."

"Yes, of course." Still groggy, I watched as Pops walked in carrying a tray of food. "Thanks so much. I had no idea how much time had passed; I'm famished."

"We thought you might be." He set the tray onto my desk and started to leave the room. "I'll go tell Riley that you're awake."

"Actually, would you mind keeping me company while I eat? Something tells me Riley's spent plenty of time up here. He probably needs a break."

A smile spread across his face. "I would love to sit with you."

"Goody."

"I'm glad that you were able to get some rest," he said as he sat down on the foot of my bed.

"Yes, I was out like a light. I don't know what Joshua gave me, but that stuff worked. I don't remember having a thought, let alone a bad dream." As I took a bite of cheesy spaghetti, my taste buds came to life. "I love it when Marme makes this stuff. It's one of my favorites."

"That's nothing. She's fixing up a whole smorgasbord down there, all your favorites."

"Bless her heart; she didn't need to do that."

"You know Molly; it's as much for her as it is for you. She needed to keep herself occupied. Otherwise, she would have been up here every five minutes checking on you."

"She could have; I wouldn't have minded."

"It would have made two of them. I think Riley wore grooves into the stairs."

"Of course, I think he takes all of this as personally as I do."

"I think you might be right." He nodded. "So enough small talk, Attiline, how are you holding up?"

"Better than I would have thought. I'm confused more than anything."

He stood and walked over to the wall of sketches. "I think we all are. It isn't natural behavior for a parent, and especially not Eddie."

"You know, when I look at that picture of my dad and me, it doesn't even seem real."

He turned to face me. "Why is that you think?"

"That's not who we are anymore, at least not since the accident. He isn't the same person he used to be. I don't know if you'd even recognize him. I sure don't."

He sat back down on the bed and watched me as I spoke.

"Did you know that he didn't even pick me up to bring me home from the hospital? He sent his nurse."

"What?" Anger and anguish surrounded his voice.

"He never came to see me in the hospital, not once. Then the day I came home, he came up with some excuse as to why he couldn't come get me. Patty dropped me off at the house and then left me there all by myself."

"Oh, Attiline, I don't even know what to say to that. You're breaking my heart."

"After the accident, it was like some switch turned off in his soul, and he became a completely different person. I went from being the center of his world to someone that he couldn't bear to be around."

"So why the Christmas picture?"

"I don't know. I came home from school, and the photographer was all set up in our living room. It took about twenty minutes to take the pictures, and then as soon as we were finished, Dad went back to work. For twenty minutes I got to see my dad the way he used to be, and I remember sitting there thinking maybe he'd woken up out of his fog, maybe we'd be back to normal. But as quickly as he came back to me, he left."

We sat in silence as we looked back at the picture for several moments.

"When he walked back out the door, I was afraid that day that I'd lost both of my parents in the accident. Pops, a man is walking around in my father's body, but he isn't my dad. He isn't the man that I grew up knowing, loving, and admiring. My dad's gone; I realize that. I woke up in the hospital an orphan, and I think that I've known it all along but didn't want to admit it."

"Attiline," he said, patting a spot next to him on the bed, "come sit by me for a minute."

I obliged.

"Did you know that apart from the doctor and nurses, I was the first person to hold you after you were born?"

"What? Nobody ever told me that."

He gave me a proud nod. "Yep, it was one of the greatest joys of my life."

"Will you tell me about it?"

He seemed excited to have the opportunity to share the story. "Well, your mom was at our house one night for dinner. Your dad was at school for something; I'm not sure what. Anyway, Elizabeth went into labor, and since the twins were so small, Molly had to stay at home with them while I ran your mom to the hospital."

"Oh my gosh."

"As you already know, she ended up having an emergency c-section, and I went into the operating room with her. When they pulled you out, you were screaming your head off."

"Not much has changed, huh?" I was still crying and screaming all the time.

"They weighed you and checked your vitals and then wrapped you up in a blanket. You stopped crying as soon as they handed you to me."

I thought of Riley. "The ability to soothe me must run in your family."

"Apparently. Anyway, I showed you to your mom, and she told me that your name would be Atticus. You started crying again…"

"Probably because I heard my name."

"Who can blame you?" He laughed. "So, to try to soothe you, I started singing an old Neil Diamond song called 'Sweet Caroline,' but for some reason I sang the words 'Sweet Attiline' instead."

"That's where my nickname came from?"

"Yep. I've called you Attiline since moments after you were born and looked up at me with those big beautiful eyes. It was love at first sight. You've always been Attiline to me."

"I've always wondered where it came from. Thanks for sharing that story with me."

"You're welcome, but I didn't tell you that story so you would know why I gave you your nickname."

"Why then?"

Picking up my hands, he gave them a gentle squeeze.

"Because I want you to know that you didn't become an orphan the day of the accident. From the first moment I laid eyes on you, I loved you like you were my own child. Attiline, God is all-knowing and all-powerful. Seventeen years ago he joined our hearts together, and now here we are helping each other, salvaging each other."

"Salvaging each other, what do you mean?"

"It's when you save or rescue something that's been damaged or rejected. They salvage old car parts or ships in order to repair them or take their most valuable parts and reuse them."

"Psalm 18," I whispered.

"Psalm 18?"

"While I was in the hospital, I kept going back to the same scripture in the Bible, but I couldn't figure out why. It was Psalm 18:16 through 19."

"What does it say?"

He reached down from on high and took hold of me; he drew me out of deep waters. He rescued me from my powerful enemy, from my foes, who were too strong for me. They confronted me in the day of my disaster, but the Lord was my support. He brought me out into a spacious place; he rescued me because he delighted in me. (NIV)

Not surprising to either of us, I started to cry. "Yes, I've been salvaged."

"We all have," he added.

"Charlie?" Riley appeared in the doorway holding Baby.

"I'll take your tray downstairs, Attiline. Thanks for letting me visit with you." He kissed me on the forehead and grabbed my tray.

Riley waited for his dad to leave the room and then walked over and sat cross-legged on the floor next to my bed.

"You okay, Charlie?"

I slid off the bed, sat on the floor next to him, and removed Baby from his arms.

"I'm better." I kissed Baby on the head and gave her a small hug before putting her onto the ground. "I believe the worst has already happened. What else could go wrong?" I tried to lighten the mood, but looking at Riley, it was apparent he wasn't going to cheer up.

"I don't know why God keeps allowing bad things to happen to you." His eyes were focused on Baby as she scampered around the room. "You'd think he'd give you a freakin' break. How much can one person be expected to take?"

"Don't talk like that."

I noticed Baby was about to head out of the bedroom and got up to grab her. Riley jumped up as well and laid my desk chair on its side in the doorway as a barrier to keep the puppy in the room with us. We then sat back down on the floor.

"I'm serious," he continued. "I can't even wrap my mind around it. What happened to God's love or his protection? You're getting the crap beaten out of you on a daily basis, and it's not like you did anything to deserve it. Enough's enough already."

"Please don't be angry; it doesn't help."

"I can't help it. My faith is shrinking by the minute, and I'm so angry I can hardly breathe."

I moved so that I was sitting in front of him and our knees were touching.

"Trust me, I know how you feel, but being angry doesn't help. Anger's what caused me to run off to New York City, and I can tell you right now, being angry and running away didn't solve anything. As a matter of fact, it caused more problems.

"There's no doubt this ordeal has been painful and very grueling. It's been tiring and I want it over, but I don't believe God's abandoned me. I still believe that God loves me and that I can depend on him. There hasn't been one second where I've felt like he wasn't with me, even yesterday out there screaming in the backyard. I was filled with so much grief that it felt like the only way I'd survive is to somehow get it all out, but even then I knew God was still with me. I saw Jesus there. I saw him crying with me, and I knew that he hurt just as much as I did and he'd have done anything for the circumstances to change. For almost a year, I didn't have anyone but him. He's been very faithful. He's never left my side."

"Your situation hasn't gotten better; it's gotten worse."

"That's not true." I grabbed his hands. "It's gotten so much better."

"How?"

"For starters, I've got you. Not to mention your parents and great new friends. God's used all of you in different ways to help me heal and enjoy life again. I don't even think I can explain how much that means to me. Plus, the nightmares are fewer and fewer. We're even getting some sleep."

"Your dad just deserted you. I would call that getting worse."

"He didn't *just* desert me; that's not a new development. He left me a year ago. I've known since I woke up in the hospital that he didn't want me around anymore.

"When I took off for New York City, I hoped that he would care enough to come looking for me ... to make some sort of effort, but he didn't."

"Is that why you were surprised that I came looking for you at the river?"

"I would have understood if you hadn't."

"I would never do that. I could never let you go that easy."

"I bet Dad didn't think he ever would either."

"I'm not him."

"I realize that. I also realize that he's been gone for a long time and I've known it all along. I just couldn't seem to admit it to myself." I was silent for a few moments as I watched Baby climb into Riley's lap. "God loves me, Riley. The fact that he brought me here is proof of that."

He didn't look convinced.

"You know, your dad gave me the best word to describe what God did for me."

"What's that?"

"Salvaged."

"Salvaged?"

"I was alone, literally in a pit. I spent hours and hours alone every day with nobody to talk to. My only hope was the Lord, his presence. Talking to Jesus was the thing that kept me from losing my mind. Although saying that out loud seems to make the point of my sanity a debatable issue."

"Don't say that. You're the sanest person I know."

Out of the blue the visualization of the word *salvaged* hit me. "God reached in, grabbed me, and salvaged me from my depths of despair. He brought me here where I could be restored, and he used you and everyone else here to do it. That's God's mercy, his grace, and his love. I can't imagine a better picture of it."

Riley was crying. "I guarantee, Charlie, you know how to turn me into a blubbering idiot."

"Crying is my specialty."

"Tell me about it." He looked up at me and grinned.

"Riley, please don't carry an offense against God on my behalf. I'm going to be fine."

"I'll try not to. It's so difficult; none of this is reasonable."

"If everything was easy or made sense, why would we need faith?"

"Okay, now you're just showing off, sounding like some dang spiritual guru or something."

I removed Baby from his lap and climbed into the spot she vacated. He wrapped his arms around me and laid his head against mine.

Several minutes passed before I spoke again. "I think I know how to make the nightmares start to go away."

"You do?" he asked.

"Yes."

"How?"

"I think it starts with making a phone call."

"Are you sure you're ready?"

"No." My chest quivered as anxiety rushed into my body.

"What are you gonna say?"

"I have no idea. I pray that God will give me the words."

I got out of his lap, took a seat at the desk, picked up the phone, and dialed the number.

Taking a deep breath, I waited for someone to answer the phone.

"Hello?" The sound of his voice made my legs go weak, and I was grateful to be sitting down. I hadn't heard his voice in months.

"Dad."

"Attie?" He immediately started crying, and although he was speaking, I couldn't understand his words.

It felt like my heart stopped beating.

"Dad … Dad, it's all right. Please don't cry."

I remained calm as my father wept on the other end of the line. I remained composed, if for no other reason than that I had no emotion left to display.

"Forgive me," he muttered. "I just couldn't tell you."

"I do, Dad, I do forgive you. I'm deeply, deeply hurt, but I forgive you."

His words continued to be unrecognizable.

"Dad, I'm going to hang up now. I just wanted to call and tell you that I love you and that I'm all right. I'm in good hands here, and I'm very happy. You can come back whenever you're ready, and if you're never ready, I'll be okay with that too. All right?"

He didn't answer.

"I'll talk to you soon, Dad. Good-bye." I hung up the phone knowing that in reality I wouldn't be talking to him anytime soon at all.

"Are you okay?"

"Yes. It's strange; as I talked to him I didn't really think of him as my dad. Like I told Pops, the man I grew up knowing is gone. The man I just talked to was a complete stranger. Even his voice sounded different. It's like there was no connection whatsoever."

"I'm sorry."

"Maybe one day my dad will come back to life. Maybe I'll see him again, who knows."

"Is there anything I can do to help?"

"Not anything you haven't done already. I think I killed my biggest monster. We should sleep more peacefully from now on."

"I hope so," he whispered.

I walked over to him and climbed back into his lap.

"So what's on the movie agenda tonight?" I asked.

"Um, Dad and Mom wanna talk to us."

"About what?"

"They figured us out."

"Figured us out?"

"Yeah, evidently we haven't hidden our interest in each other very well."

"How long have they known?"

"All summer."

"You're kidding?"

"No. Clearly, we're horrible actors."

"We haven't liked each other *all* summer," I clarified.

"Speak for yourself."

chapter 32

"There she is," Pops announced as I made my way into the room.

"Well, this is highly awkward," I admitted.

"You sure know how to draw a crowd." Nicole jumped up and gave me a hug. "Are you okay?"

"Yes." I gave her a squeeze before she released me to sit back down with the others. Pops stood up and motioned for me to take his vacant seat. "Is court now in session?" I asked.

Pops laughed. "What court is that?"

"The one that decides that fate of my relationship with Riley."

"Is it a relationship?" Joshua asked, looking at me.

"Not yet," I answered. "Maybe not ever. I guess that depends on what all of you think."

"Do you like him?" Joshua asked bluntly.

I looked over at Riley. He gazed back at me. "Yes."

Joshua looked at Riley. "Do you like her?"

"Obviously." His eyes stayed locked on mine as he spoke.

I gave him a small grin and a wink. We'd been looking forward to being together for the majority of the summer, and we were prepared to present our case to the jury.

"Well." Pops lifted himself so that he was sitting on the kitchen counter. "As I told Riley yesterday, this is no surprise to anyone in the room, Attiline. We've all known for months ... no, years, that Riley was interested in you. Molly and I discussed it when Eddie first asked if you could stay with us for the summer. We expected

Riley's feelings but weren't sure if you would reciprocate. Evidently you do."

I nodded in acknowledgement.

He shrugged. "Far be it for us to stand in the way of true love, right, Molly?"

She enthusiastically nodded her blonde head. "Right."

He continued. "I don't wanna take the joy away from the fact that you're gonna be living with us for a while. We're thrilled about that. But this does complicate things. Joshua, you wanna jump in here?"

"Of course." Joshua stood and walked over to join Pops at the counter. "We support you two. We love you, and we want you to be happy, whether that means you date or you don't. I've spent hours with each of you, and I know where you are spiritually, personally, emotionally, physically, all of it. I've told your parents that I trust you. I believe that you two will respect any boundaries that we, your support group so to speak, put into place."

"Thank you," Riley spoke, but his eyes remained locked on me.

I removed my gaze from Riley and saw Joshua pull a folded-up piece of paper from his back pocket.

"We've written down some guidelines that we would like to share with you." He unfolded the piece of paper and read from it. "First, you may no longer enter each other's rooms. If you want to talk to each other, one of you better be on the other side of the doorway."

Riley and I both nodded in agreement.

"Second, you may not be alone in any room of the house with the door shut."

I visualized the house and realized that the boundary was redundant seeing as how our bedrooms were pretty much the only rooms we went into that had doors on them. But I kept my mouth shut and nodded at the second condition.

"Third, little to no physical contact when you're in the house."

We all caught Riley roll his eyes.

"It may sound harsh," Joshua spoke directly to Riley, "but trust us, with as much time as the two of you will be spending together, touching each other all the time will not make this easier on you. The more 'familiar' you are with each other, the more difficult it's going to be to resist temptation when you're alone."

"This is beyond embarrassing," I admitted out loud.

"Don't be embarrassed, Attie." Marme reached over and patted my arm. "We're on your side. Plus, we can't ignore the elephant in the room. We've all been teenagers, and it was hard enough without living with the people we were dating."

"Fourth," Joshua continued, "each of you will meet with Nicole and me weekly. It won't be a counseling session as much as it'll be a debriefing. I would hope that if you're struggling in any way with temptation or anything like that, you'd bring it up during our time together."

Pops spoke up again. "Molly and I are your parents, so we realize you won't be comfortable coming to us with issues. Having Joshua and Nicole for that will be a great outlet for you two."

"I won't share anything with your parents unless I ask your permission first." Joshua walked over and placed his hands on my shoulders. "I don't see that needing to happen, but I'll warn you now that if I feel this spinning out of control I will intervene."

I looked up at him. "Yes, sir."

"We've already agreed that if this becomes too difficult, one of you will be living with us."

It was all common sense to me.

"Fifth..."

"There's more?" Riley was growing impatient with the boundaries.

"This is the last one," Joshua assured. "You'll attend church every Sunday and youth on Wednesday nights." His eyes darted back and forth between Riley and me. "So can we all agree to the rules?"

"Yes," Riley and I spoke in unison.

"All right then, you have our blessing," Pops announced.

"Why do I feel like we should have popped open a bottle of champagne after you announced that?" Marme asked.

"Because you're as excited about the two of them dating as they are," he informed her.

"True." She nodded her head and clapped her hands. "I really am. I think you're adorable together."

"Oh yeah, one more thing," Joshua announced as he made his way over to Riley. "You hurt her and your dad and I will hurt you. Got that, Riley?"

I giggled.

"Me?" Riley squealed. "She's the one with the power here."

"What does that mean?" I asked.

"I'm much more involved in this than you are."

"What?" I asked. We'd forgotten that there were other people in the room.

"It's true. You have a much better chance of breaking my heart than I do of breaking yours."

"That's not true. Just because I wasn't on the bandwagon as early as you were doesn't mean I'm not completely on it now. If this ship sinks, we're both doomed."

"You two better shut your mouths," Pops interrupted. "Or I'm calling the entire thing off now. That's all we need, two heartbroken teenagers moping around our house."

"There will be no heartbreaking going on," Riley announced. "We're meant to be."

"That's so sweet." Nicole was gushing. "Remember when you used to like me like that, Josh?"

"Give them time, Nicole. They'll get sick of each other before long," he teased before kissing her on the nose.

"All right." Pops clapped again to bring the room to order. "This court session is now over."

"Thank God." Riley rolled his eyes and slunk farther into his chair. "That was brutal."

Pops ignored him and continued, "So when's the big official first date?"

Riley sat back up in his chair, and a grin spread across his face as he looked back over at me. "What do you think?"

"I think you haven't even officially asked me yet," I answered.

He smirked. "So, Charlie,"—he leaned across the table as he spoke—"will you go out with me?"

"On a date?"

"Yes." He nodded. "An actual date."

Again, it was as if there was no one else in the room.

"I'd love to."

"Thank God." He laughed as he laid his head on the table. "You have no idea what a relief that is to hear."

"You're a doll baby, Riley," Marme announced. "Who could say no to you?"

Riley looked back up at me and grinned. "Tomorrow night then?"

"Sounds good."

"Goody, we get to go shopping for an outfit!" Marme said.

"Oooh, can I come?" Nicole asked.

"The more the merrier," I said.

Pops got our attention again. "Well, I have a gift for you two."

"I love gifts!"

"We know," Riley teased.

Pops walked into his bedroom and returned with two large beanbag chairs.

"What in the world?" Riley asked.

"Well, since you can't go into each other's rooms, I figured we could put them in the upstairs hallway so you can hang out up there when you wanna get away from us without getting totally away from us."

"Good thinking, babe," Marme said proudly.

"Wow, that's a great idea. Thanks, Dad."

"Trust me, you two, I've put as much thought into this as you have. Now granted, I've focused on how to keep the two of you safely away from each other rather than what you've been thinking about. I believe I even contemplated plastic bubbles at one point."

I stood, walked over to him, and gave him a hug. "We'll be good. I promise."

"I know you will." He kissed me on the top of my head. "All right, let's leave these two lovebirds alone for a little while. They've got a big date to plan."

I jumped onto the counter as everyone but Riley filed out of the room.

"Does this feel strange to you?" he asked from his seat.

"Totally. I hope the anticipation wasn't better than the reality is."

He leaned toward me and spoke in a hushed voice. "I've already kissed you twice, Charlie. I can say with one hundred percent certainty that the reality will be much better than the anticipation."

"But the mystery will be gone," I warned.

He sat back in his chair and chuckled. "Trust me, you are and always will be a complete mystery to me."

"You, on the other hand, are an open book."

"I realize that. It's disgraceful but true." He stood and walked toward me but stopped a few inches away. "So what do you wanna do for our first date?"

"I don't know. I've never been on a date before."

"That's a lot of pressure on a guy—being the first date and all."

"I'm sure you'll be the guy for a lot of my firsts."

"Good to know." He acted as if he licked the tip of an imaginary pencil and wrote in the air. "Should we start a list? For a few of these we'll have to wait until we're married."

"Riley! First of all, that's not what I meant, and secondly, we haven't even gone on a date yet, so I don't think you should be talking about marriage. That's a little overconfident and unrealistic, don't you think?"

"I'm an open book, and I'm gonna tell it like it is. Ten years from now, our kids are gonna be running around this house."

"Kids?"

He nodded. "Oh yeah."

"We won't still be living with your parents, will we?"

"No." He laughed and shook his head. "They'll be babysitting."

I put my hand on his face. "You've lost your mind, Riley Bennett."

"You're breaking the third rule," he informed.

I yanked my hand away. "Sorry." I hopped off the counter and walked past him toward the refrigerator. "Just for the record, I'm not getting married until I finish undergrad."

I felt him walk up behind me as I opened the fridge door and grabbed two bottled waters.

"You're gonna be on that accelerated program, right?" He was so close that his breath was warm on my neck, and the sensation caused chills to run down my spine.

"Riley," I spoke without turning to face him, "it's probably not a good idea to stand that close to me."

"Why?"

"It makes me want to break rules one, two, and three."

He moved away from me, and I heard him laugh as he left the kitchen.

"Don't you want the water I got out for you? It'll cool you off."

"You keep it." He laughed. "Sounds like you need it more than I do."

. . . .

"You called?" Jesus asked as soon as I put my ear buds in.

"I did. I assume you heard the conversation that took place downstairs."

He sat down on the bed next to me. "Of course."

"Well, it's great to have their permission and everything, but I wanted to run it by you too. Riley and I like each other, and we want to go out, but—"

"I know."

"So how do you feel about it? Are you okay with that?"

"Would it matter if I wasn't?"

"Yes, it would matter. If you told me not to do it, I wouldn't. I know you would tell me no if it were in my best interest."

"I appreciate that."

"It's true."

"I know it is." Jesus smiled at me. "Riley's parents, Joshua, and Nicole have been praying about this for months. As they told you, this is no surprise to them—or to me. They've put a lot of thought into their boundaries, and they've consulted me about it as well. They feel at peace about it because I feel at peace about it."

"So you're okay with it?"

"Yes, as long as you follow the rules. If you ever decide to be deceitful or not follow the guidelines, I'll feel differently, but I don't see that happening. You two are good kids, and like I said before, I believe that you're good for each other."

"I believe that too."

I was relieved that Jesus was accepting of our relationship.

"But something else is bothering you. Why don't you talk to me about it?"

My mind wandered off for a few moments, and I sat in a trance as I thought about Jesus's words to me at the river.

He read my mind. "We haven't spoken since our talk at the river. I don't think you and I ever came to any resolution about it."

"Evidently, I need to deal with some forgiveness issues. Is that what you think my nightmares are?"

"Yes. Your subconscious has a way of speaking to you even when your conscious mind doesn't want to listen."

"And you can help me with the whole forgiveness process? Honestly, I thought I'd already dealt with it all."

"Ignoring and forgiving isn't the same thing. Just because you don't think about it on a regular basis doesn't mean you've forgiven. Refusing to accept that your father has abandoned you doesn't mean he hasn't."

"I guess that's true." The reference to my father brought tears. "Why isn't he coming back?"

"Because he's hurting and he isn't thinking clearly right now."

"Will he ever?"

"I can't tell you that. But calling him today was a big step. Releasing him of any obligation to you will allow him to begin to forgive himself, which in turn will start the healing process for him.

"For you, it's the realization that you can't control another human being. The only person you can control is you. Forgiveness is a choice, Attie. It's a choice you will have to make every single day until it's no longer an issue for you. And then, even when you think you've completely forgiven, something may happen, and you'll have to start the process all over again."

"Lovely," I said sarcastically.

"When I command people to forgive others and to pray for their enemies, it isn't so the other person, *the offender*, will benefit. It's for the offended, so *they* will benefit. I want you to forgive your father *for you*, Attie, not for him. I want you to sleep at night, and I want you to be joyful again. Holding on to anger, hurt, or an offense becomes a burden and literally depletes joy from your spirit. I love you, and that's not what I want for you."

"So what, I pray for him, that's it?"

"For right now, yes. Unselfish prayers. You pray for him to return to me, not to you. It's my relationship with him that's most important, not yours. But through having a relationship with me, he's much more likely to reestablish a connection with you. You have to pray for what's best for your dad, and right now that may not be what you think it should. Being here may not be what's best for him, and quite honestly, it may not be what's best for you either. I need you to trust me in this."

"I do."

"Look at your life now, Attie. Look how far you've come in such a short time. You have so much to look forward to; don't let unforgiveness stand in your way."

"I won't. I'm ready to deal with it. How do I start?"

chapter 33

I slowly drove down East Noble Road until I found the correct house. Pulling the car to a stop, I took a deep breath before turning off the engine, getting out of the car, and heading toward the front door.

I rang the doorbell and waited for someone to answer. In less than a minute I heard tiny footsteps running toward the door, and as it opened, a small towheaded boy looked up at me.

"May I help you?" He sounded very proper for a child of only four or five.

"Is your father home?"

"He's in the garage. You can go back there," he said before the door slammed shut.

Making my way across a trail of steppingstones laying in the grass, I found the garage on the side of the house.

"Hello?" I asked as I neared the garage. "Mr. King?"

"Come on in." I heard a voice but didn't see anyone. "I'm not interested in buying anything."

I walked into the garage and found a man sitting at a workbench. His back was to me. "Oh, I'm not selling anything." My voice shook, and I was about to lose my nerve. "I just needed to talk to you."

He turned to face me, and as soon as he saw my face, he dropped his hammer. Mitchell King was in shock.

I ran over, picked up the hammer, and offered it back.

"Um, thank…thank you." He stood and removed his baseball cap. "I'm sorry. I didn't recognize you at first."

"Oh, that's all right. I know you weren't expecting me. I just decided to come by before I lost my nerve. I hope you don't mind."

"No. Of course not." He swiftly removed some newspapers from a chair. "Would you like to have a seat?"

"Thank you." As I sat down, he fell back onto the barstool. "I hope I'm not interrupting anything."

"No. Not at all."

"I don't even know what to say. I just felt like I needed to see you."

I noticed his hands were shaking.

"Mr. King," I continued as I looked down at my fidgeting hands, "I know this sounds insane, but I feel like I'm supposed to let you know that I forgive you for the accident. It may sound pompous of me, like I think I have the right to 'forgive' you or something. I wanted to make sure you knew that I'm not angry with you. I don't blame you at all for the accident. I'm selfishly doing this more for me than you, and I realize that I'm rambling, but I don't know what to say here. I just…I just want you to know that I'm sorry for any pain that you've experienced."

Mr. King was silent.

"Right." I stood and began to head out of the garage. "Well, I guess I'll go."

"No, don't go," he yelled after me. "I'm sorry; it was rude of me not to say anything."

I sat back onto the chair. "I understand. I'd be shocked too if I were in your shoes."

"I've tried to talk to you a few times, but Mr. Bennett didn't think the timing was right."

"I can imagine. He's very protective of me."

"I can't blame him for that. You've been through a lot."

"So have you, I would assume."

"I didn't lose a loved one, but I've had to try to reconcile the idea that I took the lives of a mother, wife, daughter, and sister. I'm so sorry for that."

"We're two people that are stuck in a horrible situation that we didn't cause."

"Well," he mumbled, "you didn't cause it anyway."

"You didn't cause it either, Mr. King. It was an unfortunate accident. My mom wasn't paying attention, and you didn't have enough time to respond. Nobody blames you. I know I don't."

"I appreciate that."

"Mr. King—"

"Mitchell. Please call me Mitchell."

"All right. Mitchell, I want you to feel absolved of any responsibility." He wept as I spoke. "That's a burden you don't need to carry."

"You have no idea what this visit means to me, Attie. The guilt overtook my life. This year has been a nightmare."

I laughed, and it caught him off guard. "Sorry." I shook my head. "I can relate to that statement. That's partly why I'm here. It's pretty much a nonending nightmare for me as well."

He wiped his nose and let out a small laugh. "Well, aren't we a miserable pair?"

"Yes, in fact we are. But maybe some good will come out of all this. We can only hope, right?"

"Some good has already come for me. My family started going to church. We've made some great friends there who have helped us out a lot. Our lives have changed for the better."

"I'm so glad."

He pointed over his shoulder at his workbench. "Heck, I've even got myself a new hobby."

"Oh yeah, what's that?"

"Well, come on over and I'll show you."

Hopping off the chair, I went to stand beside him.

"I make leather jewelry. I've even been able to sell some of it in a few of the local stores."

"Really? How cool." I picked up one of the pieces and examined it. "This is great. Is it hard to do?"

"Not at all. Do you want to give it a try?"

"Would you mind?"

"Nah, I'd enjoy the company. My wife got tired of it about two weeks in." Pulling up another barstool, I sat down next to him. "All right, you choose a piece of leather ... "

I spent several hours with Mitchell as he taught me how to make and decorate leather bracelets. As we worked alongside one another, we shared our experiences of the last year. I told him about my nightmares, and he shared that he suffered from some as well. Ironically, in his nightmares he saw my face just as it was before his car made impact with ours.

We were hopeful that our resolution would bring us some peace of mind and spirit. I had the gut feeling that it would help more than we could even imagine.

I left Mitchell's house with one last stop to make in my quest to completely rid the monsters from my dreams.

· ·

"Hey, Mom," I said as I sat down next to her headstone. "What a year, huh?"

I looked around to make sure nobody was in the area and would overhear me talking to myself.

"Well, you'll be excited to hear this. I'm going on my first date tonight. It's with none other than Riley Bennett. You'd be shocked; he's turned into the nicest boy ever. He cares about me a lot, and he's been great to me since I moved into his house ... "

I spent a couple of hours talking to her about my summer and all of my new friends and family. I could picture her sitting down next to me, deeply interested in all my news, but I didn't bother to talk to her about Dad. I was sure she'd already been aware of the situation, and I didn't feel the need to talk about it any further. I'd save that discussion for another time.

"I guess I'd better be going. I've got to get ready for the big event. I'll come back and tell you all about it." I stood up and brushed some grass off of my shorts. "Mom, one more thing. Um ... I wanted to let you know that I'm all right now. I think the worst is over, and I've moved beyond being angry with anyone. I don't know if that type of thing bothers you up there in heaven, probably not. But, just in case, I've forgiven you. I've forgiven you for not paying attention while you were driving and for leaving me here all alone, for all of it.

"I would have done all of this a long time ago had I known that I needed to. I'm sorry that I've withheld it from you. Would you tell Melody all of this stuff? I'm sure she'll be interested in hearing it, especially the part about me going out with her brother. She'll get quite the kick out of that.

"I miss you, but I'm much better now. I wanted you to know that."

I felt much lighter as I made my way back to the car. I'd dealt with my demons and was ready to move on with my life. I would now focus on the positive and happy memories of my dad, mom, and Melody. None of them would want anything different than that. They would all want me happy.

chapter 34

I sat folding laundry as Marme busied herself in the kitchen. It was obvious we were both excited about my upcoming date with Riley, but we weren't exactly sure how to go about discussing it.

She threw a pot clambering into the sink before turning to me. "This is killing me, Attie. I'm dying to talk about how you're feeling about the date tonight. It's your first date!"

"Me too, it's just weird. You're my mom for all intents and purposes, so I want to talk about it with you, but you're also Riley's mom, which makes it awkward."

"Well, what if we act like it's somebody else? A boy named 'Bob' maybe."

"Bob?"

"Then we aren't talking about you dating my son, we're talking about you dating Bob."

The idea sounded brilliant to me. We would have the best of both worlds. Marme and I would be able to reclaim some of the mother/daughter bonding moments we'd both been missing out on, but it would be less embarrassing because we wouldn't be talking about Riley...per se.

"It's worth a try," I said.

"Great!" She ran over to the seat next to me and plopped down. "So are you excited?"

"Very."

"Do you know where you'll be going?"

"No clue. Bob won't tell me."

"So he's keeping it all a secret then?"

"Yes. I've tried to pry it out of him, but he won't budge."

"What's he like? Does he treat you well?"

"He's the sweetest boy I've ever met. I think he'd do just about anything for me."

She leaned forward and placed her face in her hands. "He's a sweetheart?"

"And a gentleman."

She let out a happy sigh.

"His mother must have raised him well."

"I sure did—I mean, she sure must have."

We laughed just as Riley startled us by walking into the room. "What are you guys doing in here?"

"Nothing," we answered simultaneously, and I was certain we sounded guilty.

Marme and I quickly glanced at each other and then busied ourselves with folding bath towels.

"Who's Bob?" he asked. "I heard somebody mention a guy named Bob." He stuffed a cookie into his mouth and looked at us as he waited for a response.

I glanced at his mother and then back at him. "Um, just a guy."

"Just a guy?" he asked with his mouth full.

Here I'd just told his mother what a gentleman he was, and now he was talking with his mouth full. We'd have to work on that.

"Then why do you look guilty?" he asked.

I panicked at the fear that he would know I was lying. "Guilty? Do I look guilty?"

"Yes, you big liar, you look totally guilty. Spill it."

I knew it; he caught me red-handed. Riley practically knew me better than I knew myself.

"Well, Bob is the *gentleman* that's taking me out on a date tonight."

I threw my hand over my eyes and waited for his wrath to descend upon me.

"Oh my Lord! You're talking to my mother about us?"

"No, Riley." She rushed to my defense. "Attie's telling me about her date tonight with a boy named Bob."

He kicked my chair. "Atticus Elizabeth Reed, you big wimp. Couldn't you have just told her no when she asked for the details? She's my mother for cryin' out loud! How embarrassing."

My hand was still covering my face when I heard Pops walk into the kitchen.

"What's the matter?" he asked.

"Attie's spilling the beans to your nosey wife about our relationship."

"Well, that's embarrassing," his dad said dryly.

I peeked through my fingers at Riley. He was smiling down at me, so I removed my hand and gave him a weak smile back. "I'm sorry, Riley. I just needed someone to share it with; that's all."

"You've got a hen house full of friends. Couldn't you talk to one of them about it?"

"I already do. Besides, its not the same thing."

"Yeah, Riley," Marme said, snapping a towel his direction, "give us a break. This is what moms and daughters do. We're all we've got, and if you won't let us talk about it, then as long as you two are together, neither one of us will ever get to talk boys."

His shoulders dropped as he gave me a sympathetic smile. "Nothing too personal, Charlie, don't get crazy or anything."

"I won't. I mean really, there isn't much to tell."

He looked over at his dad, who waved his hands in front of him. "Don't look at me. This is your problem; I'm staying out of it."

Marme and I glanced at each other. We both knew Riley was caving.

"Fine, enjoy your girl talk," he said, turning and walking out of the kitchen. "I've got some errands to run. I'll see you later."

"Like I said, he'll do just about anything I ask," I said, grabbing another towel.

Pops hung his head in shame. "The poor boy never had a chance. I'd say it's gonna be getting interesting around here."

. . . .

"Attiline, someone's at the door for you."

"For me?"

"Yes, now get your butt down here."

"You're sounding more and more like one of my parents every day, bossing me around and all," I teased as I marched down the stairs.

"Good. And just think, in a week I'll be your principal too."

"Lucky me."

I threw open the front door and found Riley standing on the porch holding a bouquet of yellow roses. As a big grin filled his face, it felt like all those fireflies we'd captured over the years simultaneously lit up in my chest.

"You ready to go?" he asked.

I could see Pops and Marme in my peripheral vision. "Maybe you should come in and meet my parents," I joked.

Riley walked into the house and handed me the flowers. "For you."

"Thank you for the flowers, Riley. They're beautiful."

"Not as beautiful as you."

I looked over at his parents. "Have you met this hopeless boy?"

"He's practically unrecognizable." Pops shook his head. "It's sickening."

"I think it's adorable," Marme disagreed with her husband. "Here, Attie, give me the flowers and I'll go put them in water." I obliged, and the adults left Riley and me standing in the foyer.

This was the first time I'd seen Riley in something other than jeans or shorts of some kind. He wore a pair of khaki linen slacks and a brown short sleeve button down shirt. His thick mane lay in muddled, loose curls on his head. I never understood how he could pull off such a messy bed head look, but he looked fantastic. I wore a simple brown summer dress and felt plain compared to his near perfection.

He took a step toward me and then stopped.

"What?" I asked.

He walked backwards until he was standing on the porch and then summoned me with his pointer finger for me to join him. As soon as my feet were outside the house, he grabbed me and wrapped his arms around my body in a tight embrace. I laid my head against his chest and could hear his heartbeat. It was strong and fast, and I could only assume that its fierce pounding matched mine.

"I can't believe we're finally going out." He released his grip and lightly kissed me on the forehead.

"Me either."

"You ready?"

"Let me get my purse. I'll be right back; don't move."

"I'm not going anywhere without you."

He waited as I ran inside, grabbed my purse, said good-bye to his parents, and met him back out on the porch. I was out of breath, and it caused Riley to laugh. "I'm ready."

He led me to his car and opened the passenger door for me. The scent of his cologne permeated the interior of his car. I closed my eyes and took in several deep breaths.

"You asleep?" he asked as he got in the driver's side.

"No. I'm enjoying the smell of your car. It smells just like you. We should take your car more often."

"No way. Why do you think I like to take your car everywhere?"

"It smells like me?"

"Oh yeah."

"Where are we going?" I asked as he put his seatbelt on.

"You like steak, right?"

"Love it."

"That's what I thought. We're going to a place in the city that I've heard is really nice. Very fancy."

"You've never been there?"

"It's our first date. I'm not gonna take you somewhere I've already been. This will be a first for both of us."

I placed a checkmark into the air. "Add it to the list."

"Good girl." He nodded but kept his eyes on the road in front of him.

The restaurant was the fanciest one that I'd ever been to. The woodwork was dark, and there was barely any light overhead. We laughed at each other as we tried to read our menus by candlelight.

"Good grief, Riley, this place is way too expensive."

"Don't worry about it. We'll have McDonald's next time if that'll make you feel better."

"Really, you have to pay for everything separately. It's going to cost a fortune."

He glared at me but didn't say a word.

"All right, all right," I conceded and browsed the small menu.

"Do you want a crab cake to start with?" he asked.

"Yes. That sounds good. Have you decided what you're getting for the main course?"

"I think I'm gonna get this prime rib-eye. What about you?"

"Same thing. I bet it's huge. Do you want to split a baked potato or something?"

"Sure."

Our conversation easily flowed as we drank our sodas and ate the crab cake. When the waiter returned with our meal, he shined a small flashlight onto our steaks and asked us to cut into them to make sure they were cooked properly. I tried not to chuckle at the ridiculousness of the flashlight.

As soon as the waiter walked away, Riley rolled his eyes. "Why don't they just turn on the dang lights?" He'd read my mind. "Seriously, a flashlight?" He laughed. "I appreciate the whole 'ambiance' thing, but if you have to shine a flashlight on somebody's food for them to see it, there's a problem."

I giggled as I cut into my steak. "This is romantic, Riley; don't you get that?"

"Oh, is that romantic? I just thought it was stupid. This restaurant's nice, but I'd like to see you sitting across from me. I can barely see your face it's so dark in here."

"It adds to the mystery. Just go with it."

"I hate to complain, but between this and the movie, I won't be able to see you all night. It's a major disappointment."

I picked up the candle and held it up to my face. "Does this help?" I asked with a big cheesy grin on my face.

"Yes. Just hold that right there all night and I'll be good. Here," he said, reaching across the table with his knife and fork. "I'll cut your steak for you so you don't have to put the candle down."

"Don't you dare." I placed the candle back onto the table. "They'll kick us out of this place for being too white trash. We must not appreciate the finer things of life. The steak's good though."

"I'm glad." He winked at me before taking his first bite.

Conversation continued as we finished our meal. We talked about everything from school to movies and books. The awkwardness wore off, and we were free to be ourselves.

• •

(Riley)

When the movie let out, Attie and I decided to return to town and go to the park for a while. After arriving, we sat in the car talking for several minutes before I reached across the dashboard, opened the glove box, and pulled out a small gift-wrapped box.

Attie squealed. "You got me a gift?"

I laughed as I handed it to her. "Of course." I would never get tired of seeing her reaction each time I gave her a gift.

She quickly unwrapped the box and opened it.

"Oh, Riley, it's beautiful!" She removed the ring from the box and held it up to the light.

A round green peridot stone sat in a thin band and halo of tiny diamonds (at least that's how the saleslady described it to me when I bought it).

"It's your birthstone," I informed her.

"I love it." She started to place it on her finger, but I stopped her and motioned for her to hand the ring back to me.

"I wanna ask you something first," I announced.

"You're not going to ask me to marry you, are you?"

"Not yet. That'll come later." I wasn't totally kidding. "But I do wanna ask you a serious question."

She turned in her seat so that she was facing me. "All right."

"I can't believe I'm finally getting to do this," I admitted.

"Do what?"

"Ask if you will *officially* be my girlfriend."

A large smile formed on her gorgeous face. "You are?"

"I am." I nodded. "Honestly, there's nothing I want more than for you to be my girlfriend."

"I'd like that very much."

Slowly grabbing her hand, I slid the ring on her finger. "Look at that, it looks great on you."

"It's beautiful. It would look great on anyone. I love it; thank you so much."

"You're welcome."

"Okay, well now I'm sort of embarrassed." She buried her face in her hands and shook her head.

"Why?"

"I brought a gift for you, but it's nowhere near as great as what you gave me."

"You got me a gift? No girl has ever given me a gift before."

She peeked out between her fingers. "Another first."

"That's right." I laughed. "Another first. Now can I see my gift? I'm stoked."

"Please don't be overly excited about it. Really, it isn't anything that great. I'm actually starting to think it's too hokey."

"Well, let me see it … please."

She rolled her eyes and pouted a little but eventually reached into her purse and pulled out a box. I practically had to yank it out of her grip so that I could open it.

"This is so embarrassing." She covered her eyes as I unwrapped the paper. "Okay, wait," she shouted.

"What?"

"Just a warning. I made it myself, so don't have high expectations or anything."

My heart melted. "You *made* what's in this box?"

"Yes."

"There's no way I'm not gonna like it."

"Oh yes, there is."

I carefully removed the gift wrap and opened the box.

"It's a cuff bracelet," she explained.

Removing it from the box, I held it up to light so that I could appreciate it more. It was made from dark brown leather and had the word *Salvaged* stamped in it.

"Charlie, this is amazing. You made this? How?"

"Out of an old belt. It's not very hard to do."

"I can't believe you did this for me."

"You don't have to wear it. I realize it may be a little much."

"It's the coolest thing I've ever seen. I love it."

"If you'll look on the inside you can see that I branded our initials and today's date on it."

I turned it over and saw the emblem. I was speechless.

"Here, let me help you put it on." I watched as she untied the leather strip that linked the ends together, wrapped the cuff around my wrist, and then secured it in place. "There. What do you think?"

"It's amazing. Thank you so much."

"I made one for myself too." She reached into her purse and pulled out a thinner version of the same cuff. "Except this one's more girlie. I bedazzled mine." She slid it on her wrist. "See, we're a set."

"We're perfect," I added.

Attie leaned her head back against the headrest and gazed at me. Her eyes were warm and full of admiration. The way she was looking at me made all the days of waiting well worth it. I wanted to kiss her, but I couldn't muster up enough courage.

"Do you wanna get out and walk around?" I asked.

"Sure."

Holding hands, we walked in silence for several minutes before taking seats in a couple of swings.

"You don't like it, do you, Riley?"

"Like what?"

"The cuff. It's okay, really."

"I do like it. I love it; why would you think I didn't?"

"You've barely said a word since I gave it to you."

"Trust me, it's not that."

"Well then, what is it?" she whispered. "What's the matter?"

"Can I be brutally honest?"

"Of course."

I held my legs out and entwined them around hers so that our swings pulled closely together.

"I'm a nervous wreck," I confessed.

"About what?"

"Kissing you. I want to but I'm scared to death."

"Riley! Good grief, you've already kissed me twice. Why would you freak out about it now?"

"The other two times, they just happened. There was no time to get nervous, so I didn't think about. I just did it."

"Seriously? That's so cute. I'm not nervous at all."

"No?"

"No," she said quickly.

Attie unwrapped her legs from mine and stood up. Placing her hands on the chains of my swing, she leaned closely to me.

"I could kiss you," she offered in a sultry voice.

"Really?" It sounded very appealing seeing as how I couldn't move.

"Um-hmm," she whispered.

My heart raced as she slowly brought her face to mine, but instead of our lips touching, her nose sweetly grazed mine several times.

"There's an Eskimo kiss," she explained softly before kissing the tip of my nose.

"Close your eyes," she said quietly.

Of course, I obeyed and was rewarded by a small kiss on each eyelid.

"You're killing me," I admitted.

She stood back up and giggled. "Sorry."

The distance between us became unbearable. I stood and pulled her to me. "I love you, Charlie."

"I love you too." She placed her lips onto mine, and my entire body felt faint. I gently pulled my face away and placed my hands on her cheeks.

"You do? You love me?"

She giggled. "Yes. Of course I do."

"You're not just saying that because I did?"

She shook her head. "No." Her eyes searched my face as if she were looking for a sign of what was going through my mind. "Riley?" A small crease formed between her eyebrows. "Are you all right?"

I leaned down and kissed her crumpled brow. "I'm perfect."

"Good, you scared me there for a second."

"I think I need to sit for a minute."

I grabbed one of her hands in mine and made my way to the merry-go-round.

"Riley?"

"I feel a little overwhelmed." Little was an understatement, but I didn't wanna scare her to death by letting her know how overpowered I was feeling. I was vulnerable and weak.

"What are you overwhelmed by?"

"Are you joking?"

"No." She was dead serious.

"The girl I love just told me that she loved me back. I swear, I think my heart's gonna explode."

She giggled again. "Oh, you're so sweet."

"I'm whipped is what I am."

"I'm sorry," she said as she rubbed my shoulder.

"I'm not. It's the most amazing feeling ever."

"I would have to agree. I feel the same way, but I thought I was the only one."

I turned so that we were facing each other, and her hand fell into her lap. "Why did you think it was just you?"

"This is all new to me, Riley. I've never been in love before."

"This is all new to me. I've never been in love before either."

I reached over and traced the outline of her face with my fingers.

"Are you trying to memorize my mug so you can sketch it later?" she teased.

"I've already got your face memorized, Charlie. I'm just enjoying finally being able to touch it."

Once I removed my hand from her face, Attie made her way over to the jungle gym. I turned the merry-go-round so that I could watch her without needing to turn my head.

"Do you want to know one of the things I love about our relationship?"

It was wonderful to hear her say the words "our relationship" and know that she was talking about the two of us.

"Of course."

"What we feel for each other isn't clouded by physical cravings."

"I don't understand what you're saying."

I had plenty of physical cravings.

"Well..." She paused as she carefully walked across the suspension bridge. "We've been together every available moment for three months, we've slept next to each other over eighty times, and we've only kissed twice."

"Don't remind me."

She laughed. "No, seriously, Riley. I think kids our age tend to get physical too fast, before they even know if they truly like each other. Then their feelings are jumbled up because they aren't sure if they like the person or just like *being with* the person. It may be fun, like Curt said, but what's special about it?" She stood peering down over the fort wall.

I could answer that from my own experience. "Nothing. There's nothing special about it."

I walked over to the jungle gym and stood below her. The moment was reminiscent of a balcony scene from *Romeo and Juliet*.

Attie elaborated. "I want to spend time with you because you're fun and charming. Don't get me wrong, I like kissing you..." She giggled and then smiled, beaming down at me. "But I love just *being* with you. We don't need to be physical to feel connected to each other, and that's important for a girl my age that's trying to do the right thing.

"I'm sorry that you're beating yourself up over being afraid to kiss me. But there's something comforting to me about knowing that every time you're alone with me you aren't only interested in getting physical." She folded her arms across the wall ledge and placed her chin on her arms. "I feel safe with you."

"You are safe with me. I'm not gonna screw this up."

"I know." Our eyes were fixed on each other for several moments before she spoke again. "Thank you."

"Why are you thanking me?"

"For the perfect first date. The dinner was wonderful, you sat through a chick flick with me, and it was a musical too, which gets you bonus points. And now this."

"Now what?"

"You're being sweet to me. You're just being…my Riley. The boy I fell in love with."

"Don't give me too much credit. It isn't like I don't wanna be hanging all over you or anything."

"But you aren't."

"Probly not for the noble reasons you think."

"Then why?"

I jumped onto the sliding pole and climbed my way up until I joined her on the fort.

"Why don't we cop a squat?" I asked.

Attie lay down on the jungle gym floor. "I want to look at the stars."

"All right."

Not wanting to press my luck, I laid down similarly to how we'd been on the bathroom floor the second day she was here. Only this time, I placed the top of my head against her shoulder. Our cheeks were practically touching, but our bodies were horizontal, and we were facing completely opposite directions. There was no way that we could come into any inappropriate contact.

I started off. "This is beyond embarrassing."

"Since when do we not tell each other things that are embarrassing?"

"I know. It's just weird being so brutally honest all the time."

"It's who we are. I like that about us."

"I do too. I love that about us; it's just a little hard sometimes."

"So what's so embarrassing to talk about?" she asked.

"I'm seventeen years old and outrageously in love with you. Barely touching you could send me over the edge ... if you know what I mean."

"Pardon?"

Evidently, she didn't know.

"Oh, I got you." She giggled. "I know all that stuff. I'm not going to run away screaming if you get a little overexcited."

"You're not?"

"No. Girls get worked up too, you know. In any case, you'll get more and more desensitized to me as time goes on."

"I don't know about that." I couldn't imagine ever getting acclimated to touching her. I hoped the thrill of being near her never went away. "My parents set some boundaries for the time that we're under their roof. We need to set some for when we aren't home but alone."

"I agree. Let's set some ground rules."

"Okay. First, let me fill you in on a few things."

"I'm ready."

"There are times when something is sweet, and there are times when that same thing can be utterly sensual. I need you to be careful with me."

"What do you mean?"

"Call me 'my Riley' when you're ten feet away and we're all good. Whisper it in my ear and we're in trouble. Honestly, Charlie, that was one of the sexiest things I've ever heard. I about died. "

"Really? Okay." Her head was nodding next to mine. "No 'my Rileys' whispered in the ear."

I continued. "Then there are some things that are an automatic problem."

"Like?"

"Like when you kissed my eyes a few minutes ago."

She was surprised. "That?"

"It wasn't the kissing itself; it was the way you did it. Slow and…the way you were talking…well, you get the point. That's pure seduction; there's no way around it."

"You're probably right. I was trying to get you in the mood to kiss me."

"I was already in the mood," I informed her. "Trust me. With you, I'm always in the mood. Sometimes it's just best if I don't."

"All righty then, I get the point."

"It will never be a question of whether or not I wanna touch or kiss you. It'll be a matter of if I should."

"I understand."

She turned her head and lightly kissed me on the cheek.

My mind instantly went blank. "Maybe we should sit up," I suggested.

"I can't kiss you on the cheek?"

"Yes." I laughed. "Yes, you can kiss me on the cheek. I just need to think clearly right now. We need to set the boundaries."

"Okay."

We sat cross-legged and faced each other.

"You're going to have to come up with the boundaries," she said. "I've never done any of it. I would have to use my imagination to come up with no-nos."

"Well, if you have to use your imagination to come up with it, that's a big clue that it would probly be off limits."

She gave a quick nod. "Good point."

"We shouldn't kiss if we're in the horizontal position. It's a little too convenient." Again, I was speaking from experience. "And obviously no getting carried away with our hands."

"Obviously."

"If there's serious heavy breathing going on, we should stop immediately."

"Heavy breathing. Right."

She sounded as if she were writing everything down as I spoke.

I worked my way through a mental checklist of what could cause a boy my age to lose his mind in ecstasy and then realized almost anything could do it. "Ears are an iffy area."

"Kissing the ears or talking into them?"

"Both. Well, again, it's all in how it's done. If you're joking around, it's one thing. In the heat of the moment it becomes dangerous."

"I love how you say 'dangerous.' It cracks me up."

"Unfortunately, I'm not exaggerating."

Her eyes grew wide. "Oh."

"This isn't gonna be easy. We need to be on guard all the time. It'll be worth it though."

"Totally." She nodded. "How much longer until we need to be home?"

I pulled my cell phone out of my pocket to check the time. The picture of Attie and me flashed on the screen. "Ten 'til twelve. We need to get going pretty soon. I don't wanna be late the first night they let us go out."

I stood and then pulled Attie to her feet.

"Thanks again for the date, Riley. I had a great time."

She turned to go down the slide, but I grabbed her hand and turned her back to me.

"I didn't say we were leaving right now. I just said we needed to go soon. We've got about thirty minutes or so."

She looked up at me through her eyelashes and smirked. "What did you have in mind to pass the time?"

"Aren't you quite the tease? Be careful with me, Charlie."

Her face turned serious. "Sorry. I'll be as morose as possible. I wouldn't want you to—"

I pulled her to me and gently kissed her before she could finish her sentence. Her lips were soft and warm against mine.

She pulled slightly away from me.

"Riley," she whispered.

"Yes?"

"Kiss me."

I laughed. "I just was."

"No." She shook her head. "Really kiss me. Kiss me the way you've wanted to all summer."

My legs felt slightly shaky, so I leaned back against the wall.

Attie's eyes were on fire as she walked toward me. Leaning into me, she ran her fingers through my hair and then grasping it in her hands gave my head a teasing tug.

"Good grief, Riley, freakin' kiss me already."

Ignoring my pounding heart, I placed my left hand on the back of her neck as my right found its home in the small of her back and forcefully pressed her more closely to me. Casting off as much restraint as I safely could, I allowed myself to kiss her as passionately as I'd craved. Attie responded fervently, and within moments all my inhibitions melted away.

chapter 35

(Attie)

I peeked around from behind the curtain and noticed that the church was completely full. I saw Gramps and the Bennetts sitting on the front row. Anne, Tammy, Tess, and Jen were sitting just behind them.

I was panicking but then felt Nicole squeeze my hand, and my uneasiness dissolved.

"You're going to do great, Attie. There won't be a dry eye in the place."

She winked at me and squeezed my hand again.

I teasingly scowled at her. "And that's a good thing?"

"Yes, Attie, sometimes crying is a good thing. A very good thing."

Pastor Rick finished his sermon and told everyone they were about to get a special treat and then passed the microphone on to Joshua.

"A year ago Attie Reed was involved in a tragic accident that killed her mother and best friend. Someone nobody could ever identify magically pulled her from the car. Although she was critically injured, she lived. Attie stayed in a hospital for over two months, and she was left to heal and grieve alone. She remembers having a dream while she was unconscious. Attie was walking with Jesus, and he had invited her to join him on a journey. Lucky for all of us, she agreed. After she woke up, she could hear the Lord speaking to her. He was praying with her, comforting her, and encouraging her to stay faith-ful. 'You're not alone, Attie,' Jesus would tell her. 'I'm here.'

"Today, Attie is going to share with you a love song that she sings to the Lord. It is a song by Meredith Andrews called 'You're Not Alone.'

"Attie?" He turned to me as I walked on stage. Handing me the microphone, he gave me a kiss on the cheek and then left me alone on stage.

The room was hushed, and I didn't look up to see the audience. This song was to the Lord. My Lord, who had never left my side. The audience was being allowed to witness my song of gratitude.

I heard the piano begin, and I brought the microphone to my mouth. Looking down, I began to sing.

• •

Standing in the doorway of the church, I watched as people left, many still crying. Some hugged me or told me that the song was beautiful. I wasn't enjoying all the compliments, but I welcomed their appreciation just the same. All of my friends were huddled over by the youth building fooling around and enjoying each other's company.

I'd started to go join them when out of the corner of my eye I saw Jesus waiting for me back inside the sanctuary. I went to join him.

As I walked up behind him, he spoke softly, "That was beautiful."

"It was for you. I meant every word."

"I know you did. Thank you."

He gave me a half bow.

"Why you're welcome." I returned a slight curtsey. "Everything I sang was true. You've never left me. I know that."

"I never will."

"I know that too." We were silent for a few moments before I spoke again. "I wouldn't have survived without you."

"That's the point."

"Yes, I guess coming to that realization really is the point."

I was proud of myself for figuring it out.

"Attie, I have loved you your whole life. Even before you were born, I loved you. That will never change."

He patted the altar next to him, inviting me to join him.

I sat down next to him. "I know."

"Nobody will ever love you like I do. My love is unconditional, perfect. My love will never disappoint you."

He spoke so softly, and I strained to hear him.

"Thank you, Lord. Thank you for that."

"There's nothing that you did to earn my love, and there's nothing you can do to lose it."

I turned to look at him, "This isn't you dumping me, is it?" I asked sarcastically. "The whole 'you're a great girl *but*' routine?"

He laughed. "Nope. I'm not going anywhere."

"Thank God." I realized what I'd said and rolled my eyes. "I mean, thank you … both of you, well all of you. You know what I mean."

He smiled and nudged my shoulder with his. "To end this relationship you would have to walk away—but even then I'd find you."

"The shepherd and his sheep?"

"I won't lose one. Not one."

We sat in silence for several minutes before he spoke again. "What was it about that song that made you choose it?"

"It perfectly explained our time together since the accident. The story of hearing your voice tell me I wasn't alone, that you were there with me. That you'd loved me all my life and always would."

"Yes, it perfectly describes all of that." He paused again. "Why else do you think you chose that particular song over any other? Many, many songs could tell me the same thing."

"I don't understand. What are you asking me?"

"Attie, if I only wanted you to have a relationship with me, I'd have you become a hermit. You need people or a person in your life. A person you can share experiences with. A person who can show you to a small degree what I feel for you."

I was very confused. "Okay?"

"Think of the song, Attie." He softly sang the words: "I searched for love, when the night came and it closed in ... it was the sweetest voice that called my name, saying ... "

I pictured Riley holding me that second night in the Bennett home. I'd woken up from a nightmare. I could hear his voice; I could hear his words: "You're not alone. I'm here."

My body shook.

Jesus continued, "My love, I've never left your side. I have seen you through the darkest night."

Pictures of Riley and me sleeping on the floor in our rooms, he was protecting me. I felt safe with him.

"And I'm the one who's loved you all your life."

It was as if hundreds of childhood memories with Riley flooded into my mind.

"All your life," Jesus ended.

I was stunned. I turned to Jesus and stared at him in disbelief. As my heart pounded through my chest, I whispered, "Riley?"

Jesus smiled. "Your Mr. Darcy." He winked.

"Riley?"

I was motionless until I heard it, that sweet voice.

"Charlie?"

My eyes turned to find the person who was saying my name.

"Riley," I whispered and then nodded.

It was Riley. He was peeking through the sanctuary door with a large grin on his face.

"First day of school tomorrow, Charlie. How about one last adventure before reality hits?"

I looked at Jesus. "Will you come with me?"

"I wouldn't miss it. Especially with it being a whole new adventure and all."

I turned back to Riley.

"Wanna join me on a journey?" he asked with a wink.

I smiled as I got up to go to him.

"Absolutely."